In Memory of
HOWARD MARTIN SINGER
Howard was shot by an African home invader,
on his 67th birthday,
May 10th 2011,
in his home in Johannesburg, South Africa.
Howard passed away May 13th at 4:30pm.

BOOK 1, EMMA
BOOK 2, MARLA

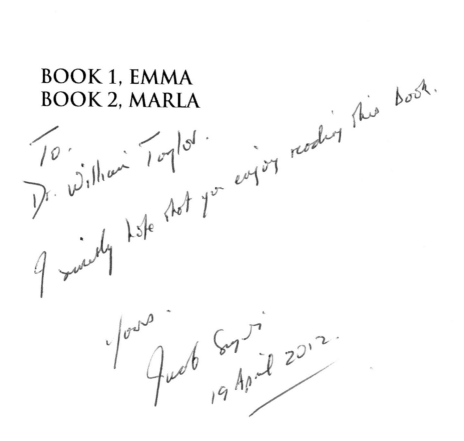

To.
Dr. William Taylor.
I sincerely hope that you enjoy reading this book.

yours
Jacob Singer
19 April 2012.

THE VASE WITH THE MANY COLOURED MARBLES

JACOB SINGER

Outskirts Press, Inc.
Denver, Colorado

The Vase with the Many Coloured Marbles
Book 1, Emma. Book 2, Marla

Cover Photo by David Crocker

Outskirts Press, Inc.
http://www.outskirtspress.com

ISBN: 978-1-4327-7544-5

Outskirts Press and the "OP" logo are trademarks belonging to Outskirts Press, Inc.

PRINTED IN THE UNITED STATES OF AMERICA

My thanks go to Dr. Jonathan Singer of London, England, who helped with the editing and factual correctness..

My thanks also goes to Lynn Thompson of Thompson Writing and Editing Corporation whose editing comments were a great help in teaching me how to write a book.

Contents

Introduction

"The fairest cape in all the world."

So said Jan van Riebeeck as he established the first permanent European settlement in South Africa, on April 6th, 1652. The Portuguese explorer, Bartolomeu Dias was the first man to round the Cape in his ship, but it was Vasco da Gama who recorded a sighting of the Cape of Good Hope in 1497. The beauty of Table Mountain with its "tablecloth", as the thin strip of cloud that forms over the mountain was called, was the perfect way-station for ships travelling to the Dutch East Indies. The city grew slowly at first as it was hard to find adequate labour, prompting the city to import slaves from Indonesia and Madagascar, many of them becoming the ancestors of the first Cape Coloured Communities. Dutch was the first language spoken, but with the arrival of British forces in 1795, English was introduced. The Dutch language spoken in the Cape over the years gradually evolved into Afrikaans, a language that became primary under the National Government of Dr. Malan in the national elections of 1948.

Cape Town today is located at the northern end of the Cape Peninsula, with Table Mountain forming a dramatic backdrop to the city. With its mild, wet winters, and dry very warm summers, it has become the vacation jewel of many South Africans. Cape Town is also where the South African Parliament sits, and is the legislative capital of the country. It is also the city in which the ship you have taken from England will dock, a magnificent welcome to a country that is remarkable in its beauty and diversity.

The Protea, a flower found growing wild in the Cape, attracted the attention of botanists in the 17th century. The extraordinary richness and diversity of species characteristic of the Cape Flora are thought to be caused by the diverse landscape where populations can become isolated from each other and over time develop into separate species. Recently, after a major fire that destroyed acres on Table Mountain, Proteas appeared that had never been seen before, much the delight of botanists all over the world.

Within approximately a thousand-mile radius of Cape Town, you can drive from the semiarid plateaus of the Little Karoo separated from the Great Karoo by the Swartberg Mountain range. You rise to an altitude of 2000 — 3000 feet of the Western Cape along the Atlantic coast, to Namaqualand on the west and the Komsberg and Roggeveldt escarpments on the southwest, merging with the high veldt of the Free State and Transvaal provinces.

As you drive, air conditioners at maximum cold, the red dust somehow seeps through the closed doors and windows of the car, causing you to cough and cover your nose and mouth with a handkerchief. The wind, unchecked by trees or shrubs, blows it about as it ruffles the wool of the sheep that thrive here. If you are lucky, and drive through a flash rainstorm, you will be overwhelmed by the botanical garden of flora not seen anywhere else in the world that seems to spring out of desert sand as the rain drops hit the dry earth. If you are unlucky you will catch a swarm of locusts that fills the outside of your car with their sticky corpses before you pull to the side of the road, waiting for the swarm to pass. You are overwhelmed as they batter themselves unceasingly into your windshield and side windows. At the nearest garage, you stop to wipe the sticky mess off your car, allowing the engine to breathe as you fill up with petrol before you continue on to the alluvial diamond fields of the Orange River Delta in the Richtersveldt.

Or you can drive along the coast of the Indian Ocean through the beautiful and captivating garden route, visiting the ostrich farms of Oudtshoorn whose farmers made untold fortunes when ostrich feathers were the rage of the European fashion market. You would make a detour and visit the Cango Caves, one of the world's great natural wonders on the way to George and Knysna before stopping at Plettenburg Bay, a prime holiday resort known for the unusual pansy shell that washes up on its beaches.

If you want to, you can continue on to Port Elizabeth, where you would sit on the rocks, opening oyster shells or mussels and slurping their contents after dipping them into the ocean for flavor, or you would decide to spend the cash you have in its large shopping centre that caters to tourists. Eventually you reluctantly tear yourself away and drive along the coast, crossing the Sundays River in an inland detour to visit the University town of Grahamstown on the way to East London, where you can spend a few days enjoying the warm water of the Indian Ocean.

You can then drive on into the Transkei, officially known as the Republic of Transkei and inhabited by the Xhosas, one of South Africa's many African tribes, a tribe that gave birth to Nelson Mandela. You would visit Umtata, its capital, today known as Mthatha, or you could decide to continue on into the heights of Hogsback, with its artist colonies, where the climate is like that of England. You would look for a room at one of the few hotels and spend your days walking the trails through forests full of blooming azaleas and rhododendrons as waterfalls thunder in the background. The adventurous can shower in the falling water like a nude nymph, the solitude broken only by a hiker whistling to warn of their approach, allowing you to quickly cover nudity and hide in the bushes. More often than not the crashing water of the falls would drown out the whistling and as the hiker came closer to the falls he would pause and rub his eyes in disbelief at the mirage of a water nymph.

Then again, you can continue north to the subtropical Province of Natal warmed by the Agulhas current, past the towns of Margate into Durban surrounded by its fields of sugar plantations and banana trees.

You would enjoy the sight of avocado trees full of monkeys that captivate your heart and make off with whatever article you may leave lying around. Driving north through Natal, you can pass through the holiday resorts of Umhlanga rocks, to the Umfolozi, and visit the Hluhulwe-Umfolozi Game Reserve, and St. Lucia Bay before driving north into Piet Retief making your way slowly to Johannesburg. Or you could continue north around the border of Zululand to Nelspruit, and the start of the Kruger National Park.

Then again you could have preferred to drive through the vineyards of the Cape, sampling wine as you slowly make your way to the town of Stellenbosch that hosts the fourth largest university in the country. You would enjoy having lunch in any one of the many early houses built in the Cape Dutch Architectural style, unique to this small area of the world and without question magnificently beautiful. With heartfelt regret you would pull yourself away from this beauty and continue on to the frontier town of Beaufort West, the oldest town in the Central Karoo and the world's richest collecting grounds for reptile fossils that today are displayed in museums throughout Europe.

After filling up your car with petrol, you would continue driving until, crossing the Orange River and driving through the dry grassland, you would eventually reach the city of Bloemfontein, the judicial capital of South Africa, a city poetically known as "the city of roses" because of its yearly rose festival. The city also boasts the University of the Free State, one of the oldest institutions of higher learning in South Africa.

Should you have driven further to the west, you would have reached the city of Kimberley, home of the largest man-made hole in the world, where the early settlers dug for diamonds.

You could continue on by crossing the Vaal River at Parys and driving through the small university town of Potchefstroom to visit the gold mines of Johannesburg with its yellow mountains of processed sand, the result of mining the vast gold fields. Johannesburg has a wonderful climate, almost 1,753 meters above sea level, shaded by cumulus clouds that look like stairways to the heavens as the sun sets in the evening. The Highveldt of the Transvaal, today known as Gauteng, is where your blood thickens to handle the lower oxygen levels in the atmosphere, a climate visited by athletes from all over the world to train months before an Olympic event; a climate where your skin tans golden brown in the ever present sun.

From Johannesburg you could travel North to Pretoria, the administrative capital and the *de facto* national capital, a city where Winston Churchill was imprisoned during the Anglo Boer war of 1899 to 1902. You could then continue East to the Lowveldt and the Kruger National Park, teeming with wild game. You would try to sleep under mosquito nets to escape the bite of the Anopheles malaria mosquito that keeps you awake all night with its singing. You could drive to, and gasp at the dramatic view of, the Blyde River Canyon, the largest Grand Canyon in the world.

Then again you could slowly make your way north to Pietersburg, and the scenic Magoebaskloof mountains, and drive on to Tzaneen with the road dropping some 600 meters in less than 6 kilometers, as you reach the northernmost point of the great Drakensburg Mountain Range that runs South and West, its influence felt in all four Provinces.

Or, instead of driving to Johannesburg, you could have veered off to the Drakensburg Mountains, that in winter are more than often covered in snow. The beautiful Drakensburg mountain range, the border between Bechuanaland, today known as Lesotho, and South Africa, in the centre of the country where one can play in the snow in the morning and after a 500 kilometer drive into Durban, sunbathe on the beautiful sandy beaches in the afternoon, with the crashing waves a picture of surfers.

This is South Africa, an ancient land at the tip of Africa unequalled in its rich diversity of fauna and flora, a country where many argue that man's ancestors walked erect for the first time. South Africa, a land where the different cultures of Africa, Europe and the East clash almost without respite even to this day; a land all the cultures agree, is richly endowed with culture, mineral wealth, natural splendour, wilderness and wildlife that is the envy of the world.

This is South Africa, a country into which Emma was born.

Book 1
Emma

Chapter 1

"Where the hell do you think you are going?" Nellie looked at her boss. He had shouted at her in Afrikaans as she left the table where she sorted and wrapped the peaches for the market. She looked down as she felt her water break, the fluid dribbling slowly down her leg.

"Baas," she cried out, "I have to go. The baby is coming." She had always thought that she was only eight months pregnant, which was why she continued going to work. "I have to get home," she shouted, her face a picture of horror at what had happened, "and quickly."

"Well, see that you are back at work tomorrow," he shouted after her as she hurried out the door, hiding the wet spot on her dress with her coat. She started running down the road towards her house as the first labour pain hit her. *'Liewe Hemel, Good heavens'* she thought as she gritted her teeth, bending over in agony. *'but this one is different from Jonas. It wants to come, and quickly. I hope I make it home.'*

Jonas was her first baby, born a year and a half earlier. She had delivered him in her bed at home, with her neighbour Patricia, as the midwife.

Another labour pain hit her, and she doubled over with the cramp, a cry of pain escaping from her lips. Her home was not that far from where she worked, but as the labour pains started to come quicker, it seemed like 100 miles away.

Nellie's meager diet had kept her weight down, and her pregnancy had not been that obvious to anyone. She started feeling the pressure of a child wanting to be born. As she passed the Peninsula Maternity

Home, she decided to walk into it rather than attempt to walk home and have Patricia help her deliver it.

Two hours after Emily had been born, her delivery helped by nurses at the Home, Nellie dressed herself, collected her belongings and with a newborn baby cradled in her right arm, walked unseen out the back door of the Home. She hobbled slowly along the cobbled Hostley street, a road climbing toward Table Mountain that dominated District Six, to her house, a three-roomed home shaded by a grapevine at the front door. The house boasted a verandah that on a long humid summer evening would see the whole family enjoying supper watching the activities of the street and waiting for the sea breeze to cool the air as the sun set over the bay. No-one was at home. She walked in, placed Emily in a cot that she brought in from the verandah, and lay down in her bed.

'*Ag Hemel,*' she thought as she closed her eyes, '*what a day.*'

She looked at Emily sleeping in the cot.

'*Somehow she looks anders (different') and she hasn't cried for a nipple yet. I hope there is nothing wrong with her.*'

District Six, as it was commonly known, was named in 1867 as the Sixth Municipal District of Cape Town. By the turn of the nineteenth century it was a lively community made up of former slaves, artisans, merchants and Jewish immigrants mainly from Eastern Europe, as well as many Malay people brought to South Africa by the Dutch East India Company during its administration of the Cape Colony. Situated within sight of the docks, where many of the Cape Malays who were Muslims and other Coloureds worked, it gradually, over the years, saw many of the Whites leave the area, moving to more affluent parts of Cape Town, areas restricted to Whites only.

Emily was classified by the South African race laws of that time as being a Coloured, a term that referred to an ethnic group of mixed race people, who possessed some sub Saharan African ancestry, but not enough to be considered Black under the laws of South Africa. Coloureds are a mixed race, more than often possessing ancestry from Europe, Indonesia, India, Madagascar, Malaya, Mozambique, Mauritius, St Helena and Southern Africa. In the Western Cape, where Emily was born, the Coloured community developed distinctive Cape Coloured and affiliated Cape Malay cultures. They constituted the majority of the population of the Western and Northern Cape provinces, most being bilingual speaking over the years, both English and Afrikaans, but with Afrikaans as their mother tongue. They developed a distinctive dialect, a creolized mixture of Afrikaans and English.

In the 19th Century, the Coloured people of South Africa had similar rights to the Whites in the Cape Colony, though income and property qualifications affected them disproportionately. In the rest of South Africa, they had far fewer rights, and although the establishment of the Union of South Africa in 1910 gave them the right to vote, they were restricted to electing White representatives only.

When Emily turned six years old, she attended the George Golding Primary school, leaving home at seven thirty in the morning after a breakfast of Cornflakes. Every morning she would walk with her brother Jonas and their friends up Constitution Street of District Six. Her father, Jeremy, would walk with them part of the way before turning off to the tobacco factory where he worked. The street would echo with laughter and shouts as the workers greeted each other on their way to work.

"Hey, Jannie," Emily looked around to see who was shouting, "we are having a braai tonight. You and the missus must come, hey?"

Jannie, who was walking in front of them, without turning around shouted out an answer, "Sure man, we will be there."

"Just bring your own beer, hey,"

"OK… see you at seven."

Nellie, Emily's mother had become housebound, looking after Emily's two younger sisters and brother. The street was always a friendly hive of activity even that early in the morning, irrespective of whether or not the cold northeasterly wind, was sweeping off Table Mountain.

Most Saturdays she and her friends would walk through Hanover Street, the soul and life of District Six, with its Peoples Dairy, fish market, Maxims Sweeteries and Jangra's grocery store and spend the one or two pennies they managed to coax out of their parents. If there were no pennies, they would look to see which way the wind was blowing and decide whether it was a good day for fishing or better yet, enjoy a swim at Woodstock Beach. They all spent many hours perched on the rocks at the beach, there to watch ships from all over the world sail in to Cape Town harbor, erupting into screams of laughter as the odd wave burst in a froth of white foam and splashed them. They would often write down the names of the ships as they steamed past, wondering which country each ship belonged to and daydreaming as to whether they would ever visit that country and what it would be like to live there.

On Sundays the family always attended the Holy Cross Church, wearing their finery. Enthused by the minister's sermon, when the service was over, they would stand in the grounds of the Church, gossiping with friends. They would slowly amble home, and sit down to a small lunch on the verandah, with a glass of homemade wine, greeting their friends as they walked past.

After a nap, they would often walk to a friend's house, usually just down the road, or they would invite them over for afternoon tea, enjoying a cake that Nellie had baked in her coal stove that Saturday morning. Their parents would all sit in the shade of the grape vine and discuss the politics of the day, while the children played in the back yard, enjoying the sound of the birds singing in the trees, a serenade broken only by the Muslim call to prayer. It was all part of the daily noise and bustle of living in District Six

Emily's grandfather, unknown to her, had been a White farmer with a farm just outside Beaufort West. Her grandmother was one of the black maids that looked after his house. She worked in the farm house as the maid by day and as the farmer's mistress by night. Whether or not the farmer's wife knew about his nightly exploits is immaterial. She probably did know, but was happy to escape his sexual demands as they both aged.

Emily's mother, Nellie, was the eldest daughter. She ran away from the farm when she was 14 years old, and made a life for herself in Cape Town. A year later, she met and married Jeremy, and raised a family of five children, Emily being the oldest daughter, with a brother Jonas, older than she.

Emily grew up a very happy child, loved by her parents, and adored by her brothers and sisters who looked to her for help as they grew older, more so than to their mother. She never knew her grandparents on her mother's side, and never really missed them. Her father's parents lived a short distance from them, and she enjoyed walking with her grandfather whenever he took part in the "Coon Carnival", as the Cape Town Minstrel Carnival was called. She would dress up in a dazzling array of shining colours, a dress her mother altered every year as she grew taller. With her grandfather looking dapper in his bright red jacket and shiny white trousers; a red top hat on his head and his face painted black and white with green polka dots on each cheek, she would bang her tambourine as he played his banjo. They would walk in the parade, singing, dancing and enjoying the crowds that lined the streets to watch them. Music and a keen sense of rhythm came naturally to her.

Emily's Coloured status in South African society as a second class citizen never bothered her. She loved her life and believed it to be the norm.

"Somewhere, sometime in your past, you had a White and a Black as a great grandparent," the teacher one day told the class at school during a history lesson, "which is why you are known as a member of the Cape Coloured Community."

That night during supper, she shocked her parents by asking, "Ma, was my grandfather a white man?"

Her mother nearly dropped the plate she was holding.

"Why… where did you hear that from?" her father asked her, looking carefully at her mother.

"Well, teacher told all of us in school today, that we all had a white man as a great grandfather, and that is why we are coloured, and not black or white. She said that this is why we are different to the Whites, who treat us badly. Is that why Jonas' hair is kroes, and mine is straight?"

Her mother sat down in her chair, her face a picture of shock. She looked at her daughter, not quite believing what she had just heard. Emily was only fifteen years old and here she was asking to explain why they were different.

Her father cleared his throat.

"You must understand, Emily," he mumbled, "as part of the Coloured Community in South Africa, we are classified as second class citizens by the government."

"What does that mean?" Emily asked, not quite understanding what he was saying.

"You have grown up in District Six, amongst both Blacks and Whites, and you have been treated as equals by them. South Africa as a whole does not treat us as equals. The Whites come first, we the Coloureds with the Indians second, and the Blacks are at the bottom with the Coolies and Chinese somewhere in-between. When you go into Cape Town proper, you have seen benches marked, 'For Whites Only.' We as Coloureds are not allowed to sit on those benches."

"But I have often sat on them, and no-one has bothered me," Emily interrupted.

"I know," her father answered, "that is because you were born with a lighter skin than any of us, and with hair that is light brown, long and straight. No White would think you were a Coloured. I know of many in our community who are angry at these laws, where the Whites squeeze us from the top, while the Blacks squeeze us from the bottom. We have to take cheap work, because the Whites do not believe that we are as clever as they are. They treat us like slaves, while many of our women are treated like whores at night, and our children age and die long before they should."

"Jeremy, that is enough," Nellie shouted at him.

"But Ma," Jeremy began looking imploringly at Nellie who was angry at what he said, "let her find it out from us, rather than in the street."

"No… that is enough," Nellie repeated. "Come on, finish your supper Emily, and then off to bed," and she looked at Emily angrily.

Emily never again had the courage to ask her mother about the family history and whether she truly had Black and White blood in her veins. For the first time in her fifteen years, she became aware that being classified a Coloured restricted her to a way of life that she could never be happy with. This was a country that she dearly loved and she began to feel the pain of being rejected in such a way. In one dramatic evening, her life had changed.

The next day at school, she started noticing for the first time that some of the girls and boys were indeed different in both their skin colour and in their hair. It was something that she had never noticed before. She saw all her friends standing in a group under one of the trees in the playground, talking to each other softly.

"What is going on?" she asked Violet as she approached them. Violet was her best friend.

Violet turned to her. "Judy was telling everyone how her brother went to Johannesburg and became a White."

"He did what?" Emily asked, not sure about what Violet had told her.

"Judy told us that because her brother's skin was white, and that he had straight hair, just like you, he went to live in Johannesburg. He told everyone there that he is a White and they accepted that he was one. No-one said he was not one."

"But how did he do that?" Emily asked.

"I don't know," Violet answered, "you must ask Judy to tell you how he did it."

Later that morning, during the school break when she saw Judy alone, Emily approached her.

"How did your brother get away with passing himself off as a White?" she asked Judy.

"He taught himself to talk Afrikaans like the White Afrikaners do, not like we Coloureds talk Afrikaans. He also joined the Dutch Reformed Church," she said sarcastically. "He told me that it was easier to better his Afrikaans than it was to learn to speak proper English. Can you believe that? I think our Afrikaans is good, but then again he is lucky, his skin and hair are like yours, not like my dark skin, and my kroes hair," and she twisted a strand that had fallen over her forehead.

What Judy told Emily shocked her. She started to spend a great deal of time looking at the people around her as she walked to and from school. She became quieter, spending less time with her friends, and more time walking the streets of Cape Town looking at everything in a different light. She would walk through the restaurants, pubs and hotels of the city, ignoring the restrictions to people of colour just to see what would happen. Nothing happened.

One afternoon, as she walked through the city, she found that the wind was blowing hard off Devil's Peak. With the winter rain that started, she was soon chilled to the bone. She looked around her at the comfort of the Whites as they sat eating, drinking and laughing in the numerous restaurants. She was so cold. Hiding her nervousness she boldly walked into one of the restaurants and sat down at a table. After reading the menu, looking carefully at the prices charged, she ordered something to eat. In the past, she would never have thought of visiting these establishments, but now she was rebelling. When she had finished eating, she remained sitting at the table, admiring the view overlooking the harbour.

'*This is what we are missing*' she thought. '*I could never bring my parents, brothers or sisters here. The only way they could come into this place would be as servants, working in the kitchen.*'

She came to a decision.

'*I must become a White, but not an Afrikaner White, an English White. I don't want to be an Afrikaner White because they hate us Coloureds. As an English White I could get away with it, but I must learn to talk English like they do. From now on, no more Afrikaans, I will only speak English.*'

She stood up from her table and paid the bill when the waitress gave it to her. She spoke to her in her broken English, stuttering as she struggled to remember the words. This caused the waitress to look at her curiously. She walked home slowly, pleased with her decision and determined to see it through.

Her parents had raised her to be a devout Christian, and although she still attended the small church every Sunday down the road from where they lived, she had gradually started to reject Christian teachings as being faulty.

'*How can the devout White with their Christian religion discriminate against people based on the colour of their skin?*' she thought to herself. '*Why has God allowed this to happen?*'

Family traditions, passed down through the generations, made her feel as much a South African as she believed the Voortrekkers felt, and she started challenging the right of the Government to discriminate against her.

'*They, the Voortrekkers*', she reasoned, '*ran away from the Cape to the Transvaal, because they wanted to escape British rule. My parents, on the other hand, accepted Britain, accepted the King and the Monarchy and the British way of life as adapted to South Africa. In my mind, I am more South African than the Boers who live up in the North, in the Orange Free State and the Transvaal.*'

She felt that her heritage was part of the British Empire, and the fact that she had mixed blood in her veins should not be a discriminatory fact. Visiting a library close to District Six, she boldly opened a library account, and started borrowing books written in English to read. She made a point of reading what the South African race laws did to stereotype the population of South Africa into the basic racial categories of English, and Afrikaners, both of whom were of White classification. The nine black tribes were classified as Black Africans who she would have avoided at any case because they looked down on the Coloured community. There were the Indians, who by their own hand divided themselves into Muslim and Hindu, and frowned on marriage between the two, and finally there were those of mixed race and mixed blood, the Coloureds, that was her racial category.

There were also the Malays and the Chinese, although many were uncertain as to the Chinese category simply because of the few Japanese that had come to South Africa and who were allowed White status.

Emily became very angry and withdrawn. She gradually stopped socializing with her Coloured friends, and they with her. She chose instead to walk and eye-shop the popular fashion stores in the city, learning to imitate the dressing habits of the Whites, and by talking to the sales ladies as though she was interested in buying an article of clothing, started improving her English. At home the family usually spoke Afrikaans with the Coloured dialect and intonation and she found learning to speak English not as easy as she thought it would be. English was taught as a second language at school, but it was rarely spoken during class. She started saving the few pennies given to her as pocket money every week by her father, and sought the odd job in the community to add to those pennies. One night, as they lay in bed, Nellie said to Jeremy in her broken English.

"Jerry, have you seen that Emily has changed?"

"What do you mean?" he asked.

"Just look at her," she answered sitting up in the bed. "She is starting to dress differently, like those ladies in the magazines."

"So?" Jeremy said, "What is wrong with that? She is a teenager, growing up."

"Ja, I suppose so," Nellie answered, her face a frown of uncertainty. "But, you know, she always used to talk to me in Afrikaans. Now, she only talks to me in English."

"Ag Ma," Jerry answered turning on his side and closing his eyes. "Leave her, she will come right."

Nellie leaned over and blew out the candle that had lit up the room. She lay back in her bed, thinking about Emily. Listening to Jeremy as he snored softly beside her, she slowly relaxed and fell asleep.

Emily began to challenge the race laws more and more. When she walked through the streets, she would often, especially if she saw a crowd of Whites, sit on a 'Whites only' bench next to those already sitting there, and wait for someone to say something. No-one did. She would catch a 'Whites only' bus to wherever, and wait for the driver or conductor to ask her to get off the bus. None of them did. She started highlighting her hair, which fell in soft brown waves to her shoulders. She no longer lay in the sun looking for a suntan that would turn her skin a beautiful golden brown tan that even then was much lighter than the darker skin of her brothers and sisters. With eyes that were the lightest of blue, she noticed that she was starting to attract the admiring glances of White men, and the odd jealous frown of a White woman.

Her racial obsession kept her awake at night as she schemed of ways to break the racial laws of the country and improve her status. At school she would listen carefully to the teachers when they discussed the new racial laws that were being introduced.

"My father says that they are going to kick us all out of our homes in District Six one of these days," Violet told her as they walked home from school one afternoon.

"That cannot be," Emily answered. "We are people. No-one can be that horrible."

"Well, my father said look what is happening to the Jews in Germany. They are being separated as a different people, like we are here. My father says that many of them are leaving Germany. Quite a few are coming to South Africa."

"Yes, but there are a lot of English living in South Africa, and I think that if the Government started doing that, there would be a war," Emma answered, troubled at what Violet had just said, "Then again, I must admit though, that even the English treat us as second class people."

What Violet had said worried her. Violet had confirmed that as a Coloured she would never be accepted by either the African community, not that she wanted to be, nor by the White community, as long as she remained in Cape Town. The fear of being recognized by a friend from the Coloured community as she continually tested the colour barrier was a major concern. As a Coloured, she enjoyed practicing the traditions handed down by her family, but every day she became even more determined to jump the colour barrier and become a White.

After a great deal of thought and introspection, she came to the conclusion that the coloured traditions she had grown up with had to be forgotten and no longer remain even a part of her memory.

On a Sunday, she would now take a bus into the city on some pretext or other and bus her way to Clifton Beach, a beach that is to South Africa what Copacabana is to Rio. She retained her modesty, wearing a one piece bathing suit with a short skirt.

Here, against the stunning backdrop of a mountain dropping almost sheer to the sea, with Devil's peak on the one side and Lion's Head on the other; where houses and apartment blocks clung preciously to the steep slopes, she would sunbathe in the shade of an umbrella on the white sandy beaches. She did it more to catch the eye of a White boy than a tan, and indeed, she started catching plenty. Emily began to realize that she was an attractive girl. She also started to realize that none of the boys even dreamed that she was a Coloured girl, and that if she were to keep up the deception, she would not only have to dress differently, but would also have to lose her instinctive lapse into the Afrikaans spoken at home with its distinct Coloured dialect.

Whenever she left the boundary of District Six she changed her name to Emma, rather than Emily, using the surname Kline. She had originally thought of spelling her surname as Klein, removing the 'tjies' from her true surname, but decided against it. Klein meant small in Afrikaans, and she wanted nothing to do with Afrikaans. When Violet spoke about extracting her two front teeth to create a 'passion gap', the fashion of the day with the young Coloured girls, she walked away in disgust.

"A sign to show that we belong to the Coloured racial group," she told Violet, her disgust showing in her voice.

She went as often as she could to the bioscope, classified for Whites only, especially when they showed British movies, and listened carefully to the dialogue. At night when at home in her bedroom, she would practice talking with an accent similar to that of the heroine in the movie.

Soon there was no end of dates with White boys, and she rejected invitations by the Coloured boys she grew up with. She would always arrange to meet her dates in the city, never bringing them home. Her mother commented on the fact that every Saturday night she was never at home, coming in late and leaving the house early on Sunday, often missing Church. She always lied to her mother, telling her that she was out at a friend's house.

The double life was beginning to tell on her at home. In the city and on the beach she was Emma Kline, and she spoke English like the Emma Kline she was slowly becoming. At home she was Emily Kleintjies, falling quite naturally into the expressions and slang of those around her as they spoke either English or Afrikaans.

One Sunday morning, sitting in her favourite spot on Clifton beach with two White boys that she usually dated, she suddenly saw Andries approaching. Andries was a boy in her class at school. He was walking around the beach selling ice cream from a container filled with dry ice to keep them frozen. As she saw him approaching, she immediately lay down and turned onto her tummy, so that Andries would not recognize her. This is what she always did when she saw someone she knew approaching her. She always lived in the fear that she would never notice them and that one day one of them would recognize her. Although Coloureds were not allowed to sunbathe on Clifton beach, they were always walking the beach as hawkers or garbage cleaners.

"Hey, boy," one of the boys next to her shouted at Andries, "over here. Would you like an ice cream?" he asked Emma looking at her back as she lay on her towel.

"No thank you," she answered, her voice muffled by her hands as she covered her face with her hat.

"You sure?" he asked, "it is so hot and the ice cream is just what I need to cool off."

Emma was scared to move. When eventually Andries moved away, she slowly moved onto her back breathing a sigh of relief, keeping her face covered until she was sure that Andries was far enough so as not to recognize her. She looked at the ice creams the two boys were eating.

"John," she said to one of the boys, "watching the two of you eat those ice creams I have changed my mind. Will you run after that boy there," and she pointed to where Andries was standing selling ice creams to another couple, "and buy me one?" She reached for her purse.

"Sure," John said standing up, "my treat," and he ran through the hot sand towards Andries. She saw Andries looking at her curiously as John bought an ice cream from him, but from that distance he did not recognize her.

A month before her sixteenth birthday, Emily passed Standard 8 at the top of her class. At prize giving, her parents were terribly proud of her when she received the award for best student in her class. The following night, at supper table her father asked her, "Now that you have finished school, where do you want to go to work?"

She looked up at him in amazement, her fork half way to her mouth.

"But Pa," she said putting her fork back on her plate, "I was hoping to carry on and get my Matric. I would like to go to University, and get a degree. I thought you and Ma would allow me to, seeing that I did so well at school."

Her brother Jonas, when he had completed Standard 8 had immediately found a job as a worker at a Pharmacy in a mall in Goodwood, a suburb of Cape Town.

"I would love to, my dear, but unfortunately we don't have enough money to keep you at school. We need you to help us so that we can educate your younger sisters and brother."

She thought about what he had said for a few minutes looking down at her plate, a tear forming in the corner of her eye. Then with a determination she never knew she had, she looked up at him and asked, "Does it matter to you where I find work?"

"What do you mean?" he asked her, looking at Nellie as she came in from the kitchen carrying a hot plate of food.

"For a long time now," Emily continued, "I have wanted to go to Johannesburg. I feel that I would like to see more of South Africa," she lied. "If you allowed me to go, and I found a job in Johannesburg, would that be O.K. with you and Ma?"

"But you have only just turned sixteen," Nellie cried out, "you cannot leave home so young."

Emily turned to face her mother. "Ma," she said with a smile on her face, "you married Pa when you were only fifteen, so at sixteen, I am one year older than you were." She turned to her father and continued. "You know, working in Cape Town, I would earn very little. I have spent a lot of time in the library reading newspapers, Transvaal newspapers, and I have seen that jobs pay much better there, than here."

"We will think about it," her father interrupted angrily. "Now let us finish our supper."

They all sat quietly not saying a word. Emily no longer felt hungry, and after a while she stood up and cleared the table, washing all the dishes in the sink, drying them and packing them away.

"*I will keep nagging them,*" she thought. "*Eventually they must give in.*"

After many arguments and a lot of tears, her parents finally did give in. Her mother, Nellie probably realizing her intentions, said nothing. Three weeks after that decisive supper, she bought a dress and a suit with the few pounds that she had managed to save up by helping out in the shops close to where they lived. She needed clothes that she felt would be suitable for Johannesburg. She planned the day she would leave Cape Town for Johannesburg, and started preparing for the big day.

The day before her departure, her parents prepared a farewell braai for her in their garden, inviting many of the neighbours and a few of her friends. She was slightly upset with this, because she had wanted to leave quietly, without too much fuss. The next morning, beaming with her newfound determination and a spring in her step in anticipation of a new life in the Transvaal, she caught the train from Cape Town to Johannesburg. Tears streamed from her eyes as she hugged her mother.

"I love you Ma," she whispered, "I will always love you, but I have to go."

Her mother kissed her on the cheek, her hand stroking her head. "I know my dear, I know" she said softly. "Just be careful."

She quickly kissed her father on his cheek, and sobbing she ran to the coach.

As the train slowly pulled out of the station, she waved goodbye to her family, her heart tearing as she watched her mother sobbing on her father's chest, his arm consolingly around her. Her brothers and sisters standing with them waved and shouted, wishing her well, not quite sure what to make of her leaving them.

She cried her goodbyes from the coach marked for Non-Whites, dressed in the long large flowery dress that enveloped her, but once the train had left the station, she walked to the lavatory, and changed into the tight fitting white suit she had bought. She freed her hair from the tight bun covered by a doek, allowing it to fall naturally to her shoulders. She made up her face, taking special care with the eye shadow and lipstick, and then satisfied with how she looked, she went back to the coach, but sat in a different seat, closer to the exit. At the first stop, Paarl, she left the Non-White coach and with butterflies in her stomach, calmly walked into the coach reserved for Whites. Weeks before, she had bought a ticket to a basic sleeper four person compartment. She walked through the coach slowly, struggling with her suitcase, looking for her compartment. Eventually finding it, she found that she was sharing it with two ladies.

"Good morning," she said as she reached up and placed her small suitcase in the overhead rack, standing on the seat to do so. She smiled at them as she sat down.

"Good morning," the lady she sat next to replied.

"Good day," the lady in the seat opposite said to her in Afrikaans.

She relaxed, her nervousness slowly dissipating as the click-ety-clack of the train soothed her. She was sitting in a Whites-only compartment with two white ladies. From this day on she would be and would live as a White. She was now Emma Kline.

When the conductor came around to examine tickets while the train was travelling through the Karoo, he smiled at her, and then said in Afrikaans,

"Ladies, do enjoy your trip. If you should need anything, please let me know."

At sixteen, Emma had grown to be a very beautiful young lady. She was slim and had taught herself to be very poised and full of confidence, something remarkable for a young woman of her age, but something

she knew she could achieve. Anyone who may at any stage have doubted her racial qualification was stared down by her into embarrassment
at even doubting that this beautiful woman, with her bright blue eyes,
was anything but a White. Had they only known about the butterflies
in her stomach! But then, nearly one year of Clifton beach associat-
ing with, joking and even necking with good looking White jocks had
given her the confidence to pull off her change.

Chapter 2

Emma looked carefully at the two ladies in the compartment. The lady sitting next to her was reading a magazine. She looked matronly, wearing a brown dress cut to show off a large bosom with a deep cleavage. Her arms, almost bursting from the sleeves of her dress, were heavy, but her hands were small, with well kept fingernails painted dark red. Her brown hair, falling on either side of her face, was slightly disheveled, and she kept brushing strands of hair away from her eyes. Emma looked at her face, as the woman looked up from her magazine and smiled at her. It must have once been a very beautiful face, with eyes that boasted many laugh lines on either side. Age was, however, starting to take its toll.

Emma looked at the lady sitting opposite her. She was thin, almost to the point of being too skinny. She was wearing a dress of dark floral buttoned up to her throat with the long sleeves of her dress fastened at each wrist by a single button. Her thin face gave her a very stern look that was accentuated by her graying brown hair tied in a bun behind her head. Her lips were thin, with not even a hint of lipstick or lip gloss, and were pursed as she looked out of the window as the veldt swept past them.

In an attempt to break the ice she felt in the compartment, she asked, hesitantly.

"Where do both of you come from?"

They both looked at her as if seeing her for the first time. Then the lady sitting next to her smiled, and said as though she had been waiting for the silence to be broken, "I come from Johannesburg."

The lady sitting opposite her looked up from the magazine she was reading. "Oh, I come from a town called Klerksdorp," she said in Afrikaans, assuming that they would both understand her. Without waiting for either of them to introduce themselves, she continued.

"I have a daughter who lives in Hermanus, and I spent three weeks with her." Hermanus is a small fishing village on the garden route, a seaside resort very popular with holiday makers.

Emma had never been to Hermanus, but she had heard from friends that it was a very beautiful seaside town.

"I know Hermanus," the lady sitting next to Emma exclaimed, "but I must say I have never been there. I travel down by train to Cape Town and then on to Muizenburg every year for a holiday. I have done so for the last 12 years."

Emma had often taken the train from Cape Town to Muizenburg. The train always stopped at every station on the way to pick up passengers, almost emptying when it reached Muizenburg station, leaving a few passengers to carry on to St James, Fish Hoek or Simonstown. Sometimes, when the South Easter, nicknamed The Cape Doctor because it cleared the air of pollution, blew too strongly she would stay on the train enjoying the scenic ride to Simonstown and back.

At Muizenberg she enjoyed the beach amongst all the holiday makers. Often some boy, seeing a girl all by herself, would approach her, and then, not receiving a cold shoulder, would sit and talk to her. She enjoyed listening to them as they tried to charm her.

'They have manners,' she thought, 'different from the boys at home.'

She liked Muizenberg, because the waves were small, and the sea warm, unlike the cold water of Clifton Beach. She also felt more secure there, not having to worry about any hawker recognizing her.

"By the way, my name is Carole Lipshitz," the lady next to her interrupted her thoughts. "You are...?" and she looked at Emma.

"Oh, I am Emma Kline, on my way to Johannesburg for the first time." Emma answered smiling at her.

"I am Mrs. de Klerk," the lady who sat opposite her said primly, "Tinnie de Klerk."

"Now that we all know each other's names, we can enjoy our trip," Carole said with a smile on her face, a little bit of sarcasm tinting her words.

Emma and Carole were soon chatting away like old friends. Emma was, however, continually mindful of only speaking English. With one of the ladies being Afrikaans, speaking English with a bad accent; struggling to find the words to express herself, Emma found that she often had to remind herself not to slip and start thinking and speaking in Afrikaans.

Emma asked Carole questions about Johannesburg, especially where to stay.

"Hillbrow, of course," Carole answered. "It is not far from the city centre, and for a young girl like you, it is a suburb filled with young people. You will love it there. How old are you?"

"Uhh, nineteen," Emma lied.

"Why are you going to Johannesburg?"

"It is not that easy to find decent work in Cape Town. I thought Johannesburg could be easier."

"Look, I have a daughter, Chrissie Stead, who is in charge of some type of department at the OK Bazaars. I will introduce you to her if you want me to."

"Oh, thank you so much," Emma said gratefully, "That would be wonderful."

"Well…" Carole said, scornfully, "I really don't know how wonderful. Chrissie can be a bit of a bore, especially when it comes to her work. She is some head of a department and it has gone to her head, ha…ha…ha…" and she laughed at her own joke, "but I will do my best. Just keep in touch with me once you are in Jo'burg," She took out a pen and paper and wrote on it. "Here is my phone number. Call me when you have settled in," and she pressed the note into Emma's hand.

That night, they all slept in the bunks in the compartment, with Emma sleeping in the upper bunk. She slept badly, scared that she may have a bad dream, roll over and fall out. The next morning, after dressing, and washing in the basin in the cabin, they went to the dining car for breakfast. Emma was tired. Her eyes felt gritty with black soot from the smoke the engine spewed out as it roared down the railway tracks.

'*Pull yourself together, you will give yourself away if you don't,*' she kept admonishing herself nervously.

At breakfast, Carole could not stop talking, often repeating herself. Tina, openly irritated at Carole's incessant chatter, took her leave from them as soon as she could, leaving Emma alone with Carole at the table. Emma felt that she had to be polite and nice by just listening, because she wanted that introduction to her daughter.

'*She must have swallowed a gramophone sometime in her life,*' Emma thought, smiling to herself, '*because she just simply doesn't stop.*'

"My daughter Chrissie met and married a very nice man. His name is Issy Stead. What did you say your surname was again?" Carole asked Emma, taking a sip from the teacup she held in her hand.

"Oh, I thought I had told you," Emma answered, the clickity-clack of the train which was so soothing last night irritating her this morning. "My surname is Kline…"

"Good heavens! That's right, I'd forgotten. You did tell me. I didn't even remember that you were Jewish," Carole interrupted her.

Emma frowned. '*Jewish?*' she thought, '*what does she mean by thinking I am Jewish? Is it because of the surname I chose? A crazy woman! Then again, is it an advantage or a disadvantage to be Jewish?*' She didn't pursue it. She looked out of the window at the veldt, a bare russet-coloured dust-swept plain, with many thorn trees showing their large white thorns against a thin green leaf. It was a very different picture to the dry Karoo of the Cape.

When they returned to their compartment, Tinnie de Klerk was preparing to leave the train.

"We will be in Klerksdorp shortly," she said in her broken English, and then slipping back into Afrikaans as though English was too difficult for her, "Please, whenever you are in Klerksdorp, do look me up. I am in the phone book." Taking her suitcase she moved out of the compartment to the carriage exit as the train pulled into the station.

"Not a very nice woman, that," Carole remarked. Emma said nothing.

An hour later, the train stopped once again, at a town called Potchefstroom.

"What a beautiful old station," Emma said as she pulled down the window of their compartment.

"Potchefstroom was one of the first towns settled by the Boers when they came up north," Carole told her. "At one time, it was the capital of the Transvaal, but they lost that to Pretoria. My uncle, who lives on a farm here, loves the town. It has plenty of water that runs in furrows through the streets, so the gardens are always green and beautiful, even when there is no rain, and the veldt is dry."

The train started moving again, slowly leaving the station. Emma sat with her eyes glued to the town.

"That is a part of the University they have here," Carole continued pointing to some buildings they could see in the distance, and there is the Potchefstroom dam." She pointed to a large body of water that appeared on their left. As the train clattered over an iron bridge spanning a river they had a much better view of its size.

Emma sat fascinated. The countryside was so flat, with the occasional koppie (hill) breaking the horizon, so different from the Cape with its mountains. The train stopped at Randfontein, and Krugersdorp, two mining towns not that far from Johannesburg.

"You had better start getting ready," Carole said. "We will soon be in Johannesburg."

Emma couldn't move. She was looking at the yellow mine dumps that started to appear as the train closed in on Park station, the central station in the city center.

"What are those yellow mountains?" she asked Carole.

"My dear girl, those are the mine dumps," Carole answered. "Johannesburg is known throughout the world for them. That is the sand that has been processed to remove the gold, after it has been dug out of the mine."

"But it is yellow," Emma said.

"Well, isn't the sand on the beach yellow?" Carole answered.

"Yes, of course," Emma answered, "but not this yellow, and not in mountains like this. Just look at those buildings, they are so much taller than the ones we have in Cape Town."

The train pulled into the station. To Emma it was dark after the bright sunlight. The platforms, shaded from the sun by a roof to protect the passengers, were filled with people, some boarding the train, others getting off, and very noisy as the engines let off steam. They left the train, and walked to the taxi rank, a porter following them with their luggage.

Carole turned to her. "Well my dear, this is where I must leave you. Please, don't forget to phone me. I will talk to my daughter about giving you a job, so do make sure you phone me."

Giving Carole a hug, Emma said goodbye to her promising to phone her as soon as she had settled in. She caught a taxi and asked the driver to suggest a place she could stay.

"I would suggest you stay at Raema Court."

"Why do you recommend it?" Emma asked him, suspicious of his motives.

"Ma'am," he answered. "The boarding house is owned by Mrs. Rowe. She is a nice lady and always gives me a big tip. Also, it is close to the city, a short walk through a tunnel under the railway line, and you are in the city itself. Most people coming to Johannesburg for the first time come to see the city, so it is convenient. Finally, it is a beautiful and a very clean accommodation, and as I said earlier, Mrs. Rowe is a lovely lady and gives me a big tip."

Emma laughed. "Ok, Raema Court it is then."

The boarding house was a beautiful white building, with a large veranda that ran the length of the house, shaded by a Castor Oil tree in one corner. Emma took to Reena Rowe almost immediately, liking her pleasant smile and her joyful friendliness. She was a small woman, with sparkling eyes and a mouth that never stopped smiling. Her gray hair was cut in a page boy style that made her look very businesslike in the dark dress she was wearing.

"I don't have a room facing the front at the moment," Reena told her when she asked for accommodation. "I only have one at the back, a bit dark but comfortable. Depending on how long you want to stay, I will move you to a sunny front room as soon as one is available."

"Thank you, I really appreciate that," Emma answered. "I am here in Johannesburg to find a job, and once I have one, I will probably be here for a long time."

"Do you know where to look for work? I have a niece who lives across the road. She could help you find something."

"Thank you, that would be nice," Emma answered, happy that she had found a place to stay where she could be comfortable and at home. She felt secure.

She learned from Reena Rowe that the city was a short walk through a subway tunnel down Wanderers Street, just as the taxi driver had told her. However the next day, even though she was happy with her accommodation, she went to Hillbrow to see what apartments were available, and especially what the rent was and whether or not she could afford to live there. She had to catch a bus to Hillbrow, finding that it was further from the city centre than Raema Court. She did like the hustle and bustle and the liveliness of the shops, with the streets full of young people sitting outside at restaurants, music blaring into the street. She checked the rents at two apartments, and although they looked comfortable, they were far larger and more expensive than what she could afford.

She walked past the shops, looking in the windows to see if any advertised for staff. None did. She decided, for the moment, to stay at Raema Court. She just felt more secure there.

That night she phoned Carole Lipshitz. "Hello Mrs. Lipshitz, this is Emma from the train," she said uncertain of whether it was Carole she was talking to.

"Oh yes, Emma, and how do you find Jo'burg?"

"So far, very nice," she answered, but very different to Cape Town. People are rushing everywhere. No-one walks slowly like in Cape Town." She could almost feel Carole smiling.

"Well, my dear,' Carole answered, "you will soon get used to it. By the way, I spoke with my daughter, Chrissie, and she said that you should come in and see her. I told her how charming you were."

"Oh, thank you, thank you so much" Emma answered, relieved that she may soon have a job. "Where does she work? I know you told me, but I have forgotten."

"She works in the buying department at the OK Bazaars in town. It is on Eloff Street; anyone can direct you there. She says that you must just ask for her, and someone will tell you where her office is."

The next morning, after a most enjoyable breakfast, Emma walked into Johannesburg city centre. It was not as far as she first thought it would be. She found that Johannesburg was very different from Cape Town. Where Cape Town's horizon was dominated by Table Mountain, Johannesburg's skyline was dominated by manmade mountains of yellow sand that were the mine dumps.

Everything Emma had learned at school about South African history, which she had found interesting, flooded back. She remembered how the class had debated whether Britain would have invaded the Boer Republic if gold had not been discovered by George Harrison, an

Australian prospector, in 1886. His discovery had led to a feverish gold rush as fortune hunters from all over the world rushed to the area. Within a short time there were more 'Uitlanders' as the foreigners were called, living in Johannesburg than there were Boers living in the whole of the Transvaal.

President Paul Kruger had established a city at the site, with Churches and schools to bring law and order to what was then a wild prospector's collection of tin shanties. After much discussion, her class had concluded that the refusal by President Kruger to allow the 'Uitlanders' to become citizens of the Transvaal unless they had resided there for 14 years, plus the gold fever that made many of the Boers, especially Government officials, extremely wealthy, was the reason why Britain declared war on the Boer Republic in 1899. The war was known as the Anglo Boer War, and lasted until 1902, a war where Boer women and children were confined to and died in British concentration camps. A war that even today arouses animosity towards anything English by many of the Boer descendents.

Emma found that she enjoyed walking through the streets. She enjoyed the business vibe of the city; the rush of smartly dressed women and men walking the streets; the shops full of buyers with a feeling of liveliness that was not found in Cape Town. As she dawdled along she window shopped, admiring the latest fashions in ladies' dresses in the shop windows, all beautifully displayed.

On Rissik Street she had her photo taken by a street photographer called Sam Gluckman opposite the Carlton Hotel, a beautiful building that resonated with the history of the city, and that thrilled her.

'*I shall definitely come here for lunch one day,*' she said to herself as she watched a chauffeur-driven Rolls Royce unload its passengers at the entrance to the hotel and drive away.

When she eventually found the OK Bazaars, on Kerk Street, it was early afternoon. She walked up to the lady at the first counter she saw that was close to the entrance.

"Could I speak with Mrs. Chrissie Stead?" she asked.

"Who is she?" the assistant answered.

"I understand she works here," Emma said puzzled.

"Oh then, ask that man over there, he is the assistant manager," and she pointed to a tall man at the next counter with his back to them. Emma walked up to him gingerly.

"Excuse me, sir," she said. He turned and looked at her. He saw a very beautiful girl, exceptionally well dressed and beautifully made up. He could see drops of perspiration on her upper lip probably a result of the heat outside. It just made her all that more attractive.

"Can I help you?" he asked politely.

"I am looking for Chrissie Stead," Emma asked hesitantly.

"Oh... you want Mrs. Stead," he answered smiling at her. "She is head of the lingerie buying department. I am on my way there if you would like to walk with me."

"Thank you," Emma replied, and they walked towards the lifts.

"By the way, my name is Eric O'Neil, and you are?"

"Emma, Emma Kline," she said, her heart fluttering in her chest from nervousness.

He looked at her and smiled. "Nice to know you, Emma," '*Very nice to know you,*' he thought.

Chrissie had received a phone call that morning from her mother telling her that she had sent a young girl to her, looking for a job. "*Oh, not again,*" she thought, but being polite to her mother, she listened to all she had to say. When her mother paused to take a breath, she excused herself and told her that she would phone her Saturday night as usual. Her mother continuously sent her young girls she had met in the course of her very active social life, daughters of friends and acquaintances all looking for work. It had almost become a joke with her friends, but to please her mother she would talk with them, and then fob them off to some other department head.

That afternoon, while she was having her tea break, she caught sight of Eric O'Neil walking to her office with a very attractive, well-dressed young woman. '*This is a first*,' she thought assuming that Emma was his girlfriend. '*I must say that he does have good taste. She does look a bit young, though.*'

Eric was tall, six feet one inch, thin, with black hair and thick black eyebrows joining together above an aquiline nose. His eyes were dark brown, and with high cheekbones and dimples on either side of a fairly large mouth, he was very good looking. Chrissie was amused as she watched the girls in her department all turn to look at him. He had a wonderful personality and was quick to learn, with a very pleasant way of handling both staff and customers. This had served him well in the company, allowing him to move up the ranks far quicker than most. He was now a junior trainee manager, and would probably be promoted to assistant manager at a branch in the near future. Everyone liked him, and Chrissie felt herself softening as he walked towards her office. She tried not to smile. She stood up and walked toward him. Eric looked around her office, and not finding her there, turned to look for her.

"Hello, Chrissie," he said when he saw her walking towards him, "let me introduce you to…" and he hesitated looking at Emma.

"Emma Kline," she said nervously, her heart beating in her throat.

"…Emma Kline," Eric continued. "She is looking for a job. I hope you can help her."

"Oh, you must be the girl my mother phoned me about," Chrissie said, smiling at Emma. "Let me see what we have," and looking at Eric, she raised her eyebrows as though questioning him as to the importance of finding a position for this girl. He smiled and nodded, and she read in his face that he hoped she would have a place for Emma. She looked away from him, cleared her throat and started ruffling the papers on her desk as though looking for something.

"Well," she said to Eric, "Let me have a chat with Emma, and I will see what we can do," and she smiled at him, as though to say that just to please him, she would find something.

Chrissie was a tall very thin woman, with brown hair combed into a bun at the back of her head. She wore glasses perched on the tip of her nose, and was inclined to look over the top of them when she looked at a person, yet looking through them when she had to read something. This caused her to frown, filling her forehead with lines that were slowly etching themselves into permanence. Her lips were thin, with no lipstick to suggest any fullness and with no make-up she looked like a stern manageress. Her dress was dark brown, stretching below her knees, and her shoes were of the same colour, with only a slight heel. She had a pen tucked behind one ear, and spoke in a voice that had a rasp in it. Emma wondered whether her dress reflected the lingerie she wore because she thought that as head of the lingerie department, she did not appear to be very fashionable.

To please Eric, Chrissie did find something for Emma, as a saleslady on the lingerie counter. '*She won't last long there,*' she thought, '*nobody has, they all find it too consuming but, to please Eric...*' and she smiled to herself.

Emma was thrilled. She was surprised that the department had not asked for any papers of identity when she filled out her employment form. This was something that had worried her, not that she had needed any when she worked part time in Cape Town. There, they simply classified her as a Coloured by her dress, and the way she talked. Here, at the OK Bazaars, all they wanted was her name, address and any previous sales experience.

Her salary was far more than she expected, and would have allowed her to rent a flat in Hillbrow, but she decided instead to continue staying at Raema Court. She liked the ambience, the feeling of belonging to a family; the feeling of being in a place where she wasn't alone, where at breakfast and dinner there were others sitting in a dining room with her and often talking with her. She needed that.

Over the months, she became very friendly with Reena Rowe.

Reena took a liking to her, and one day introduced her to her daughter Lilly, who was visiting with her new grandson.

"Come and meet my daughter," Reena shouted at Emma as she walked in one afternoon after work.

"Lilly lives in Potchefstroom and has come to stay for a week with my grandson, Josh. Her husband is a pharmacist there." They were all sitting on the front verandah, enjoying the coolness of a breeze after another very hot day, sipping lemonade.

"Hello," Emma said walking up to Lilly. She was tired. It had been another hard day at the counter and she needed a bath to freshen up. "You know, coming to Johannesburg by train, we passed through Potchefstroom. It looks like a beautiful town, with a large dam."

Lilly stood up as Emma spoke. She was as tall as Emma, and as thin, with black hair that showed a thin strand of grey at her temples. Her eyes were dark brown, under carefully plucked eyebrows. She was beautifully dressed.

"My mother has told me such nice things about you," Lilly said to her, holding out her hand to touch Emma's shoulder. "If ever you are in Potchefstroom, you must visit us. My husband is a pharmacist there. It is a small town, where everybody knows everybody else, unlike Joh'burg. We love it there."

After chatting for a few more minutes Emma excused herself, saying that she needed a bath and a lie-down before supper.

"Do join us at our table," Lilly said, "I would love to find out more about Cape Town. We have never been there, and from what I hear it is a beautiful city."

Emma had been working at the OK Bazaars for just over a year. She loved her work. By working very hard at her job, her life in Cape Town was soon forgotten with the exception of the weekly letter she wrote to her parents. She never told them where she lived, or where she worked. They assumed that she was working as a cleaning lady, or some other low-paying job in the city, and that she was living in Riverleigh, the township for Coloureds.

As a lingerie saleslady she made a point of knowing the lingerie presently on the counter; she quickly learned which garments sold and which did not, often requesting a change or making a suggestion to the buying department. She was very pleasant to customers, talking Afrikaans when addressed in Afrikaans, but making sure that she did not slip into the Coloured dialect. She was dedicated to her work and always very well dressed. Her efforts started to pay dividends.

Chrissie Stead, pleased with her progress and the improvement at the counter, promoted her to the buying department as a junior buyer. She was given the additional responsibility to keep an eye on the counter and make sure that sales were maintained.

Most Saturday nights she went out with Eric. He took her to the theatre, and to the bioscope, and on one evening, after she had mentioned it in a casual conversation, he took her to the Carlton Hotel for dinner. She enjoyed his company, and although he was becoming quite serious towards her, she would not allow him too much leeway with her affections. 'Eric could one day be my boss,' she thought to herself. 'I like him, but I want to experience a bit more out of life, before I become serious with anyone.'

With this in mind, she decided to go out with any number of young men at the branch who asked her out. It did not matter who they were or what they looked like, as long as they were White, but she would not allow herself to develop a serious relationship with any one of them.

'I will go out with whoever asks me out,' she decided, 'that way I will meet people, and understand Johannesburg society better. I must simply not get serious with any of them, not yet at any rate, and above all, no necking, no matter how much I like my date.'

Eric was soon transferred to the Pietersburg branch as assistant manager, so she only saw him on the odd occasion whenever he came to Johannesburg for a managers' meeting. She found that she missed him.

The other buyers, including Chrissie, often came to work in casual attire. But Emma always made a point of going to work well dressed as though she were on the cover of *Vogue* magazine. She felt that by doing so, she would distance herself from her Coloured heritage. It was not a cheap decision. Her dress sense was outstanding and her choice of dresses expensive, so she spent many hours at sales looking for something she liked that would meet her budget. She received many a compliment from customers, which she enjoyed. She felt that watching her P's and Q's when she spoke was enough to worry about without having to worry about dressing in casuals. She never had a 'Henry Higgins' or a 'Colonel Pickering' to coach her. She only had 'Emma Kline'.

One morning, after she had been with the company for almost two years, as she was in the lift going to the floor where she worked, the President of the OK Bazaars walked into the lift. He looked at her as though appreciating what he saw. She cringed into a corner trying to hide from his curious look.

"Whose secretary are you?" he asked. She looked up at him, then looked down at the floor and replied a tremor of nervousness in her voice.

"Sir, I am not anyone's secretary. I am a junior buyer in the lingerie department, and I look after the lingerie counter."

"Oh" he replied, "then you work with Mrs. Stead."

"Yes, " she answered nervously.

"Mmm, I see," said the President looking her up and down. After a few moments he asked, "And what is your name?"

"Emma Kline," she answered, her knees shaking. '*Oh God*,' she thought, '*I have been found out. I am going to be fired.*'

"Miss Kline, thank you," he said, as the lift reached her floor and the doors opened. Trembling and quite sure that she had been found out, she walked out of the lift, as dignified as she could, holding back her tears.

The following morning, she was called into Chrissie Stead's office.

"Emma" Chrissie said, "I have a memo from Mr. Gersh, the MD."

'*Dear God,*' Emma thought, '*here it comes.*' Tears started to form in her eyes. She leaned forward in her chair, ready to stand up and run from the room.

"He told me that I am to give you your own range of lingerie to handle," Chrissie continued, "and that I am not to influence you in your choice of buying." She looked at Emma with a quizzical expression on her face. "Do you by any chance know Mr. Gersh personally?"

Emma couldn't believe what she had heard. She looked at Chrissie in amazement, tears of relief streaming down her face.

"N..N..No" ,she stuttered, "I met him in the lift for the first time, yesterday."

'*Strange,*' Chrissie thought, '*I wonder what made him decide to promote her.*' She then looked at Emma as though for the first time. She saw a very attractive young woman sitting in front of her wiping away her tears with a handkerchief, her hair tastefully groomed, beautifully made up, and extremely well dressed. When she thought of all the other girls in the department who came to work in casuals, she shuddered. '*Well I sincerely hope that Mr. Gersh is not going to make a pass at her,*' she thought, '*but I can definitely see what he saw in her.*'

"Well," she said, "I will be giving you a new range of lingerie to promote. It is a new range introduced by a lady, Irma Rosen. I have a few samples in that suitcase over there," and she pointed to a suitcase next to her desk. "Familiarize yourself with the range and next Monday you will join me in visiting her showroom. I will introduce you to Mrs. Rosen, as a new buyer and promoter of her lingerie within the organization. You must still look after the counter, though." She shook her head and looked at Emma. "Are you sure you have never met Mr. Gersh before yesterday?" she asked. "Perhaps your parents know him, or do you attend the same synagogue?"

'*Synagogue? What is that?*' Emma frowned and shook her head. "No", she said, "no, they don't." Her knees felt weak, and she trembled slightly, feeling the blood rushing to her face.

"Thank you Mrs. Stead," she replied her voice trembling. "Thank you very much. I will do my best to make you proud of me. Thank you."

"Your area," Chrissie Stead continued as though she had not heard her, "will be the whole of Johannesburg, and the branches in the suburbs. You will also be calling on the branches in Germiston, Boksburg and Benoni, as well as Pretoria, although I wonder whether Pretoria is not too conservative a city for the range... well, we will see. Once we see whether the range is established and moving, then you can go further afield, to Krugersdorp, Randfontein and even as far as Potchefstroom and Klerksdorp.

The company will give you a company car with a driver to help you carry your suitcases." She looked at Emma as she said this, still not quite believing that this young girl could have pulled off such a coup. '*She must be dating one of his sons*' she thought. She looked away, and then looked at Emma again. '*I must admit though, she really is a lovely girl,*' she sucked in her lips, '*and she does dress well with exceptionally good taste, but I simply cannot believe that Mr. Gersh would go for somebody as young as she is. She is definitely dating one of his sons.*'

"Do you have a driver's licence?" she asked as she started filling in forms on her desk.

"No, I don't have one," Emma replied.

"Well, you will have to get one. Take that suitcase with you, to your desk," she continued pointing at a large suitcase at the far wall of her office, "but try not to let the other girls see the range, not just yet at any rate. I will give you a note so that security will allow you to take the suitcase home."

That night, Emma returned to Raema Court, walking on air. The suitcase was not as heavy as it looked, but she still struggled with it as she walked, resting ever so often. She couldn't believe what had happened to her that day… it was all like a dream.

"Mrs. Rowe," she shouted as she walked onto the verandah and saw Reena sitting there sipping a glass of wine. "I have been promoted. Can you believe it? I am now a junior buyer."

"I am not surprised," Reena answered, "You have worked very hard. You deserve that promotion. Can I offer you a glass of wine to celebrate?"

"Thank you, but not yet, I am still a bit too…" she stopped before she said the word 'young', "but I would love a lemonade if you have one."

"Let me get you one," Reena said and went inside.

Emma sat down, still not believing what had happened to her. It was all like a dream. Reena returned with a glass of lemonade.

"What is in your suitcase?" she asked.

"They have given me a range of samples to look at. I have to decide whether I like them or not. Tell you what, I will put them all out in my room, and have you look at them with me. Would you like that?"

"Yes, thank you," Reena answered, "I would enjoy that. I would like to see what the OK Bazaars has for its customers."

After sitting a little while longer, finishing her lemonade and talking to Reena about the weather, she went to her room. She opened the suitcase and laid out its contents on her bed. She was impressed. The lingerie was unlike anything she had ever seen. The garments were beautiful, flimsy, trimmed with lace and, she smiled to herself, 'more sexy than anything out there at the moment.'

Reena walked in and looked at them on the bed. "Good heavens," she said, "I could never wear this. These are for young girls and I wonder whether they would have the courage to wear them. My bloomers have served me well over the years, thank you."

Emma laughed. "They are all the latest fashion in Europe," she said.

"South Africa is always a bit behind on fashion, but I know these will sell like hot cakes. They are very, very fashionable."

After spending about two hours studying them, Reena gradually began to accept that there may be a small chance that she could try and possibly wear one or two of them. Blushing as she said this, she left Emma laughing. Emma started making notes and, finally exhausted after the day's tension, threw herself down on her bed and fell asleep almost immediately.

The next morning she woke up determined to be successful in her new position. She spent more time than usual on her dress and makeup, not that she needed it, but she felt that it gave a feeling of confidence knowing that she looked her best when the mirror took up more time. She took the suitcase of lingerie and walked quickly to the branch.

When she walked into the buying department, she could feel the frost as the other buyers treated her coolly, looking at her from the corners of their eyes, but she greeted them with her normal cheery good nature, and they soon thawed. Had they only known how knotted her stomach was. Chrissie looked up disapprovingly from her desk, but said nothing.

Emma walked to her office, and knocked on the door. Chrissie looked up. "Yes, Emma?" she said.

"Mrs. Stead, I looked at the range last night. I must say that the lingerie is very different from what we are selling at the moment, and very beautiful. I have made some notes. I would like to show the range to the other girls in the department, and listen to what they have to say."

"Sure, go ahead," Chrissie said after a moment, and returned to her work.

Emma walked to each of the girls in the office and asked them to look at the range, which she had displayed in the corner near her desk, and give her their opinions. At first they looked at her with suspicion and disapproval, but they gradually drifted over and started examining the lingerie. Their oohs and aahs brought a smile to Emma's face. She noted what they said, often surprised at how they disagreed even with each other. She observed that those who spoke excellent English and had an English background, and were therefore less conservative, liked the garments far more than the Afrikaans-speaking girls. This didn't surprise her, but it did confirm what she had already concluded, that she would have to classify the branches in the different towns as to their conservatism.

A few days later she noticed that a few of the girls started to dress smarter than usual and she smiled to herself, pleased that she was no longer as isolated.

Chapter 3

Benjamin Weiss arrived in Johannesburg in March of 1936, with his parents and sister Irma, fleeing a Nazi Germany in which they could no longer live. Their family home had been in Berlin, and growing up there, he had always considered himself more German than the Germans. The family were sixth-generation Germans and his father, Abie (Abraham) had served as an officer in the German army during World War I, and with distinction.

Once the war had ended however, and in spite of the hyperinflation that decimated Germany, his father returned to running a very successful and prestigious gents and ladies outfitters; a business his mother had managed to keep alive while he was away fighting a war. He was a respected and well-liked man in the Berlin community and their house was always filled with friends and guests.

As a boy, Benjamin had worked in his father's store every Saturday during the school term, and every day over the school holiday period since he was nine years old. His father paid him a pittance for his work, but he loved working there and did not consider a salary as an incentive to work. When Benjamin finished school, rather than go to University, he decided that he would prefer to join his father in the business.

Benjamin was extremely athletic. He had always been tall for his age and above average in his class at school. He was also good looking, very popular with the boys and more so with the girls. Although never wanting for a girlfriend, when he was 23 years old he fell in love with Irene Tannenbaum and as far as he was concerned, that was it. She was only 15 years old at the time, but he knew that she was the partner he wanted for the rest of his life. He promised himself that he would one day marry her.

Irene was small for her age, very petite and delicate, like a porcelain rosebud on a fine piece of Dresden china. She had an infectious laugh. With her bright black eyes, and ever smiling face framed by a golden halo of curls, she was always the centre of attention at any function. Irene's exceptionally wonderful sense of humor, her witticism and beauty drew Benjamin to her the day he realized that the little girl he had always seen in the playground, and hardly noticed, was now a very beautiful young lady.

Irma, his sister, was a pretty girl, but rather on the plump side and very shy. She was two years younger than him, and exceptionally artistic. With her snow white skin and rich black hair always braided and wound around her head, as was the fashion of the day, she did attract a number of Benjamin's friends who asked her out, but she was simply not interested. She had enjoyed drawing and designing dresses ever since she had discovered pencil and paper. Rather than holding hands on some date she did not enjoy, she preferred spending her hours sketching. She took to studying French because she had made up her mind at a young age that Paris was where she wanted to be, working for one of the famous French fashion designers, setting her heart on Chanel.

With the leaning of Germany towards Nazism in the years following WW I and the passing of the Nuremberg Laws that stripped Jews of their citizenship in 1935, Benjamin began to feel uneasy about living in Germany. He consoled himself in the belief that his German patriotism would be accepted above the anti-Semitism that was becoming more prevalent throughout the country.

"I am a German first and a Jew second," he would tell his friends. He would stubbornly refuse to believe otherwise. His uneasiness grew however, especially as anti-Semitism within the country became more prevalent.

Before WW I, anti-Semitism was confined to the fringe of right wing political groups, but after the war, anti-Semitism slowly moved into the mainstream of European politics. Those nations that lost the war -- Germany, Austria and Hungary -- attributed the dreadful carnage on the battlefield, to internal traitors working for foreign interests, primarily the Jews. This was because of the belief that Jews, spread throughout all the nations of the world, with their religious teachings were loyal to each other, putting their religion first and the country they lived in second.

This legend was deliberately fed by the German military leadership, who were looking to cast the blame onto a third party for the consequences of their own failure.

"They are blaming us, the Jews in Germany because they lost the war. We did not start that war; Germany, Austria and Hungary did," his father shouted angrily one night at dinner after reading the editorial in the local Jewish newspaper. "Now we all have to pay damages to those who won the war. It is all here," and he thumped the newspaper with his hand.

"I fought in that war, and I was decorated. I didn't want to go and fight, but I served my country. Now in the provisions of the Versailles Treaty system, we in Germany more than the other countries, are starting to suffer a period of hyperinflation. Every day in the store I have to remark prices because the Reichsmark is becoming worthless. This is being blamed on us, the Jews that live in Germany. This newspaper says this," and he read,

'The flames of anti-Semitism are being fuelled even more, and preparing the ground for the fascist party and the birth of Nazism.'

Many of the Jewish families in Germany and surrounding countries like Poland and Hungary, fearing the growth of anti-Semitism, started to emigrate to any country that would accept them, often selling their assets at a pittance to their true worth. Early in 1933, Irene with her family realizing the way Germany was going, emigrated to the United States of America. Benjamin's heart was broken. He was terribly hurt when he said goodbye to her. For the first time, he started to realize that perhaps after all, anti-Semitism in Germany was here to stay, and could even get worse. He promised himself that whatever it would take, he truly loved Irene, and that in spite of his love for Germany it would not be long before he joined her in America.

Benjamin found that he simply could not pack up and leave without his parents or his sister, Irma. He started pestering them, arguing that it was time to follow Irene and her family, and leave Germany. He started to fear for their safety. His father, however, was obstinate, believing that his German patriotism, the fact that he had fought for Germany in WW I and had been decorated, would be acknowledged by Germany above the growing anti-Semitism.

"I am a German," he shouted at Benjamin when Benjamin begged him to leave. "My father was born in Germany and his father before that. We, the Weiss' have lived in Germany longer than many of those who call themselves German today. Why should we leave?" and he walked out of the room, angry that Benjamin had even suggested such a thing. Then he put his head back into the room and shouted, "you want to leave? Then go! There is nothing stopping you."

"But the Nuremberg Laws that were passed last year..." he shouted after his father, but his father simply ignored him.

Benjamin was upset that his father would not listen to him. At first he even doubted his own reasons for wanting to leave Germany. Then something happened that convinced him that he and his family had to leave.

He was walking down the street with his mother on their way to the shop. A group of Nazi youth in uniforms, walking down the pavement in the opposite direction, pushed them and everyone else on that pavement into the gutter. He was furious, but his mother held him back.

"Don't," she said holding his arm. "Please don't, they are only young boys and don't know what they are doing."

He calmed down, and taking his mother's arm, carried on walking to the shop.

"What if they had hurt you?" he asked.

"They didn't," she answered. "Let us leave it at that."

The incident led him to realize that Nazism was gaining strength, and that being German without being a Nazi meant nothing. Being a Jew as well meant even less, especially now that he was no longer considered a citizen of Germany. To the Nazis, they were simply Jewish first and foremost and as such were no longer German citizens. German patriotism and a love for the country meant absolutely nothing. He decided then and there that somehow he had to start making his own plans to leave Germany.

Then about three weeks later, when he went to the municipal swimming pool for his daily early morning swim, he was refused entry.

"Why?" he asked the manager of the swimming pool, "why? I have been swimming here all my life and I always thought of you as a person to admire and respect. You have known me for years. You even taught me how to swim when I was an eight year old child, and now... now you turn me away as if I am a piece of garbage. What have I done to you that you now adopt this attitude? I haven't changed...I am the same person you have known for the past 16 years. Look at me... and tell me what is different, other than the fact that I have grown taller and older?"

The manager looked at him, his face showing no emotion. He opened his mouth to say something, and his hand reached forward as if he wanted to touch Benjamin, but then a stranger entered the ticket booth, and he turned away without answering him. Benjamin became very angry and upset.

"Is it because I am a Jew?" he shouted after him as he walked away. "You have known that I am Jewish all the years I have been swimming here. Why should it matter now?" He didn't receive an answer. He stood for a few minutes, totally dejected. Then, trying to hide the tears in his eyes, he slowly walked home.

He also noticed that the few non-Jewish friends that he had made at school stopped inviting him over to their houses. Whenever he invited them to his house, they would always offer some reason why they could not come.

"My parents said..." was the stock answer.

He had learned from one of his close friends that a Jewish underground had been formed, to help Jews leave Germany with as many of their possessions they could carry, which was hardly anything at all. He contacted them and they helped him open a bank account in London. He started to transfer all and any spare cash he had. He even asked his father to start paying him a proper salary. He told his father a lie, that he was saving to buy a motor car, and lead a decent social life. In return, he acted as a messenger for the underground, travelling throughout Berlin and the surrounding villages.

After living like this for about five months, he decided that enough was enough. He had to leave Germany and somehow convince his father to leave as well. He spoke to his mother about his fears and asked her to talk to his father. She said she would.

A few days later, he broached the subject once more with his father over dinner. He looked at his mother imploringly, but she stood up from the dinner table and walked into the kitchen, leaving the three of them.

"Pa," he said, "Pa, we have to leave Germany, and soon. If you won't leave, then Irma and I will. I have asked Ma to come with us, and although she wants to, she says that she cannot leave without you."

"The Nazis will not last," his father shouted at him waving his fist in the air. "The Germans aren't stupid. They are a clever people. They will realize that the Nazis will destroy the country, and they will vote them out of power."

Benjamin looked at his father, and then shook his head. "Pa," he said, "I cannot agree with you. I have tried to see things the way you see them, but I can't. I have spoken with Irma, and as much as she doesn't want to, she and I will be leaving as soon as I can arrange it."

Then a week later his father decided to go on his yearly visit to the Carlsbad Hot Springs in Czechoslovakia. No sooner had he left than Benjamin was arrested by the Gestapo.

Benjamin's first thought was that his assistance to the Jewish underground had been discovered, but he was surprised when they interrogated him about why his father had left Germany and gone to Czechoslovakia. They questioned him through the night and he began to feel that he would never see his family again, but he was very persuasive and convinced them that he was not aware of what his father was doing.

"If you keep me here, my mother will become suspicious, contact my father in Carlsbad, and he will not come back. It is him you want, not me."

With this argument, they let him go early the following morning. He was tired. They had kept him awake all night, hoping that the lack of sleep would break him. The first thing he did was go to the store, where he emptied the cash register of all and any cash available. He then emptied the safe, placing the cash and documents in a brown paper bag. Slipping out the back of the store, in case he was being watched, he went to the house of Goltz Kritz, the window dresser. He told him that he was going to Carlsbad to fetch his father on a matter of urgency. That he should look after the store for a few days while he was away. Goltz had been in their employ ever since the store opened, and was a good and loyal employee.

Benjamin then drove home, told his mother and sister what had happened to him and that they should come with him exactly as they were dressed, taking nothing with them. This was to allay suspicion in case they were being watched. He contacted his friends in the underground, who took them into hiding while plans were being made to smuggle them out of Germany to London. The members of the underground would contact his father in Carlsbad, tell him what had happened and that he should make his way to London and not, under any circumstances, return to Germany. At first Abie doubted their story, but then they gave him a letter from Bertha telling him what had happened to Benjamin.

"It will be better if you don't come back to Germany. All passports issued to us have been restricted. You were lucky to get out." she wrote. "We are going to the family in London, and we will meet you there."

Less than one week later, the family was reunited at the home of a relative in London.

While they waited for their father to arrive, Benjamin sent Irene a telegram, asking her to marry him. She was now 18 years old, he was 24. After a long discussion with her parents, they agreed to allow her to marry, and she telegraphed Benjamin that she would marry him, but that he had to ask her father for her hand in marriage. He went to the nearest post office, and immediately sent a telegram to her father asking for permission to marry his daughter.

The next day he received a telegram.

IRENE TELLS ME THAT YOU ARE GOING TO LIVE IN AFRICA. THEY ARE CANNIBALS THERE. CAN YOU LOOK AFTER MY DAUGHER?

Benjamin immediately returned to the post office and replied with a telegram.

SIR, WE ARE GOING TO SOUTH AFRICA. IT IS CIVILIZED. I LOVE YOUR DAUGHTER AND WILL PROTECT HER.

A day later he received a telegram stating,

YOU HAVE MY BLESSING.

Benjamin applied for a marriage license and arranged with a Rabbi and a Synagogue to marry them. Two weeks later Irene and her mother arrived in London. Four days after that, they were married.

What made the family choose South Africa rather than America was probably more an accident than preplanned. They had applied to the United States, Canada and England, but because of limitations to the number of European immigrants each country accepted, they were put on a waiting list which, from what they gathered, was a long list. In the meantime their length of stay in England was nearing the end of the time that they were allowed to stay. When the South African Embassy in London accepted their application to emigrate, they were glad that their problem was solved in that they would not have to return to Germany. They had also been scared that without being allowed to work in London, they would use up all their available cash, cash they would need to start a new life in whatever country accepted them.

During the two weeks on board the ship taking them to South Africa, they planned their future. Benjamin, Irene and Irma would look for jobs bringing income to the family, while his father and mother would look for and make a home for the family.

While in London they had learned that Johannesburg was the business centre of South Africa, and without even resting in Cape Town, where the ship docked, they caught the train to Johannesburg. Once there, they immediately looked for and found a house to buy. The money they had was enough for a deposit on a small house in Germiston, a town not that far from Johannesburg, because prices there were so much cheaper. They slowly settled in, living frugally and counting each and every penny, a very different lifestyle than what they had lived in Germany.

Benjamin soon found work as a window dresser with a gentleman's outfitters in Booysens, one of the suburbs of Johannesburg, while Irma found employment as a saleslady at John Orr, a large department store on the corner of Kerk and Eloff Streets. Irene decided to find work closer to home, in a ladies' clothing store in Germiston. They pooled all their earnings, which were managed by Abie.

Their mother, Bertha, looked after the home, preparing meals and cleaning the house with the young African girl they employed as a maid. She found it difficult teaching her how to cook the German recipes they were accustomed to so it wasn't long before she left the maid to clean the house while she worked in the kitchen. The maid, a young girl, Meisie slept in a quarters especially built for servants in the back yard, quarters that had their own toilet and shower. This shocked Bertha. She found the racial discrimination that was accepted as the norm in South Africa too much like the discrimination that was now in force in Germany.

Living in Johannesburg and Germiston was very different from Berlin, but they were pleased to be away from the anti-Semitism of Germany. They found the racial discrimination in this new country un-settling, a custom that went back to when the Dutch first settled in the Cape. Had they known that discrimination existed; had they known that races of color were classified as second class citizens, restricted from owning property and discriminated against in all walks of life, they would have persisted in trying to emigrate to North America. Believing that South Africa was like other countries in Africa, a colony, run by Britain and other European countries with no racial discrimi-nation. they were horrified to find it otherwise.

"One day this country is going to implode," Benjamin told Irene. "In Germany, we Jews were a minority. I don't believe we were even a million. Here in South Africa, they tell me that the ratio is four Blacks to one White. The Government simply cannot succeed in oppressing and discriminating against the black population in the way Germany discriminated against us Jews. Sometime in the future, the blacks will take over, and they will exact a vengeance for all that has been done to them. We must work hard, earn a living and try to save as much as we can. When we have saved enough money, we must leave this country."

The family joined the Germiston synagogue, attending services every Friday night. They soon found that there were a number of Jewish families living in the area and in the surrounding towns of Boksburg and Benoni who, like them, had escaped from Germany. All soon became good friends because they shared a common heritage. A few had started clothing factories, something they had done in Germany. But with the little cash they had, growth was slow.

Irma pleaded with her father and Benjamin to allow her to start her own business, a dream she had had all her life.

"I am 24 years old," she said to them, "I feel I must start doing something before I become too old to do anything on my own."

After a great deal of persuasion, they agreed. She started sewing a sample range of fashionable lingerie, from designs she had enjoyed drawing over the years. She showed what she made to the John Orr's buying department. They liked what they saw and they started giving her small orders. She employed four seamstresses, all of them Blacks who lived in the Location, a township outside Germiston where all Blacks were forced to live by the racial segregation laws of the country. Working from a small room in Germiston, she started her factory. Her range was called Irma's Lingerie.

In observing the young women of South Africa, she noticed that although they dressed conservatively, they were inclined to buy seductive underwear. The days of tight girdles and bloomers were becoming a fashion of the past. She found that the underwear and lingerie she designed and manufactured found a niche market and started to sell exceptionally well through select ladies' stores.

On September 1, 1939, Germany invaded Poland. France and Great Britain, with the Commonwealth countries, immediately declared war on Germany. South Africa was at war.

"I told you that the world would not accept what was happening in Germany," Abie said to the family over dinner, excited at the prospect of returning to Germany. "This war won't last long. When it is over we will all go home."

Benjamin looked at his father, and slowly shook his head. Irene looked at him, so he said nothing.

Irma's company continued growing in spite of the war. She had to employ more seamstresses. She asked Irene to join her in managing the company, which Irene did.

Unexpectedly, fate played its hand. She had made a number of friends at the synagogue, but very rarely went out with anyone. She was far too busy with very little time to socialize. Although the hard life in South Africa had made her lose weight, highlighting her loveliness, she was still extremely shy. One of her friends asked her over for dinner to meet a good friend of theirs. That is where she met Solly Rosen. Solly was a South African, a physician with a small practice in Orange Grove, a suburb of Johannesburg.

Irma was 24 years old, a reasonably successful business woman with no time to go out with friends. Solly was three years older than she, too involved in his practice to ever think of meeting someone. They started dating, and when five months later he asked her to marry him, she agreed. Her parents were absolutely thrilled.

Irma and Solly bought a house close to his practice with a large garden that boasted a swimming pool. She was extremely happy, both with her business which continued to grow and in her marriage. Because she now lived in Johannesburg, she decided to move her business. She found an empty floor space at a reasonable rent in a building on Eloff and Commissioner Streets. She employed more seamstresses and with Irene's help, increased production considerably.

It was then that Benjamin, walking through the city during a lunch hour to fetch Irene for lunch, saw an opportunity to make a great deal of money. He was looking in the window of John Orr waiting for Irene, wondering whether they would employ him at a far better salary than he was presently earning, when he noticed that they were displaying rolls of material used for tailoring gents' suits. He looked at the price, frowned, and then carefully examined each roll on display. That night, after a great deal of thought, he came to a decision.

"Pa, I want to take you to Johannesburg, now, after supper," he said while they were all seated at table eating.

"Why... why now?" his father asked, looking at him curiously.

"Well, I saw something in the window of John Orr that I think could make us some money."

"Like what?" his mother asked, "What is so important that you have to take your father out this late at night?"

"Ma," Benjamin said looking at her, "it is not that late. I saw something and I need Pa's opinion. I cannot take him tomorrow, so it must be now."

He drove his father and Irene into Johannesburg in the small car they had bought. They parked in Eloff Street, and walked to window where Benjamin had seen the material. His father looked at the rolls closely, and studied the prices.

"You are right," he eventually said to Benjamin who was standing next to him with Irene. "You are right, these prices are too cheap." He turned to Irene. "Can you find out how many rolls they have at this price?"

"Yes, Pa, I will find out tomorrow, and let you know," she answered.

Driving home they concocted a plan. They would use whatever savings they had. They would borrow from the bank as much money as they could, and buy as much of the material as possible.

The next night, Irene told them how many rolls were available.

They then worked out how much money they would need to buy as many rolls as they could without raising any suspicion. Taking a day off from work, Benjamin went with his father to their bank in Germiston, and asked the manager whether they could have an overdraft, pledging their house as security on a second mortgage. After much thought, and after they assured him that within three months the loan would be repaid, he agreed. With the money, they then bought a large number of rolls of the material over a number of days, which turned out to be almost the entire stock John Orr had. They stored the rolls in the lounge and dining room of Abie and Bertha's house. They spent many hours repacking the rolls of material, so that they would look different from what they had purchased.

Three months later, acting the part of a salesman for a prestigious European company, Benjamin sold the rolls back to the John Orr buying department at three times the price they had paid. His guess that the buying department did not spend enough time familiarizing themselves with the inventory for sale had been correct.

Abie and Benjamin now had enough money to start a gent's outfitting store in Germiston, on Knox Street. With the war in Europe, stock was becoming difficult to find. They spent many hours visiting the clothing factories their friends had established in and around Germiston.

The clothing store Benjamin and his father started succeeded in growing remarkably quickly, far quicker than even Benjamin had hoped. They soon opened a second store in Johannesburg, on Pritchard Street, where they discounted clothing that did not sell in their main store.

"Irene tells me that you are becoming really busy," Benjamin said to Irma one Sunday as they all sat in the garden having lunch at Irma and Solly's house.

"Yes, we are, "Irma answered, "but I am struggling to find enough cloth of type I like to meet the demand."

"Let me see what I can do for you. One or two of the chaps I know may have something on their shelves that is not suitable for their needs. They could be happy to get rid of it at any price."

"Price does not matter at the moment," Irma answered. "I could use whatever they have as long as it is fine and silky, if possible. Irene knows what we need."

"Uh, by the way Irma, I will have to take a leave of absence soon," Irene said walking behind Benjamin and hugging him, "we are going to have a baby."

"How wonderful," Irma said, "when are you due? "

"In about five months' time."

"Well, I must say you don't show it."

"It is all the tennis I play," Irene said, "and the hard work at the warehouse. It keeps my weight down."

Irma's Lingerie kept going from strength to strength. The War in Europe did limit supplies of cloth needed to manufacture her range, but the public loved her style, and she struggled to keep up with demand. Benjamin helped her with the cloth she needed as much as possible, but it was her style and the fact that she turned large 'bloomers' into tiny thin panties trimmed with lace that were her success. The rest of her range of lingerie was just as skimpy, as she stretched what material she had as far as possible.

She expanded her range, bringing out new styles and fashions that she had dreamed up on her sketch pads. It was to view this new range that Chrissie Stead took Emma.

Chapter 4

Emma was nervous as she walked next to Chrissie Stead down Eloff Street, towards Commissioner Street. The City was busy, and she often fell behind Chrissie as she threaded her way through the shoppers. She never said a word to Chrissie, and Chrissie never spoke to her, obviously thinking about something. She still couldn't believe that she, Emily Kleintjies, now Emma Kline, was to have her own range of fashionable lingerie to promote and sell. That she had been given so much responsibility.

"*If Ma could only see me now,*" she thought as she caught a glance of her reflection in a shop front display window. "*She would be so proud of me, but I cannot tell her, I dare not tell her. I just cannot take the chance.*"

She did not look her age, being very careful to dress conservatively, fashioning her hair and make up to present an older, more mature image.

Chrissie Stead was frowning and agitated as she walked, giving Emma the impression that she was wasting her time by taking her to meet Irma Rosen, but she had to introduce them to each other. She was also curious to see the entire range that Irma was promoting, to come to a decision whether or not it was suitable for the OK Bazaars. The few pieces that Irma had sent her, that she had asked Emma to look at, were truly something very different than what they normally sold, but would they sell at the OK Bazaars? People came to buy at the OK because they offered a cheaper range of clothing than that at John Orr or Anstey's. She wondered whether the range was not out of character for the company. Irma Rosen had told her that she was manufacturing a range more in line with what the OK would sell, but Chrissie felt that she had to see the full range to make a decision. However, now that she had promoted Emma to the job of making the choice… well, it would be interesting to see what she chose.

"*She is definitely dressed for the part,*" she thought looking at Emma out of the corner of her eye as she walked beside her. "*I will soon find out whether Mr. Gersh's decision to give her the range was correct or not.*"

The entrance leading to Irma Lingerie was between two very fashionable shops, one a ladies' clothing shop and the other a gents' outfitters. Their display windows were beautifully prepared, and both stores looked very busy. Chrissie found the door locked. She had to ring the bell. A young African girl opened the door for them.

"Can I help you Ma'am?" she asked.

"We are here to see Mrs. Rosen," Chrissie said. "We have an appointment."

"Do come in," the African girl said, opening the door to allow them to walk in. "Mrs. Rosen is on the second floor." She pointed to the stairs.

They started walking up two flights of stairs, the young girl following them. Elephant trading was on the first floor. The door was open, and Emma peeked inside as they walked past, but all she saw were offices with people sitting at their desks and working. The steps circled an industrial elevator shaft, and while they continued on to the second floor, the elevator started rumbling past them on its way to the ground floor. Chrissie was panting and sweating badly as they reached the second floor. It was very hot in the stairwell. She looked at Emma, who looked as cool as a cucumber.

'The advantages of youth,' she thought as she wondered why they had not taken the elevator.

The young girl who had followed them up the stairs opened the door to the warehouse, leading the way to Irma's office. The floor was brightly lit when compared to the dull light of the stairwell. They walked in and Emma was surprised at how large the area was. There were three offices on her left, with rows and rows of clothes hanging on racks on her right. Tables with lingerie displayed on them were arranged between the offices and the racks. At the far right, she could see a number of girls folding and packing garments into boxes while towards the back of the factory there were 30 to 35 girls all working at sewing machines. Soft music was playing while they worked, lending a relaxed atmosphere to the floor, but the noise of the sewing machines and the talking and laughter of the girls drowned out the music. Three large fans kept the air, scented with a soft perfume, circulating. The temperature was far cooler, adding to the pleasant ambience. Emma felt that the whole scene was a very relaxed and happy one.

Chrissie turned to Emma and said, "This is a new range of ladies' lingerie that we have been asked to look at. The designer, Irma Rosen, is a friend of Mr. Gersh. We have held her products before, but never in great quantity, as it is not quite our style... not our market... a bit too fancy and pricey. The samples I gave you to look at last night were but a few pieces from the range. Look through her range, and choose what you feel we can sell." She never told Emma that she had rejected the pieces as being far too daring, something she felt the company would have difficulty selling. She never mentioned that Mr. Gersh had overruled her decision, and insisted that she look at the complete range, and that he felt that they should upgrade the lingerie of the store as a test to see whether the company could handle a more exclusive and expensive product.

They walked into Irma's office. Irma rose from her desk where she had been talking on the telephone to greet them. "Hello, Chrissie," she said with a strong German accent, and turning to Emma smiled and held out her hand, "and you must be Emma. How lovely to meet you."

'Good heavens,' she thought, 'this girl looks so young. Well, she must be good if they have given her the position she has,' and then looking at the way Emma was dressed, 'I can see why.'

"Hello, Irma," Chrissie answered, and looking around continued, "and my, but your factory has grown since I was last here."

"Thank you, Chrissie," Irma replied, "we are very busy with clients all over the country, even into Rhodesia and Mozambique, where the John Orr branch has placed a very large order. Those Portuguese girls must have a more modern taste than the girls in South Africa, perhaps because they do visit Portugal and are influenced by European fashion." While she spoke she guided them to her office, seating them in two chairs close to her desk.

"Can I get you something to drink? Tea, coffee, a Coke?"

"Tea, thanks," Chrissie said seating herself.

"And for you, Emma?" Irma asked.

"Coffee would be lovely, thank you," Emma replied and then nearly jumped out of her skin as Irma shouted out the door,

"Emily… two teas and one coffee, please."

"Yes, Ma'am," came the reply from the young girl who had escorted them up the stairs.

Irma took her seat at her desk, and then said to Emma, "Emma, my dear, I will take you to examine the entire range. Have a look through it, and let me know which of the pieces you like."

"Emma looked through the sample range you sent me," Chrissie said, "and chose a number of garments."

"Ah… that is nice," Irma said, "but there are a lot more than that small sample range that I sent you. I chose them after Leonard Gersh said I should send you some pieces to look at, and I just chose a few rather quickly."

Emma stood up, and walked to the door of the office.

"They are all on the table over there," Irma continued pointing to where the tables were. Put what you like onto that empty table near the office, and do look at the hangers," and she pointed to a row of hangers with dresses on them. "This is something new we are trying. If you like anything," and she smiled looking at the way Emma was dressed, "and I am sure you will, put them on the hanger next to the table."

Emma chose with care, enthralled with what she saw. She knew that Chrissie Stead was watching her carefully, but decided that she would take the plunge, and so chose only what she liked and what she thought customers may like. What she chose was not excessive, a small sample of the entire range, that she felt was different, and very stylish. While she was making her choice, Irma Rosen had walked up quietly behind her, watching her with interest, and impressed at what she had chosen. Emma had been concentrating and had not noticed Irma watching her.

"I must say that I find what you have chosen out of the range very interesting, because they are something new in fashion, something that we have been working on for some time. A little bit more daring than what we normally make."

Emma turned and smiled. "The range is very beautiful, Mrs. Rosen," she answered. "They should sell well among the younger set in Johannesburg. I'm a little bit uncertain about the surrounding platteland though."

Irma nodded in agreement, "I am inclined to agree with you," she said, "but you never know until you have tried."

They were soon talking about the range, with Irma asking Emma why she had chosen certain pieces and why not others. Emma forgot her shyness, and the two of them were soon chatting like old friends discussing each and every garment, with Irma noting everything Emma said. Chrissie Stead looked on with surprise. Irma Rosen had always been polite to her, but never over friendly. That she and Emma hit it off so well puzzled her.

"I must add that I really do like your dresses as well," Emma said, pointing to the racks filled with dresses. "I have chosen a few that I especially like, and put them on the rack as you suggested. Who is the designer?"

Irma looked away, "Oh, they are something I have wanted to do ever since I was a little girl. I decided to make a few of my styles, and see whether buyers would like them or not."

"Well, they are very fashionable," Emma said moving to the rack of dresses she had chosen, "but I wonder whether they are not too fashionable for the OK Bazaars."

"They were not designed for the OK," Irma said, looking at the dresses Emma had chosen, "more for the up market private boutiques. I was curious to see whether you," and she looked at Emma, "with your excellent taste in dresses, would like them."

Emma blushed and looked at the ground. "Thank you," she said.

"I wonder, "Irma continued, "if you ever have the time, whether you would like to model them for me. You do dress beautifully, and would be a perfect model. I would really appreciate it."

"Oh, thank you," Emma said, "but I work full time at the OK, and I will soon be travelling a lot to the branches, showing off your range of lingerie."

"Oh…that is no problem, just let me have your schedule and I will arrange mine to fit in with yours. It will be about once every three months, usually in the evening."

"Thank you," Emma replied, "that is most considerate of you."

"By the way," Irma asked, curious, "forgive me for asking, but you are Jewish aren't you?"

"No," Emma said, "My parents are Christian. For myself, I don't want to say that I am an atheist, but I am not religious at all."

"Oh…" Irma replied, surprised, "It is just that your surname, Kline, is usually associated with a person that is Jewish. I have a good friend with that surname… rather my husband has." She hesitated for a moment. "My husband and I are Jewish, and I just…"

"So that explains it," Emma interrupted her and smiled. "You are not the first who assumed I am Jewish. Now I know why," and she laughed.

A month later, the first of Irma Rosen's range that Emma had chosen appeared in the Johannesburg stores. They sold out within the first week. Emma increased the order quantity and started visiting the East Rand branches. She was given a company car with a Black, James, as her driver. She was still too scared to apply for a driver's license.

At each branch she was welcomed by the manager, who led her to a display room next to their office. She would arrange the garments on the tables provided, then watch the assistants as they looked, chatting with them and getting their opinion on what they thought. She started placing orders with Irma for the branches, spending time at each branch making sure that the lingerie was displayed in the way that had proved so successful at the OK Bazaars in Johannesburg. Sales soared.

Emma soon found that she was spending almost as much time visiting the branches, talking to the sales ladies and listening to their suggestions, as she did with Irma Rosen in discussing styles, fashions, and enlarging the range. They would often have lunch together, with Emma carefully copying Irma's table manners and listening very carefully to what she ordered, while they discussed new fashions for the product range.

Every three months, usually on a Saturday night, she would model at a fashion show Irma held to display her dresses. Emma enjoyed walking the runway, and the attention she received. A very close friendship developed between them. Emma spent a great deal of time at Irma's house on weekends, and often joined her and Solly at a social function. She was becoming a celebrity in the fashion industry in Johannesburg, and she did not know it.

She went on many dates, having decided early on that she would go out with anyone that asked her out, but she made a point of not going to bed with them. She still went out with Eric whenever he was in Johannesburg, which was seldom. She enjoyed his company.

And then a photograph of her modeling one of Irma's dresses appeared in the *Sunday Times* newspaper. She was shocked and scared.

She realized that if she continued with her present lifestyle, someone in Cape Town would recognize her in one or other photo and her secret would then be out.

The next evening, after a sleepless night, she took a taxi to Irma's house. She had reached a decision to stop the modeling, and she had to talk with Irma. The previous night she had tossed and turned in bed, agonizing over what she would tell Irma. She thought about the stories Irma had told her of their life in Germany, in Berlin, and how they had to escape from the country. At how shocked the family was to have found racial bias in South Africa, and that, sometime in the future should things get really bad, they intended to leave the country. She decided to tell Irma the truth about her background.

"Irma," she said when Irma answered the door to her, "I need to talk to you privately."

"Solly is not here, he is still at the hospital. Let us sit in the garden," Irma said, "I will make some tea, and then we can talk."

Emma walked into the garden. It was beautifully designed, with a number of fruit trees strategically placed so as not to cast too much shade on the flower beds. Irma loved gardening, and spent a great deal of time working in it. Emma made her way slowly to a garden table with four chairs shaded by a large Jacaranda tree, its purple flowers a beautiful contrast to the orange of the setting sun slowly drifting down into the horizon. The smell of roses as they cast their evening scent charmed her nostrils. As the sun sank, a bird, started chirping its evening serenade.

"*What a beautiful country to live in,*" Emma thought, "*what a beautiful...*" and she put her hand to her mouth and stifled a sob.

Irma carried a tray to where Emma sat. She placed it on the garden table, then sat down in one of the chairs and started pouring the tea. She looked up at Emma, shadowed against the setting sun. "*What an incredibly beautiful girl,*" she thought, "*I am so pleased that we are friends.*"

Emma added a little bit of milk and two spoonfuls of sugar to her cup, stirred it and took a sip. Then she put down her cup in the saucer, and said to Irma.

"Irma, what I have to tell you may hurt our friendship, but because of your experience in Germany, I feel that I must tell you because I know you will understand. I sincerely hope that it will be a secret just between you and me."

The first thing Irma thought when she heard Emma say this was that Emma was going to tell her that she was pregnant. She looked at Emma and said softly.

"Emma my dear, you do know that I love you dearly and regard you as a dear friend. Whatever you have to tell me, my lips will be sealed." She stretched out a hand and cupped it over Emma's hand that was on the table.

Emma looked at her and saw that indeed, Irma was serious about what she said. "Well," Emma started, "you ran away from a country because of religious bias. I have run away from a city because of racial bias."

Irma looked puzzled. "What do you mean?" she asked.

"Well, you see," Emma began softly, and she leaned back in her chair turning her face away from Irma, "I was born into a Cape Coloured family in Cape Town. My mother and father are both Coloureds."

Irma was shocked, and then as if the words Emma had spoken lit a fire within her, her face lit up and she almost shouted, "How wonderful! How absolutely wonderful! You must tell me everything! I want to know how you did it. How you managed to get away from this horrible system we live with. Tell me everything."

For the next hour, Emma told her the story of her life, how she simply could not live with the racial discrimination against her and her family. How, ever since she was a child, she had rebelled against being classified as a second-class citizen in a country that she loved. How she had taught herself European customs, and learned to talk English without a trace of a coloured accent. The hours she had spent talking to herself, and reciting poetry, mimicking the accent of announcers she heard talk on the radio. How she had made up her mind to come to Johannesburg and make a new life for herself as a White European. How easy it had been in some aspects, but how difficult it had been in others.

"... and I nearly died when, on that first day in your office you shouted, 'Emily... will you make some tea'. You see, my true name is Emily, and for a minute I thought you had found me out."

All the time she spoke, Irma never said a word, listening intently to what she said. "I have always thought you were a beautiful, well-dressed, wonderful person," she said leaning forward, tears in her eyes. "You just cannot imagine how much I admire and respect you, even more so now, after what you have told me. Your secret is safe with me."

"So do you understand why I can no longer model for you?" Emma sobbed.

"But of course, of course I do," Irma said. "Don't worry about it. What are the chances they will see your photo in the *Sunday Times?*"

"Fortunately, the *Sunday Times* is not that well read in the Cape," Emma answered, "and at any rate my family do not read the papers, but someone else in Cape Town that knows our family, just might recognize me. It is just not worth taking the chance. I live almost daily in the fear that I will somehow give myself away."

"I think that there is very little chance of that," Irma replied smiling at her and trying to calm her fears. "You are in more ways, more a White than many White South Africans I have met. You are always tastefully dressed, with impeccable manners. Bravo to you."

When she eventually left with Irma driving her back to Raema Court, she knew that Irma would protect her secret. That night she slept more soundly than she had in a long time. The simple act, sharing her secret with a good friend who truly respected her was a comfort she had desperately needed.

Chapter 5

Emma had never been interested in the affairs of the world, outside of her home country. When South Africa declared war on Germany on September 6, 1939, she had recently been promoted to lingerie buyer. She was only 19 years old and she had more important matters on her mind than world politics. The fact that J.B.M. Hertzog, a Boer general who became Prime Minister of the Union of South Africa, lost the vote on his motion in the United Party caucus by 80 votes to 67 votes, that South Africa remain neutral in the war, didn't interest her at all. When General Jan Christiaan Smuts became leader of the United Party, and then Prime Minister of South Africa, had anyone asked her who the Prime Minister of South Africa was, she would have answered, "I don't really know."

However, her friendship with the Rosens changed that. Whenever she was invited to their home, she would listen carefully when they excitedly spoke about the countries of the British Commonwealth that were now at war with Germany. They were also shocked that General Smuts had not enforced conscription, relying on volunteers to join the army.

"He is scared of angering the Afrikaner," Benjamin said. "He is protecting himself so that when he fights the next election, he will have a good chance of winning."

"Is that why he hasn't armed the Cape Corps?" Solly asked, walking to the liquor cabinet to pour Benjamin a whisky. The Cape Corps was drawn from the Cape Coloured and Indian populations.

"Look," Benjamin answered, "he needs fighting men, so he armed the Whites. The Cape Corps is there to do the labour, and clean the barracks, that is all. They are there to do the manual labour while the Whites fight and get shot. From what I hear, he has also formed a Native Military Corps manned by Blacks to do exactly the same thing. Probably not enough Coloureds and Indians joined up. They are all good enough to work in line of fire, but they are not good enough to be trusted with weapons. How cynical."

When Emma heard Benjamin say the word 'Coloured', her ears pricked up. She was sitting with Irma and Irene drinking tea, half listening to them as they spoke about the lingerie fashions. She began to realize that she needed to pay more attention to what was happening in South Africa and in the world.

She started reading the newspapers and listening to the news on the radio, especially when she was travelling in her car. She also started to notice that many of the young men that dated her were suddenly no longer around. They had joined the army of their own free will.

Eric phoned her in July of 1940. He told her that he had volunteered for the army and would be stationed at the military camp in Potchefstroom for the next six months. He was doing his basic training before he was sent overseas. When Emma heard this, she couldn't wait to get on the road and visit the branch in Potchefstroom.

Both Irma and Chrissie were very pleased with her success. At Emma's suggestion, they both agreed with her that it was time to test the range in the more conservative Pretoria and Western Transvaal. Emma started to rearrange her schedule to visit the branches in Pretoria, Krugersdorp, Randfontein, Potchefstroom and Klerksdorp.

By now she had become a sophisticated representative, known and respected by all who met her. Her salary increase had allowed her much more freedom in buying her clothes, but her friendship with Irma Rosen gave her access to Irma's dresses, which Irma sold to her at a pittance. Irma wanted Emma to wear them as a form of advertising.

As Emma's salary improved, she started sending money to her parents in Cape Town, telling them that she had a position as a maid in a wealthy household in Johannesburg, and that her employer paid her an above average salary. The first thing her mother asked her, in a letter that upset Emma terribly, was whether she was the mistress of her employer, and was this the reason he paid her a good salary.

'*Please my dear,*' she wrote in one of her letters, '*you must not fall pregnant, until you are married. Go to a Pharmacy and buy a thing called a French Letter. Make sure that your lover uses it all the time, and also wash yourself thoroughly after you make love.*'

She then listed a number of recipes made with plants that grew in the veldt. They made Emma laugh through her tears.

'*Just like Ma,*' she giggled, wiping the tears from her eyes, '*she does not reprimand me for sleeping with the man, but rather gives me a recipe on not falling pregnant, a recipe that her grandmother's grandmother probably gave her,*' and she shook her head.

She had taken the precaution of renting a post office box so that all and any letters coming to her from home addressed to Emily Kleintjies were private. She also developed the habit of opening the letter immediately, and destroying the envelope so that it would not be found lying around.

She wrote to her mother that her employer was a woman called Irma Rosen, consoling herself that in a way she was not telling a total lie. When she thought of it, Irma did employ her. She just did not pay her a salary. She enclosed an above average cheque and asked her parents to install a telephone. Telephones in individual houses in District Six were most uncommon. After a long three-month wait, it was installed. When she received a letter telling her that they now had a telephone number, she phoned her parents in Cape Town at least once a week, talking to them in Afrikaans, as she always did, unconsciously lapsing into the Cape Coloured dialect. She refused to give them her telephone number, telling them that she always phoned them from a telephone booth.

Over Christmas, when she usually took her three week yearly holiday, she travelled by train to Cape Town. When the train stopped at Paarl, she changed her clothes and scrubbed her face clean of all the makeup she wore. With a 'doek' around her wet hair and wearing a plain dress, she would change coaches, moving to the coach marked for non-Whites only, so that when the family met her at Cape Town station they would suspect nothing.

The family always grilled her about Johannesburg; "Where do you live? Isn't it too hot... too busy... too..." it never stopped. She would skate around the questions, telling them that she was sorry she had moved there, and that living in Cape Town was so much better.

"If it were not for the job I have, which is paying me a much better salary than I could ever earn here, I would be back tomorrow," she would lie. "Life there is not pleasant, the Afrikaners treat you badly, and the natives even worse. Sometimes when I go home at night..." and she would concoct a story that would grow more gruesome every time she told it. The last thing she wanted was for a brother or sister to join her.

She enjoyed being with the family and always cried when she left her mother, whom she loved dearly, always leaving her as much money as remained in her purse after buying the family anything they needed in the two weeks she was usually with them.

"Here, Ma," she would say handing her an envelope, "I earn plenty where I am. I don't need this." Her mother never refused what was given to her, but always sobbed, proud to have such a wonderful daughter.

Her fear of being found out never left her. On her last trip to Cape Town, when returning to Johannesburg, she changed her clothes at Paarl as she usually did. Her heart sank as she heard someone shout as she was entering the carriage marked 'Europeans only'.

"Hey you, you don't belong there."

She turned, her face white with apprehension, her knees shaking.

Then she saw that the man who had shouted was shouting at a young White boy entering the toilet marked 'non-Europeans.' She walked to her compartment and collapsed in a seat, sobbing with relief.

With the excitement of the entry into the war and the relaxing of morals that goes with a war, she was still too scared to form a close relationship with the few boys who dated her. She found that her feelings started to lie with Eric more and more. In Eric, she found an emotion that she was not sure how to handle.

In listening to the conversation at the Rosens whenever she visited them, she started to become concerned that Germany would conquer the world, and that the racism she so hated in South Africa would become the norm.

"Why has America not declared war on Germany?" Benjamin asked everyone one night as they sat in the garden. "Is it because of the high amount of racial bias within the country? I like Franklin D Roosevelt. I believe that he is a good president and an honest man, so why has America not allied themselves with Britain in their war against Germany? I just don't understand it."

They had told her how they had escaped from Germany because of hatred for the Jews by the Germans. That they had been classified as second class citizens, losing the vote and that here, in South Africa, they were shocked to find the same thing happening to anyone that was not a White.

"South West Africa was a German colony before the First World War," Benjamin continued, showing his agitation by walking up and down the room, unable to sit in his chair. "They had a brutal policy towards the natives. After the war South Africa became responsible for its administration. Parliament allowed the integration of its White citizens with their pro-German feelings, into South African society. Will the same thing happen now should Germany win this war? Will they be as brutal to the natives, and anyone that they consider non-Aryan in South Africa, as brutal as they had been when they ruled German

South-West Africa? The more I think about it, the more scared I become." He took a sip of the whiskey glass he held in his hand.

Emma, in listening to him, started to fear for herself and her family. To overcome this fear, she worked even harder than before, determined to follow the example set by Irma in making and saving a great deal of money, so that sometime in the future, somehow she and her family could leave the country.

She had very little trouble setting up the line of lingerie in Krugersdorp and Randfontein, and although the branches were far smaller than in Johannesburg and the Rand, sales were very good, far better than expected. Pretoria however, was a different kettle of fish. Pretoria was the administrative capital of South Africa, and was a very conservative city with Afrikaans the dominant language.

Emma loved Pretoria. With James driving the new Chevrolet the OK Bazaars had given her, she sat in the back seat, enjoying the almost hour drive from Johannesburg. The road was an avenue of tall blue gum trees that changed to the purple flowered Jacaranda as they approached the city. Pretoria had a far warmer climate than Johannesburg, with a much smaller city center. She found that the people who shopped there were relaxed in their shopping, spending more time in their choice of merchandise.

James was a Zulu, tall, well built with a skin blacker than black. He was always well dressed, with a black jacket and a chauffeur's cap that he enjoyed wearing when on duty. Somehow, whenever she needed him, or looked for him, he always appeared, as though instructed to keep her always in his sight. He carried her suitcases with the sample range, placing them next to her wherever she had to display them. Then he would leave the room, and wait patiently within calling distance. He very rarely spoke to her, and she learned not to try and talk to him, not that he couldn't talk. It was simply because he only spoke Zulu, with the few English words that he needed in his work.

The manager of the OK Bazaars in Pretoria, Mr. Grobelaar, was an Afrikaner, and she was pleasantly surprised when he treated her far better than she had expected. She had thought that all Afrikaners were anti-English, and here was a man that, although he spoke English badly, always tried to speak to her in English. She had always had the impression that in coming to Pretoria, the home of the Afrikaner, she would have to dress far more conservatively than she did and was pleased to find out that her assumptions were wrong.

While she displayed her range, she was amused that Mr. Grobelaar kept interfering when she spoke with staff about how to sell the lingerie. She started to feel that perhaps he was making a pass at her. Then he introduced her to his wife, who happened to be in the store, a lovely woman, soft spoken and conservatively but beautifully dressed. Emma watched carefully as Mrs. Grobelaar looked through the range and loved what she saw, something that Emma had not expected. She decided that on her next visit, she would bring lingerie that was far more daring.

"You know, Mr. Grobelaar," she said to him as she was packing up her range, "I was very nervous about coming to Pretoria with this range. I expected that there would be difficulty in presenting it to your staff."

"Please," he replied in his broken English, "Pretoria is a conservative town, yes, you are right there. Where Johannesburg is the English city, with a very big university for the English speaking students, Pretoria is an Afrikaans City, and the university here is for those who talk Afrikaans. But there are many like me, who talk Afrikaans at home, and try to talk English at work. We are liberal in our thinking. Our women like beautiful clothes," and he smiled as he thought about the choices his wife had made.

"I am going to Potchefstroom next week," Emma said."I understand that Potchefstroom is even more conservative than Pretoria."

"I suppose so," he answered. "They do have an Afrikaans University there as well. The Potchefstroom University for Christian Higher

Education is supposedly more religious and far more conservative than ours here in Pretoria, but I really don't know for sure."

"Well, we will see," Emma said as she picked up her suitcase. "I will be back about the same time next month and I will bring the full range. Do give my regards to Mrs. Grobelaar."

A week later, quite early in the morning, with her driver James, she embarked on what she felt would be a long 72 mile drive to Potchefstroom. She wanted to visit the town, because Eric was there. He had been given a two-day leave. She had arranged her schedule so that she could be with him for those two days.

The drive from Johannesburg to Potchefstroom was terribly slow. Leaving Johannesburg, the road was tarred up until Baragwanath Hospital, a hospital that treated Coloureds, Indians and Blacks. Medical students from all over the world came there for experience, because all types of diseases surfaced there. The hospital was always short of medical and nursing staff. Wait times were long, with many patients bedding in the corridors.

As soon as they passed three towers steaming from the top, towers that supplied gas to Johannesburg, the road became a gravel road. It was long and boring with a forest of newly planted Blue Gum trees on the left, the trunks of which were harvested and used in the mines. The forest soon gave way to farms of either mielies (corn) or sunflowers, their huge yellow blooms with their black seed center always facing the sun as it crossed the sky. The road was lined with colourful Cosmos, in the last stages of their flowering. A flock of Guinea fowl ran across the road. James slowed the car and Emma watched them as they ran for cover under a Mimosa tree growing next to a large Aloe plant.

They could only travel at 50 miles per hour because of the numerous corrugations. After what seemed like an eternity, they came to the Kraalkop Hotel, nestled on the side of the road, just before the turnoff to the town of Fochville. She told James to stop, so that she could buy something for them to drink. It was terribly hot in the car, and they were both thirsty. As she climbed out of the car, she saw that her dress was covered in red dust that had seeped into the car. Emma concluded that American cars were not geared to African dirt roads.

Refreshed by the drink, they continued on to Potchefstroom. After another hour of a hot, sweaty and bumpy drive, feeling tired and dirty, she saw, in the far distance, a row of what looked like fully grown blue gum trees with a small opening that the road appeared to go through. The trees grew larger and larger as they approached and the road became even more corrugated, as if to say, 'come closer at your peril.'

Eventually with a drop and a bump, they drove onto the macadamized surface of the town's road, and the car settled smoothly. A row of willow trees welcomed them, beckoning them to drive over a small bridge crossing the Mooi River. As James drove slowly over the bridge, Emma looked down and saw clear blue water that rippled as the branches of the willows fingered the surface. She felt a lot cooler.

The town was an oasis of greenery amongst the yellow, dry fields of the surrounding khaki veldt that had accompanied them most of the way from Johannesburg. She was charmed by the beautiful trees and gardens that lined the streets.

'What a beautiful welcome', she thought as they drove up Lombard Street past a golf course. They continued on past a row of small shops and garages to King Edward Street, with the OK Bazaars on the corner opposite the Royal Hotel. Not quite sure where to go, she told James to park the car. She walked into The Rendezvous Café immediately opposite the OK Bazaars, diagonally across from the Royal Hotel, where James sat in the car waiting for her. She was tempted with the thought of something to drink, but decided to rather find the Kings Hotel where a room had been reserved for her and freshen up before exploring the town. Chrissie Stead had told her that the hotel was on the corner of King Edward and Potgieter streets, so she asked for directions from the owner.

"Turn left, and drive up King Edward Street." He pointed up the street. "You should find the hotel on the left side at the next corner."

She walked back to the car, looking down King Edward Street in the direction they would have to go as she crossed the road. There was a huge snow white cumulus cloud hanging high over the buildings that lined the street. No building was higher than two stories. '*What a beautiful picture*' she thought. '*I must take a walk through the street and look at all the shops.*'

She told James to turn left, and drive slowly to the next corner where he should find parking. She noticed as he slowly steered the car down the street that there were not that many pedestrians around.

'*Could be because it is lunch time.*' she thought.

Tired from the trip and feeling dirty from the dust that had seeped into the car, she looked forward to having a hot bath. At the next corner, James turned left and parked the car in front of the Kings Hotel. He helped carry her suitcases to the foyer as she checked into the hotel.

"I have an African driver with me," she told them at reception. "Do you have accommodation for him?"

"Yes Ma'am," the receptionist said. "We have spare rooms in the servants' quarters. We will show him where to go."

"James," she said as he was led away. "Take the rest of the day off. I will only need you tomorrow morning."

"Thank you, Missus," James said, saluting her.

The hotel on the outside appeared as old as the town itself, but it was beautiful in its grandeur, with a wood paneled entrance, broad and spacious, but beginning to show signs of wear and tear. The wooden staircase leading to the first floor, the only floor, was broad and grand. After she had checked in, and a porter had taken her luggage to her room, she drew a bath. Relaxing in the warm water, thinking about the long drive, she hoped that it was something she would not have to do that often. Feeling refreshed after her bath, she walked to the hotel restaurant for some lunch. She had arranged with Eric that if he could, he should phone her at about six o'clock that evening. If she were not there for some or other reason, to try again before seven o'clock the next morning.

After a most enjoyable lunch, and feeling energetic, she decided to walk down King Edward Street, looking at the shops that made up the main street of the town. She walked the length of the street to the OK Bazaars. Not introducing herself, she pretended to be a shopper and watched with interest the way the staff sold merchandise and the type of clientele that visited the store. Walking to the lingerie counter, she pretended to look at the garments, eavesdropping as a staff member told the assistants that the buyer from Johannesburg would be there sometime tomorrow. That they should tidy the counter before the store closed. Emma smiled to herself and turned her back to the voice, not wanting the staff to know that the buyer was already in the store. Pretending to shop, she studied the style of feminine merchandise they stocked. A sales lady approached her.

"Can I help you with anything, Miss?" she asked in Afrikaans.

"No, thank you," Emma replied in English, "I am just looking."

When she felt that she had seen enough, she walked slowly down the street back to Annette's, a dress shop she had seen earlier. After admiring the dresses in the window, she walked in on an impulse and asked whether she might try one on. Mrs. Lowenstein, the owner, who was seated at her desk, working on her books, stood up and smiled.

"You are Mrs. Lowenstein, am I right?" Emma asked, walking up to the desk.

"Why yes," Annette Lowenstein answered, "and you are?"

"I am Emma Kline, and I bring you greetings from your sister, Reena Rowe."

"How wonderful," Annette answered. "How is she? How do you know her?"

"Well," Emma said smiling, "I live at Raema Court in Johannesburg. When I told her that I was coming to Potchefstroom, she said that I must look you up."

Before long the two of them were chatting away about life in Potchefstroom, how different it was from life in Johannesburg, and how trying the drive down could be.

"The city council have been nagging the province for some time now to tar the road, especially now that the camp is so full of soldiers. With army trucks travelling between here and Johannesburg so often, and with the war on, I don't think they will do it that soon," Annette said disdainfully. "I hate travelling by car to Johannesburg, one of the reasons why I don't visit Reena as often as I would like to. I only go when I have to stock up and then I go by train."

"May I give you an address to visit?" Emma asked. "The showroom for dresses, very stylish, is run by Irma Rosen, and I am sure you would love her fashions," and Emma handed her one of Irma's cards. "In fact," she continued, "I am wearing one of her dresses," and she spun on her heels.

"Hmmm," said Annette looking at her, "I will see if I have the time next time I am in Johannesburg," and then looking at Emma as she turned, "I must admit though, that I do like what you are wearing."

"Do you know Lilly Stern?" Emma asked

"Of course I know her," Annette answered, "she is my niece."

"Can you tell me where I can find her? I promised her that whenever I should come to Potchefstroom, I would look her up."

"Well, her husband, Alf, owns the Mooi River Pharmacy. It is just down the road. She may be there."

"Thank you, I will go there and have a look," Emma answered. Then saying goodbye, she promised to see her before she left and take a parcel from her back to Reena.

The pharmacy was small, with counters on the left side, and display cabinets on the right. Emma looked at the display of cosmetics, chose a lipstick and nail polish, and then made a point of talking to the young woman who served her.

"Is Mrs. Lilly Stern perhaps here?" she asked.

"No, I am afraid not," Marie Stuart replied.

"Oh…" Emma answered, "I am from Johannesburg, and I have greetings from her mother. Can I possibly see Mr. Stern then?"

"Mr. Stern is busy with an eye appointment. He is the only optometrist in town and is always busy," Marie answered. "He should be about another 15 to 30 minutes."

"Is it alright if I wait?" Emma asked.

"Of course" Marie replied, and because the shop was not at all busy the two of them started chatting.

"Where are you from?" Marie asked.

"Jo'burg," Emma answered as she paid for what she had chosen. "I work for the OK. I am here to introduce them to a new range of lingerie. I live at Raema Court, in Joh'burg, the boarding house owned by Mrs. Stern's mother, and promised her that whenever I was in Potchefstroom, I would drop in to say hello."

"That is so nice of you," Marie answered, and then excused herself to serve a customer who had walked in the door.

Emma waited a few minutes, and then waved at Marie, "I will be back a little later," she said, and left the shop.

Marie waved back.

Emma walked to the hotel which was across the street, to see if Eric had perhaps phoned and left a message. He had not. She walked into the lounge, and sat at a table to read a magazine.

'If Eric does call tonight, the earliest I can see him is tomorrow,' she thought as she ordered a pot of tea from the waiter.

She looked forward to Eric's call. If he could meet her early enough, she would ask him whether he could join her on her trip to Klerksdorp.

"He could be a great help," she decided, "because he knows the branch."

Emma finished drinking her tea, and decided that rather than spend the evening alone, she would ask Marie Stuart to join her for dinner. She liked Marie. To have a friend in Potchefstroom would be nice.

She walked back to the pharmacy. Marie was finishing with serving the customer, charging her purchase. Emma waited for her, looking around to see if she could see Alf Stern.

When Marie was free, Emma asked her, "Marie, I would like to learn more about the town. Will you have a drink with me after work and join me for dinner? I am across the road at the King's Hotel."

"I would love to," Marie smiled.

"What time do you finish here?" Emma asked, pleased that she would not be alone for the evening.

"About half past five," Marie answered, but rather let me meet you at the hotel. I would like to go home first, to change and freshen up."

"OK," Emma said, "I will be sitting in the lounge, waiting for you."

"I won't be that long," Marie answered. "We don't live far from the shop."

Chapter 6

Marie had been born in Potchefstroom, the youngest of four children to Charles and Christa Stuart. Charles had come to South Africa from Scotland as a young lad to fight in the Anglo-Boer war for England. Rather than return to Scotland at the end of the war, he decided to remain in South Africa, a country he had learned to love. He chose Potchefstroom to settle in, simply because that is where he met and fell in love with Christa Angelina Schoeman.

The Schoeman family were horrified that their daughter wanted to marry a Scotsman, the enemy as they put it, but Charles' ebullient personality and love of fishing soon won them over. Charles refused to be put off by their initial antagonism. His love for Christa overcame any anger he may have felt. She loved him as well, their need for each other overcoming all the bitterness the Schoeman family felt for the English. Of course the fact that he was Scottish and not English helped, as did his technique of casting a rod for trout, a skill he had learned from his father during his childhood in Scotland. Charles taught the technique to his future father-in-law, and was convinced that it played a big part in his acceptance by him. Though, to be quite honest, there were no trout in the Mooi or Vaal rivers, nor in the Potchefstroom dam where they did most of their fishing and drinking, sitting on stools in the reeds at the north end, where the Mooi River ran into the dam under the railway bridge.

Old man Schoeman, as he was known to all in Potchefstroom, was won over by his son-in-law. Although he spoke Afrikaans to him, and Charlie, as everyone called Charles Stuart, could only speak English with a smattering of Afrikaans that brayed with his rolling 'r's', they became inseparable. Charlie, although a good Presbyterian, married Christa in a Dutch Reformed Church, and to please his father-in-law, sat with the family in their pew every Sunday, hardly understanding a single Afrikaans word thrown to the captive congregation by the Dominee. He would more than often try to hold Christa's hand during the service, but she would brush him off with an "ag man, not in Church," and then smile at him suggestively.

Marie was the youngest of four children. Her two elder brothers, Petrus and Andries, were fishermen from an early age as they accompanied their father and grandfather on their many fishing expeditions. Her elder sister, Lucinda, was more interested in cooking and baking with their mother than the more adventurous life of the various river banks. All the Stuart children were educated in Afrikaans schools, going to the Hoer Gimnasium.

Marie, as she grew older, reminded Charlie so much of his late mother that he decided she should have an English education. After a heartfelt discussion with Christa, promising her everything but the world, she consented. Marie was sent to Central School and later to the High School for Girls. Because of this, she was thoroughly bilingual, speaking both English and Afrikaans fluently. Marie was not a student who excelled however, and at 16 years old, left school after she had completed and passed Standard 8. She found employment at the Mooi River Pharmacy as a sales assistant. Her fluency in English and Afrikaans was a big asset in a town where both languages and cultures were divisive.

Marie had grown up to be a home town girl, never going beyond the borders of Potchefstroom. She had never visited Klerksdorp, Ventersdorp nor any other town close to Potchefstroom. The furthest from the town she had ever been was when the family had gone to the eye of the Mooi River, about 22 miles out of town, for a picnic. She was nine years old and the car ride had been a nightmare for her, with her head out of the back window as she continually threw up. At the picnic site, she did nothing else but rest, throwing up once more on the way back to Potchefstroom. It was nothing but bile, as she had not eaten anything while picnicking. Johannesburg was to her a world apart, never to be visited. The people, mostly salesmen and saleswomen who came into the pharmacy were to her aliens, as though from a different planet.

Marie had been working for the pharmacy for more than four years by the time Emma walked in, enjoying her job talking and socializing with the customers. She loved her work and everyone loved her. She had grown to be an ample young girl, with comfortably large breasts and hips that promised to spread even more as she aged and bore children. With a smile that captivated many a young man, her family morals had trained her to slap any and all hands that groped her inviting bosom. She would only allow the odd kiss when on a date, but that was as far as she would go.

Marie became curious about this sophisticated woman who had walked into the pharmacy. Admiring her hair style and clothing, she was pleased that makeup had been used sparingly, to highlight a very beautiful face. Emma, on the other hand, was intrigued by Marie's wholesomeness. Wanting to learn more about the town, she had enjoyed chatting with the local girl while she shopped.

"Oh, I love it here," Marie answered, and then with a frown on her face looked at Emma and said, "and I don't think I could ever leave Potchefstroom."

"Well, I work for the OK Bazaars in Johannesburg," Emma continued, "I am here to introduce the local branch to a new range of lingerie, and would like to know more about the people of the town. Are the women very conservative? Would they like to wear something that is a bit more daring?"

Just then a customer walked in. Marie looked at Emma, then at the customer, and said in Afrikaans, "Good afternoon Mrs. Conradie, I will be with you in a second," and then to Emma in English, "excuse me, Mrs. Conradie has come to pick up her parcel," then walked to the counter.

When she had finished helping Mrs. Conradie, she came back to where Emma stood. Emma had decided the color nail polish she wanted and held it out to Marie.

"Ag...Sorry," she said in Afrikaans, forgetting for a moment that Emma spoke English.

"Not at all," Emma replied, handing her the nail polish, "let me pay for this." She walked to the counter where the cash register stood and reached into her handbag for her purse. It was then that she asked Marie to join her for dinner at the King's Hotel.

"Look, she said, I enjoyed talking with you. Would you like to join me after work for some tea, and perhaps some dinner? I would really appreciate it if you did."

Marie hesitated, and then looking at Emma's smiling face, said, "I would like to very much."

As soon as the Pharmacy closed at 5:30 p.m., Marie rode home on her bicycle as fast as she could. She was looking forward to meeting Emma at the hotel, but didn't want to arrive wearing her white shop uniform. Running into the house, she showered and dressed. Telling her mother in a few words about Emma and that she would be home late and not to keep dinner for her, jumped on her bicycle and cycled back into town. Her heart beating with excitement, she walked into the foyer of the hotel, looking for Emma.

Emma hardly recognized her. Her hair was windswept from the bicycle ride, and she was wearing a very pretty dress. She looked like the country, with a windblown freshness in her cheeks that emphasized her broad, lovely face. Her wide smile showed a row of beautifully white teeth, almost stretching from ear to ear. Her forehead was moist from the bicycle ride, and her eyes sparkled at the excitement of being invited to the King's Hotel for tea and dinner.

"Sorry I am late," she said breathlessly as she walked up to Emma, "but I wanted to change into a dress."

"Not at all," said Emma with a smile and then admiring her. "My, but your pharmacy uniform really does hide your loveliness."

Marie blushed.

They walked into the lounge, found two armchairs and ordered tea from the waiter. Marie was not used to the dignified way Emma poured the tea, and when Emma asked her whether she would like "one lump of sugar or two," Marie felt very much like the country bumpkin she really was. She tried extra hard not to show it.

Emma quizzed her about Potchefstroom and what the young girls were like. Marie, on the other hand, was curious about life in Johannesburg. Before the two of them noticed the time, it was already dark.

"Let us go in for dinner?" Emma suggested, still full of questions.

"Thank you," Marie replied. "I will just have to phone home and ask my Dad to fetch me afterwards. I came down by bicycle, but don't have a night light on it. At any rate, he doesn't like me riding home alone at night."

"Tell him that I will bring you home in my car," Emma said.

"Will you?" Marie replied. "Oh, that will be nice."

She left the table and went to the front desk in the foyer asking to use the phone. Emma waited for her at the entrance to the dining room.

The waiter seated them at a small table in the corner. Emma allowed Marie to order for her, and enjoyed her dinner. Marie spoke non-stop, talking about the town and the people who lived in it. She gave Emma all the local gossip and the politics that went with it. Emma was surprised to learn that the most eligible bachelor in town was the manager of the OK Bazaars and that he had only been manager for about six months, coming from Bloemfontein.

After dinner, they adjourned to the lounge where they sat talking over coffee, with Marie telling Emma even more about Potchefstroom and its history.

"My Dad has made a study of the town," she said, "and he loves it here. He helped Mr. Jenkins with some of his research for the book written about the town by the Commemoration Book Committee. I have the book at home. It is written mostly in Afrikaans, which you may find difficult to read," Emma smiled, but said nothing. Marie continued, "but there is a chapter in English, about the Commercial Section. He helped Mr. Jenkins with that section."

"What does your dad do here?" Emma asked. "Is he a school teacher?"

"Good heavens, no," Marie answered. "He is the chief of the traffic department. He and Sergeant Pottie Potgieter run it."

Emma swallowed. She would have to tell James to take greater care with his driving. Not that he drove badly; in fact he drove extremely well, but it was not worth taking a chance.

When the large grandfather clock in the lounge struck ten o'clock, Marie looked at it, wondering where the whole evening had gone.

"I must go home now," she said, "I have to get up early tomorrow morning. We open the Pharmacy at 8 o'clock, and Mr. Stern likes us to be there early."

"Come, then," Emma said, standing up, "my car is parked just outside the front door. Let me see if I can find James and drive you home." Fortunately James had not gone anywhere. The concierge soon found him. They put Marie's bicycle in the boot of the car.

"Where do you live?" she asked. Marie leaned forward, and gave the simple instructions to James. "Drive down to the end of the next block… to River street, turn right and we are the fourth house on your right, a house with a huge front yard, and a large oak tree in the driveway."

The Stuarts' house was on River Street, overlooking the golf course. It was a large rambling structure, probably built at the turn of the century, and added to as the years passed. A broad verandah framed in white-painted wood, overgrown with red and yellow rambling rose vines welcomed them to the front door, a proud entrance with double doors, designed to allow the house to breathe in the hot summers. The verandah, during the day, was shaded by the enormous oak tree in the middle of the circular driveway. Two rocking chairs and a porch swing contributed to the welcome mat at the open front door, guarded by Charlie Stuart sucking at his pipe in one of the rocking chairs, an Alsatian dog lying on the deck at his feet. He rocked slowly back and forth, enjoying the aroma of his favorite mix of tobacco as he watched the car drive in the front gate, the fallen acorns crackling as the car made its way around the oak tree to pull up at the steps leading to the veranda. He stood up to welcome them as the car doors opened.

"That's my Pa," Marie said to Emma as the car pulled up in front of the house. "Ma won't allow him to smoke inside the house. She says that the smell of the smoke sticks to everything, and then it stinks."

Christa, Marie's mother, a tall matronly woman in her late 40's, came to the front door. She stood next to her husband, a broad smile on her face. "Welcome to our home!" she shouted in a broad Afrikaans accent. As Emma walked with Marie up the stairs she said, "Marie, *liefie*, you didn't say that Emma was so beautiful." And then to Emma, "Ag, Marie told me nothing about you, she was in too much of a rush." Before Emma could say anything, she was clasped into arms that gave her a breathless hug. "Come… come in" Christa said in her loud voice, dragging Emma through the front door where she shouted, "Anna, come and take Miss Emma's coat. Marie, show Emma a comfortable chair," and before Emma knew what was happening, "it is so nice to meet you. Magdalena has made some coffee, come on and have a cup."

Emma smiled. "Thank you, I would love to," she said, "but I can't. I have a busy day tomorrow. It is late and I have to get to bed."

"Nonsense, there is plenty of time. A nice cup of proper *boere* coffee will do you no harm." Emma was almost carried into the lounge and seated in a huge armchair that buried her in its softness.

"Could your maid take James, my driver, something to drink as well?" Emma asked.

"Magdalena, take a cup of coffee to the boy in the car," Christa shouted.

Emma cringed at the word, 'boy.'

Half an hour later, after enjoying every minute with the family, Emma, stifling a yawn, excused herself, saying that she must leave. She could see that Marie was just as tired.

"Well then, Marie, you see that tomorrow night she comes to us for supper. Not to some hotel. We will have a *braai*, and I will bake some *melk tert* tomorrow morning."

"Thank you Mrs. Stuart," Emma said, "I am meeting a friend stationed here in the army. He has been given a two day leave pass."

"Then you bring him with you. I am sure that he would love some good proper food."

"Thank you so very much," Emma said, walking to the front door and out onto the veranda, with Christa and Marie behind her. "What time should we be here?"

"About seven o'clock will be good," Christa said. Turning to Charlie where he stood sucking a fresh pipe, "Hey, Pa, you will be home by then, won't you?" and without waiting for Charlie's answer, "*Ja*, seven o'clock is fine."

"Thank you so very much, you are very kind," Emma answered, and turning to Christa and Charlie, "It is so nice to meet you both, and I am looking forward to tomorrow night." She turned and walked to her car with Marie. "You have a lovely family," she said to Marie as she opened the car door, "see you tomorrow night if I don't see you at the pharmacy before then." As James pulled away, acorns crackling beneath the tires, she waved to them where they all stood. They all waved back at her.

'*What a wonderful, friendly family,*' she thought.

Chapter 7

Eric O'Neil was the youngest son of George and Ingrid O'Neil of Johannesburg. George was an insurance salesman who had, all his life, struggled to bring in a decent income and support his family of two sons and a daughter. When Ingrid died of cancer at the young age of 44, he was devastated and looked to alcohol to handle his grief, becoming an alcoholic and so destroying his family.

Eric, who was in Standard eight at the time, was forced to leave school because there was nobody at home and no money to look after him. His brother had left home a few years earlier, and his sister married the first boy who proposed to her just to escape a father that she could no longer live with. Eric was 15 years old and lying about his age when he applied for and was employed as a salesman at the OK Bazaars.

Working hard, with long hours because he dreaded going home to a drunken father, he slowly worked his way up the ladder over many years to floor manager at their Krugersdorp branch. At each yearly manager's conference, he presented his ideas and thoughts on how to improve sales. At first, Johannesburg head office listened to him with amusement and did nothing, but his endurance and determination gradually impressed them and the company started moving him around their many Transvaal branches as a way of giving him a general understanding of the way the company operated. They liked his enthusiasm and his ideas started to prove themselves. Head office began to take him seriously. He was transferred to the Johannesburg branch where he was allowed to test his sales ideas. They then sent him to the branches in the surrounding cities and slowly with each manager's permission he adapted the branch to his methods, with remarkable success. Head office watched him closely.

Eric grew to be tall for his age. At 16 years old he was over 6 feet 1 inches, thin, perhaps a bit too much on the skinny side, because he enjoyed running. He ran as many marathons as he could, but as he grew older, his body put on muscle, so that at 24 years old, he was well built with an almost rugged look. His long black hair tended to fall over his forehead, just short of thick black eyebrows that framed his deep brown eyes. His nose was aquiline, perhaps a bit too much so, leading many to think he was Semitic, until they learned his surname. O'Neil is an Irish name, definitely not Jewish or Arabic.

If his features had one flaw, then it was his facial hair which no razor blade, no matter how sharp, could remove completely. His strong square jaw was always covered with a five o'clock shadow that highlighted his pink lips and white teeth, giving him a smile that set many a female heart fluttering.

When Emma met him, he was a floor manager at the Johannesburg branch. He enjoyed taking Emma out in the two months before he went to Pietersburg as assistant manager, and was sorry to leave Johannesburg. He had had his share of girlfriends, but somehow, when he saw Emma, he knew that she was the girl he wanted to marry. He had never believed in love at first sight, and had often laughed cynically in a bioscope when the story line had moved that way. It was as though he were being punished for this cynicism when he first saw Emma walking through the counters looking for Chrissie Stead.

War was declared and it was only in 1941 that he decided he must serve his country. South Africa did not have conscription. It was left to the individual within the country to make the decision as to whether or not he wanted to fight in a war against Germany, a country supported by a vast majority of Afrikaner South Africans. He resigned from his position at the OK Bazaars to join the army and was posted to the Potchefstroom military camp for his basic training.

He returned Emma's call at 6 a.m. the next morning.

"Hello," she said sleepily into the phone.

"Good morning, Emma," he said, "I am downstairs."

"Oh, Eric!" she exclaimed, sitting upright in her bed. "Just give me a few minutes to get dressed. I will join you for breakfast."

When she walked down the staircase, he was standing in the foyer, looking up at her.

'*My God,*' he thought, '*not only is she beautiful with her golden tan, but she is so regal in the way she holds herself when she walks.*'

"Hello, Emma," he said softly as she walked up to him. He took her in his arms and kissed her lightly on her mouth.

She smiled, pleased to see him. "Hello, Eric," she answered. '*He looks so handsome in his uniform,*' she thought. '*It is as though he were made for the army.*'

"It is really good to see you. I had forgotten how truly beautiful you are." He looked into her eyes to see if she returned his feelings, then he smiled. Without taking his eyes from hers he said, "I must add that the dress you are wearing is very fashionable."

"I bought it yesterday from Annette's." Emma laughed, pleased that he noticed.

"Ah, from Mrs. Lowenstein," he said taking her arm as they walked to the dining room. "She has beautiful dresses and in a slightly classier range than the OK's. They are the lower end of the market, but you never heard that from me."

"That is what I am here for," she replied, becoming businesslike. "We have introduced an upscale lingerie product on the Witwatersrand and it's going very well. I came to see if it is something the Potchefstroom branch could handle. This morning I was planning to visit Klerksdorp; I would be pleased if you would join me…"

"I would love to," he answered.

"…and this evening we have been invited out to the Stuarts'," she continued. "Marie Stuart's mother, Christa, has asked us over for a *braai.*"

"Marie Stuart?" he asked as they sat down at a table. "Who is she?"

"Oh, she works at the Mooi River Pharmacy. We had dinner last night. She is a lovely person. I drove her home and met her family. I told them that I was meeting you today, and was not sure of your plans, but they insisted on us coming. She has a brother studying medicine at Stellenbosch University and a sister doing a B.A. at Pretoria University. I promised to look her up whenever I visit Pretoria."

"Well," he answered, "it sounds good to me. How do you like Potchefstroom so far?"

"So far, very much. A nice, friendly and very beautiful town."

"Well," Eric said, "You haven't met all the people. Potch. is very society conscious. By that, I mean that they have their different levels of snobbishness, all based on which church you belong to. If you are a member of the Dutch Reform Church you are one class, and if you belong the Hervormde Kerk, you are another class. Then you have the university professors…well, they are a class of their own, and the English speakers? They are entirely a different kettle of fish. You will soon find that out."

Emma sat quietly finishing her breakfast and thinking about what Eric had said.

He finished drinking his tea and stood up. "Well, if you intend to get to Klerksdorp and back in time for dinner, we had better move it. Let me help you load the car."

She was tired. The trip to Klerksdorp and back, although only 30 miles one way, had been just as dusty and as full of corrugations as the trip from Johannesburg to Potchefstroom. Eric had driven all the way. James had been given the day off. The staff at the Klerksdorp branch were very enthusiastic about the range, and she was pleased with that.

Back at the Hotel in Potchefstroom, a bath refreshed her. She invited Eric to her room, where he also freshened up after using the shower that was just down the passageway from her room. With a few hard slaps at an open window, he removed as much of the red dust from his uniform as he could.

"We had better go now," he said. "If we don't, I do believe that I will be tempted to keep you here, all to myself."

She looked at him, a puzzled expression on her face, not quite understanding what he meant. She had dressed in a new style that Irma Rosen had designed. A pair of black slacks offset with a white polar neck jersey, an outfit that she felt was casual enough for a *braai*.

Her car was parked on the other side of the street. He took her hand as they crossed the street, and noted the smoothness of her skin. '*These hands do not wash dishes,*' he thought. He opened the door for her. She climbed into the motorcar, gracefully. '*I am definitely going to marry her,*' he said to himself as he walked around the car to the driver's side of the car, '*and before I go to war. If I don't, she will surely marry someone else while I am away. But then again, what if something should happen to me?*' and he left the thought where it was.

Christa met them at the front door of the Stuarts' house, wearing an apron. She had been preparing the salads with the two maids in the kitchen. A black and white English sheepdog ran up to them. Emma leaned over and patted it.

"Welcome to our home," Christa shouted in a broad Afrikaans accent. "Ag man, but you look more lovely than yesterday," she said to Emma, and then turning to Eric, "and you, you young skelm, I suppose you took one look at her, and immediately fell in love with her. But I don't blame you, she is enough to make any man's head spin."

Eric looked at her sheepishly as he stood next to Emma.

"Christa," Emma said turning to Eric, "This is Eric who I told you about yesterday."

"Ag, Ja," Christa answered, "I thought so. He does look good in his uniform. He will get on well with Charlie, who was a soldier in the Boer war."

Before either of them could say anything further, she turned and shouted up the stairs in Afrikaans, "Marie *liefie*, Eric and Emma are here." Turning to them, she led them through the house towards the garden at the back.

"Come... come in," she said in her loud voice, dragging Emma through the hall, where she shouted, "Anna, come and take Miss Emma's coat. Marie, come on quick and get Emma and Eric something to drink. Pa is at the back with the *braai*," then turning to Eric she smiled and said as though he didn't know, "We are having a *braai*; would you like a steak or is it *wors*, OK? Pa, *liefie*," she called to her husband who was busy starting a fire before Eric could answer her, "find out what Emma and Eric like," and off she rushed back to the kitchen.

Emma took off her jacket and handed it to the maid. She looked around the room, admiring it with pictures of the family on the fireplace mantelpiece. The walls were filled with paintings surrounding a huge stuffed fish mounted over the fireplace. She recognized a Pemberton and a Sydney Carter, both paintings of Cape Dutch Homesteads.

Marie walked into the room, pleased to see both of them. "I am so glad you came," she said, hugging Emma. Then, looking at Eric, continued, "You must be Eric. Emma told me so much about you." She guided them through two French doors into the back garden where the open fire burned, tended by Charlie Stuart. The back *stoep* was shaded by a trellis almost overgrown with a grape vine, the purple grapes hanging just above their heads waiting to be picked and eaten. At the far corner, the fire was a pit in the ground, its hot coals covered by a huge wire mesh grill.

Charlie Stuart walked towards them to welcome them. He turned to Emma who stood admiring the scene, and said, "Good evening, Emma, you look lovely tonight. And you young man," he said to Eric, "I hardly recognize you. I only see him," he said to Emma, "when he is driving an army truck. Tell me, what would you prefer, my dear, *borewors* or steak?" not even considering that she could have been a vegetarian.

"Steak, thank you," she answered. He took four steaks and a string of *boerewors* and carefully placed them on the grill covering the hot coals. They sizzled as they hit the grill, and he quickly gave the meat a turn to sear the opposite side.

Marie took them to a long table groaning under the weight of dishes and bottles of beer. A few bottles of homemade wine with wine and beer glasses littered the table.

Marie smiled at Eric, "What would you like to drink?" she asked as she walked to Emma's side. "A glass of wine? Red or white? Or would you prefer a beer?"

"I would prefer the beer, thank you," Eric said, taking a beer off the table.

"And you, Emma?" Marie asked.

"A red wine, thank you."

The sun was a large orange ball slowly drifting westward, as it sank towards the quince hedge that separated the Stuart property from that of their neighbour. Emma relaxed in a chair, sipping her wine. The hectic day, especially the trip to Klerksdorp and back, was starting to take its toll on her. But she was comfortably happy and content. Somehow, for the first time since leaving Cape Town and her family, she felt accepted for the Emma she had become.

A young man walked into the garden. "Hello, all," he said in Afrikaans.

"Hello, Johan, how goes it?" Charlie Stuart said in English, looking up from the barbecue.

Marie walked up to him, and he leaned forward and kissed her on her cheek. "Johan, come and meet Emma and Eric," she said, taking his arm and introducing him to them.

Johan was slightly taller than Marie, with curly blonde hair that framed a broad forehead. He had a beautiful smile with dimples in his cheeks. His whole manner exuded a friendliness that made him many friends. He was dressed in a white shirt and short khaki pants, with socks almost to his knees, a pipe showing from the top of one of his socks. Emma could see why Marie was attracted to him. He shook hands with Eric. Taking Emma by her shoulders he kissed her on each cheek.

"It is good to meet you both," he said in broken English. "Marie has told me a lot of good things about you, Emma."

After they had had a most enjoyable meal, they sat in a semicircle in front of the dying coals of the fire, glasses of red wine in their hands. Emma had enjoyed her steak, basted in a sauce formula that Marie told Emma was her father's secret recipe. The red wine made her even more relaxed, and feeling full after having eaten far more than she usually did, she half listened to the men as they spoke about the war in Europe.

"So, Eric, what do you think about the war? What was it that made you enlist?" Charlie Stuart asked.

"Well," Eric answered, "I am a bit scared to tell you why, because I understand that a lot of Afrikaners throughout South Africa have given support to the Nazis and are very much against the war. I have my reasons, which may not be what everyone would like to hear." Eric looked at the bottle of beer in his hand. He felt that what he had just said was not as tactful as he should have been.

"Yes," Charlie answered carefully, "many have formed a branch of the pro-Nazi *Ossewabrandwag* here in Potch., but I understand that they are known and are being watched. I don't think they will be much trouble that cannot be handled." He looked at Johan to see if there was any reaction to what he said, and was pleased when he saw none.

"Ag, but that war is so far away," Christa said, "it won't worry us here, in South Africa."

"Of course it will *liefie*," Charlie said," take Eric there, he is wearing a uniform, and will soon be going to war. Just think, here in South Africa it is all volunteers only, because too many Afrikaners are against the war, and Smuts is scared that if he starts conscription, it will be bad for the morale of the army. There is always the fear that crazy political things could start among the troops. The last thing we need is a Nazi-inspired fifth column in the army. Eric, when do you think you will be sent overseas?"

"Well," Eric answered, "probably in a month's time."

Emma's heart stopped. She really liked Eric. She felt that he was perhaps the only man she could be comfortable with, and now he was leaving, to fight a war in some godforsaken place. When she sat with the Rosens, listening to them talk about the war and that Nazi Germany must somehow be stopped, she always agreed with them, but she was never emotionally involved other than to keep the Nazis out of South Africa. Now she was learning that in Potchefstroom there were a large number of Nazi sympathizers, and more than that, Eric would be fighting in the war. It was all catching up to her, and although she politely listened to what Charlie was talking about, she found that she was more interested to hear what Eric said and felt.

"You see," Eric continued, "a man must serve and defend his country. Sure, I understand the point of view of the Afrikaner, and why they are anti-British, because of the Boer war and the horrors of the British concentration camps. But Adolph Hitler and his fascists are terrorizing the people of the world, and I cannot accept that. I have always felt that not voting is a vote in favour of the party that wins. Staying neutral is to me like not voting, a vote in favour of Germany."

"But Ireland is neutral," Johan said, "and so is Switzerland, and they are not in favour of the Nazis, so why should we not be neutral?"

"I can only answer that by saying that there are too many Brits here in South Africa, who still consider themselves part of England, and feel a loyalty to the home country."

"But what about America? Are they not colonialists? Was America not colonized by England?" Johan persisted, "I don't see them going to war."

"They are not a member of the Commonwealth," Eric answered,

"We have benefitted from that membership. How can we now, at a time of danger to England, turn our backs on them? As to America, I am sure that when things get tough, and they will, America will join England in the war."

"You seem quite sure about that," Johan replied sardonically.

"Yes, I am."

"What do you say, Emma?" Charlie asked turning to Emma, who had sat quietly listening to them and patting the head of the sheepdog that had crept to her asking for love. Charlie asked the question not expecting Emma to say anything.

Emma looked at Charlie as he sat enjoying his pipe. She wasn't sure whether she should say exactly what she thought. Would she give herself away? She made a decision. She simply could not say nothing.

"The lady whose lingerie I am promoting to the various branches is Irma Rosen," she started hesitantly, but seeing that Charlie turned to look at her with interest, she continued. "Irma and her family are German and they fled Germany a few years ago because as Jews, they were being persecuted and discriminated against by the German government. From listening to them when they talk," and she smiled, "and they often speak German amongst themselves so I struggle to understand them, but I have gathered that they were deprived of German citizenship even though their parents, and their parents' parents were all born in Germany, and even fought for Germany in World War One."

They all sat quietly listening to her, waiting for her to continue. She looked at the dog that was licking her hand.

"Now I have heard that a large number of Blacks and Coloureds have joined the army to fight the war alongside the Whites. This surprises me, and I ask myself, 'Why? Do they feel threatened by the Germans?' I am sure they do, because if the Germans can discriminate because of a person's religion, can you imagine how they will persecute them because of their skin colour? But then I argue against myself, and say, isn't that already happening in South Africa?' Aren't people of colour discriminated against and even by all of us as we sit here?" She frowned, and waited for somebody to say something. Nobody did. She continued, "So, it cannot be that. I believe that they have joined the army because they need the job. They joined because they cannot find work somewhere else, and the army gives them a good salary. They need the money to feed their families."

They all listened to what she was saying, not saying a word.

"Is it right?" she asked, looking up from where she had been look-ing at her hands that were clenched in her lap. "Is it right" she repeated with tears in her eyes, "that people, no matter what colour their skin is, have to go to the army, to fight and possibly even die in a war to earn a living wage because they cannot earn one in normal society?"

No one said anything for a few minutes. Then Christa burst out,

"*Genoeg*! Enough! The war is the war! Tonight, let us talk of some-thing much nicer."

"So you feel that you could be sent to the front in a month's time?" Charlie asked Eric.

"From what I understand," Eric replied, "I can be sent to North Africa at any moment."

Johan looked at Marie, and she at him, and then at her parents. "Ma... Pa..." she started, "Johan has also enlisted. He will be report-ing next week to the air force base in Pretoria, but..." she hesitated and looked at Johan, and she nodded.

"Mr. and Mrs. Stuart, uh... Charlie and Christa," Johan mumbled, "I have always wanted to learn to fly, and although I am an Afrikaner, and my Grandfather was killed in the Boer war, I have to go to war, because I do not believe that what the Germans are doing is the right thing."

"You then feel strongly about this?" Charlie asked, leaning forward in his chair, interested in what Johan had to say.

Johan thought for a minute. "I have spoken to my parents about my thoughts, and at first they argued with me not to go to war, but after I explained my feelings they started to agree with me."

"And those feelings are?" Charles interrupted.

"Sir, allow me to finish. I believe that the British started the war against the Boer Republic, not because they wanted land but because they wanted the gold of the Witwatersrand. The *Uitlanders* as we called them, who all lived in Johannesburg, came there because of that gold. They outnumbered the Afrikaners in the Republic so President Kruger made it difficult for them to get citizenship. I don't think that I have to explain why. They, the *Uitlanders*, influenced the British to invade us. They wanted the gold.

"We were a Republic, a peaceful nation, we didn't want war and we didn't look for it. Now to Adolf Hitler, he is exactly the same as the Brits were. He wants to conquer Europe and the world. He wants to become another Napoleon Bonaparte, an Emperor. Under him, and after the depression of the First World War, Germany has become strong again and that is a fact. Yet, why isn't he satisfied with what he has accomplished? Why does he want to conquer the world? I cannot understand that, and I cannot accept that. That is why I must go to war. Hitler's principles are not my principles, nor are they Boer principles. They are more English principles and I feel that I must fight that. Remember that saying, 'my enemy's enemy is my friend.' Well Adolph Hitler has become my enemy, and by going to war with England he has become England's enemy, so England is now my friend. Germany is wrong, not England."

They all listened to him and kept very silent. Charlie sat quietly sipping his beer. Christa looked at her husband, but said nothing. She knew what he was thinking.

Unable to contain himself, Charles said, "Johan, you seem to have forgotten that I was one of the rednecks that your grandfather fought against. You are right about what you said that the war was fought over gold, and that we were creating an Empire throughout the world. It was the age of colonialism; the Boer Republic to us was just another country that we needed for the Empire and a rich one at that. Cecil

John Rhodes, and there were many like him at that time, was probably the instigator of that war, something the world seems to have forgotten. But for tonight, let us forget the war and enjoy the *braai*. God has given us a wonderful country and it is our duty to protect all who live in it, whatever their race, creed, or colour and let us say thank you."

Turning to Emma he asked in Afrikaans, "Would you like another glass of wine?"

Without thinking Emma replied in Afrikaans, "No thank you, I do believe that I have had enough, and have said more than I should have." Then, realizing that she had answered in Afrikaans, she put her hand to her mouth. *'What have I done? I hope that I did not give myself away,'* she thought. *'Oh, God, please, please!'*

"Not at all my dear, you have reminded us of some facts that we would prefer not to think about. What would you like, Eric?" Charlie asked in English turning to Eric.

Eric laughed, and his laugh broke the tension. "A glass of red, please."

Then Johan stood up, and said. "Mr. and Mrs. Stuart," the formal tone in his voice made Charlie sit upright in his chair. "I know that I shall be away from Potchefstroom," Johan continued, "and it could be for quite some time, but..." he took both of Marie's hands in his, "Marie and I love each other, and we would like your permission to marry."

Christa's face lit up, then fell. Her hand moved to her mouth and she looked at her husband.

"Marie..." Charlie asked, looking closely at his daughter. "Is this what you want?"

"Yes, Pa," Marie answered. "I love Johan very much. I would very much like to be his wife."

"Well, then," Charlie said, a broad smile on his face, "You have my permission," and turning to Christa, "but you must now get your mother's permission."

"Ag, Marie," Christa laughed both her eyes glistening with tears, "of course you and Johan must get married. Welcome to the family, Johan," and she walked to him and gave him one of her bear hugs that took the breath out of him.

Eric looked at Emma, and she at him. They both felt like intruders on this very intimate family moment.

Later that night, as Eric opened the hotel door for Emma, he asked, "Emma, what are your plans for tomorrow?"

"I planned to meet the local branch manager," she replied with a smile. "But where are you sleeping tonight? Are you going back to the military base?"

He thought for a moment before answering. Had she given him an invitation? He looked at her carefully. '*I don't think she has realized what she has just said,*' he thought.

"I reserved a room here this afternoon, on our way out to the Stuarts'," he answered carefully. "It is just down the corridor from you."

He took her in his arms, believing that her concern as to where he was sleeping was not an invitation. "I was proud of what you said tonight," he said, and then he kissed her. She was so surprised that she kissed him back and then realizing what was happening she pushed him away.

"I am too tired," she said. "I am not thinking straight. I think I may have had too much wine. I will see you tomorrow at breakfast. Good night." Turning, she almost ran into her room and closed the door.

That night, when she went to bed, she found that she couldn't sleep, the thought of Eric and a developing relationship with him worrying her. At about 3 a.m. she came to a decision. She would go out with him, because she enjoyed his company and liked him as a person. '*Why not?*' she reasoned, '*when he goes off to war, overseas, then he will be out of my life,*' and with that thought she fell into a troubled sleep.

Chapter 8

The following morning, after breakfast, Eric joined Emma when she visited the OK Bazaars, spending time with the manager while she showed the range to the staff. They liked what they saw and placed a sizable order. This surprised her, for Potchefstroom. Perhaps the town was not as conservative as everyone had led her to believe.

At lunch that afternoon, Eric told her that he had to report to the base by five o'clock. "Would you like to see a little bit of Potchefstroom before then?" he asked.

"That would be nice," she said. "It does look like a beautiful town, and I would love to see it."

He drove up Tom Street, with its avenue of oak trees that led one to the dam. Halfway there, he pulled over and parked the car. He pointed to a house across the road.

"Do you see that house over there?" Emma looked to where he pointed. She saw a house surrounded by a hedge of hawthorn, with a wrought iron gate leading up a path of crazy paving stones lined with rose bushes. The path took one to a small verandah that protected the front door from any thunderstorm, a weather pattern that was not uncommon in summer.

"I love this town so much," he continued, "that I bought that house. When I come back from the front, this is where I want to live."

"It looks lovely," she said, looking at the house he pointed to.

"I would love to show you the house, but I have rented it out, and I don't like bothering the tenants. The house is very beautiful and spacious inside. It has a lounge that opens up onto a large garden at the back with a number of fruit trees. There are three bedrooms and two bathrooms with a shower. I absolutely love it."

He then put the car into gear, and drove slowly to the dam. Once there, he parked the car in the parking lot next to the water. They got out and walked to the restaurant which was built in such a way that every table gave one a full view of the dam. Emma threw bread crumbs into the water and watched the fish scramble and splash, fascinated that there were so many of them.

"No wonder Charlie likes fishing here," Emma said. "The dam is full of fish. With a few breadcrumbs and a net one could catch quite a number of them. There is no need for a fishing rod."

"It is not so much the fishing that attracts the fisherman," Eric laughed. "It is what goes with the fishing. Me? I prefer to do my drinking at home."

They sat and talked over coffee that they had ordered. Before they knew it, it was 4 o'clock.

"I am sorry," he said, "I haven't shown you Potch. at all and now I had better start making my way back to the military base. When can I see you again?"

"I will try and see if I can be here more often," she said as he held her hand.

"Can I see you whenever I am in Johannesburg? Every so often I have to drive a truck through to Pretoria. I may be able to work out something."

Once they were back at the hotel, she arranged for James to drive Eric to the military base. She had enjoyed spending the day with him.

Driving back to Johannesburg the following morning after a sleepless night, she could not stop thinking about Eric. '*In fact*,' she thought, '*after two days in a small town I think that I am madly in love. I have made some very good friends*.'

On those weekends whenever he was given a pass, she would pay James to drive her to Potchefstroom, or Eric would hitch a lift to

Johannesburg. When he was not allowed to leave the base, he would phone her. She would phone back to the number he gave her, and they would talk on the phone for hours.

She started to make a point of visiting Potchefstroom during the week, either on a business visit to the OK Bazaars or on a Thursday, staying over a weekend and returning on a Sunday evening, hoping that Eric could organize a pass. She spent a great deal of time with Marie, eventually staying at the Stuarts' house at Christa's insistence, whenever she was in Potchefstroom. She couldn't believe where the time had flown when three months later she had James drive her to Potchefstroom for Marie's wedding.

Marie looked beautiful in her wedding dress. It was the dress that Christa had worn when she married Charlie, and that Christa's mother had worn when she was married. The lace adorning the dress was old, '*probably from Bruge,*' Emma thought when she saw it. Johan was dressed in his air force uniform looking very handsome and dignified as he waited for Marie at the alter. They married in the old Nederduitse Herformde Church that had been built in 1842. The Church was across the road from the Municipal buildings, on King Edward Street. It was a small church, and every pew was filled with guests. A few men who couldn't find a seat were even standing in the aisles.

Emma was her maid of honor, and during Marie's honeymoon she was a daughter to the Stuarts. Eric was given leave to attend the wedding. Emma wasn't sure whether he would be able to attend, but when she walked following Marie to the alter she saw him sitting in one of the pews. He was on a three days' leave pass before being sent to Pretoria for further training. He had rented a room at the King's Hotel, as had she because the Stuart house was overflowing with relatives.

Later that night, after the reception, he drove her back to the hotel. As he parked her car, and before she opened the door to get out, he asked her to marry him. She looked at him in amazement. This was the last thing she expected and she started crying. In comforting her they started to make love. She pushed him away. "Not here," she said, "not in the car," and getting out of the car she led him to her room at the hotel.

The next morning she woke to find him standing at the window, looking out at the street below.

"What would you like for breakfast?" she asked, yawning and stretching herself, wiping away the sandman from her eyes.

He turned to her, looked at her for a few seconds, and then turned back to the window.

"I am sorry I slept with you last night," he said softly, "I truly am."

Emma lay looking at him for a few minutes. "I am not sorry," she said, and started to get out of bed.

He watched her as she walked to the bathroom. She had wrapped the sheet around her to cover her nudity. He then walked to the bed and sat on it. When she returned, he took her into his arms.

"I am being sent to the front in a few days, to fight in a war that no one wants. I would like to marry you before I leave, but there is simply no time left. I am asking you to wait for me so that we can marry when I get back. If, on the other hand, something should happen to me..."

"I will wait for you," she said kissing him on his cheek. "There is no one else in my life, nor is there likely to be anyone else, so don't worry about that," and she moved out of his embrace, but he held her tighter.

"But..." he said, "I love you. I love you very much, and I know that I will never be happy unless I make you my wife. Emma, I will try and get permission to marry you before I leave. If I do get that permission, will you marry me now, before I go to fight a war, and if I cannot arrange it, will you wait for me to come home?"

She looked at him, and saw the entreaty in his eyes. "No", she said, "I love you Eric, I love you very, very much, and I will wait for you, but I cannot marry you now."

"Why not?" he asked, looking at her imploringly. "Why won't you marry me now? I could try and arrange a special license, if that is what is worrying you."

"Please," she answered, tears streaming down her cheeks, "please don't ask me why. I just cannot marry you now," '*or ever for that matter,*' she said to herself.

"You have said, 'cannot'," he took her face between his hands, and forced her to look at him. She looked into his eyes and then closed hers. "You didn't say 'will not,'" he continued. "Why not, why can't you? Are you already married? Is it because I am going away to fight a war? Do you….'"

She broke away from him, and pulled the sheet tightly around her.

He leaned forward, and took her in his arms, kissing her passionately. "I love you so much" he whispered. "so, so much."

"Please don't," she said, trying to avoid his kisses. "Let us stay as we are. Know that I do love you, but I simply cannot marry you, not yet at any rate. Hopefully one day and hopefully soon. Please don't ask me why. I just cannot at the moment."

He looked at her, studying her face, recognizing the determination he saw in it.

"I will never stop asking you," he said, "Even while I am away, I will always love you. I understand that you don't want to be tied to someone who may not come back."

"That is not the reason," she cried, her love for him showing in her face, "I know you will come back," and she leaned forward and kissed him deeply. "You have to come back."

He took her in his arms, and they made love again.

Chapter 9

James drove Emma and Eric to the military base on the Ventersdorp road. He stopped the car in front of the gates. Eric leaned over and kissed Emma who was sitting next to him on the back seat.

"Take care as you drive back to Jo'burg," he said. "I will try to phone you as soon as I can and let you know what is happening." He leaned forward and kissed her again, quickly, before running to the guards at the gate. She watched him clear himself with them, walk through the gates and run up the road leading to his barracks. He did not look back. He did not tell her that he was leaving for the front in a few days time. He had written it all down in a letter, and she would receive it sometime during the week.

"Okay, James, let us go back to Johannesburg," she said, trying to hide her tears.

James did a U-turn, drove back into Potchefstroom on von Wielligh Street, turned right onto Berg Street and two blocks later turned left onto Lombard Street which led to the Johannesburg highway. By now he knew Potchefstroom well, and Emma no longer needed to guide him.

She had a great deal of time to think as he drove. He never drove fast, and the trip took close to two hours. Memories of the previous night kept playing over and over again in her mind. The depth of her love for Eric had never occurred to her until then. She had refused his proposal because she was scared to get married, scared that in applying for a marriage license he may discover that she was born a Coloured. She did not even have a birth certificate, because her mother had not waited at the hospital, sneaking out of before she had been given one.

She decided that she was happy to be Eric's lover, but that she could never marry him.

When earlier that morning, Eric had asked her whether he could meet her parents, she told him what she told everyone who asked her about them, that they had died; that she was an orphan, alone in the world. She felt terrible about this lie, almost as if in the telling of it, her parents were sure to die.

When she arrived back in Johannesburg, she did something she had never done since leaving Cape Town. Walking from Raema Court to the OK Bazaars every morning, she had always passed a church. It was an old church, probably built before or just after the Anglo Boer war. On an impulse she walked up the stairs to the two heavy wooden double doors. One of the doors opened at her touch. The church was beautiful inside, with large stained glass windows casting a rose coloured glow on the empty beautifully carved wooden pews. On her left side was a small table with a number of candles. She lit one, putting a one pound note into the box asking for donations. Bowing her head, she prayed that God would give her the strength to continue to be a part of the White community of South Africa; she prayed that the politicians and the people of the country would realize that they were not following God's will by persecuting others because of the colour of their skin.

Nothing scared her more than being found out. She had always been scared of having sex, and had planned that should she ever feel that she wanted to make love with someone, she would always take extreme precautions to make sure that she was well protected. She had made up her mind that, should she ever marry, she would never fall pregnant, because it was common for Coloured families in Cape Town to have a child born with orange 'kroes' hair identifying an ancestor as being an African. What did worry her though, about having made love to Eric the previous night was that, in the heat of passion, they both forgot about protection. Exhausted after their love making, they had laid in the comfort of each other's arms and fallen asleep. When she woke up, she realized what had happened. She rushed to the bathroom to bathe, to cleanse herself.

She thought about Marie, and Pa and Ma Stuart, and how close they had become. Marie had decided to stay with her parents in Potchefstroom, and continued working at the pharmacy while Johan was overseas fighting in the war. Emma loved Marie dearly. They had become almost like sisters, talking and confiding in each other often until early in the morning, but she had never told Marie her secret. Her visits to Potchefstroom had become far more frequent than were necessary, so much so that even Chrissie Stead had remarked about it.

When she missed her first period, she thought nothing of it; it had happened before, especially when she was stressed with her work. When a month later she missed her second period, she started to become worried.

A few weeks later on a visit Potchefstroom to show a new range, Marie invited her to the Stuart home to stay the night. That evening, over supper, Marie noticed that there was something wrong with her. Emma was far less cheerful than she normally was.

"Emma", Marie asked her once they were alone, "what is wrong with you? Something is worrying you. You are not your usual self."

Emma started crying. "Oh Marie," she cried, the tears streaming down her face, "I think that I am pregnant."

Marie thought for a minute then asked, "Is Eric the father?"

"Yes" Emma answered between tears.

"The bastard," Marie said angrily, "making you pregnant, and then rushing away without asking you to marry him."

"But he did ask me to marry him."

"And you turned him down?" Marie interrupted, amazement all over her face.

"Yes," Emma answered.

"But why?" Marie asked, her eyes questioning, "Don't you love him?"

"I do," Emma answered, "Oh Marie, I love him so very, very much."

"Then why don't you marry him? Why did you refuse him when he asked you? How could he be so careless as to make love to you and not use protection, knowing he was going to be sent to the front?"

"It was my fault," Emma answered, "I forgot to be careful. Oh, Marie," she cried softly, "I just don't know what to do. I will have to resign from my job and go home, back to Cape Town. My parents will accept me, and look after the baby."

"Parents?" Marie asked in amazement, "but, you told me that both your parents were dead."

Emma looked at her, and started crying again. She reached into her handbag and took out a tissue wiping the tears from her eyes. "I lied to you, "she said.

"You lied to me? But why?" Marie asked, confused. "How can you lie about your parents being dead?"

"I had to," Emma answered blowing her nose, "I just had to."She wiped away her tears. She sat back in her chair, avoiding Marie's questioning eyes. Then she made a decision.

"Marie, you don't know how lucky you are," she said softly, looking for some sign of expression on Marie's face. "I am going to tell you something I should have told you a long time ago, but was scared to. Please forgive me, and whatever I tell you, please…please try to understand."

She stood up and walked toward the window, looking at the garden outside. She was not sure where to begin, and then finding the strength, she said. "Marie, you were born into this White community of South Africa. You accept the way you live as natural. You have grown up that way, with servants in your house, and *piccanins* in rags begging for money at Christmas. When you go to the bioscope or the swimming pool, where only Whites are allowed, you have never had a brother or a sister with you who have been turned away because they looked like Coloureds and are Coloureds with a dark skin and *kroes* hair while you, because your skin is lighter than theirs, and your hair straight, you have been allowed in.

"Did you ever ask yourself, when you went to school, why there was no person of colour in the school? Or, did you ever wonder why, to have a person of colour serving clients at the Pharmacy alongside you and earning the same salary you earn, is a no-no? That is your normal way of life, the way you have grown up, and you don't even think that it could be otherwise. But what if that way of life is something that is abnormal, something that is hateful and that is almost like a form of slavery? What if you simply don't know what the 'otherwise' is, or even thought about it?"

"Know the 'otherwise,' Emma? What do you mean?"

Emma walked back to where Marie sat, and sat down next to her. She took both of Marie's hands in hers. "Marie," and swallowing heavily, she asked, "have you ever heard of District Six in Cape Town?"

"Yes," Marie answered, "that's a suburb in Cape Town where Whites and Coloureds live side by side, isn't it?"

Emma looked her straight in the eye, and then said in a monotone voice. "That is where I was born, and that is where my parents and family still live."

"So? That means that as a White you and your parents lived in a Cape Coloured community? As a White, you must have found it difficult living there."

"That is exactly my point," Emma said, her eyes blazing. "You said 'you must have found it difficult living there.' Why? Why would it have been difficult living there? Is it because Whites are living amongst the Coloured community? Why are the Coloureds different from you? Is it because of their skin colour? They are people, just like you. They have emotions, they feel, they love, they cry just like you do, and when you cut their skin, they bleed, just like you do, and strangely, their blood is even red, the same colour as yours."

Emma looked at her and saw the puzzlement in the eyes. "We didn't live there as Whites, Marie, we lived there as part of the Coloured community. My parents are Coloureds. I was born a Coloured. I am a Coloured pretending to be a White, and that is why I cannot marry Eric."

Marie stood up suddenly, her feelings plainly visible on her face. She looked at Emma, and then stifling a sob she rushed out of the room, leaving Emma sitting there, feeling deserted. Emma hid her face in her hands, sat for a moment and then resignedly stood up and taking her handbag walked to the front door of the house. She opened it, making her way to her car, and climbed in sitting next to James in the front seat, rather than in the back seat where she normally sat. She was sobbing uncontrollably with disappointment. She closed the car door behind her. James started up the engine, put the car into gear and prepared to drive away, then slammed on the brakes. Marie was standing in front of the car. For a minute the two girls faced each other and then with a sob, Marie rushed forward, opened the car door and took Emma into her arms.

"I love you Emma… I love you as a sister and I love you as a friend. I am sorry I ran away just now and left you, but I love you, and I am sure we can do something."

Emma slowly pushed her away. Then very calmly she said. "Marie my dear, there is very little you can do. We live in a society where the colour of one's skin decides what is to be. I had a very, very happy childhood as a little Coloured girl living in District Six. It was only as I grew older that I realized that everything in South Africa is hateful for a person with a skin that is not White. Over the last few years, I have tried very hard to integrate myself into the White community, and I succeeded until I met Eric. I did not want to fall in love, but I did, and now I am pregnant, carrying Eric's child. I'm afraid there is very little I can do about it."

"You are wrong," Marie said taking her hand, "you could have an abortion. There are a couple of ladies in the Location…"

"No Marie, I could never do that, Emma interrupted, "I love Eric too much to destroy his child. I will have to go back to Cape Town, and have my baby there."

"No," Marie said firmly. "I don't want you to do that. Let me talk to my father; he is a man with a lot more influence than even I know. I once heard Ma say to him that if ever he was found out he would be arrested and go to jail, so he must be doing something unusual. He has always helped others when they have had a problem with the security police. I am sure that there is something he can do for you."

"But he is your father," Emma cried, "I am not his daughter. Please don't tell him. It will just get me into more trouble than I am already in."

"You don't know my father," Marie said. "He knows how to keep a secret. For one, he is a Freemason, whatever that means, and he travels around a lot to various secret meetings. He seems to know a lot of people in different government jobs. I think he is a very special and respected man." She paused, thought for a minute and then continued, nodding her head, "I know he will help you."

That night, after her mother had gone to bed, Marie tentatively knocked on her father's study door. He looked up from where he was preparing a fly for fishing. When he saw the absolute despair in his daughter's face he asked her.

"*Liefie*, what is bothering you?"

She looked at him, studying his face carefully. "Pa," she said hesitantly, "how do you feel about the Coloured community in South Africa?"

"Ah" he said looking down at the fly he was working on, "so you found out."

"Found out what, Pa?" she asked,

"That Emma...."

She didn't let him finish, "but how did you know?"

"My secret," he answered. "Does it change your love for her?"

"No, Pa," Marie said, "it just makes me love her more."

"Good, I am pleased to hear that," he answered. "Now, tell me, what is the problem?"

She told him everything. He looked at the teary face of his daughter in front of him, took her in his arms and said, "Don't worry, I will fix it. Tell Emma that in a week's time I'll have the correct papers ready for her. They will show that she is a Caucasian of European descent. She can then marry Eric without being scared. I will even get her a civil marriage license if she wants one, showing that she is already married to him."

"But Eric is away in the army," she said.

"Then she can marry him in a church as soon as he gets back."

Marie hugged him, overjoyed with what he had told her. "Thanks, Pa," she said, "I love Emma like a sister. She is a wonderful person. It is just a pity that in this beautiful, but stupid country that we live in, people are separated by the colour of their skin."

"I know, I know," Charlie said, "I know that all too well which is why…but one day I will tell you."

"Tell me what, Pa?" Marie asked.

"Well," he answered hesitantly, thinking carefully about what he was saying. "I don't want to say too much, but you have heard of the Broederbond and the Ossewabrandwag, haven't you?"

"Yes Pa, I have. Mr. Stern at the Pharmacy told me all about them."

"Well, all you need to know is that they are not the only secret societies in South Africa. Just remember that for every action, there is always a reaction. Where the Afrikaners have their secret societies, so do we English."

Emma continued to work for the OK Bazaars for a further six months. She watched her weight carefully, but when signs of her pregnancy started to become obvious, she handed in her resignation to Chrissie Stead.

"I am sorry to see you leave," Chrissie said, unaware and not seeing that she was pregnant. "You have been a pleasure to work with. I shall have my secretary prepare a letter of reference for you. Should you ever decide to return to us, be assured there will always be a position for you."

"Thank you, Mrs. Stead," Emma said, "I have enjoyed working here."

"Now that you are leaving, please call me Chrissie," Chrissie said, smiling.

"Thank you, Chrissie," Emma answered, "You have been very kind to me. I shall never forget that."

She then went to find James. "James," she said handing him an envelope, "I am leaving the OK Bazaars. I would like to thank you for all the help you have given me. Please take this as a small token of my appreciation. I am going to live in Potchefstroom. If you ever need anything, do contact me." She took his hand and shook it, not quite sure whether he understood what she had said to him or not, but knowing that he would appreciate the one hundred pounds in the envelope.

That night she joined Irma Rosen for dinner and told her why she was resigning from the OK Bazaars. She told her that she intended to marry a soldier who was on the front fighting, and that she was moving to Potchefstroom to take care of his affairs.

"Why live in Potchefstroom, of all places?" Irma asked, "You know that it is a very conservative town."

"I am pregnant, Irma," Emma said, feeling that it was better if Irma knew the truth rather than to hear it from some third person at the gossip table.

"You are pregnant?" Irma said, shocked. "Who is the lucky man?"

"You remember Eric who was with the OK Bazaars?"

"I have heard you mention him when he took you on a date, but I have never had the pleasure of meeting him," Irma answered.

"Well, he is the father. He owns a house in Potchefstroom, and he wants to live there when he leaves the army. He asked me to marry him, and I will, as soon as he gets back."

"Well, my dear, that is wonderful, and I wish you all the success in the world. You are a wonderful person, and an excellent saleslady. If ever you decide that you want to go back into the business, join me, and not the OK. I will always have an opening for you."

"Thank you, Irma," Emma said, I will take you up on your offer once I have settled down and have my life in order."

When she told Reena Rowe that she was moving to Potchefstroom, Reena was very sorry that she was leaving. "Do make a point of seeing Lilly as often as you can. That way, I will always know about you," she said as she gave Emma a hug. "You are a lovely person, Emma, and I know that Lilly likes you and will be happy to help you with anything you might need."

When Emma moved to Potchefstroom, she had to travel by train. A moving truck brought what little furniture she had accumulated to Potchefstroom. Charlie and Christa Stuart insisted that she live with them in their house until she had the baby and was able to work again. They were wonderful to her in the last months of her pregnancy, and she truly felt spoiled. She and Marie had now become more than sisters, both emotionally involved with soldiers fighting a war and in keeping a secret, Emma's secret.

One week after Emma had moved in with the Stuarts, Charlie called her into his study.

"This is for you," he said. He handed her a large brown envelope.

She took it from him, looked for a name and saw the envelope was blank. "What is it?" she asked frowning.

"It is a present from the Stuart family to you. Open it and have a look."

Emma did not see Marie walk in softly behind her as she opened the envelope. She took out the papers that were in it, and read them slowly. She then looked up at Charlie, reread them and felt faint. Marie took her in her arms, and led her to a chair. Emma read them for a third time, and started crying.

"Where did you...?" she started.

"Don't ask questions that I will not answer," Charlie said. "By the way, this cheek needs a thank you."

Emma stood up, and rushed to him, taking him in her arms and kissing both of his cheeks. "Thank you, thank you. Oh, thank you," she cried.

Charlie had given her a birth certificate showing that she had been born Caucasian of European descent, as well as a marriage license which showed that she and Eric had been married in a civil ceremony ten months earlier.

"By the way," Charlie said to her as she was about to leave, "tomorrow be at my office at 8 a.m. You will start your first driving lesson... that is, if you want to learn how to drive."

"I will be there," Emma smiled through her tears. "You bet, I will definitely be there."

Marla was born in the Potchefstroom Hospital on April 8, 1943. The first thing Emma did when the baby was handed to her was remove the blanket around her head and look at her hair. Marla was born with a thick crop of light brown hair, and it was straight. Emma started crying with joy. Her fears of a baby with kroes hair that would give away that they were Coloureds were no more. To Emma, this pink bundle she held in her arms was the most beautiful baby she could have ever have wished for.

She registered Marla with Eric's surname, and adopted his surname as her own. Emma Kline had now become Mrs. Emma O'Neil. Her life was now totally devoted to her daughter, Marla.

Chapter 10

It took Emma almost three days to settle herself with the Stuarts in Potchefstroom. She found that over the years living at Raema Court she had collected a considerable amount of bits and pieces of furniture and various odds and ends, all with memories that she could not part with. She hired a moving truck and it took them a day to pack up everything and drive to Potchefstroom.

Charlie Stuart suggested that she approach the elderly couple who rented Eric's house. He told her that as far as he knew, they did not own a motor car. They might be very happy to lease their garage for storage. When she approached Mr. Cronje, the tenant, he told her that he and his wife intended to leave in a few months' time. They could no longer live on their own and wanted to move into an old age home in Vereeniging, close to where their daughter lived. They did not know where to contact Eric to tell him. Emma told them that they should talk with Eric's lawyer, Lionel Herz, and inform him of their intentions.

As soon as she had left them, she rushed over to Lionel Herz' office and told his secretary who handled the rental agreements, that she would like to rent the house when the old couple left. She was just too happy to have a home in Potchefstroom, and the fact that it was Eric's house made it even more of a home.

Emma did not want to return to her family in Cape Town, especially now that she had a baby. Too many questions would be asked, questions that she did not want to answer. Until the Cronje's moved out, she and Marla would stay with Marie and her parents. They had offered her a home and she was grateful. Her family was now Marla,

Marie, Charlie and Christa. Their love for her and Marla, shown in so many ways, mirrored her own for them.

Living frugally in Johannesburg, she had saved a considerable amount of money. She felt that she would like to be a stay-at-home mom to Marla for at least the first six months, but she felt restless and continually looked for part time work.

Living in Potchefstroom, being fluent in Afrikaans was very necessary. She was still scared that talking too much Afrikaans would betray her Coloured heritage and was very careful of what she said and how she said it.

Because she felt that God heard her prayers and had given her a Marla that did not betray her, she became very religious, joining the Methodist Church, finding part time work cleaning the sanctuary and preparing the church for Sundays or any other religious day if necessary. Every so often she was asked to do a lay reading from the Bible during the service. She enjoyed that. With her radiant personality, she was very soon accepted by the English community as one of their own.

When Marla was about five months old, the couple that rented Eric's house moved out as they had said they were going to. Emma was happy to move from the Stuarts' home into Eric's house. She did miss living with the family, but she enjoyed having her own home. She started fixing up the garden, neglected by the old couple, and employed a repair man to work on the house itself, repainting and renovating. But her cash was running out and she felt that she had to find a full time job.

She considered taking up Irma Rosen's offer, but she felt that working for Irma would take her away from home too often, and she did not want to be away from Marla, "not yet at any rate, perhaps when she is a little bit older."

Christa Stuart had offered to babysit Marla while she worked, so she looked around and eventually found work at Smit and Muller, an egg brokerage owned by two local men. Annetjie Louw, who had been with them for close to ten years, had resigned. Rumour had it that she was mistress to one of the partners, and he had broken off their relationship.

The owners of the business, Gerrie Smit and Kris Muller, learned very quickly that any flirting with Emma was out of the question. She soon became part of the office furniture, but an integral part of their business. With the salary she earned she bought a second-hand Chevrolet and employed a maid to look after and clean the house.

She wrote letters to Eric once a week, telling him about her life, and life in Potchefstroom in general, but she never mentioned Marla in any of her letters. She felt that she did not want to burden him with a responsibility and obligation of being a father. She received very few letters from him, at first addressed to the OK Bazaars, then to the Mooi River Pharmacy, where Marie would pass them on to her. She wrote and told him that she was renting his house. She never told him that she was using his surname.

He wrote about life at the front, about the war and about how much he missed being with her. She treasured his letters, keeping a scrapbook with whatever news she could find about where he was fighting.

The offices of Smit and Muller were on Wolmarans Street, very close to the Potchefstroom Store, a supermarket run by the Grobelaar family. Gerrie and Kris were brokers, buying and selling eggs. They were continually travelling around the countryside visiting the various poultry farms in the area, buying up eggs, with prices varying as to size and demand. Often they would be away days at a time, leaving Emma to run the sales side of the business. She very quickly learned her prices and her market, and would more than often negotiate a price with a buyer that they could never have done themselves. Being a beautiful, well-dressed woman had its advantages.

After working for them for about two to three months they started to rely on her to the extent where they would be lost if ever she left them. They paid her a comfortable salary, and told her to simply write out a cheque, which they would both sign, if ever she needed extra money. They trusted her and above all they appreciated her ability as a sales woman, something that Annetjie, her predecessor, was not. She was Emma, and very soon many in the town who knew Gerrie and Kris joked that she employed them.

Both men were regarded as astute businessmen in Potchefstroom. They were well liked, and always the life and soul of any party. What the townspeople did not know was that in spite of Emma's success in managing them and their office, this was not their main source of income.

Kimberley, the most famous diamond city in the world, was not that far from Potchefstroom. The veldt around Kimberley, from Lichtenburg to Wolmaranstad was prospected for diamonds deposited by water many thousands if not millions of years ago. Rivers must have flowed through the area, eroding the Kimberlite pipes and spreading its precious contents all over the veldt. Many of the diamond diggers working on the mines at Kimberley or with mining companies that looked for stones in the surrounding veldt, would conceal the odd stone in some or other way and then look for a buyer. Because of this, Potchefstroom had become known as the largest diamond smuggling center in the world. Illicit Diamond Buying (IDB) was a major criminal offence in South Africa.

Almost all the Africans who worked in the Kimberley diamond fields and surrounding area knew that as a last resort, if they could not place their uncut diamonds at a better price, Gerrie and Kris would always buy them.

Emma suspected that her employers were in some funny business not associated with eggs, but did not want to become involved. She kept a blind eye, said nothing and made a point of knowing nothing. She managed their office and sold eggs, and that was that. They did the buying of eggs, she did the selling of eggs. She did her work, and every day at about four o'clock from Mondays to Fridays, she would close the shop and go to the Stuarts' to collect Marla, often spending the evening with them.

Gerrie and Kris may have suspected that she knew of their illegal activity. But having been in the business for many years, they had grown complacent and overconfident. Kimberley was over 200 miles from Potchefstroom, after all, and they never ever visited there. Then, they made the classic mistake of believing in their own cleverness, convinced that their IDB business remained efficiently concealed from everyone around the town by their legitimate egg brokerage.

They would accumulate small parcels of uncut diamonds, and when they had a big enough parcel, usually amounting to what they had calculated to be in the region of one million pounds, they would, on one of their many country trips, drive to Johannesburg to offload the stones at a jeweler who was known by them to be a buyer. By restricting their visits to only once or twice a year, they felt that they were not drawing any attention to themselves, and that they were safe to continue their illegal business.

They had a few rules that they followed, religiously.

Never talk about IDB to anyone.

Never spend money too freely.

Do NOT own the latest top-of-the-line ostentatious Mercedes Benz. Stick to buying smaller, cheaper motor cars.

Always pay your bills promptly, and always let your wife believe that you are short of cash. (Most times they were, as they accumulated cash so that they could always buy any parcel offered them, always hoping for "the big one.")

At any one time, never be in the front of the shop together.

Cash and diamonds were kept in a safe hidden in the egg cool room at the back of the shop. They were always prepared that should they ever be raided by the police, the person who was in the front of the shop would keep them talking, while the person in the back would remove the stones from the back safe and leave by the back door. That way, should the police search the premises, they would find no diamonds.

The front office boasted a small safe, with Emma holding a key. She also had another key that was used to lock the cool room when she went home at night but she never had a key to the safe in the cool room. For a number of months she was not even aware that another safe existed in the cool room, because it was well hidden, usually behind some cardboard boxes that were used to pack the eggs. When she did one day discover it accidentally and asked about it, they told her that many farmers wanted cash when they sold their eggs. This way, by receiving cash rather than a cheque, they could avoid paying income tax.

Life for Gerrie and Kris was good. They both had beautiful homes with wonderful families. They bought the eggs that Emma sold and without her knowing it they also bought uncut diamonds at bargain basement prices, and sold them in Johannesburg.

Now, it was the custom for an African policeman to occasionally test every businessman in Potchefstroom as to whether or not they would buy uncut diamonds. He would take a small parcel of uncut stones, dress as though he were a miner, and walk into a shop, looking for the owner. He would spin a sob story, and try to get the owner to help him, by buying the parcel.

By this time in their lives, Gerrie and Kris had their regular sellers, and they stuck with them. When Gerrie who was in the front shop at the time, was approached by the young African policeman who offered him a small parcel of stones, he turned him away because he did not know him.

A month later, when the African policeman approached Gerrie who happened to be in the front shop again, offering him a much larger parcel, Gerrie mistakenly felt that he recognized him as one of the regulars. He bought the parcel, paying cash, calling to Kris to give him the money from the back safe. He then gave the parcel to Kris to put with their other stones. No sooner had Kris walked back to the safe in the cool room than the police walked in.

Now it so happened that Emma had brought Marla to work with her that day because Christa had a dental appointment. With both Gerrie and Kris in the store, she had gone next door to the grocery shop to buy groceries for her house. She knew nothing of what had happened.

"Can I help you?" Gerrie asked the policemen in Afrikaans, standing up and walking to the counter.

"Ag yes, please," the very overweight man replied. He was dressed in a rather shabby grey suit and wearing a black felt hat pulled low over his forehead. The second man also wore a grey suit, but he was more smartly dressed, without a hat and much younger looking.

"You are Mr. Smit, correct?" the very overweight man asked.

At that moment Emma returned with Marla. The two men looked at her as she walked into the shop, wheeling her pram.

"There are two policemen in the front talking to Gerrie," she said to Kris as she walked to the back of the shop.

Kris turned as white as a sheet. "How do you know they are policemen?" he asked, his voice quivering.

"I have seen one of them occasionally visiting Charlie Stuart," she replied. "They are very friendly."

Composing himself, Kris ran to the back safe knowing that Gerrie would keep the two men busy while he hid the stones. Marla started crying, and to soothe her, Emma picked her up.

Kris took the two small brown paper bags of uncut diamonds. Walking so as not to be noticed by the men in the front shop, he moved to the back door. As he opened the door, he saw the African that Gerrie had bought the diamonds from standing in the yard. He quickly closed the door and looked around the office. He had to hide the diamonds somewhere. He spotted the garbage bin next to Marla's pram and dropped the packets in it, covering them with a piece of paper. He did not notice that one of the packets broke, the uncut diamonds spilling out into the bin. He then walked casually into the front shop and stood next to Gerrie.

"Good afternoon, sirs," he said to the two men that stood at the counter.

"Good afternoon," they replied.

"These two men are policemen," Gerrie said to Kris, then turning to them asked, "Well, how can I help you?" Emma had walked to the front shop with Kris, curious as to what was happening. She was holding Marla in her arms. Then Marla began to cry again.

"Please excuse me," Emma said to them, "I have to take care of the baby," and she carried Marla to the back and placed her in the pram. She lifted up her nappie bag and placed it on the garbage bin next to the pram, looking for a bottle to give to Marla. It was quite a large bag, holding a number of toweling nappies as well as the bottles of milk. She then rocked the pram to soothe Marla trying to get her to sleep, and without being aware of it, hid the garbage bin.

"Mr. Smit," Detective van der Merwe said in Afrikaans. "About ten minutes ago, you bought a parcel of uncut diamonds from one of our boys. You know that dealing in uncut diamonds is illegal. We would like to search your premises." And before Gerrie could say anything, he continued, "Jannie," he said to Sergeant Pretorius, "search the place."

Jannie walked behind the counter, "Could you please open that safe?" he said pointing to the safe Emma used.

"I think it is open," Kris shrugged. Sergeant Pretorius walked to the safe and started looking through it.

Gerrie stood there, not knowing what to say. Then he asked, "Are you sure that he sold them to us? I have no recollection of buying anything from anybody today, especially illegal diamonds." Turning to Kris he continued, "Did you buy anything from anyone Kris?"

Neither of the policemen said anything.

"You know," Gerrie continued, "it is your boy's word against mine. Are you sure he sold them to us and not to somebody else? Are you so sure that he even sold them to somebody, and hasn't kept them for himself?"

Sergeant Pretorius looked Gerrie in the eye. His eyes were light blue and quite cold. He said nothing. He looked around the front office, and started rummaging carefully through Emma's desk. Finding nothing he walked to the office at the back where Emma was trying to get Marla to sleep. She showed her annoyance.

"So sorry to trouble you Ma'am," he said. "I would just like to look around."

Emma turned her back to him and continued rocking the pram.

"Ssshhh," she whispered, turning to him and holding her finger up to her mouth, "she is nearly asleep."

Sergeant Pretorius pointed to the cool room door.

"What is that?" he whispered.

"That is our cool room," Emma answered softly, guessing what he was pointing at. "That is where we keep the eggs."

"Will you open it, please?" he asked walking towards the door.

"It is open," Emma answered.

Kris walked into the back office and looked questioningly at Emma. She pointed to the cool room where the Sergeant was looking at all the eggs. The shelves were stacked with eggs, because Gerrie and Kris had been on a buying spree the last two days. In the far left hand corner, after moving some cardboard boxes, the Sergeant saw the small safe. "Could you open that, please?" he said to Kris, who was standing in the door of the cool room.

"With pleasure," Kris said. He walked to the safe, inserted his key into the lock, and opened it. Sergeant Pretorius stood next to him.

"Why do you have two safes?" he asked. "What do you use this one for?"

"Well," Kris answered," the safe in front is for our invoices and books. This safe is for cash. Many of the farmers we buy our eggs from insist on being paid in cash and we keep that cash here."

"I see," said Sergeant Pretorius. "Can I look through it?"

"Go ahead," Kris said.

He rummaged through the safe, carefully handling the money tied in bundles of one hundred pound notes.

"How much money do you have here?" he asked casually.

"Well, Kris replied, "We usually keep about a thousand pounds there, but we bought some eggs this morning, so there is only about four hundred pounds at the moment."

Detective van der Merwe walked into the back office followed by Gerrie. "Found nothing in the cool room, sir," Sergeant Pretorius said.

"Well, then, search the office more thoroughly. The parcel must be here somewhere."

They began a thorough search of the back office, avoiding Emma as far as possible, but turned up nothing.

"Have you found anything?" Gerrie smiled at Detective van der Merwe.

"No," he replied, and then addressed his partner, "Well then, come on, Jannie," he said to Sergeant Pretorius, his frustration quite obvious to all. Then looking at Gerrie he said angrily, "we will be back, Sir," and they both walked out of the back office.

Gerrie and Kris followed them to the front office.

"So you found nothing," Gerrie said, "I told you that there was nothing to find, that we never bought any stones."

"We will see about that," Detective van der Merwe said. "Jannie, go and ask Piet to come in here." He pulled up a chair and sat down. Gerrie sat down at Emma's desk. Kris stood at the door. Sergeant Pretorius walked out of the front door and called to Piet, the African policeman, to join them. Piet was rummaging in the outside garbage bin.

Emma walked to the front office and said to everyone in the room,

"You don't need me now, do you? I have to take my baby home. It is after four o'clock, and her bath time."

"That is OK with me," Gerrie replied, "and with you?" he gestured to Detective van der Merwe.

"Sure, Ma'am," he answered. "Go ahead."

Emma picked up her nappie bag, and placed it on the pram. She then picked up the garbage bin on which she had placed the nappie bag to empty it, as she did every day when she closed the shop. Saying goodbye to Gerrie and Kris, she walked out the back door to the large garbage bin in the yard, the bin that Piet had searched a few minutes earlier. She looked at the office bin curiously, the glass stones lying on the bottom of the bin catching her attention. She opened the brown paper bag and found more of them.

'That's strange,' she thought. 'These crystal pebbles are really beautiful. I wonder why they threw them away? I will buy some marbles and mix them together. They would look lovely in a vase of flowers.'

She placed them in the nappie bag, then emptied the bin into the garbage and returned the empty bin to the office.

A half hour later, the three policemen left.

'So... clever of you,' Gerrie said to Kris. "Where did you hide them?"

"Where did I hide what?" Kris asked not quite sure whether any of the policemen were perhaps eavesdropping. He walked to the front door, looked up and down the street and saw no-one.

Gerrie, impatient and not realizing what Kris was doing, shouted, "You know what! Don't fool with me!"

Thinking he saw a shadow at the window, Kris answered, "Quite honestly I don't know what you are talking about." He walked to the window, looked out carefully and saw no-one. He turned and looked at Gerrie's face, which was purple with anger, and laughed.

"Well," Gerrie shouted, angry at Kris. "Where did you fucking well hide them?"

"In the garbage bin by the inside desk," Kris laughed.

Gerrie walked to the back office and looked in the bin that Emma had emptied. "You are bullshitting me!" he shouted angrily. "The bloody bin is empty."

Kris walked into the back office and took the bin from Gerrie. He looked in the bin, and then at Gerrie, "but I hid them here, under some paper," he said, puzzled. "I couldn't go out; that black policeman was there, watching the back door."

"Are you sure?" Gerrie exploded. "Another one of your fucking lies?"

"But I did hide them there," Kris said, starting to doubt himself, "I know I did, I promise you, I did. I wouldn't lie to you."

Gerrie looked at him, ready to explode. "If you don't tell me where you hid them I will…"

"You will what?" Kris shouted back at him, becoming angry. "I tell you, I placed them in the garbage bin. Are you sure you never took them? You came here while I was in the front office and looked in the bin. How do I know that you haven't taken them?"

Then it struck Kris, "Oh my God, Emma must have emptied the bin as she left. She always cleans up before she leaves. She usually empties it in the big garbage bin outside. Go look outside," he shouted at Gerrie. He rushed outside with Gerrie following him.

They rummaged through the two garbage bins in the yard, but found nothing.

"But I know she dumped the garbage here like she always does," Kris whispered hoping that no-one was listening. "I saw her leave through the window… but… but shit man, earlier I also saw that fucking black policeman rummaging through the bins."

"And you expect me to believe all this crap? Gerrie whispered angrily. "Kris if you don't tell me where those stones are, I will…"

"You will what?" Kris, becoming angry, started shouting, "Report me to the police? Go ahead. Do that. I tell you that that bloody black policeman took them. When Pretorius went to call him, he was outside, rummaging through the garbage, and the bloody bugger never said a fucking word. I will kill him if I ever see him again. We have been taken, man."

"I don't believe one word you have said," Gerrie shouted at him. "You had better find those stones and fast!" He walked back into the office, slamming the door behind him.

That night, after Emma arrived home, she bathed Marla and put her in her cot. She then went outside and picked some roses from the garden. Going to the kitchen she took down a tall vase. Taking a small brown packet from her diaper bag, she poured the coloured marbles she bought at Shellards Toy Shop on her way home, into the packet. Shaking the packet well she then poured the contents into the vase, which she then filled with water. She arranged the roses beautifully, their stems held by the marbles and the crystal stones. Placing the vase with the flowers on the mantelpiece in the lounge, she stood back to admire her work.

"*I must say those pebbles that I found in the garbage look very beautiful with the marbles, and they are holding the roses just perfectly,*" she thought.

The next morning, when she went into work, neither Kris nor Gerrie were there. This was not unusual, because they were often in the field leaving her alone to manage the office. Neither of them showed up at the office for the next three days. On the fourth day, Kris walked into the office. He came to Emma where she sat at her desk behind the counter.

"Emma," he said, "Gerrie and I have decided to break up our partnership. I am taking over this business, and I would like you to stay on and help me. I am a little short of cash at the moment, so please do realize this and do your best with your sales. I would really appreciate it. If Gerrie should approach you to join him, I will meet any offer to you that he makes. I would very much like you to stay."

Emma found what he said strange, especially seeing that he had one black eye.

She continued working for Kris, but hardly ever saw him, because he was always in the field.

About six or seven months later, she invited Marie, Christa and Charlie over for dinner. She had spent a great deal of time in repainting and furnishing the house, and wanted to show it off. The evening with them was most enjoyable, far better than she expected, with Charlie insisting on managing the barbecue. At eleven o' clock that night, having all drunk too much wine and feeling very relaxed, Charlie called Emma to him as he stood in front of the vase.

"Emma," he said smiling at her, "this is a beautiful idea, displaying the roses in a vase with many coloured marbles. But tell me, where did you get those other colourless stones from?"

"Oh," she said, "they are unusual aren't they? I found them in the garbage bin at the shop.

"Very pretty," Charlie laughed. "You don't know, of course, that they are uncut diamonds?"

"Uncut diamonds?" Emma said, amazed, "but they look like glass stones."

Charlie started laughing. "Well I must say that the joke is on them. Kris and Gerrie had a fight about those stones. Gerrie thought Kris had stolen them from him, and Kris believes that Gerrie and some African policeman had a deal, and that he stole them to share with Gerrie."

Turning to her with a smile on his face he said. "My dear, keep them, and above all, do not give them back to either Kris or Gerrie, and please, don't ever think that you stole them. You found them where they had been thrown, and it is the old rule, finders are keepers."

He pointed to the vase, "You have an absolute fortune in that vase. Look after those stones and one day, if ever you are short of money, let me know, and I will refer you to a buyer." He then laughed so loud and hard that his sides ached. But he would not tell Marie or Christa what the joke was.

After they had left, Emma stood in front of the vase. "*The best place to keep them hidden is exactly where they are right now,*" she thought, "*in plain sight of everyone. And there my darling Marla, is part of your inheritance. Most of it will go to support your grandparents in Cape Town, to give them the life they should have were it not for the hate that lives in this beautiful country of ours.*" She heard Marla crying in her sleep. She saluted the vase, and went to comfort Marla.

Then, in August of 1943, she received a phone call.

Chapter 11

Emma was bathing Marla when the phone rang. She wrapped a towel around Marla. Carrying her in one arm, she walked to the telephone and answered it.

"Good evening, Emma O'Neil speaking," she said.

The voice at the other end of the line said, "I am sorry, I must have the wrong number, I am looking for Emma Kline."

Emma recognized the voice immediately, "Hello," she said hesitantly, "Chrissie, this is me, Emma," she placed Marla on the floor next to her. "It is so wonderful to hear you. How are you and how is the family?"

"We are all fine," Chrissie said. "My mother keeps asking after you. I am pleased that I found you. I looked all over for you. I misplaced your phone number and phoned Irma Rosen hoping that she might have it. She gave me this number. She never told me that you and Eric were married. How are things with you?"

"I am very well," Emma replied, "so far enjoying Potch. and very happy here. How is the OK? I must say that I do miss it." Emma was puzzled. Why should Chrissie Stead, of all people, phone her?

"The OK is fine," Chrissie said hesitantly, "just remember, there is always a position waiting for you." She paused, and Emma listened carefully to make sure that she was still on the line. "Hello... hello...?" she spoke into the receiver.

"I am sorry, I am here," Chrissie answered slowly, as though she were thinking. "Emma, the OK management received a phone call from a lawyer in Potchefstroom. He is trying to find you. His name is Lionel Herz."

"Oh, I know Lionel Herz," Emma said, "Did he mention what he wants?"

Chrissie was puzzled. "No, he did not," she answered, "but if he knows you, I can't understand why he should phone us looking for you."

"Neither can I," Emma said. "I will contact him tomorrow, and find out what he wants."

Emma and Chrissie then chatted about the O.K. and Emma promised to visit Chrissie the next time she was in Johannesburg.

Lionel Herz's office was a short walk down the street from the Mooi River Pharmacy. Emma walked into the Pharmacy to say hello to Marie because she was a few minutes early for her appointment. Marie was busy with a client, so Emma waited in the pharmacy, playing with the perfume testers. Alf Stern walked up to her and asked her if he could help her. He must have been a very good looking man in his youth, but his hair was now completely grey, with a bald spot at his crown. He had put on a lot of weight, and could no longer button the white linen jacket he wore in the pharmacy over his stomach. His cheeks were jowls on either side of his mouth, drooping slightly with the extra weight he was carrying. He smiled, and his eyes lit up his face. Emma could see why he was so popular with his clients. He simply exuded friendliness.

"Oh, I am just waiting for Marie," Emma said, "I would like to ask her something.

Alf nodded. "So how are you and how are you settling down?" he asked.

"I love Potch," Emma said, "far more than I expected. "It is a beautiful town, with beautiful gardens and houses. Most of the people are very friendly, and I have made a number of very good friends."

"Well," Alf said, "How about joining us for dinner on Friday night? It is usually a special evening for us, and we always have people over. You could meet someone new."

"Thank you," Emma answered, smiling at him, "Is it alright if I bring my baby daughter?"

"But of course," Alf answered, "I am sure that Lilly would love to see her."

Marie finished serving the client and walked to where Emma and Alf were chatting.

"Hello, Emma," she said.

"Hello, Marie," Emma replied putting down the perfume tester she was holding.

"Well, see you Friday night," Alf said. "Don't forget, now."

Emma smiled at him as he walked away, "I won't," she said. She turned to Marie. "Marie, I am on my way to see Lionel Herz. He phoned the OK in Johannesburg, looking for me. I don't know why he wants to see me, but I am nervous. Is it possible that you come with me?"

Marie looked at her watch. "Well, it is nearly 4 o'clock. Let me ask Mr. Stern. With the shop closing in an hour, he just might let me go." Marie was worried that Lionel Herz may have discovered Emma's secret.

Fifteen minutes later, both girls walked into Lionel Herz's office. Emma approached the lady that sat at a desk in the reception room. "Good afternoon. Could you tell Mr. Herz that Emma O'Neil, I mean Emma Kline, is here?" she said nervously.

The lady smiled at her. She was not the woman Emma had spoken with when she rented the house. "Please take a seat over there," she said, and picked up her phone. She spoke into it, then put it back in its cradle and said to Emma, "Mr. Herz asks if you could wait just a few minutes."

Emma smiled and nodded and walked back to where Marie was sitting. Marie picked up a magazine and pretended to read it.

"Don't worry," she whispered, "He is a nice man. He is a customer at the pharmacy, and he and his wife, Trudy, are very nice people."

"I cannot help being nervous," Emma answered. "I don't like lawyers at the best of times, they always want to know too much of everything. When I spoke to him on the phone, he sounded very serious. I hope that he hasn't found out anything about me."

After about five minutes, the phone at the lady's desk rang. She picked it up and looked at Emma and Marie. "Mr. Herz will see you now," she said, smiling at them. They stood up, with Marie placing the magazine she was paging back on the table. They walked into Lionel Herz's office, Marie leading the way. He stood up from behind his desk to greet them. He was a tall thin man, with a long face that accentuated his thinness. His eyes, though, were friendly and warm as he looked at the two women who stood front of him. He smiled, trying to appear relaxed, something he found difficult because he always had more work than he could handle, often staying late into the night just to catch up with his daily business.

"Ah... Miss Kline," he said to Marie, frowning, recognizing but not quiet placing her, and turning to Emma, "and this is?"

"Oh," Emma answered, "I am Emma Kline. This is my friend, Marie. You know her from the Mooi River Pharmacy. I asked her to join me. I hope that you don't mind."

"Not at all, not at all," Lionel replied, slightly embarrassed by his faux pas. "Of course I know you, Marie, I should, but in a different setting, well..." and he shrugged his shoulders. He then gestured towards the two chairs in front of his desk. "Please, do take a seat."

They both sat down, Emma still feeling very uncomfortable. She crossed her legs, pulling down her skirt to cover her knees. Marie in her white pharmacy uniform looked at her and whispered, "Don't worry." Emma smiled at her.

Lionel looked down at his desk and ruffled some papers, then frowned.

"Miss Kline," he said to Emma, "somehow your name rings a bell." Emma looked surprised. "Well," she answered, "I am presently renting Eric O'Neil's house, which your office handles. I must say that I never spoke with you when I signed the lease, but spoke with one of your secretaries."

"Ah, yes," Lionel replied, smiling at her, "Now I remember. I saw the copy of the lease, and I wondered who you were. I always thought that I knew everybody in Potchefstroom. I hope you like the house?"

"Very much," Emma replied.

"Well," Lionel said, looking at the open file that lay on his desk, "I don't quite know how to say this, but I have some good news for you."

"Good news?" Emma asked, puzzled.

"Well, yes," Lionel said. "You see, the owner, Eric O'Neil has left the house to you in his will. I received notification last week that he had been killed..." he never had a chance to finish.

"Oh my God," Emma cried, "In his will? Eric is dead..?" She started crying uncontrollably.

"Good heavens," Marie said, and then almost shouted at Lionel. "Mr. Herz, how could you be so tactless? Emma, darling... Oh, Emma," and she took Emma in her arms to comfort her.

Lionel sat quite still, struck by this outburst from Marie. He had expected Emma to be pleased with the inheritance, not cry they way she was. He sat, not sure what to do next.

Marie turned to him, "You could have been more sympathetic. Emma is Mrs. O'Neil. She and Eric are husband and wife."

Lionel was distraught. "But... but ..." he said, "I didn't know Eric O'Neil was married. There is no mention of it anywhere. I have a letter from the military..." He rummaged through the papers on his desk. Finding one, he held it up and continued, "... that said Eric was single, not married. That he corresponded with an Emma Kline who worked for the OK Bazaars in Johannesburg, and that I should please find her. That was the only name they had on record besides that of his father and sister, as well as my name, as his lawyer."

He stood up and walked around the desk to where Emma sat sobbing. Taking both her hands in his, he said, his voice breaking with emotion, "I am so sorry. I am so terribly, terribly sorry. If I had only known."

Emma started to recover herself. She looked at Lionel dully, her eyes not focusing. "You could not have known," she said softly, her voice not betraying her feelings. "Please, tell me what happened."

Lionel walked back to his chair and sat down. He looked down at the papers that lay in an open file in front of him. Then he looked up at Emma, who was staring at him with no emotion on her face, her eyes blurry from her tears.

"The army apparently did not have any record of you as his wife. As I said earlier, his records only show you as Emma Kline, not you as Emma O'Neil. They have the OK Bazaars in Johannesburg as your mailing address. They had no one to contact to tell of his death. Apparently his father has passed away, and Eric had only listed a sister whom they could not find. All correspondence to the address he gave them for her was returned. There were no other relatives that they could contact. They had me on record as his lawyer and contacted me. You were not listed as a relative, but as a friend.

"They sent me all his effects, which showed that he had worked at the OK Bazaars before enlisting. There was a letter among all the papers that showed that you were also an employee there. I contacted them and asked if they knew where I could find you. I simply never put two and two together, that the Miss Kline that rented Eric's house was the same Emma Kline I was looking for. The manager at the O.K. Bazaars told me that you were once in their employ, and passed me on to..." and he looked down at the papers in front of him, "to a Chrissie Stead. She knows you, but did not know where to contact you, but she told me that she would try and find you." He looked up at Emma and said without thinking, trying to lighten the situation, "You appear to be a very secretive person, Miss Kline."

Emma looked at Marie, and Marie at Emma. Both were shocked

with what Lionel had just said even though he was not aware of the implications.

"Yes, Mr. Herz," Emma eventually said, her face lined with worry about how much he knew or did not know about her. "I am known in Potchefstroom by my married name, Emma O'Neil, but I rented the house using my maiden name."

"Emma and Eric were married," Marie lied, "just before he went overseas. He probably forgot to tell the military authorities that he now had a wife."

Emma looked at Marie and frowned, but she said nothing.

"Well," Lionel continued, "I am truly, truly sorry that you had to hear about your husband's death from me so tactlessly. If I had only known,,," and he shook his head with remorse. They could see that he was very upset with what had just happened. "Please forgive me, and accept my deepest and most sincere condolences on his death."

Emma looked at him to see if he meant what he said. Lionel's face reflected his sympathy at her loss. She started crying softly and rummaged in her handbag looking for a tissue. He reached into his desk and took out a box of tissues which he passed to her. "Thank you," she said taking one, wiping away the tears and blowing her nose.

"Could you, could you tell me," Emma hesitated, looked down at her hands clasped in her lap, "Is there to be a funeral?"

"From what I understand," Lionel said, "Eric was buried overseas, in a military grave. I don't have the particulars, but I will try and find out for you."

"Thank you," Emma said. Collecting her things she stood up as though to leave.

"Please, please sit down," Lionel said, "There is more to tell you."

Emma turned in surprise and sat down on the edge of her chair, worried about what Lionel Herz had still to say.

"Can I get both of you something to drink?" he asked.

"Tea would be lovely," Emma answered.

"For me as well," Marie said.

Lionel picked up his phone and asked his secretary to bring in two teas.

"Mrs. O'Neil," Lionel started, accepting her as Eric's wife. "Eric came to me and changed his will naming you, Emma Kline, as his heir two days before he left Potchefstroom. Up until then he had left everything to a sister who lives in Pietersburg. I tried to contact her to see if she knew you, but could not find her. Please forgive me for asking, but why did you rent your late husband's house under the name of Kline, and not simply live in it as his wife, without paying any rent?"

"Well, you see..." Emma started looking at Marie, "we were married in such a hurry. Eric managed to get a day's leave before being sent overseas. There was simply no time to do anything. I had already come to your offices to look into renting the house and thought well, by paying the rent, in a way it is a form of saving. Your office was handling all the expenses and taxes with regard to the house, let me leave it that way, rather than take it on myself. Either way, the money I paid in rent stays in the family as a sort of saving."

"Yes, I suppose so," Lionel agreed. "Now, please forgive me, but I must ask you a strange question. Can you prove to me that you are the Emma Kline Eric referred to in his will?"

Emma looked at him, disbelief on her face.

Marie looked at him shocked. "But hasn't everything Emma just said, isn't that proof enough?" she blurted out.

"This is just a formality," Lionel answered embarrassed. "It is a question I have to ask."

"Well, I do have an account with Barclays Bank that I have had for years as Emma Kline...." Emma started.

"Will my father's word be acceptable that she is Emma Kline, now Emma O'Neil?" Marie interrupted.

"And who is your father?" Lionel asked.

"Charlie Stuart, I am sure you know him."

"Charlie? Of course I know him," Lionel answered. "Everyone knows him. Your father is an honorable man. His word is good enough."

They left Lionel's office still in a state of shock, went to the Stuarts' house, and waited for Charlie to come home. Christa, who had been babysitting Marla, was comforting, a mother helping a daughter, Emma, with her grief. When Charlie came home, they told him what had happened. He was shocked at Eric's death and expressed his deepest sympathies to Emma. He picked up the phone and confirmed Emma's identity with Lionel Herz.

"Lionel is a good friend," he said to them, "I like him very much, but one must never forget that he is a lawyer, and lawyers can be, well, let us say not that easy to handle. They tend to stick to the law."

He looked at both the girls sitting in front of him. "Both of you look awful," he said, "Emma, I can understand the shock you have been through, and know that Christa, Marie and I will always be here for you when you need us. Now, I do think that you should spend the night here and that you definitely need something strong to drink." Going to his liquor cabinet, he poured both girls a stiff brandy.

That night, lying in bed at the Stuart house, Emma thought about Eric and how much she had loved him, but how little she had known about him. She sat up, and leaned over the cot that was next to the bed. Marla lay fast asleep. "My darling Marla," she said as she stroked Marla's head. The baby smiled in her sleep.

"You have lost a father that you never knew. Somehow, I promise you, I will try to be both father and mother to you. I just hope that I don't disappoint you. Your father died in a war started by a hateful group of people that practice religious and racial hatred. They succeeded in brainwashing their nation to follow their hateful ideals, and those that did not follow what they preached, they killed.

"South Africa is very similar to them. The government here also divides its nation, but on racial colour, not yet on religious beliefs. I cannot understand why they don't realize that they can only practice these hateful policies for a limited time period. The Whites here are in a minority and, like the Nazis, they will sometime in the future be overpowered. But it will be from within, not from without like in a war, although I do believe that the outside world will help in some way. I feel that the Africans who live in South Africa will take over the country, and being uneducated, will take this country back to its tribal origins. That is wrong. The Government must educate the Africans, even give them a better education than they give the Whites if necessary. Then when they do take over - and they surely will, because time is on their side - they will continue to maintain the westernization of South Africa, and instead of destroying it, build upon the foundations that the Whites have given them. You my darling, you have lost a father who went to war to fight this hatred. I now promise you, my Marla, that I will spend the rest of my life fighting this racial hatred with every breath that I take."

She leaned over the cot and kissed Marla on her forehead, then lay back in her bed. She pulled the blankets over her, punched the pillow the way she liked it and lay on her side facing Marla. She then pulled her knees up to her chest, lying in a foetal position and closing her eyes, cried herself to sleep.

Book 2
Marla

Chapter 1

The school bell rang its final peal. The boys tumbled out of their class rooms, cheering and shouting.

"Hey Josh, what are you doing these holidays?" one of the boys shouted at Josh as he walked from the classroom. Josh didn't answer him, but walked as fast as he could to the school gate, disappointment written all over his face.

'*I hope my Dad will let me go to Habonim camp next year,*' he thought as he walked. '*Every year it the same reason why I cannot go.*'

School was over for the year, breaking up on a sun-filled Friday, with the hint of a grey thunderstorm staining the white cumulus clouds that hung like balls of cotton wool in the sky. Josh walked home slowly, carrying a heavy schoolbag on his back feeling sorry for himself. His home was a block away from the Potchefstroom High School for Boys. He always enjoyed the walk, shaded from the hot sun by the three willow trees that lined the water furrow floating down the left side of the sidewalk. A small boat that he made out of a twig curled its way over the waterfalls of crab-hiding rocks that lined the furrow bed. A frog croaked at him from a moss lined bank of the furrow. He jumped back in fright, and then laughed at his own fear.

"Hey Josh, hang on a sec!" Jaapie shouted at him. He stopped, turned and waited for Jaapie, riding his bicycle, catch up to him. Jaapie was one of the boys in his class, the son of Albert van Wyk, manager of a farm in the Tuli block, on the Limpopo river.

"Did you hear that Pietjie cannot go to Boys High? He has to go to Volkskool."

Pietjie was Jaapie's younger brother. Without waiting to hear Josh's answer, Jaapie continued.

"A new law saying that that if your home language is Afrikaans, you can only go to Afrikaans schools has stopped Pietjie from joining us. What are you doing this holiday? Are you and your dad coming to the farm?"

"No, I don't think so," Josh answered. "It is too hot, and my Dad is always worried about malaria."

"Ach… he shouldn't worry," Jaapie answered, "garlic keeps the mosquito away. See you next year," and he cycled off.

For the next five weeks, over Christmas and New Year, there would be no school because it was summer holidays. Exams had been written and passed. It was December 1955. When the new school year started again in January, Josh would be going into Standard 9. He walked slowly, wondering how he would spend the long, hot, languid days of the summer. All his friends were going to Habonim camp, at Leaches Bay, with its beautiful white sandy beach, close to East London in the Cape. That meant he would be alone, with no friends for almost three weeks of the five-week holiday.

They were a group of four boys and three girls, all more or less the same age; friends since they first met at Mrs. Myers' Kindergarten, on Kruger Street, when they were three and four year olds. A close friendship was started, a friendship that lasted a lifetime.

In the year he turned six, Josh attended Central school, feeling proud to be in grade one, with Miss Broekhuizen, a stern but loving teacher. Two of his friends were already in grade two, waiting eagerly to teach him the do's and don'ts of the school. It was only when he went to high school that they split up, with the girls going to the Potchefstroom High School for Girls with Miss Ramsbottom as the principal; the boys attending the Potchefstroom High School for Boys with Mr. MacDonald, a stern and strict but kindly man as the principal.

All of them were now at the age where they enjoyed Tommy

Dorsey or Benny Goodman. They had only just started learning to ballroom dance. Josh knew that he would miss the Saturday nights when they would meet at one or another's house to play the latest record releases. Taking one of the girls in his arms, he would slowly practice the foxtrot or the waltz. He still blushed as he remembered the first time he took Yvonne in his arms and placed his hand under her armpit, his palm feeling the softness of her breast.

"What do you think you are doing?" he remembered her saying as she slapped his hand away angrily. She had not pushed him away, and continued with the dance lesson.

For as long as he could remember, he had been in love with Yvonne, but every year when she went to camp, she came back with a different boyfriend, a relationship that always lasted about five months. Those five months always hurt, watching her moon after a boy in another city, but by now he was used to it.

They had not yet left for camp and he hoped to see them before they went. They would catch the train as it passed through Potchefstroom from Johannesburg early the following morning, but already he was feeling lonely.

It was December. In South Africa, December was the middle of summer; hot, sweaty, and usually boring. Too many of the Jewish families went on vacation to Muizenberg in the Cape, a city nick-named "Jewsenberg," as it filled with Jewish families from all over the Transvaal. They gathered there every year to meet friends and family and gossip about family and friends. With their teenage children in camp, mothers and fathers felt they needed a well-earned break from parenting.

Josh would have loved to go to camp, but this year, he hadn't asked his parents, because he knew that the expense was more than they could afford. It was the summer of 1955. They had survived the war years in their pharmacy and the change in the government with the rise of Afrikaner nationalism, with difficulty. At supper, Alf, Josh's father, would always talk about how difficult the day had been, then "with a bit of luck business will soon start picking up," he would always smile, and then ask him how his day had been.

What Josh hadn't worked out for himself, was that the war ended when he was 5 years old, 10 years ago, and that the reason business was so bad was because they were English speaking and above all Jewish, living in a predominantly Afrikaans-speaking town. With the Afrikaner nationalist Daniel Francois Malan's administration that took over from General Jan Christiaan Smuts as Prime Minister at the first election after the war, Afrikaner nationalism had become a strong emotional force. Many of Mooi River Pharmacy's previous customers began boycotting them, in favor of the Afrikaner-owned pharmacy that had recently opened opposite the OK Bazaars.

The Mooi River Pharmacy had always been located on King Edward Street. But with the new political scene, the street was now renamed Kerk Street. Although small, the pharmacy was well managed. Hope MacDonald, was the sales lady, Piet Pienaar the apprentice with Winkie Bezuidenhout the bookkeeper. They, with his dad, ran an efficient shop.

Of course the fact that Alf was the only optician in town brought them business they would not have had, but there was a flaw in the business. The flaw was Alf himself; he was a very soft touch. He could never bring himself to sue for non-payment of an account. Many of the town's labourers would run up large credit bills that went unpaid. If any of them presented Alf with a prescription, especially for one of their children, he never had the heart to turn them away. The cost of the medicine simply added to their ballooning debt.

Alf was the youngest of three sons. His elder brother, Bernard, was a well-respected doctor practicing in Potchefstroom, a very likable man with a gruff rasping voice and yellow nicotine-stained moustache who often accepted chickens instead of cash for services rendered. He was as yet unmarried, and to him cash was not a necessity. That would only come much later, when he would meet and marry Ruth.

His second brother, Joe, set up a dental practice in Johannesburg. Unlike his two brothers, Joe charged for his services. He often visited them in Potchefstroom over a weekend with his latest girlfriend, always driving the newest and most expensive motorcar advertised. He was a very heavy man, prone to wearing white pants and an old boy's blazer from Potch Boys High, the buttons straining over his ballooning tummy. He was always bubbling and enjoying life to its utmost, the life and soul of any social gathering.

Josh remembered that when he was a young boy, the whole family would drive down to the Swartzberg farm in Boskop every Sunday afternoon. They would bathe in the Mooi River, under a waterfall built to spin a water wheel that crushed the grain in the mill.

Alf was a well-respected man in Potchefstroom and liked by all who met him. He was comfortably built, with black hair greying at the temples, eyes that were always smiling set in a face characterized by a large very Semitic nose that sometime in his youth he had broken. He was spoiled by a loving wife, Lilly, who was a very beautiful woman and an excellent cook. Her Sunday morning bagels, fruit and butter cakes were to die for.

Josh knew that he had to be home no later than 5:30 every afternoon, because that is when the shop closed, and his father wanted supper. After the meal, Alf would always sit in his favourite armchair and eat two or three oranges. He would then read a Zane Grey book, carefully marked with a dot on page 26, his birthday, so that Lilly would be able to identify it at the library as one that he had already read. Every Monday, Wednesday and Saturday nights at exactly a quarter to eight, his parents would drive the one block down to the local bioscope, always sitting in the same seats in the gallery, without even knowing or caring what was showing.

Alf had qualified as a pharmacist in London, England, at the Chelsea Polytechnic. While studying there, he'd had a three year relationship with Veronica Sybil Smith but on returning to South Africa, he had fallen head over heels in love with Lilly Rowe. The two were married in a civil ceremony in Potchefstroom, a year before their religious ceremony at a synagogue in Johannesburg. When he married Lilly, she was beautifully slim, slowly putting on weight comfortably over the years as she gave birth to three children.

They were a very happy family, though always hard up for cash, yet they lived comfortably. On a Friday night, after attending synagogue, Alf would always bring home any of the young soldiers who had attended, so that they could enjoy a beautifully prepared Sabbath dinner.

Then of course, there was Dr. Tom with offices above the pharmacy. He was a very popular doctor and his patients often brought their prescriptions to the pharmacy rather than walk to another one further down the street. Dr. Tom also had rooms at the back, where he would examine his Black, Indian and Coloured patients, rooms that were separate from the Whites. Rather than writing prescriptions for them, he dispensed mixtures prepared at the pharmacy at greatly reduced prices, but just as effective in curing disease. Josh knew the names almost by heart; *Mist. Expect Sed.* for coughs, *Mist Expect Stim.* for who knows what, with *Mist. Alba* and *Ulcer Balm* being the most commonly made and dispensed.

On most Saturday afternoons, after synagogue, Josh would walk to the shop and help Jeremiah, the Coloured boy who worked in the store at the back, prepare those mixtures that Dr. Tom dispensed, of course always under the supervision of Piet Pienaar. Although Jerry had been there long enough to be trusted to prepare the powders and basics without ever making a mistake, he was not a qualified pharmacist. Piet had to supervise him, checking what he had prepared before the mixtures were made.

Of course, when a customer wanted them to put down a dog with puppies, or a cat with kittens, then that was Jerry's job as well, without any supervision. Josh had once watched how Jerry had placed the dog and puppies in a large tin can, and how he had closed the lid after throwing in a wad of cotton wool soaked in chloroform. He never forgot how the animals had whimpered before they died. For many a month afterwards, he had woken at night with nightmares, crawling into the bed between his parents. What he did not know then and only learned years later was that it was all a big bluff by Jerry. No animal died by his hand. He always pretended to kill them, putting them to sleep and then smuggling them to the Location, giving them to his friends and family.

But that was the pharmacist's job in those days. They were persons respected in the community, helping all customers with all their problems, and referring them to the doctors only when they diagnosed a major ailment.

Josh still remembered when at supper one evening, his father told them that he had examined a man for eyeglasses.

"I could see when I looked at the retina in his left eye, that he had a tumour on the brain. I asked him who his doctor was, told him to go there immediately. I then phoned his doctor and told him what I suspected."

Alf was correct in his diagnosis, and months later, after the man had been operated on, successfully, he came to the house to thank his father, dragging a sheep as a gift behind him. It made Josh so proud.

Josh cherished his Saturday mornings at the Pharmacy, working as best as he could. When it rained he would jump over the puddles of rainwater that collected in the yard between the shop and the storeroom where Jerry worked. He would help Jerry unpack the boxes, then carry the stock after they were priced into the shop and help Hope pack them neatly on the shelves. When he received his payment at lunch time, he would rush to the OK Bazaars to buy stamps, stopping on the way at Shellard's Hobby Shop to admire the newest Dinky Toy motorcar.

Josh had a very happy childhood growing up in Potchefstroom, a town situated on the banks of the Mooi River, which started as a trickle of water out of a rock face some 15 miles to the north. The river fed the dam that kept the town green when the rest of the countryside died to a *vaal* colour in the hot summer days.

Potchefstroom was a Boer town, captured by the British during the Anglo-Boer war. Street names were changed to English, even though the town council was predominantly Afrikaans speaking. However, once the National Party won the election, the street names were changed from English names to Afrikaans names; King Edward Street became Kerk Street; Berg Street, where Josh lived was renamed van Riebeeck Street after the Dutch founder of the fairest Cape in all the world.

Surprisingly though, in 1954 his father was elected to the town council, winning a fight against an Afrikaner councilor who was an ex-mayor of the town. Conservative Afrikaners, although they would not do business with him, respected him, because he was a man who was just and fair to all. He would serve more than 30 years as a town councilor, more often than not re-elected unopposed. In 1955, at the height of Afrikaner nationalism, he would be elected mayor of the town simply by pulling the short straw in a tie break. For many years thereafter, Alf often served as vice mayor, but was never re-elected mayor.

But now it was the summer with school holidays. His father had said that he should work at the shop for a salary of a half crown a week, but Josh decided to take up the offer only after the second week.

"Let me relax and play for a week," he told his dad. "I will start at the shop in a week's time."

What he actually had in mind was to go very early every morning to the municipal swimming pool, to practice his swimming. He had nearly made the swimming team at school, and felt that if he practiced hard and long enough, he would easily do so when school re-opened. So early the next morning, after grabbing a bite to eat, rather than visit the station to wish his friends a pleasant trip as they caught the train to camp, he went to the municipal swimming pool, a twenty-minute walk from the house.

At that time in the morning, The Baths, as they were commonly called by the townspeople, were usually empty, with workers sweeping and cleaning the pool. There were usually only one or two determined swimmers attacking the 100-yard length. Josh dived in and started swimming, hoping to complete at least two lengths before he tired, not the five or ten lengths the others were casually swimming.

'*If I do this every day,*' he thought as he swam, '*I should be able to build up to six lengths by the time school starts.*' By the end of the first length he was tired, having swallowed quite a bit of water. He turned to swim back, his swimming style slowly deteriorating the further he swam. Near the end, he was gasping for breath with every stroke. He stumbled up the ladder and out of the water. Stretching his towel out on the freshly cut grass beside the pool, he lay down on his stomach with his arms cushioning his head. As the warm early morning sun started drying him, he fell asleep.

He woke to the noise of screams and shouts as children splashed in the water. He stood up and stretched, shaking off his sleep. With a back itching slightly from new sunburn, he took his towel and walked slowly to the deep end where there were fewer children. He looked around to see if he knew anyone, but he saw no-one that he knew. Then recognizing the head of black hair with a stocky muscular build, he walked slowly forward where it lay on a towel on the grass.

"Hi, Costas", Josh said shyly as he walked up to him.

Chapter 2

C ostas, as everyone called him, was Gerasimos Bouras. He was 17 years old and lived a few houses away from Josh but on Lombard Street, not van Riebeeck Street. Roula, his sister, was Josh's age, and they had known each other ever since their mothers had tucked them in the same perambulator next to each other when they were still babies. Costas's family was originally from Greece, the island of Ithaca, his parents moving to Potchefstroom sometime in the early 1920's.

His father owned the restaurant the Rendezvous Cafe on the corner next to Barclays Bank, close to the Mooi River Pharmacy. He had moved the restaurant from the corner opposite the OK Bazaars when the new building had been completed, because the building his restaurant was in was being demolished. The restaurant was a popular one, with tables and chairs where one could sit and enjoy a light meal of food that was very Greek, the grilled calamari being the favourite. The smell of the spices used in the food, coming from the kitchen, was everywhere.

When one walked in, you were always greeted by Mr. Bouras' smile as he stood behind the counter. Behind him were shelves filled with sweets, cookies, packets, boxes of every cigarette and cigar available for sale in South Africa. The top shelf, though, had a row of bottles, each one with a label on which was written a name. Some were filled with bank notes, but most of them were empty. Josh had often wondered what they were for. One day, after asking Roula, she told him.

"That is my father's lending tree," she said, frowning. "My mother hates it, but in a way it does seem to work. People are always coming in to borrow money from my dad. He then goes to the bottle with that person's name on it and if there is money in it, he gives it to them. If the bottle is empty, he says, 'Sorry, your bottle is empty. I can only loan you money when you pay back what you took out of the bottle.'"

Josh laughed. "Very clever," he said. "That must solve a lot of problems."

What Josh didn't know was that when Mr. Bouras refused the loan, they would then go to his father and ask him for a loan. Alf always found it difficult to say 'No', which was why he drove an old Oldsmobile, when all those who borrowed from him drove brand new Mercedes Benzes.

At 17 years old, Costas was exceptionally good looking. He was built square, five foot nine inches tall, and probably two foot ten inches wide, all muscle, and not an ounce of fat. He played first team rugby at Potchefstroom Boys High, as a lock forward, and was vice captain of the team. He was popular with both the boys and the teachers, a brilliant scholar, top of his class and expected to pass his matric year with six distinctions. He was very popular with the girls and liked to visit the municipal pool, where he showed off his muscular build glistening with suntan oil that allowed his skin to burn to a beautiful brown tan. Costas was a good catch, and he knew that and played it to his best.

With all his good looks and achievements at school, he was also a brilliant jazz pianist, memorizing countless tunes effortlessly. At any and all parties, if a piano was present, he always took over, entertaining his friends with whatever tune they asked him to play. The trick was to find one that he didn't know. If one were found, whistling a few bars would cause him to improvise and play it as though he had played it a hundred times before.

He was a remarkable boy, a prefect at school, and an example that many boys tried to emulate. Josh always looked up to him, greeting him respectfully whenever he saw him even though he visited their house often, doing homework with Roula.

He was therefore surprised to find Costas lying on his towel alone, with no girls around him.

Plucking up courage, he asked, "Is it ok if I lie next to you?"

"Sure," Costas answered. "Help yourself."

Lying with Costas, in a way, he did feel protected, because here, at the municipal swimming pool there was always some anti-Semitic Afrikaner boy calling him names.

Josh spread his towel on the grass and lay down on it, his back to the sun. After a few minutes in an attempt to start some conversation, he asked, "Where is everybody?"

"Probably on holiday somewhere," Costas answered, and yawning, turned his face away from Josh as though to end the conversation.

Josh closed his eyes, enjoying the heat of the sun on his back and legs. After about five minutes, his skin started to burn. Standing up, he dove into the pool to cool off, not wanting to experience the sting-ing sensation he always felt on his skin when he bathed in hot water at night, before bed time. He was never scared of the sun, because he always burned dark brown, but he had to collect his tan slowly. When he was a child, his mother would rub him down with olive oil. He would then tan almost black. She was once asked by a man in the street, "Ma'am, why are you looking after an African baby?" After that, she stopped giving Josh a suntan, shading him from the sun with an enormous shade umbrella when he lay on his blanket on the back lawn of the house, playing.

"Why do I burn so dark in the sun?" he once asked his Dad when he was older.

Alf had looked at him, not quite sure how to answer, then he said, hoping that Josh would understand.

"Well, your mother's maiden name was Rowe. Although her father came to South Africa from Russia, somewhere, sometime in the past they must have been one of the Spanish Jews that ran away from the Spanish Inquisition, so there must be some Moorish blood in your veins. That is why you burn so dark."

Josh had only understood a little of what he said. But later, as they studied the Spanish Inquisition in history at school, he recalled the story and finally grasped the full meaning of his father's words.

He swam the width of the pool and stopping to take a breath, holding onto the side, he looked up and noticed that Charlene and Erica had walked in. They spread their towels near the bushes that hid the pool's filtration plant, close to the baby pool.

'Strange' he thought, 'I always thought Costas and Charlene were dating. I am surprised she did not look for him. I wonder whether they have broken up. Perhaps that is why he is so grumpy.'

He swam back slowly to where Costas lay. Costas had now turned onto his back, his chest and muscle-strong stomach facing the sun. Josh admired his build, vowing that he would start doing weights. He looked down at his brown skin, darkening even more in the morning sun, and knew that in a few days his skin would be almost mahogany brown. Summer to him was always a problem, not due to the fact that he burned so dark, but because he then had to convince the ushers at the Grand and Lyric bioscopes, that he wasn't a Coloured or an Indian, but a White, and therefore they could let him in. The Lyric Bioscope did allow Blacks, Coloureds and Indians, upstairs, but the Grand Theatre was for Whites only.

Once, when he went to the Lyric bioscope, despite almost dropping his pants to show them his tan line, where he didn't burn, they still insisted that he sit upstairs. When he told his father what had happened, his father was furious, phoning the manager and telling him off. So he was very careful not to burn too much, and did not use the olive oil his mother always gave him as a sunscreen, knowing that he burned blackest after he rubbed it on.

He pulled himself out of the water, grabbed his towel, and rubbed himself dry. Then he sat on his towel, looking around to see if anyone else he knew had come into the pool grounds. Costas slept beside him, snoring ever so slightly as he lay on his back.

'Must have had a late night,' Josh thought, envying Costas that his parents allowed him to stay out so late. Josh's parents insisted that he be home by 10:30 p.m. Of course, now that all his friends had gone off to camp, he didn't have anywhere to go at night, anyway.

He looked across the water to where Charlene and Erica sat in their two-piece bathing suits. Charlene was stunning with her blonde hair and slim figure, always with a bevy of boys around her. Erica, her elder sister by one year, was not as slim nor as pretty, but she was the conversationalist who attracted boys with her charm more than looks. Both girls were very popular, with many a boy claiming to have broken their virginity. The problem was that so many had claimed to have been the first, that no one believed them anymore.

Two young men walked out of the men's changing room and joined them, laying their towels on the grass next to them. Josh didn't recognize the boys but they looked more like young men than young boys. *'Must be from Pukke,'* he thought. Pukke was the Local University, short for Potchefstroom University for Higher Christian Education.

Josh looked at Costas. Costas had woken and had sat up. He was looking at the two boys with Charlene and Erica, a slight sneer on his face.

"When I was at Boys' High, and they had just moved to Girls' High," he said, "they wouldn't leave me alone. Now I am no longer good enough for them...too young." He gave a snort and lay back on his towel. "They will learn very quickly" he mumbled, disappointment showing in his voice, and closing his eyes he pretended to go back to sleep. Josh looked at him, recognizing his disappointment. He turned over to lie on his back. He put his hands behind his head and closed his eyes, thinking about how much he missed his friends, especially Yvonne.

After a few minutes Costas said, "Did you hear about Richard Sternfeld?"

"No," Josh answered, sitting up. Richard Sternfeld had matriculated from Boys High six years previously, and was now helping his father managing a garage. He was a fitness fanatic, and often came to the pool early in the morning before starting work.

"Well," Costas said in his gruff voice, "I must take my hat off to you Jew-boys."

Josh tried not to be offended by his remark. "What did he do?" he asked coolly, pretending not to be interested.

"Well, you know Robie Leibrandt," Costas continued, "Richard apparently gave him a damn good beating yesterday here at the pool."

Josh sat up straight. He couldn't believe what he had just heard. "Richard gave Robie Leibrandt a beating?" he said, amazement in his voice. "But that is impossible. Robie was an Olympic boxer…"

"…who became a spy in South Africa for the Nazis during the war," Costas said, contempt in his voice. "He was caught and sent to prison, but when the Nats came to power they released him. I was told that yesterday morning he was here at the pool shouting about how much he hated the Jews. They told me that Richard approached him and told him to shut up. Robie tried to hit Richard, but you know Richard has been going to that new class on that style of fighting from Japan. From what the guys told me, Richard used it on Roby and beat the shit out of him."

Josh felt proud. Everyone knew Richard Sternfeld. Whether what Costas had just told him was true or not, did not matter. Richard was now a hero to all who knew him.

There were plenty of Afrikaner boys around who called Josh 'Bloody Jew,' and other anti-Semitic names, but he had learned to ignore them. He got his own back on one of his worst name callers, a boy called Bennie Oberholtzer, who had beaten him up a couple of times. Bennie had been cycling down the street as Josh was about to cross it.

"Hey, you bloody Jew-boy!" he had shouted as he aimed his bicycle at Josh intending to run him down. "Get out of my way!"

Josh jumped back, but at the same time pushed the ruler that he was carrying in his hand into the spokes of the front wheel of the bicycle. Bennie nosedived over the handle bars, broke his nose and knocked out his upper front teeth. He ran home crying, leaving his bicycle lying in the street. Josh felt good. He had gotten his own back on Bennie.

The sun was really hot by now. The pool had filled up with kids, screaming and shouting at the shallow end. Costas was still dozing next to Josh.

"Feel like a drink?" Josh asked. He always brought some money with him to buy a sandwich and a drink for lunch whenever he came to the pool.

"Thanks," Costas answered. "A lemonade would go down well."

"Would you like something to eat?"

"No," Costas answered. "Just a drink."

Josh stood up and walked towards the canteen. He stood in the queue waiting to be served. In front of him stood a young girl in a one piece black bathing suit faded by the sun. She had brown hair, long and flowing down her back. Her skin had been burned dark brown by the sun, slightly darker than Josh's. Her body was slim, and when she turned he saw that her breasts were small, still developing, with her nipples showing softly through her wet bathing suit. Josh looked at her as she turned her face to the side.

"*What a beautiful girl,*" he thought. "*I have never seen her here before. I wonder where she comes from?*" He knew almost everyone in his age group that visited the pool. He bumped her as though by accident. She turned.

"Sorry," he said.

"That is alright," she answered, smiling at him, and then turned as the sales assistant asked her what she wanted.

Josh felt as though he had been hit in the stomach. "*Good heavens,*" he thought, "*Give her a few years and she will make Charlene seem like a plain Jane.*"

Chapter 3

Marla, at 12 years old turning 13 in five months, was tall for her age. She was already three inches taller than her mother, inheriting her height from her late father. She was also very slim, probably because she was extremely picky with what she ate. From an early age she had refused to eat meat of any kind.

Emma would laugh, "As a baby she had always reached for everything with her feet, rather than her hands. She became frustrated when her long toes were not able to grasp whatever she was reaching for. In her previous life she must have been a monkey, and monkeys are vegetarian."

Marla had inherited her father's height, but her mother's beauty. Her face was beautiful, so much so that when she walked down the street, many who looked at her turned and looked at her again as she walked. She had the lithe body of a dancer, having started ballet lessons when she was three years old. With a smile that boasted perfectly shaped teeth, she was the envy of many a friend forced to visit their dentist for braces. Her lips were full and naturally coloured.

Once before a dress rehearsal, Marla's ballet teacher told her students,

"All of you should wear lipstick when you make up for the stage, but it must be the colour that Marla is wearing."

"Mrs. Zeller," Marla said, not quiet understanding, "I am not wearing any lipstick."

She remembered how Mrs. Zeller had looked carefully at her lips as the girls in her class laughed. "Then try and buy a lipstick the same colour as her lips," she said, turning her back to them.

Her eyes were a light blue, the same color as her mother's eyes, a sharp contrast to her skin color which was much darker than Emma's, giving her a permanent suntan which heightened her beauty. She was maturing early, and her figure was very feminine even at this age. With her thick dark brown hair falling to her waist, she was never short of an admirer who thought she was much older than her twelve years.

Emma had cautioned her about boys, and she was fully aware of the facts of life. If a boy asked her out alone, that would be a date, and she would politely refuse. Going out with her friends in a crowd was much more comfortable for her. Often she would walk next to the boy that took her fancy, even flirting with him, as long as other girls were present. Also, she knew that if Emma ever found out that she was going out on a date, there would be hell to pay.

Lying in bed at night, she would often daydream about how and when she would start dating. After talking with other girls in her class, she came to a decision that a date, when it came, should be with a boy not older than 15 years old. They would also have to pass the Mom test, which meant coming over to the house so that Emma could get to know them, and then give her approval. So far no boy had made the attempt, being a bit scared of Emma's very strict and firm assessment.

Emma was a wonderful mother. Raising Marla as a single mom, a war widow, was not easy, especially with a daughter growing more beautiful by the day and one that was always the leader of the pack. Marla was not at all shy about voicing and giving her opinion.

Listening to and obeying Gran'pa Charlie was another matter. Emma always turned to him whenever she felt that Marla needed guidance from a man. Gran'pa Charlie was Charlie Stuart, more a father to Marla than a grandfather, and he enjoyed watching her grow up, probably more than he had with his own children because he had a parental and responsible feeling toward her mother, whom he had helped in establishing her life.

Marla had once asked her, "Ma, why do other kids have a father who lives with them at home, and I only have Gran'pa Charlie?"

Emma was taken aback at this question. After a few minutes thought, she answered cautiously, considering every word. "Your father fought in the war to keep the world free of hate. He was killed in that war, and was a hero. Gran'pa Charlie has taken his place. He is to you, both a father and a grandfather. You are a very lucky girl."

Emma never told her parents in Cape Town about Marla. She still wrote to them every month, but phoned them less often than she used to. She had told them that she had moved to Potchefstroom from Johannesburg; that she had changed her employment. They never questioned her, or asked her why. Every year, but now in May and no longer December, she would still catch the train to Cape Town, spending only a week with them. Marla was always left with Charlie and Christa when she was away. She never asked her mother where she went or why.

Living on Tom Street, which was closer to the Potchefstroom dam than the municipal swimming pool, Marla would cycle to the dam to swim during the holidays, usually with two or three friends, enjoying the well kept lawns and fresh river water, rather than the chlorinated water of the municipal pool. Her friends were all Afrikaans speaking, friends she made at school; a clutch of boys and girls, with the girls being her age but the boys one or two years older. She went to school at Gimnasium Hoer Skool, an Afrikaans school not far from where she lived. Although they only spoke English at home, Emma had insisted that she attend an Afrikaans school.

"The ultra conservative Afrikaners have ruined this country with their racial distinction," Emma would tell her, "but you must remember, not all the Afrikaners are bad. There are many, and I say again, many that are good and are wonderful people. You must learn Afrikaans because we are a nation with many languages, and you must meet those Afrikaners who do not feel like the Verkramptes (Conservatives) that enforce the apartheid. There are many who want to see a change for the better. You, my girl, have to learn and become fluent in Afrikaans; that way you will become one of them and hopefully influence them and make them realize that apartheid is not a benefit to this country."

All Marla's friends were Afrikaans speaking. She was often invited to their homes for meals and parties, meeting their parents and immediate family. They enjoyed their friendship and the special love, as young girls, they had for each other. Many an older brother had tried to date her, but she always turned them down unless her friend, their sister, came with them.

This spring, as was usually the case about every three or four years, the Potchefstroom dam had been drained by a considerable amount of water so that water weeds in the swimming area could be removed before the start of the holiday season. The dam had not been drained as much as previous years but Marla found the water was still too shallow. She enjoyed diving, but found that she could walk to the diving boards, the water only reaching up to her waist. When the dam was full, the diving boards boasted 20 feet of water, a safe enough depth for the high board divers.

Many of Marla's friends were away on holiday, or visiting family ahead of Christmas, and this year, more than any others she felt alone. Most years, she and her mother went to the Stuarts' for Christmas. This year would be no different, but she was now at an age where she could cycle, on her own, throughout the town, and she enjoyed exploring.

She woke up one morning and decided that rather than cycle down to the dam, which at Christmas time was usually filled with caravaners from the surrounding towns, she would cycle down to the municipal swimming pool. It had been many years since she was last there, and she was curious to see if it had changed in any way, hopefully for the better.

It was a hot day, and after the ride, she cooled off by jumping into the shallow end of the pool, but soon found that she did not enjoy the rowdiness of the young children playing there. Swimming to the deep end, and after practicing her dives off the three tier diving board, she decided that she had had enough.

'I need something to drink,' she said to herself. 'It is so boring here. I don't know anyone.'

Standing in the queue to buy her drink she was surprised when the boy behind her spoke to her after he had rudely bumped her.

"Do you come here often?" Josh asked her, thinking of the weak cliché as he spoke the words.

She turned to look at him, and then spoke in English with a slight Afrikaans accent.

"Excuse?" she answered, looking puzzled.

"Uuhh.... I am sorry that I bumped you," Josh apologized. "I asked you if you come here often. I almost live at this pool, and I have never seen you here before."

"Oh, no," she answered coolly, "I usually go swimming at the dam, much closer to where I live, but today I thought I would have a look here."

"And..." Josh asked, looking around, "do you like it here?"

"No," she answered. "It is too noisy. I prefer the dam," and she turned her back on him.

"Well," Josh replied, hurt by her snub, but not wanting to give up, "early in the morning it is nice and quiet, but then it fills up and does become quite loud." He looked at her, hesitated for a moment and then said, "Excuse me, but you know, somehow I feel I know you. Your face looks familiar. My name is Josh Stern, and..."

Marla turned and looked at him. She was slightly taller than he was. "Of course you should know me," she said. "My mother and I used to come to your house for supper when I was a lot younger. I remember you now..." she looked at him, "but I must say that you do look different."

"Come to our house for supper?" Josh asked, puzzled. Too many people came to their house for supper for him to remember them all.

"Oh, yes," Marla replied, "my mother is Emma O'Neil. She told me that she always enjoyed the Friday night dinners with your parents. She told me that she loved the Jewish religious ceremony before eating. Alf and Lilly Stern, are your parents, right?" and she looked at Josh to confirm the names.

"Right," Josh answered, puzzled. "Then you are...?"

"Me? Oh I am Marla, Marla O'Neil. You and I often played together when we were smaller, but you always thought me a bit young to play with."

Josh still struggled to place her.

"Well, I am sorry to say that I cannot remember you," he said with a frown, "but look, before you leave why don't you join Costas and me? We are sitting over there," he pointed to where Costas was lying, "and enjoy whatever you are buying."

She looked in the direction he pointed. Costas looked so much older. She hesitated and thought before answering. Josh seemed pleasant enough, and with him there and Costas, well, actually when you think about it, she would not be breaking any of Emma's rules. "Sure," she said slowly, "that would be nice. It is always good to make new friends."

They bought their drinks, and walked back to where Costas lay. Josh watched her as she walked slightly in front of him. She walked like an athlete, heel to toe, with a long lissome stride. Her legs rippled with muscles as she walked. She turned to him and smiled.

"Of course, now I know you," Josh replied, still not certain who she was. He remembered a woman whom his father had mentioned had lost her husband in the war. He always had to play with the little girl, who was so much smaller than he was, so boring. Could Marla be that girl? He shook his head. "You and your mom came over quite often when you were much younger. I always had to play with you."

"That is right," Marla smiled. "I will never forget that night, on

Guy Fawkes night, when the sparkler landed in the box of fireworks, and everything exploded."

"Good heavens," Josh answered as they walked to where Costas lay, "I had forgotten that." He frowned. "You were there? No wonder I seemed to know your face when we stood in the queue."

"And here I thought you were chatting me up," Marla laughed. "You didn't want to play with me then because I was younger than you, and I still am. "I am twelve, turning thirteen in April. And you are?"

"Well, I am fifteen, turning sixteen in February," Josh answered, "but gosh, you look so much older."

Marla smiled, pleased with what he had said. They walked to where Costas was lying.

"And this is my friend, Costas, "Josh said with a gesture in Costas' direction. She looked at Costas as they drew closer.

"I hope he won't mind me joining you. He looks a lot older." she said, hesitantly.

"Please...I know he won't mind," Josh replied. "I will tell him that you are a good friend of mine."

"That is not the point," she said, looking at Costas, "it is just that..." She looked at Josh, then at Costas, and gave Josh a quick smile. Costas lay on his stomach, sweating slightly as the sun burned down on him, totally unaware of their presence.

"OK," she said, spreading her towel next to where Costas lay.

"Costas," Josh said as they sat down, "this is Marla, a good friend."

Costas opened one eye, looked at Marla, then turned around and put his hands behind his head. Watching Marla's face, Josh knew straight away that she was attracted to Costas.

"Marla?" he asked, looking at her carefully and frowning, "Marla who?"

"Marla O'Neil," she answered.

"Well, Marla O'Neil," he replied, "any friend of Josh's is a friend of mine." He stood up, walked to the edge of the pool and dived into the water. He swam to the opposite side where Charlene was sitting with Erica and a group of boys, looking at her and hoping that she would greet him. She had been watching him, but when she saw that he was looking at her, she turned her back to him. Noticing this snub, he swam back slowly. Climbing out of the water, he took his towel, dried himself, and then mumbled rather sarcastically, "I hope I am not too young for you."

Marla looked at him disdainfully, ignoring his sarcasm.

And so a strange friendship was born, a friendship that remarkably lasted all that summer. Josh fell in love with Marla. Marla was intrigued with Costas, even though she felt Costas was much too old for her. To Costas, Marla was just another little girl, a friend of Josh's that he should put up with.

Costas, Marla and Josh spent that whole Christmas holiday season together. In the morning they would sit with each other at the pool, or on occasion, when Marla persisted, meet her at the dam, which she always preferred. But Costas wanted to be at the pool, because that is where Charlene would be.

She learned from Costas how to handle and talk to older boys, but could never understand what the attraction to Charlene was. One day, after about a week, when her curiosity got the better of her, Charlene happened to be in the locker room as she was changing into her bathing suit. She started talking to Charlene and came to the conclusion that Charlene was nothing but an empty head with a beautiful body and a very clever, manipulative sister.

"*I think I know what Costas sees in her,*" she said to herself, admiring Charlene's two-piece bathing suit that captured a trim body, leaving very little to the imagination. On an impulse, she made up her mind to help Costas.

"You know," she said to Charlene a few days later, sitting down next to her without waiting for an introduction, and making sure that Erica did not hear her, "Costas really is a wonderful guy. I could really go for him."

Charlene looked at her, not quite sure what to make of her, quite taken at her effrontery. "He hasn't asked me out yet," Marla continued, "only because Josh is always there and he thinks I fancy Josh, but you never know, one of these nights…" and she stood up, leaving her sentence hanging in the air. "See you," she said, waving a hand and walking back to where Costas and Josh sat, made sure that her hips swayed seductively.

Later that afternoon, when the three of them left the pool, Charlene stood up to leave, almost pulling Erica with her, leaving the three boys that were sitting with them. When Costas walked to the exit door of the pool, he found Charlene was removing an imaginary stone from her shoe. Erica shouted to her to hurry up.

"Hello, Costas," she said coyly as Costas walked out the door, and then she ran to where Erica was waiting for her. Costas stood there, dumbstruck.

They always had lunch in one of two places. Sometimes it was at Costas' house, where Mrs. Bouras would prepare them a delicious Greek dish while Costas played the piano for them. Other times it was at Josh's. Maggie, the Sterns' maid, was always ready to prepare something for the three friends. Marla on the other hand, never invited them to her house, because Emma was at work. She was also worried what her mother might say about Costas being so much older.

By now, Costas and Charlene were talking to each other again. Every second or third afternoon, when Costas was not with Charlene or when there was a change in a movie, the three of them, with Charlene and Erica tagging along, would go to the Grand bioscope, where, like Josh, Marla had to prove that she was White. Soon it became a standard joke with the ushers when they appeared. On occasion, some people buying tickets were shocked when Marla lifted her blouse to show a small piece of her tummy that had been protected by the swimming costume, not that her skin was pearly white, but it was paler than her sunburned skin.

On those afternoons when they didn't go to the bioscope and they were not at the pool because of the weather, they sat on the back stoep at Costas's house or at Josh's house playing board games, or just simply talking or listening to Costas as he played the piano. He accepted both of them as friends, and although they were both much younger than he was, Marla noticed that he spent less time with Charlene and more time with them.

And so they spent their five-week summer holiday together, with Josh dreaming about Marla every night and Marla intrigued with Costas, who she looked up to as someone she could learn from. Costas, well if he wasn't dreaming about Charlene, then it was enough for him to put up with "these two kids."

When the summer holidays were over, their friendship, although cooling, remained. Costas left for Johannesburg to study teaching at Witwatersrand University. Marla went back to her Afrikaner friends, a lot older and wiser. Whenever she saw Josh or Costas, she would always go up to them and talk to them, pleased to see them, but their halcyon days of that summer were over. And Josh? Well, he could not stop dreaming about Marla, and whenever he saw her his heart would skip a beat.

Chapter 4

"*T*hank God her hair is straight, and not 'kroes.' God has given me such a beautiful child. One cannot help but love her. Eric would have been so proud of her.*"*

Those were the thoughts that continually went through Emma's head whenever she saw Marla. Marla was growing up, and growing more beautiful with every day that passed. She very soon learned how to twist all who knew her around her little finger. Charlie Stuart always boasted, "You see that little finger on her right hand? That is my finger. I have been twisted around it from the day she was born. One smile from her and she has me doing whatever she wants, even at my old age."

He started taking her fishing to the dam with him, usually early on a Saturday or Sunday morning. She very soon learned how to cast a rod, boasting about her first catch to anyone who listened when she was only four years old. The people of Potchefstroom were always amused to see Charlie drive around town with Marla sitting in the seat next to him, even when he was on duty. They enjoyed his affection for this little girl.

When Marla turned six years old, Emma enrolled her in a primary school, the closest to their home being the Afrikaans-speaking President Pretorius Primary School. She wanted Marla to learn to speak Afrikaans fluently, and Marla picked up the language very quickly. Emma herself made a point of never speaking Afrikaans to Marla. But Christa Stuart without much thought, whenever she saw Marla, would only speak in Afrikaans to her, and Marla would reply in Afrikaans, the two chatting away like grandmother and granddaughter.

Emma had rejoined Irma Rosen. Irma had seduced her with a very attractive salary and the pick of her samples of lingerie and dresses that Irma designed and sewed at the end of each season. Her sales area stretched from Johannesburg to Bloemfontein, with Potchefstroom being in the centre of the area. This was ideal because it meant that although Emma travelled a great deal, she was only away from home for most of a day, and one or two nights a month. The roads to Bloemfontein and Johannesburg were now tarred, so the journey by car was a pleasure. On those occasions when she visited Bloemfontein, a three hour drive away, Marla stayed with the Stuarts, loving it and looking forward to being with them, because they spoiled her terribly.

Emma employed a maid called Kathy who looked after the house and slowly became Marla's surrogate mother. Kathy was a Coloured woman. She with her family lived in the Old Location, at the southern end of King Edward Street, on the way to the town of Parys on the Vaal River. Emma had heard about Kathy from Lilly Stern, at one of their many Friday night dinners. Kathy had worked for a friend of theirs for the past nine years, but the friend and her husband were moving to Johannesburg and Kathy was looking around for employment.

She would cycle up every morning from her house at the Old Location, arriving at about six o'clock and prepare Marla for school in the mornings, making her breakfast, and walking with her the two blocks to the school. Emma was usually preparing for her daily sales trip. At one o'clock in the afternoon, when school closed, Kathy would wait for Marla and walk home with her to a lunch that she had prepared. When Marla started riding a bicycle, the two would cycle to the school together, until Marla was old enough to cycle alone.

One afternoon though, when Marla was nine years old, Kathy on an impulse took her to her house in the Old Location. She wanted to show off this child she had come to love to her parents who lived with her and her husband. Her house was a mud house, the outside walls painted white with whitewash. A thick grape vine trellis greeted you at the front door, acting like a screen protecting the house from the dust of the dirt road. Although all the streets of Potchefstroom were tarred, not one street in the Old Location had been tarred. The roads were scarred with tire tracks and furrows that rain water had carved into them.

The inside of the house was dark, because the windows were small, letting in very little light. None of the houses in the Location had electricity. Everyone used candles or paraffin lamps to light their houses at night and they were never lit during the day.

Kathy's mother, dressed in her usual blue flowered coverall, greeted them at the door with, "*Yislike*, but this is a very beautiful child, and her skin, why, it is darker than mine. She could be a little Coloured girl," all said in Afrikaans with the broad Cape Coloured accent.

"Sshh, Ma, 'Kathy whispered, "she talks Afrikaans, so can understand you. Be careful what you say, because she is very clever."

"But she is a beautiful child; no wonder you like working for them. She could be your daughter," and guiding Marla through the front door of her house she shouted out, "Pa, come and look who Katrina brought to visit us." She had always called Kathy "Katrina", a name she gave her at birth, shortened to Kathy by her brothers and sisters who found it difficult to say Katrina when they were children.

Marla spent the afternoon playing with two of Kathy's children who were still at home, a boy nearly twelve years old, and a little girl close to her age. They played in the back garden, a very large vegetable garden with a cage full of chickens in the one corner.

Later that afternoon, when Marla and Kathy cycled home she asked, "Kathy, why is the lavatory a room at the end of the garden? Why is it not in the house like at home?"

Kathy looked at her, not quite sure how to answer her. "Well, that is the way it is in the Location," she eventually said hesitantly.

"It stinks terribly," Marla said pulling up her nose. "You must tell them to change it."

Kathy smiled but said nothing.

When Marla was in Standard two, and eleven years old, she looked around at the parents and grandparents who sat, proud of their children as the prizes were handed out at the school prize giving.

"I wish I had a real father sitting here, with a real grandfather and a real grandmother," she said to Emma who was sitting next to her.

Emma was shocked. She put her hand to her mouth, as a sob escaped her lips. She had only just that afternoon spoken on the phone with her mother in Cape Town. As usual she had told her nothing about Marla, or her life in Potchefstroom. Her mother had told her that her father was starting to show the first signs of dementia. This upset her terribly.

Once a year, she still caught the train to Cape Town to see them, changing her visit from December to May, because she wanted to spend Christmas with Marla and the Stuarts. She always dressed down on the train so that when she arrived at the Cape Town station, she would look the way the Coloured women in Cape Town would look. She never ever told her parents anything about her life in Potchefstroom. After spending a week with them, she was always sad to leave yet happy to be returning home to Marla.

"But you do have a grandmother and a grandfather," she said to Marla, "You have Gran'ma Christa and Gran'pa Charlie."

"No, Ma," Marla answered, "Gran'pa Charlie is more like a father to me, and Gran'ma Christa another mother. Most of the kids in my class have two lots of grandparents, and they look like grandparents with their white hair." Emma wiped away a tear, then hugged her and said, "Gran'pa Charlie and Gran'ma Christa love you very much, and they are very much your grandparents."

Emma enjoyed working with Irma Rosen. She enjoyed the travelling and meeting her clients in the various towns she visited. She hated leaving Marla alone at home with Kathy, but she knew that Marla was in safe hands, and that Kathy would take care of her. If a problem should crop up, Kathy always had Charlie's phone number as an emergency.

Often, over a weekend, especially after the road to Johannesburg had been tarred, they would spend a weekend with Irma Rosen and her family. The Rosens owned a beautiful home in Houghton, a suburb of Johannesburg, boasting a swimming pool and a tennis court set in two acres of lawn. Fruit trees lined the driveway to the house, a double story that boasted six bedrooms, with the front stoep shaded by a huge Jacaranda tree. Every so often, Marie and her family, which was growing by the year, would join them, making for a very pleasant weekend. Marie lived in Pretoria, her husband, Johan, remaining as a pilot in the air force after the war.

Irma, knowing Emma's story of the uncut diamonds, introduced her to a Mr. and Mrs. Alberts, who were diamond merchants in Johannesburg. Every year, before she took the train to Cape Town, Emma would take one uncut stone from the vase, a vase that was always on the mantelpiece in plain sight; a vase that Marla and Kathy were forbidden to touch on pain of death; a vase always on display with fresh flowers beautifully arranged. She would sell the stone to the Alberts' and then give the money, usually a sizable sum, to her mother. The Alberts never asked questions and she never offered any explanation as to where the uncut stones came from.

When Marla was twelve, she graduated from the President Pretorius Primary school and started preparing herself for the Gimnasium Hoer Skool. The school was close to where they lived and she was looking forward to going there, because many of her friends would be with her. It was during that summer holiday, before she started at 'Gimmies' that she met Josh and Costas at the municipal swimming pool.

"What are you doing going out so early in the morning? Kathy tells me that she never sees you 'til about five in the afternoon." Emma asked her one evening. She had come home after calling on stores in Krugersdorp and Randfontein to see if they needed anything. With the Christmas buying season in full swing she was sure that they could be sold out of certain garments.

"Well, Ma," Marla answered, "I spend my time with Josh Stern and his friend Costas, either at the dam or at the municipal swimming pool. They are great fun, and I enjoy being with them. Sometimes we go to the bioscope, and every now and then we play either at Costas's house or Josh's house."

"Who is Costas?" Emma asked, worried by the fact that her daughter was spending time with two boys rather than girls her own age.

"Oh, he is Costas Boukritis, or something like that." Marla answered offhandedly, not remembering Costas' surname.

"I think you mean Bouras," Emma said frowning. "His father is the owner of the cafe. He is a lot older than you." She thought for a minute, and then said, "I am not happy that you are with two boys all the time. Why aren't you with your girlfriends?"

"Ach, don't worry, Ma," Marla said, turning away, "sometimes Costas' girlfriend and her sister join us. Sometimes even his sister Roula sits with us. Everything is quite OK."

"Well," Emma said, "I must worry, that is my job as your mother. Who is the Josh you mentioned?"

"Oh, you know his parents. We used to go there for supper on a Friday night when I was little. They always had that religious ceremony before we ate anything."

"Do you mean to Lilly and Alf Stern's house?"

"That's right."

"If he is like his parents, then he is a nice boy." Emma said, happy that here was one family that she knew.

"He is a nice boy," Marla said, '*but Costas is so much nicer*' she thought.

Marla enjoyed that summer. Her mother was travelling less than she usually did. In the evenings they would decorate a Christmas tree, with as many lights and baubles as the tree could hold. They would spend hours arguing what to buy the Stuart family for Christmas, Emma usually giving in to Marla's choice of presents. Christmas Eve was spent at home with friends, but every Christmas day was a day with the Stuarts, enjoying a huge lunch that Christa would prepare. She always had a house full of family, with Marie, Johan and their children driving down from Pretoria. Petrus, Andries and Lucida, Marie's two brothers and sister, would also be there with their families.

"Gran'pa, what does snow look like?" Marla asked Charlie one Christmas.

"Snow is just like you see in the pictures, only a hundred times more beautiful," he answered. "You know," he said to Emma, "one June or July, if we have a really cold winter, we should drive into the Drakensburg, just so that Marla can see snow. It should take about three hours by car. We could all spend a couple of nights at Cathedral Peak Hotel...that is, if we can get through the snow. It is really a beautiful hotel."

When school started, a new school, going into Standard six, Marla made new friends, and although Costas and Josh were never forgotten they slowly faded from her social scene. Whenever she did meet Josh, or Costas, she found that she was always pleased to see them.

Two years later, when out of the blue, Josh invited her as his partner to his matric dance, she was thrilled. Emma allowed her to choose one of the sample evening dresses that Irma Rosen had given her to show. Marla felt very adult, and proud. She spent the afternoon at the hairdresser, and after she had dressed, Emma made up her face. When Josh rang the doorbell and Marla walked into the lounge, Emma couldn't believe that this beautiful woman standing in front of her was her daughter. Josh had brought her a corsage of orchids, which Emma carefully pinned to Marla's dress.

The school dance was held in the Boys High School hall. Josh was ever so proud as he walked in with Marla on his arm and introduced her to Mr. MacDonald who stood at the door with his wife, welcoming the students. The hall was decorated with flowers. Tables were numbered so they all knew where they were to sit. Dinner, prepared at the hostels, was served by Standard 9 boys, all dressed up as waiters. Between courses Josh and Marla would join the crowd on the dance floor, dancing to the music of a local band.

Marla thoroughly enjoyed the dance, not quite understanding why so many boys asked her to dance, and why Josh often looked so angry.

"Now that you have written matric, what are you going to do?" she asked Josh as they sat down for one of the dinner courses.

"I have been called up into the navy as a ballottee for a three-month stint," he answered. When I am finished, then I am going to London to study pharmacy at Chelsea Polytechnic, the same school where my father studied pharmacy."

"London, England?" Marla asked, her eyes widening with surprise.

"Yes," Josh answered. "I wrote to them three months ago and received a letter of acceptance last week. I haven't told my folks yet, so they could be surprised."

"I am sure they will be," Marla answered. "I would love to go overseas, around Europe when I've finished school -- that is, if my Mom will let me. Just see that you write to me, so that when I do go, I will know where to find you."

Three weeks later, Emma and Marla went to the Stuarts' to celebrate Christmas. Marie and Johan with the children had come down from Pretoria, and Emma looked forward to seeing her. As usual, Charlie took over the barbecue, and although Emma and Marie offered to help Christa and Lucinda in the kitchen with her two maids, she chased them away.

"You are both my guests today," Christa said in Afrikaans, "get out of my kitchen and go and gossip."

They all sat around the table under the grapevine, in the back yard, with Marie's husband, Johan, helping them to drinks. After lunch, having eaten far more than they should have, they relaxed sipping wine, drinking beer and talking politics.

"So what do you think of this new act going through Parliament?" Charlie started.

"Ach, Pa," Marie said looking at Emma, "must we talk politics?"

"But of course," Charlie said, "what can be more exciting? We either talk rugby, or cricket, or politics. There is no rugby at the moment, and cricket will only start again next month, so it must be politics. What do you say, Johan?"

Johan smiled and looked at Marie, who nodded her head. "A couple of us guys in the air force are finding that our promotions are not happening because of our liberal political views, but as I have told Marie, I am not prepared to change how I feel."

"And how DO you feel?" Charlie asked, sipping a brandy.

"I feel that the government is starting something they could regret; that they are making enemies of the people," Johan answered, his voice shaking with emotion. "The world is turning against us, especially since they have seen what happened in Germany with racial hatred. They will not be in favour of any law that promotes racial hatred."

Marla sat in her chair quietly listening. The politics of South Africa had never bothered her before, but as she was growing older, she found that she was beginning to disagree and argue against a number of the students in her class at school.

"Well, consider," Charlie said, "there is racism in all the countries of the world, with America perhaps being among the worst, where negroes are discriminated against, especially in the southern states like Alabama."

"Ach yes," Johan interrupted, "but South Africa is the only country in the world where the Government, in a systematic way, is formalizing that hatred between the races into law. I mean, think of it: in

1949, one year after Dr. Malan's victory over Jannie Smuts, they bring in a law prohibiting marriage between the Whites and the other race groups. Then a year later, they come out with the Immorality Act, where adultery between Whites and people of other colour is prohibited. Hell, man, are they going to put a policeman in every bedroom? And then to top it all, they create the National Register, where they record everyone's race."

Charlie looked carefully at Emma.

"It is like making the Jews wear yellow stars on their clothes in Germany during the war, to show they are Jews," Emma said softly. Marla looked at her mother. She had never heard Emma discuss politics.

"They don't need that yellow star," Johan said. "They have the colour of their skin."

"And how do you feel about the Group Areas Act," Charlie said carefully, looking at their faces to see their reaction as he spoke, "where people are forced to live in certain areas? I mean, just think about it. Take for example District Six in Cape Town, home to thousands of Cape Coloureds for centuries. They will probably soon be forced to move and go and live outside of Cape Town, in some godforsaken place far from their jobs, while the houses they have lived in for a hundred years are bulldozed to the ground."

He carefully looked for a reaction from Emma. She had told him that her parents had been forbidden from enlarging their home, and were forced to live in the small house that did not have the living comforts of a normal home. Their toilet was still a room at the end of the garden, without sewage; their bathroom, a tub with a shower. Their house was falling apart, and the city refused them permission to repair it. With the money she gave them, they had tried to build on two extra rooms, so that the family could enjoy a little bit of extra comfort, but their application had been refused.

"And the Pass Laws and the Education Act brought about by the

Minister of Native Affairs, Hendrik Verwoerd. What did he say?"
Charlie thought for a minute. "The aim of the law, if I remember correctly, is to prevent Africans from receiving an education that will
provide them with skills to serve their own people, so that they must
only work as labourers under the Whites." He stood up and angrily
poured himself another brandy. "How sick can this form of slavery be?
That is what he is doing, making slaves of everyone of colour."

"Isn't Verwoerd the man who was against the admittance of Jews
escaping from Nazi Germany in 1938 and 1939 into South Africa?"
Emma asked, "I remember Irma Rosen telling me about it. She told
me that Verwoerd was editor of the Transvaaler Newspaper at the
time, and that is what he wrote about in his editorials."

Charlie Stuart raised his eyebrows, and looked at her. "I never
knew you were so up on politics, Emma," he said.

"This Irma Rosen, is she Jewish?" Johan asked.

"Yes," Emma answered, turning to Johan. "She and her family escaped from Nazi Germany long before 1939. They still had family in
Germany and managed to get some of them into South Africa before
the war started, but she says it was not easy. Those that never came, or
left Germany, were murdered in the gas chambers at Auschwitz." She
clasped her hands together, so that her knuckles stood white as they
lay in her lap.

"Today I read only bad things in the newspapers," she continued.
She paused, her face showing her emotion as she said softly, "I just
wish I could do something to help. We, as people, must always stand
on the side of freedom for all, and especially human dignity. To de-
base a person because of their skin colour, that is being just as bad
as the Nazis."

Marla looked at her mother. She had never ever heard her talk
this way. Marie and Johan sat quietly listening. Christa came from the
kitchen carrying dishes filled with dessert.

"It is going to get a lot worse," Charlie said. "Prime Minister

Strydom is a sick man, and talk is that when he resigns, the person who has the best chance of taking his place will be Hendrik Verwoerd, and I am telling you, he is as bad as they come."

"You know, Pa," Johan said thoughtfully, "that is just what my father thinks. He is very worried about the way the country is being segregated, that so many of the people are not free. He feels that somewhere, sometime the Blacks will stand up and fight, especially the Zulus, perhaps even the Xosas, because they are both fighting nations."

"That is not quite what he said," Marie interrupted. They all turned to look at her. Up till now, she had been very quiet, listening to what they all said.

"Your Dad said that the way things are going, we could soon have a war on our hands. He said that it won't be long before the African National Congress will go to a country like Russia, who will want to get their hands on our diamonds and gold, and ask for help. He said that if they didn't do that, they would be stupid, and he does not think they are."

"Mmm," Charles said, "I don't think he is that wrong with what he says."

They all sat quietly digesting Marie's words, not saying anything. Marla looked at Emma, who was biting her bottom lip. Emma stood up.

"It is late," she said. "Unfortunately, we have to leave. I promised the Sterns that we would join them for dinner, their Friday night Sabbath dinner. We haven't been for a long time. Josh, their son, took Marla as his partner to his matric dance, and the Sterns asked us to join them. It was difficult to refuse the invitation." She stood up.

"Come on, Marla, go and kiss your Grandfather and Grandmother goodbye." She then turned to Marie. "Will we see you tomorrow?"

"Definitely," Marie said, "we are only leaving Sunday afternoon."

In the car driving home, Marla asked Emma, "Mom, is it really going to get bad here?"

"Not if we can help it," Emma answered, "but there are only a few of us, and we do not govern the country. All we can do is try and help wherever we can."

Marla did not ask her what she meant.

Chapter 5

Josh had not seen Marla as often as he would have liked after that summer holiday. She was too busy growing up, learning how to handle a large number of boyfriends that continually pestered her for a date. He, on the other hand, was very busy at school, but whenever they met, they greeted each other like old friends.

When Josh matriculated, and Marla agreed to be his date for the matric dance, he was thrilled. His father had offered to drive them to the dance in his Oldsmobile, so Josh had spent the whole afternoon washing and cleaning it, so that it sparkled in the afternoon sun. He then showered and shaved the few whiskers he had. Dressing in a new suit bought especially for the occasion, he went to say goodnight to his parents. They were listening to the news on Springbok Radio.

"This Treason Trial is probably the most stupid thing I have ever heard," his father was muttering as he walked into the lounge. "They will all be found guilty of being communists whether they are or not, and sentenced to life in prison. Does anyone even think it will be otherwise?"

"My, but you do look handsome," his mother said, standing up from where she sat knitting. "Who is the lucky girl that you are taking out?"

"Her name is Marla O'Neil," he said, "She and her mother came here a few times on a Friday night for dinner when she was a little girl. She still treasures those evenings."

"Well," his mother answered, "I bought this for you to give to her. I thought you would forget to buy something," and she handed him a small orchid corsage.

"Oh, thank you, Mom," he answered, taking the orchid. "That is wonderful," and he kissed her on the cheek.

"And here is some cash you may need," his father said gruffly, "you may decide to go out after the dance."

"Thanks, Dad, but I already have some cash," he answered.

"But still take it, you may need it."

Josh pocketed the twenty pounds, gave his mother a hug and walked out the front door to the car parked in the driveway with his father. At 17 years old, Josh he was still too young to apply for a driver's license even though Jerry from the shop had given him lessons. He had to wait another two months, for his 18th birthday. His brother and sister both watched him, wondering who his date was.

His father drove very carefully to Marla's home, parking under the oak trees that lined the street in front of the house. Emma opened the door when he rang the doorbell and welcomed Josh into the living room where Marla was standing. He couldn't believe that this beautiful woman standing in front of him was a girl three years younger than he was. He stood with his mouth open, unable to say anything, and then he pushed the orchid corsage awkwardly into her hands.

"This is for you," he mumbled, then regaining his composure, and shaking his head with amazement, he continued, "you look absolutely beautiful."

"Thank you," she answered and smiled at him. Turning to Emma, who stood behind Josh, watching her, she held out the orchid. "Ma, this is what Josh has given me."

"Come here," Emma said, "it is quite beautiful. Let me pin it on." She took the box from Marla, took out the orchid and carefully pinned it to Marla's dress at her left shoulder.

At the dance, Josh was amazed at how many friends he suddenly had. Boys who had previously ignored him at school were now fluttering around his table like a swarm of bees, or talking to him on the dance floor as he danced with Marla. It was an evening that he would remember for the rest of his life, an evening he enjoyed with the most beautiful girl in Potchefstroom. If he had ever had feelings for Marla in any way before that evening, he was now totally besotted by her.

His father had continually asked him during his matric year what he had chosen as a profession. He had never been sure whether he wanted to become a pharmacist and join his father in his business or whether he should study medicine, which was where his preference lay. The three-month service in the South African Navy, three months away from home, would help him make up his mind.

Josh turned 18 at the end of February and a week after his birthday he was on his way to Durban by train. He entered the Navy as a boy, but three months later, as May turned into June, he left the Navy as a man knowing what he wanted from the world, and how he would go about getting it.

Much to his surprise, he enjoyed the naval basic training. Everyone had told him that it would be hard, but he found the marching and drilling an exercise that his body needed. The puppy fat he had grown up with was quickly removed and his figure slimmed and hardened with muscles he never knew he had. He found the ocean training on S.S. Transvaaler, a frigate sailing from Durban to Cape Town, something he would never forget, even though he was terribly seasick for the first few days at sea. He joked with his friends that the only food he would eat was chocolate because, he laughed, "it tastes good going down and just as good coming up."

Towards the end of May, two weeks before he was discharged, he and two friends were given a two-day shore leave. They decided to do a tour of the wine farms surrounding Cape Town. They would catch the train to Paarl, hire a car and slowly drive back to Cape Town, touring the vineyards on the way back. They bought their train tickets at the ticket booth and as they made their way along the platform to board the train, Josh saw a woman who looked familiar.

"She looks like someone I know?" he thought his eyes screwing up as he tried to get a better look. "Now who? I have definitely seen her somewhere."

He pretended to bend down to tie a shoelace and have a good look at her without her seeing him. The woman was walking with an old Coloured woman at her left side and an older Coloured man on her right. She was dressed in a very simple linen dress, the type usually worn by household servants, with a 'doek' (cloth) wrapped around her head, covering her hair. She looked very plain with no makeup on, a complete contrast to the woman he knew in Potchefstroom. He thought of approaching her and greeting her, but she started hugging and kissing the old couple as she boarded the train.

What surprised Josh and put doubt in his mind was that she boarded the train in the coach reserved for non-Europeans. He watched her as she leaned out the window talking to the elderly couple, tears streaming down her face. She looked up in Josh's direction but never recognized him.

His friends called him to the coach reserved for Europeans where they were sitting, and he settled in the seat next to the window as the train started to pull away. Out of curiosity, he looked for and found the old couple on the platform, waving goodbye. The old lady crying and he heard her shout in Afrikaans, "Goodbye my darling Emily, please write as often as you can. We love you and miss you so very, very much," and then he watched her turn to the man next to her and sob on his shoulders as he comforted her.

When the train reached Paarl, Josh and his friends left the coach. As they walked down the platform, Josh looked back at the train and saw the mysterious lady leave the non-European coach and rush to the restroom of the station. He stopped at the restaurant to buy a chocolate bar. When he walked out to rejoin his friends he saw a woman that looked like the Emma he knew walk out of the restroom and enter the coach reserved for Europeans only. She was smartly dressed, beautifully made up. He wanted to greet her, but his friends called out to him to hurry up.

When he arrived home after his three-month stint in the Navy, the first thing he did was visit Marla. Emma opened the door to him. A large black dog greeted him at the door, with Emma struggling to hold him from leaping on Josh.

"Gamboo, to the kitchen," she commanded. The dog looked at her and then with its tail between its legs, crawled back into the kitchen.

"Sorry about that, Josh," Emma apologized. "Marla fell in love with Gamboo, so we bought him. He is a Bouvier des Flandres. We got him as a puppy about 7 months ago, not realizing how big he would grow. We usually lock him in the kitchen when the doorbell rings. He is a good watch dog and, as you can see, scares everyone that comes to the front door by jumping on them, although I think he would more likely lick them to death than bite." She stood back, suggesting by her action that he come inside the house. "It is wonderful to see you, Josh. Marla is still at school, and should be back at about five o'clock. I think I have forgotten, but I remember Marla telling me that you were in the Navy. Did you enjoy it?"

"It was great, thank you, Mrs. O'Neil," he answered, "I loved it more than I ever thought I would. They asked me to sign up for the permanent force, and I was very tempted, but I will never forget what my father taught me."

"And what is that?" Emma asked, smiling at him.

"He always said that whatever you want to do, first get a degree from a university, then you can become a bum if you still want to, but when you are tired of that, you will always have your degree to fall back on."

Emma laughed. "That is good advice," she said, "I will remember to pass it on to Marla."

"You know, Mrs. O'Neil," Josh said hesitantly, "When we were in Cape Town, I saw a woman at the railway station that looked so much like you, that I couldn't believe my eyes. She was with an elderly couple, but boarded the train in the non-European carriage, so I knew it wasn't you. It was quite amazing."

Emma turned white at his words, clutching at the door frame as her knees gave way. "You must have been mistaken," she said hurriedly, and before he could say anything further, she blurted out, "I have never been to Cape Town," and visibly shaken, she turned her back to him. "I shall tell Marla you were here," she said as though dismissing him.

"That's OK, Mrs. O'Neil, I shall come back later," he said, leaving the house wondering why she looked so upset.

That night, after supper he approached his father and asked him how much he had budgeted to send him to university.

"Why do you want to know?" Alf asked him.

"Well, I have made a decision to study pharmacy," he answered. "It is a matter of deciding which university I want to attend."

"I have budgeted for £25 a month," Alf answered.

"O.K. That sounds good to me. Does it matter to you where I study?" he asked.

"Well," Alf answered looking at him suspiciously, "I had always hoped that you would study pharmacy and join me. You could study here at the Potchefstroom University."

"Does it matter where I study?" Josh asked for a second time.

"Actually, not particularly," Alf answered, thinking that he was going to say Grahamstown University rather than Potchefstroom University.

"Well, then, if it is all right with you, I would like to go to London, England and study at Chelsea Polytechnic. I wrote to them some time ago, and they accepted me. I have enough saved to buy my passage."

Alf was surprised, and in a way pleased, but said nothing. Josh's mother, however, was upset at first that he would be leaving home, but he promised her that he would write once a week and tell her everything about his life in London.

"When do you intend to leave?" Alf asked.

"The new term starts in September, "Josh said. "I need a few months to settle down and find accommodation. With the ship taking two weeks, I think I should leave sometime in July."

That same night, when he saw Marla, he told her what his plan was. He also told her that he loved her very, very much and asked her if she would wait for him until he came back.

She laughed and said, "Josh, we are still so young… and I love you, too, but as a friend."

Hiding his disappointment, he said, "I will write to you once a week." He leaned forward to kiss her, but she turned her cheek to him.

Three weeks later he boarded the Edinburgh Castle bound for London, England.

Four weeks later, Emma had an unexpected visitor.

The doorbell rang. It was after six o'clock in the evening and Emma and Marla were having supper in the kitchen. Kathy had already gone home. Emma stood up from the table muttering about how inconsiderate people could be to disturb them at a meal, and went to the front door, Gamboo running and growling ahead of her. She opened the door, holding Gamboo back by the collar. A man in a police uniform was standing on the stoep, his back to her. He turned as he heard the door open and did a double take when he saw the large black dog.

"Good evening, Mrs. O'Neil," he said in a very broad Afrikaans accent. "My name is Brigadier Grobelaar. I am with the security police. May I come in?"

Emma stood shocked. Her first thought was that the police had found out that she was a Coloured woman living as a European. She opened the door wider and in her shock nearly let go of Gamboo who was straining at her arm.

"I am really sorry to trouble you," he continued, looking apprehensively at Gamboo, "but I need to ask you a few questions about a donation you have made."

"Do come in," she said, regaining her composure. My daughter and I are having supper. Gamboo, into the kitchen," she commanded. "To the kitchen!" She pointed in the direction of the kitchen and the dog humbly crept away. She led the Brigadier into the lounge and waved at one of the arm chairs. "Please take a seat. I will be with you in a second." She started to walk to the kitchen, then turned and looked at him. "Can I get you something to drink?"

"Thank you," he answered, removing his cap and running a hand through his blonde hair. "Unfortunately I am on duty."

"A cup of tea then?" she asked.

"Thank you, but no thank you," he said sternly. He walked into the lounge. It was beautifully furnished with a maroon Persian carpet on the floor, the two antique armchairs and a sofa covered in a reddish floral design placed around a small table. The curtains were a pale crème lace that contrasted beautifully with the furniture. He looked at the arrangement of flowers in the vase on the fireplace and admired its beauty.

Emma's heart skipped a beat as she saw him looking at the vase, but he turned away and seated himself in one of the armchairs.

She walked into the kitchen, where Marla was still eating. "I have someone in the lounge," she said. "Finish up, and I will join you as soon as I can get rid of him." She walked back into the lounge and seated herself opposite the Brigadier, on the sofa. "Well, then, how can I help you?" she asked.

"Mrs. O'Neill," he started, "you are aware of the Treason Trial?"

She looked at him, and breathed a sigh of relief. "Of course I am," she answered, "the news broadcasts and newspapers are full of it."

"Well, I understand that you have made a significant donation to their legal costs."

"Who hasn't?" she answered smiling at him, trying not to laugh. Then she became serious. "When a group of people are unjustly accused of treason, then anyone with compassion will help them fight that unjust charge." She smiled at him and asked, "Don't you agree?"

"Are you a communist, Mrs. O'Neil?" he asked gruffly.

Emma was taken aback by the question. "Good heavens, no, "she answered, "I am definitely not."

"Then why did you make such a sizable donation to this trial of communist members?"

Emma thought for a minute. "Brigadier Grobelaar," she said slowly, with a determination and courage she did not know she had, "are you suggesting that anyone and everyone who opposes false accusations brought about by the Nationalist Government is a communist?"

"Not at all," he answered, his steely blue eyes penetrating her expression, looking for an answer to his questions, "but we would like to know the reason for your involvement."

"I have Jewish friends in Johannesburg who escaped from persecution and racial prejudice in Germany before the war. From what they have told me, life for them was similar to the life the present government is inflicting on the people in this country that are not White. I find that unacceptable, especially when charges are trumped up with false accusations. I am against racial and religious prejudice in all its disgusting forms. The Afrikaans word apartheid is very apt. It is apart hate, another form of Nazi discrimination that has found its way into this wonderful country of ours. Thank God we have a separate individual judiciary in the country and I hope they come to a just verdict. How long they will remain independent, however, is a matter of speculation."

She looked at a shadow she saw in the doorway to the lounge, and saw that Marla was listening to them.

The Brigadier watched her as she spoke, his eyes narrowing.

"I understand that you are very friendly with Charles Stuart," he asked, looking at her carefully.

"Of course I am," she answered, "he is family to me and my daughter."

"Are you aware that he is a part of the defense fund that paid the bail of the accused?"

"No, I was not," she answered, "but now that you have told me, I am proud of him. Is it a crime to pay for the defense of men wrongly accused? I don't think so."

"Do you have the names, or do you by chance know of anyone else that is a part of that fund?"

"No, I don't," Emma answered, angry at his question, "and if I did know," she continued, "I would never tell you."

"I see," he said, his anger at her answer showing in his voice. He stood up, placing his cap firmly on his head. "Mrs. O'Neil," he said coldly, walking towards the front door, "I would just like to warn you that if there is any person or persons in Potchefstroom who take it on themselves to act against you in any way because of your involvement with these people, we shall not defend you," and he walked out of the house.

Emma was shocked. "Good night Brigadier Grobelaar," she shouted after him, stressing every word. "Make sure you have a good night," and trembling with anger, she closed the door.

Marla came to her. "What was that all about, Ma?" she asked.

"Just some donation I made," Emma smiled. "Don't forget to put Gamboo out before you come to bed." Gamboo had his kennel by the back door and always spent the night sleeping in it, occasionally waking them up with his barking whenever a cat trespassed.

The next morning she was surprised when she went to the kitchen to make a cup of coffee. Gamboo was not scratching at the back door asking to be let in as he usually did. She opened the kitchen door wondering where he was. Then she saw him. He was lying on his side in the back yard, his legs moving in spasms, scratching furrows into the grass where he lay. Both his eyes were wide open, looking at her.

"Marla, come quick!" she shouted. "Get dressed. I think Gamboo has been poisoned. We must get him to the vet." She rushed to her bedroom, pulled on a dress, then ran outside. Marla joined her. They lifted Gamboo onto a wheelbarrow, his legs still jerking in spasms. Wheeling him to the car, they placed him carefully on the back seat. Emma then drove as quickly as she could to Dr. Johanssen, the town veterinarian's house. He was dressed, preparing to leave for his surgery. He examined Gamboo where he lay.

"I am sorry to tell you, but your dog is dead," he said to them.

"But... but his legs keep moving," Marla cried, tears streaming down her face.

"That is a sign of strychnine poisoning. The body will react with muscular spasms for a short while after death. He must have been poisoned sometime this morning, not long before you found him. I am terribly sorry."

Marla took Gamboo in her arms, and buried her face in his neck. "Oh, Gamboo, my Gamboo," she cried. "Who would do such a horrible thing to you?"

They drove to Dr. Johanssen's offices and laid Gamboo's corpse on a table. After what seemed like an eternity, they tore themselves away from the dog they had both come to love so much and drove home, tears streaming from their eyes, leaving Gamboo's body with Dr. Johanssen, who promised to take care of it with respect.

"Do you think this is the result of what you said to that man last night?" Marla sobbed.

Emma looked at her through her tears, not quite sure how much she had heard of her discussion with Brigadier Grobelaar. "I don't know," she said. "I sincerely hope not."

Chapter 6

In January 1959 Marla read in the *Rand Daily Mail* newspaper that she had passed her matric exam, an external exam prepared by the School Board, with four distinctions. She was absolutely thrilled. It was customary for the Board to publish the matric results in both the English and Afrikaans newspapers. Schools were closed for the holidays. Students needed to know their exam results to assist them in being accepted into the university of their choice.

Emma was so very proud of her. As much as Marla had loved school and all the friends that she had made at Gimmies, the year 1958 had not been the same as previous years. She'd had to spend more time studying and doing homework with far less time to socialize. Her friends were discussing politics with greater emotion than before. Many students in her class tended to be cool towards her and this hurt her. They knew that she came from an English-speaking home that was far more liberal with feelings towards the Black, Coloured and Indian peoples in South Africa than they were. Hendrik Verwoerd had been appointed Prime Minister in August. Influenced by their parents, many of her classmates believed he would be the savior of the Afrikaner in South Africa.

Marla, on the other hand, was influenced in her thinking by listening to discussions between her mother and Charlie Stuart. They believed Verwoerd's policies would be detrimental to the country.

"Do you know that of all the European countries that helped the Germans murder the Jews, Holland was the worst," Charlie told Emma as they sat sipping their wine one Saturday evening. "Adolf Eichmann, the director of the Final Solution, said of his local Dutch helpers, 'It was a pleasure working with them.'"

"No, I did not know that," Emma answered. "I thought the French were the worst."

"Never forget," Charlie continued, "The Afrikaaner is descended from the Dutch. Hendrik Verwoerd was born in Holland, and even though he left the country with his parents when he was only two years old, he grew up in a Dutch family."

"So you believe that they influenced him?"

"But of course they did," Charlie answered. "All children are influenced by their parents, especially when it comes to politics. Don't forget that in 1926 Verwoerd went to Germany, to study at the Universities of Hamburg, Berlin and Leipzig. During those years he must have come under the influence of National Socialism, which was starting to rear its head in Germany."

"Are you saying that he is a Nazi?"

"No, I don't believe that he is, but I do believe that he was influenced by its basic principles when they were still being argued and formulated. Germany was trying to find its national pride after being defeated in a war and there must have been a great deal of debate at the various universities Verwoerd attended."

Marla listened carefully to what Charlie and her mother were saying. She realized that Hendrik Verwoerd was not the angel her friends thought he was.

She was disappointed with her matric dinner. Her partner was one of the boys in her class, and the evening did not have the same atmosphere as the matric dance she had attended with Josh when he matriculated. The venue was the Town Hall, with speeches and boredom. After the dinner, there was a 'lekker kuier', (a pleasant visit) at various students' houses. She chose the party given by a good friend who lived close to where she lived. She lost many friends that evening. Rather than keep her mouth closed as she usually did when her friends discussed politics, she expressed her opinion quite vehemently, telling them what Charlie Stuart had said about Verwoerd, without mentioning Charlie's name. At the height of the argument with a couple of the boys calling her names, she walked out of the house very upset, walking home alone.

Emma started spending more time than usual away from home in the evenings. Marla was more than often alone at home, with Emma only coming in at 10 p.m., if not later. She did not mind this, as she was busy studying for the matric exams. Since the poisoning of Gamboo, Emma had seemed to have become more involved in something other than her work with Irma Rosen.

One evening, when they went to Charlie and Christa Stuart's for dinner, Marla was surprised when Emma and Charlie became involved in a heated argument.

"He intends to create homelands for each of the eight ethnic groups in South Africa, separating them with each tribe living in a separate homeland," Charlie grunted angrily. "It is obvious that he is trying to reignite their ancestral hatred for each other. He is basing the concept on the United States and Canada, where tribal reserves exist for each of the various Indian tribes that live in the country. He is even forcing factories to build plants close to the homelands, the Bantustans, so that jobs are created with a fictitious economy within the homeland."

"What is wrong with that? "Emma asked him, "Perhaps he is more enlightened than we think." She sipped at the glass of wine he had given her, listening carefully to what he said.

"By the way," he continued, holding his glass to the light and studying the red hue of the wine as he twirled the glass, "the wine is a Cabernet that I have found very pleasant. Give me an opinion."

"I cannot agree with what you said," Emma answered shaking her head. "In the United States and Canada, the Indians have equal rights outside of their reserves. If they do not wish to live in the reserve, they may leave it and live amongst the population as taxpayers. The incentive to live in a reserve is that they do not pay taxes on what they earn. Can you see Hendrik Verwoerd and the National Party allowing that here? Remember, too, that Blacks in the United States, although in some States confined to the back of the bus, in other states they have equal opportunity. They can move around the country, find employment and buy a house wherever they want to. Can you ever see that happening here? Can you ever see a Black, Coloured or Indian owning and living in a Houghton mansion?"

She took a sip of the wine, rolled it around her tongue, and then swallowed it. "This is really good."

"No, I suppose you are right, "Charlie agreed, "but think, where Blacks settle, they seem to create a slum. Look at Harlem in New York City."

"That slum is created because they are not given equal opportunity in New York, and because of crime and the lack of police protection," Emma answered, surprised at Charlie's words. "When they are given what they need to succeed in life, with a decent education, they succeed. One day, America may even have a black president."

"You could be right, but I seriously doubt it," Charlie snickered. "There is still far too much prejudice in the world, especially in America, for that to happen. I think I have got to that stage in my life where I am looking for and hoping to see an end to the apartheid injustice before I die." Charlie sat for a minute, looking at the wine in his glass. "I have been working unsuccessfully against racial discrimination for so long now, without success, that I am really becoming disillusioned."

"With Hendrik Verwoerd, I can see why you have become so disillusioned," Emma said taking another sip at the glass of wine Charlie had given her. "Don't forget, this is the man who, when he was editor of the *Die Transvaaler*, spoke out against allowing Jews to escape from Germany before the war, into South Africa. The man is as bad as Hitler was. The only difference between him and Hitler is that Verwoerd will never be allowed to get autocratic control over the country." She bit her bottom lip and thought for a minute. "God help us if he ever does."

Marla listened carefully to what they said, but she said nothing. Many of her school friends had constantly told her, in spite of her arguments, that their parents thought Verwoerd was a wonderful man, the savior of White South Africa and that his part in shaping the implementation of apartheid policy when he was Minister of Native affairs was the right thing to do. They felt he had introduced a strategy of massive economic development to make South Africa less dependent on Great Britain, a strategy that would create thousands of jobs amongst the Blacks.

"Have you had any more visits from the security police?" Charles asked thoughtfully after a few minutes.

"No," Emma answered shaking her head. "After they murdered our Gamboo, and I know it was them, I am a great deal more cautious than ever before."

"But I understand that you made a sizable donation to a school hall in Ikageng." Ikageng was the new black township developed on the hills overlooking Potchefstroom.

"Yes," she answered, "but I did it with the Mooi River Pharmacy. I did not want my name to appear on any plaque. They, in return, have picked up a great deal of business from it." She thought for a minute and frowned."But I thought it was a secret. How did you know?"

"I have my sources," he smiled.

Christa came in from the kitchen with a milk tart and a bowl of sliced biltong. "Come on, you two, enough politics for the night, and with this little one listening," she nodded her head towards Marla, "it might not be that good."

"So, what are you going to do next year?" Charlie asked Marla.

"Well," Marla answered looking carefully at her mother, "I think I would like to attend Wits, to do a B.A. degree."

"Wits," as the University of the Witwatersrand in Johannesburg is known, was an English-speaking university that appealed to Marla because it was a lot more liberal than any of the Afrikaans Universities, or so she thought. She was not certain as to what she wanted to study, so she chose to study for a Bachelor of Arts. Most girls thought of pursuing a B.A. as a year of fun and a way to find a husband. Marla took it to be a year to find herself; to decide what she wanted to become and where her direction in life lay.

Living in Potchefstroom, with her mother, she had always been under her protective eye. Since the death of Gamboo, she felt almost overly protected. When she had told Emma that she would like to attend Wits, rather than Potchefstroom University, Emma was horrified that her daughter would be leaving home. But with a number of promises as to what she could and could not do, Emma had finally agreed to let her go.

"Promise me that you will phone me every night," she demanded, "and promise me that if you should ever need anything at all urgently, you will phone Irma Rosen. Look at her as if she were your grandmother."

"I promise, Ma," she had said, giving Emma a hug, "and I am sorry to leave you on your own at home. You do have Kathy, you know."

"Kathy is not you," Emma answered. "Definitely not you."

Marla found her first year at Wits challenging. Going to an Afrikaans school in Potchefstroom, where her every need was controlled by the teachers of the school, made the free society at Wits at first difficult to cope with. The students in her class, most of them from Johannesburg, dressed, spoke and acted differently than the conservatism she had grown up with. For the first few months, she kept away from them. Staying in the hostel, however, helped her adapt a lot quicker than if she had lived in a flat close to the University, as many of the students did. Her roommate was a girl from Lichtenburg who had chosen to study medicine and had to keep her nose in her books because only the top students were selected. Fortunately for her, Costas Bouras, after Josh had told him she was at Wits, took her under his wing and introduced her to the social life of the University. He was studying law, and had made many friends. He was also very popular, and well known to both lecturers and students on the campus.

She was surprised when almost six months later talking to Emma on the phone, Emma said, "I have decided to sell up in Potch. and buy a house in Johannesburg."

"Why, Mom," she asked, "don't you like Potch. anymore?"

"No," Emma answered, "that is not the reason. I love the town, but I have nothing here anymore. You are in Johannesburg, and I would like to give you a home there."

Marla was just too happy that her hostel living would soon be over. That December, during the summer holidays, she and Emma spent their time house hunting, and eventually found a beautiful home in Parkhurst, a suburb of Johannesburg, less than a 30 minute drive from the university.

"Why are you moving to Johannesburg?" Charlie asked her when she told him. "I always thought you were so happy in Potchefstroom."

"I was, and still am," Emma answered him as they sat in their usual seats in the garden sipping wine, this time a Merlot. "I love the town, and I love all the people in it, but I miss my daughter. Also, since the visit of Brigadier Grobelaar, I have always felt that I am being watched, and I can't take that. By living in Johannesburg, I can hopefully lose myself in the crowd."

Charlie understood, but he was sad. He had grown to love Emma as a daughter, and especially Marla, who had grown up in front of him.

"You will keep in touch with us," he said to Emma, reaching forward and taking both her hands in his.

"I will always keep in touch with you," Emma answered. "You and Christa are my family. Don't ever forget that. Just promise me that both of you, whenever you don't go and visit Marie in Pretoria, will come and visit us, or better yet, Marie can come to us, and then you won't have to drive so far."

The house Emma bought in Parkhurst was on the only street with a name in the suburb, Parkhurst Street. All the other streets were numerical. The house was a newly built double story, not very large, but large enough for the two of them and on a very comfortable property. It overlooked the *spruit* that divided Parkhurst from Victory Park. Walking the *spruit* on the hot summer days was a pleasure, as it was always full of residents either walking their dogs, or running or cycling on the paths that led one into Delta Park, bordering Blairgowrie, Linden and Victory Park.

The house had a beautiful lounge with a large fireplace. On the mantel piece above the fireplace, the first thing Emma did was display her vase filled with marbles and stones of all colours, boasting a beautiful arrangement of roses. Next to the vase, she placed a small framed picture of herself, taken many years ago.

"Why the picture, Ma?" Marla asked her, looking at it. "You look so young in it."

"I was," Emma answered, "I had only just arrived in Johannesburg, and was walking to the OK Bazaars to apply for a job, when a street photographer took the photo."

"Here is his name," Marla interrupted, "on the back. Sam Gluckman."

"I met him when I went to collect the photo at his studio," Emma said, taking the photo from her and looking at it. "He was a very charming man. I spent some time talking with him. I often saw him on the street taking photos and we would stand and chat. The photo brings back very pleasant memories."

"But why have you only put it out now?"

"When I started packing up everything in Potchefstroom, I found it. It brought back memories of how anxious I felt in those days."

"Anxious?" Marla asked. She had always thought of her mother as being determined and very much in control.

"Yes," Emma said, looking at the photo. "I was very young. I had arrived in Johannesburg a few days before and was very anxious about everything. Things, however, worked out far better than I could have ever foreseen."

In the evenings, she and Marla enjoyed sitting on the back veranda, next to the swimming pool, dripping water from a cooling swim. They air was filled with the singing of birds in the trees around them, the sun setting slowly, pinking the clouds with its orange glow. They loved living in Johannesburg, 6,500 feet above sea level, known to have the best climate in the world.

Marla was happy living with her mother, glad to be out of the hostel. Emma had bribed her with a car, an Austin Westminster, that Marla enjoyed driving. '*Had Ma only known that I would have moved back home simply on a kiss,*' she laughed to herself.

She would drive to class every morning, often picking up friends and classmates on the way, and more often than not bringing them home for a swim, or supper. They enjoyed playing Elvis Presley records, much to Emma's annoyance. She simply could not get her teeth around rock and roll.

During her first year at Wits, Marla had decided that she wanted to do social work. She applied for and was accepted for second year. Like all the students with whom she associated, she had started to attend conferences on world peace, and on opposing racial segregation and the apartheid that was South Africa.

When, in January of 1960, before University started, the government announced that it wanted to hold a referendum on turning South Africa into a Republic within the British Commonwealth, she and her group of friends became very disappointed.

"This had always been one of the aims of the Nationalist Party, to make South Africa independent of Britain and British influence," they debated with each other. "The benefits the country received financially by belonging to the Commonwealth will be lost."

"My mother's friend, Irma Rosen," Marla told them, "says that this is just the beginning. She with her family lived in Germany before the war. She says that the pattern happening now is just the same as what happened in Germany. Verwoerd is copying exactly what Hitler did. He is starting to stimulate national pride."

Two weeks after the announcement of the referendum, Harold Macmillan, the British Prime Minister, visited South Africa. In an address to Parliament he made his famous Wind of Change speech, which was interpreted as an end to British support for White rule.

'The wind of change is blowing through this continent. Whether we like it or not, this growth of national consciousness is a political fact."

"National consciousness?" Costas said to Marla and Emma one night at table. Marla had invited him to join them for a swim and supper. Costas was very involved in the political scene at the university, and could always be found at any and every meeting.

"What he means is Black national consciousness, not the White that Verwoerd wants. That is what will happen. What Britain originally started when it took the Cape from the Dutch has come to an end. The horrors of Nazi Germany's racial and religious persecution, of mass murders in the concentration camps, has come home to roost.

"Just look around, through Africa and the world," he continued. "Colonialism throughout the world has come to an end. The nations of Europe are pulling out of Africa and the Far East. Unfortunately, they have not considered the consequences of their actions. Mark my words, by granting independence to the countries they have ruled for centuries, they will create countries that sink into decay, while their leaders fill their Swiss bank accounts. Watch, and you will see that I am right."

Emma sat eating her meal. She said nothing. Later that evening, after Costas had gone home, she said to Marla, "Costas is very emotional about the political situation in the country. Please, I beg you, don't let him involve you."

"But Ma," Marla said, not understanding her request. "You and Gran'pa Charlie are always talking politics. I thought you would enjoy chatting with Costas."

"I found it interesting listening to what he had to say," Emma replied, "but he may be overreacting, as most students usually do. Please, don't let him influence you. Don't become involved."

In order to bolster support for a republic, Verwoerd reduced the voting age for Whites from 21 to 18, counting on the younger Afrikaans voter who he felt would more likely favor a republic. Marla and her friends suddenly had the right to express their opinions in a ballot box. This led to further serious debate amongst them.

"There are not enough of us liberal kids to vote against this country becoming a Republic," Costas argued at a meeting called by students to discuss the reduction in the voting age. "Verwoerd knows that. Do you honestly think that he would have reduced the voting age if he had known that he would lose the vote? Stupid he is, yes, but not that stupid."

Marla had attended the meeting without telling Emma that she was going to. Her friendship with Costas made her curious to hear more of what he thought.

When the government then extended the franchise to Whites in South West Africa, most of who were German and Afrikaans speakers, they were shocked.

"That is wrong," students debated at the numerous political meetings Marla went to. "South West Africa is not a part of South Africa. It is a separate country, administered by South Africa. What right do the White residents that are citizens of South West Africa have to vote in our affairs?"

On March 21, when Marla arrived at the University, she found that many of the students had gathered in groups and were thinking of organizing a march to protest the issuing of identity books to all the citizens of South Africa.

"The pass laws must be abolished," she heard one group of students shout above the noise as she passed them. "Would you like to walk around with a book that lists your name, birthplace, tribal affiliation with your picture and a serial number?"

"Do you know, it also has a place for a receipt to prove that you have paid your taxes?" she heard another student shout. "They also want the book to record how many times you have been arrested. My father tells me that unless he signs it every month, our maid can be taken from her home and sent to a native reservation. How long will it be before that applies to Whites as well?"

Then, at 1:20 p.m. while she was in the canteen having lunch with her friends, it was announced over the radio that police started firing at a crowd of 20,000 Africans that had collected at the Sharpeville police station, 28 miles southwest of Johannesburg. They were protesting the pass laws, demanding to be arrested. In two minutes between 72 and 90 Africans were killed, with more than 200 wounded.

Marla and her friends were shocked.

"My God, is this what our country is coming to?" Marla said to Costas when she saw him. They were standing with a crowd of students that had gathered around the radio to listen to the news.

"The murder of innocents? Killing men, women and children to enforce an inhuman pass law?" the announcer said.

That night, the *Star*, a Johannesburg newspaper, wrote in its editorial:

"This is a pathetic faith in the power of machine guns to settle basic human problems."

When Marla arrived home that night, she and Emma spent the evening listening to the radio. They heard how over 500 students at the University of Natal carried banners that read, HITLER 1939, VERWOERD 1960; that all British and South African flags had been lowered to half-mast.

"Oh, Mom," Marla said to Emma. "Can you imagine what it will be like at Wits tomorrow? It will be a madhouse."

The Sharpeville Massacre, as it came to be known, was condemned throughout the world. Verwoerd justified the massacre by saying, "nothing would be done" to abolish the pass laws. "They had shot first," he said.

When Marla went to university the next morning, she found that students were joining in the demonstrations against the Sharpeville massacre.

"Bullshit!" Carlos shouted to the crowd that had gathered on the campus. "No one found any arms on the Blacks. Hendrik Verwoerd has lied. Verwoerd feels that he can use the pass laws as an instrument to arrest and harass us, his political opponents. The man is a crazy murderer."

Protest marches flared up all over the country with the government eventually declaring a state of emergency to control the strikes and riots. The African National Congress and the Pan Africanist Congress were banned. Both organizations shifted from passive resistance to armed resistance.

Marla could not help but become caught up in the events at the university. She joined the protest march, even though Emma had begged her not to become involved in politics. She felt that she had to. All her friends took part, and she was just as emotionally angry at what was happening in the country as they were.

Then, on April 9, when Hendrik Verwoerd opened the Union Exposition on the Witwatersrand to mark the jubilee of the Union of South Africa, David Pratt, a farmer from Natal, attempted to assassinate him by firing two shots from a .22 automatic pistol at point blank range into his cheek and ear. Once again, Marla found that she spent more time at students' meetings discussing and arguing the politics of the country than she did studying.

At nineteen, Marla was 5'9" tall, with an hourglass figure that was the fashion. She was beautiful enough to warrant the occasional wolf whistle when she walked through the campus. Her dark skin, with not quite almond shaped eyes, above a petite nose and full-lipped mouth that smiled with perfectly shaped white teeth, took many a breath away. She had allowed her rich dark brown hair, highlighted by the sun, to grow almost to the middle of her back, and in a slight breeze it looked like a stream behind her as she walked. She knew she was beautiful, and with her naturally tanned skin, was the envy of many of the girls in her class.

Whenever she stood up to speak at any of the political meetings, no one took her seriously. It was only when, taking the advice of Costas, she started to dress down with hair tousled and wearing no makeup that students started to notice what she said.

Marla was a girl with an opinion that had to be expressed. She had been fortunate enough in her school years to live with and understand the view and fears of the Afrikaner. At Wits she learned the views and fears of the English. In many debates, she was inclined to defend a few of the government policies, especially when views were emotionally expressed that she felt were totally out of sync with what was truly happening within the country. After one debate, where a few highly radical students called for another protest march about the latest government policy, she could not contain herself.

"I agree with what has been said," she started nervously, standing up in spite of her nervousness. "My name is Marla O'Neil," and she looked around her for some support. "Many of you know that I come from a town called Potchefstroom, a very conservative Afrikaans town. I am sure that you all know the town, because it was the first capital of the Boer Republic, and many of the Boers still live there. I have listened to what you have debated at this meeting, but I am afraid I simply cannot agree with you on everything that has been said.

"Yes, apartheid must be abolished, but hatred among the various racial and religious groups must also vanish at the same time. I do not want to see a civil war start within the country, because that will destroy it. You simply cannot ignore the feelings of the Afrikaner, many of whom believe that racial discrimination is the will of the God they pray to."

A few in the audience snickered, and she looked around at them.

"Yes, I admit there are extremes, just as there are extremists in this room, sitting in the seats around me. And yes, I agree that Hendrik Verwoerd is a man whose racial policies are deplorable. But tell me, sir," and she addressed the chairman of the meeting, "does everyone in this room want a civil war? Do we want a war with the ANC and the PAC taking up arms on our borders against us, with many of the boys in this room being drafted into the army to fight them against their will and even face the possibility of being killed? Let us face it, Africa and the world will support all opposition to apartheid in all its forms. Do we truly need this isolation from the world?"

She looked around the room. Everyone sat watching her. "I don't," she continued, "and I know just by looking at your faces that you also don't. So let us temper our anger at the present government policies, which I agree are horrific. Let us instead look for sensible and above all peaceful and constructive arguments that will benefit the country and all the people who live here. Direct confrontation hurts, and has always hurt. Peaceful negotiation is the only answer."

"You try and negotiate with Hendrik Verwoerd!" someone shouted. "He only knows how to shoot and kill. He is no different from Adolph Hitler."

She sat down, not quite believing what she had just said, then someone started clapping. Soon the clapping reverberated around the whole room. Were they clapping for Marla or for her heckler? She wasn't sure.

After the meeting, Costas congratulated her on what she had said.

"You spoke well, and with emotion," he told her. "You must keep it up. You impressed them and you got your point across."

When she told Emma about the meeting, and how well she was received, Emma was angry.

"Marla, I have begged you to stop taking an active part in the political meetings at the university. Please, don't attract attention to yourself. Remember what happened to Gamboo?"

"Mom, I know that I must say what I feel," she answered. "I simply cannot sit back and say nothing when all these horrible things are happening."

"I understand how you feel," Emma replied, "but do try and be discrete and a lot less visible. Try not to attract too much attention to yourself. Please, do listen to what I ask."

Marla had started dating a fourth-year medical student, Phillip Barnard, inviting him to the house for a swim over most weekends. Emma was absolutely thrilled that her daughter was dating Phillip, not only a medical student but a good-looking young man from a distinguished Johannesburg family that lived in Houghton, not that far from Irma Rosen. For the first time, she felt that all of the torment of leaving her family in Cape Town had been worth it.

She hoped that the friendship between Marla and Phillip would develop into a lasting relationship.

"A nice boy, Phillip," Emma said to her one evening while they were having supper.

"He is alright, but he wants to become serious, and I don't want that, not yet at any rate," Marla replied, sipping at her coffee.

Emma was surprised. "What do you want?" she asked.

"Well Ma, once I have my degree, I would like to tour. I would like to see the world. You remember Josh from Potchefstroom? He is in London studying pharmacy. From his letters, London sounds fantastic. I would like to visit him."

"Are you in love with him?" Emma asked, her eyes widening at what Marla had said.

"Good heavens, no!" Marla answered. "He is just a friend. That is all. A couple of girls in my class at Wits want to hitch-hike around Europe, once they are qualified. If you would let me, I would like to join them."

Emma thought before answering her. "This is a decision we can make when you have your degree," she said. "By then you may have other plans."

And so, Marla became more determined than ever to concentrate on her studies, and obtain a degree in sociology. Politics, as much as she was against the government's policies, she felt was not her forte. She applied her nose to her books. With four months left before her exams, she was determined that her grades would be exceptional. She was also determined to see the world before looking for a job.

Chapter 7

Josh loved London almost from the minute he arrived at Victoria station. It was July and summer. With the sun shining, London was at its best. His uncle, Alfred Wise, was waiting for him. Alfred recognized him by the South African flag he held in his left hand.

Alfred was a taxi driver. He drove a black Austin FX4 cab. Josh had brought a trunk with him, with clothes for five years, something Lilly had insisted on, quite convinced that he would not recapture the weight he had lost in the navy. They placed the trunk on the luggage platform next to where Alfred sat. Josh climbed into the back seat and Alfred started driving through the city to Whitechapel, where he lived with his wife, Kaye, and daughter, Wendy.

"I will not take you past the tourist spots," he said in a broad cockney accent that Josh found difficult to understand. "I will take you straight home. Kaye has prepared lunch. Tomorrow, when we look for digs, I can show you a bit of London."

Josh lost his sense of direction almost as soon as Alfred left the station. They drove down a broad road, past a beautiful church, to the Thames.

"That there is Westminster Cathedral," Alfred said, pointing at the church. "That is where Queen Elizabeth was crowned in 1953. There in front of us are the Houses of Parliament and Big Ben."

Josh sat not saying a word. He was looking out the cab's windows, admiring the beauty of London. None of the pictures he had looked at in South Africa to familiarize himself with the city could capture the London that they were passing. The Thames was a great deal wider than he had ever imagined, with large ships unloading cargo at wharfs on the opposite side from where they were driving.

"I will take you past St. Paul's Cathedral," Alfred said. "Sometimes driving along the back roads is faster."

The cathedral with its huge dome was beautiful.

"During the war, this whole area was bombed," Alfred told him, driving slower so that Josh could take in the scene. "I remember how we all marveled that the bombs missed the cathedral, but the buildings around it were all destroyed. When they started rebuilding, they found the ruins of a Roman temple, the Temple of Mithras.

"This is the business center, and that building over there is Lloyd's of London," Alfred continued as they drove a little further. "At night this whole area closes down, with nobody on the streets. It is like a morgue. Over there, you can see a bit of Fleet Street. You know what Fleet Street is famous for?"

"Yes," Josh answered. "That is where all the newspapers are."

They drove into Whitechapel Road, a busy street, filled with people shopping at the different shops lining only one side of the street, the other side being a large white building.

"And that is the London Hospital," Alfred said pointing at the building. "There, across the road, is the Underground Station you will arrive at when you come to visit us by tube. Just walk down New Road to Varden Street and we are here." He pulled up in front of a door, one of many on a long white façade broken with windows and doors. Each door was painted a different colour. The door to their home was painted green.

"Welcome to London," Kaye said in an accent as broad as Alfred's as they walked into the house. "Do come in, and this is our Wendy," she said as a little girl pushed herself forward under her arm.

Kaye was a big woman, taller than Alfred by a few inches, with auburn hair and what must have been, in her youth, a very beautiful face. She had made fried eggs and chips for lunch. Josh ate as though he hadn't seen food for weeks.

"Thank you for a wonderful meal," he told Kaye when they had all finished eating. "I don't know what you did to those eggs, but they were absolutely delicious."

That night, for the first time, he watched a television program on a small black and white television.

"South Africa does not have television," he told them when they switched it on. "The National Party, the ruling party in the country, compares TV to atom bombs and poison gas. The Minister for Posts and Telecommunications, Dr. Albert Herzog, argues that TV would show interracial films and make Africans dissatisfied with their present situation." After about an hour, Alfred excused himself, saying, "I have to get back to work. See you hopefully at five o'clock."

Josh sat talking to Kaye and Wendy the whole afternoon. Kaye told him that he would be sleeping on the sofa, in the lounge. The house was a small one, with only two rooms; no bath, only a wash basin.

"We go to the public baths just down the street, once a week," Kaye told him. "If you would like a bath, I will take you there."

"No, it is not necessary," Josh told her. "I had a shower on the ship early this morning."

By the time Alfred came home, Josh was tired. As soon as supper was over, they all went to the lounge to watch the news on TV.

"Nothing fantastic that anyone I cabbed never told me," Alfred said.

The next morning, with Alfred's help, he found digs in Battersea, close to the Battersea Park. Chelsea Polytechnic, where he was en-rolled, was a half hour walk across the Albert bridge that stretched majestically across the Thames.

He spent his first week in London, walking the city, studying the underground system and bus routes, losing himself in Hyde Park. He became fascinated with the number of people simply lying on the grass, enjoying the sun.

"*This huge park is in the middle of a large city,*" he kept thinking, "*quite remarkable and absolutely wonderful.*"

At Hyde Park corner he stood and listened to a man standing on a box talking about the heavy taxes they all had to pay, and that a new government should be formed that would work for them, the people. A policeman with his tall helmet stood watching the crowd of onlookers. By the look on his face, Josh felt that he was slightly bored as he watched him stifle a yawn.

He walked slowly through the park, listening to the birds as they chirped, the noise of the traffic softening. Crossing a bridge that spanned the Serpentine, a large artificial lake, he stood for a while, watching the boaters as they slowly rowed down its length. He walked further into the park towards the south end, and was surprised to see two horse riders trotting along a bridle path.

"*Good heavens,*" he thought, '*and this is all in the centre of London?*'

Walking slowly out of the park, he made his way to Knightsbridge and into Chelsea, enjoying the vibe of Kings Road, feeling his way through the shoppers. He stopped for a coffee and a biscuit that was his lunch, and then slowly made his way to the Albert bridge and back to his digs.

The next day he caught a bus to Trafalgar Square, feeding the pigeons at Nelson's column. He then walked into South Africa house that was across the road from the Square, and registered his arrival in England.

"We are having a cocktail party tomorrow night to welcome visitors from South Africa," the receptionist told him. "It starts at six o'clock in the evening. We would be pleased if you could attend."

Leaving the Embassy, he walked through St. James' Park, making his way to Buckingham Palace. The park seduced him. He sat for almost two hours, feeding the ducks and swans under willow trees whose branches fingered the water of the pond that floated in the park. He sat wondering how anyone could not want to live in London permanently. Eventually waking from his daydreams, he walked into the circle in front of Buckingham Palace and sat at the Queen Victoria

Memorial watching a shiny black Rolls Royce approach the wrought iron gates of the palace. He was sure that the young Queen Elizabeth was sitting in the back seat of the car. Whether or not she was, it didn't matter. Here was a story he lived with for weeks.

A week after he arrived, he wrote to Marla, telling her all about the two week boat trip on the Edinburgh Castle and meeting the famous ballerina, Maryon Lane, who was travelling back to London after visiting family in South Africa. He told her how much he loved London and how he planned to see as many shows as he had money, before he started at the Polytechnic. He missed her and although he had flirted with a couple of girls on the ship coming over, both of whom were nurses returning to England, Marla was always in his thoughts.

For the next few weeks, he did nothing else than walk London, from Drury Lane where he looked to see what plays were on, to Covent Garden where he bought some fruit. He stood on the sidewalk, watching the shoppers buying flowers, delighting in the hustle and bustle as they negotiated prices.

He walked to Piccadilly Circus, enjoying the shops of Regent Street, and looking in all the shop windows wishing he had enough money to buy what he liked. At the moment, not sure of what his monthly expenses could be, he was counting his pennies.

With a limited monthly income out of which he had to pay university fees, board and lodging, he soon found that the last week of every month, no matter how careful he was with his money, he lived on bread and tea for his meals. Every now and then his mother would send him five pounds, and he usually used that money to go to a show, or spend it on a trip down the Thames to Kew Gardens, or even walk through an art gallery. Having met Maryon Lane, he went to a performance where she was the lead ballerina at Sadlers Wells. After the performance he went back stage to see her, and was welcomed by her, but as a young student, he felt uncomfortable among all the dignified people around her.

The university semester started the sixth of September. He had to enroll at the Polytechnic the day before. Standing in the queue with hundreds of students presenting themselves, he signed the numerous forms that were necessary for registration. When he returned to his lodgings, he found that another student had taken a room in the same 'digs'. Mr. and Mrs. Jones, the owners of the house, earned an income by renting out rooms to students.

John Williams was English. He came from Slough, on the outskirts of London, where he lived with his stepfather, Reg Crosby, his sister, Anne, and her husband, Paul. His mother had passed away a few years earlier from cancer.

"Hi, my name is Josh Stern," Josh said, holding out his hand when he met John the next morning at breakfast.

"Hello," John said in a very British accent, taking Josh's hand. "I am John Williams. Where do you come from with that strange accent?"

Josh laughed. "I am a South African," he said. "I am here to study pharmacy at Chelsea Polytechnic."

"So am I," John answered. "Not a South African of course, but studying pharmacy. I am in my second year."

John was tall, blond and handsome, the absolute cliché of manly good looks. His manner, behavior and speech were as English as English could be. He was a brilliant student, planning to enter one of the large drug companies in their research laboratories once he was qualified.

That first Sunday, John invited Josh to join him in Slough. They took the underground to Uxbridge, and then a bus to the top of the road where they lived. The lane leading to the house was an avenue of oak trees.

The house, set back from the road with a driveway, was beautiful, with a large garden in front leading to a larger one at the back. Both gardens boasted a well kept lawn circled with rhododendron and azalea bushes in the last stages of flower. This was something that Josh had never seen before because the South African climate was too hot for them to grow. The back garden bordered a large field surrounded by trees, offering a walk that was very inviting.

Soon, if Josh was not spending a Sunday with the Wises', he was enjoying the hospitality of John and his family, in Slough. He spent many a weekend walking through the fields behind the house. It was on one of these walks that he and John decided to climb to the top of what John called the 'ivory tower'. The tower was in the centre of the field next to the one that they usually walked through, tall and thin like a white needle pointing skyward. They had often walked past it, with Josh wondering what it was for.

"What is that tower?" he finally asked John.

"We think that it was built as a watch tower a couple of centuries ago. Don't know for sure." John answered, looking at it. "Would you like to have a closer look?"

"Sure, why not?" Josh answered, breaking through the hedge that separated the two fields.

They walked to the tower and found a small wooden door hanging on rusted hinges. The door opened to a winding staircase that climbed to another wooden door leading onto a platform giving them a view of the surrounding countryside.

They stood and admired the beauty of the fields around them, with John pointing out various landmarks to Josh.

"There , in the far distance," he pointed, "you can see Windsor Castle. That is where the Queen lives."

"I thought she lived at Buckingham Palace," Josh said.

"Not all the time," John answered. "I think she spends more time here, than there."

They walked around the platform and were surprised to find a little girl of about twelve years old, sitting in silence, watching them curiously.

"Hello," John said, surprised at seeing her sitting there. "I am John. I hope we haven't frightened you."

"I am Josh," Josh added.

The little girl said nothing. John and Josh looked at each other and, feeling uncomfortable, started walking back to the door.

"Oh, don't go," the little girl said. "My name is Livvy, and I am hiding up here. I always do."

"Hiding from whom?" Josh asked, "from your parents?"

"I like to have some quiet time alone, so I always come here," Livvy continued, as though she had not heard Josh's question.

Both John and Josh thought this a bit strange, but said nothing.

Livvy stood up and followed them as they continued walking around the tower, chattering as only a girl of twelve years old could. When they left the tower, she walked with them, at one stage taking John's hand. John was a bit surprised, but behaved more like an older brother than otherwise. She left them when they came to the road.

"I live just a little way down there. Thank you for walking with me," she said politely. "Do come again."

John and Josh looked at each other, surprise on their faces.

From that day on, whenever John and Josh went to Slough, Livvy would often be waiting for them hidden in bushes close to their house or watching for them from the top of the tower and running down when she saw them. This did not happen every time, but Josh was surprised at how often Livvy was there, almost as if she knew when they were to visit Slough.

One Sunday, when they walked into the field, they found Livvy waiting for them, as usual, but with a young man standing next to her.

"This is my brother, Albert," she said, "I told him about both of you. He very much wanted to meet you, probably to check you out and make sure that you were not kidnapping me," and she smiled, looking slyly at John.

Albert questioned John, as though interrogating him as to who and what he was in society. When he learned from John that Josh was a South African, he turned to Josh.

"Tell me," he asked as they crossed a small brook, stepping carefully over the stones, "how could you grow up in a country that legalizes racial discrimination? You did read the article in the *Readers Digest* about the Tomlinson Report a few years ago, and how the report concluded that each of the eight South African tribes should be separated into their own homelands, and that apartheid was the only solution to South Africa's racial problem?"

"No, I did not," Josh answered, "I don't follow politics that much. My father, who does, believes that Hendrik Verwoerd, as the minister of Native affairs, introduced all these laws. That, as Prime Minister, he will become even more restrictive. He is very worried about that because of a speech Verwoerd recently gave in Potchefstroom, our home town, where he referred to the Blacks of South Africa as the shrewdest, cleverest and most dangerous of all South Africa's enemies."

"Well, the Tomlinson report was published a couple of years ago. We debated it in my class at Oxford," Albert continued. "When I read it, I thought it was horrific. That was the conclusion the debate reached. We wondered how anyone could accept the report's recommendations, and live in a country that practiced racial hatred, especially after what has happened to the Jews and others in Germany."

"Albert," Josh said, frowning as he thought carefully thought about what he wanted to say, "you must understand how we were raised there as kids. To me, as a young boy growing up, the way we lived with racial discrimination was the norm. My parents never raised me. I was raised by an African girl. She was my surrogate mother, waking me and dressing me in the morning and then playing with me all day. At night she would bathe me and put me to bed. I was about four years old when she was employed to look after me. The only time I ever saw my parents was at supper, at 5:30 in the afternoon, and on a Sunday. My dad played lawn bowls in the morning and then drove us to the Swartzberg farm in the afternoon for a swim under the waterfall."

"When I started school, the girl, her name was Dolly, who was by then probably between 16 and 18 years old, would walk me to school every morning until I was old enough to walk to school on my own."

"But didn't it worry you that these people, these servants, were restricted in the way they were?" Albert asked.

"That was the trouble," Josh answered. "When you grow up believing that this is the way of life, it becomes the norm. I was raised by Dolly, my brother by a black girl whose name was Sally, and my sister had Emily as her maid. All were substitute mothers, and Emily, the youngest of them all, I don't believe was more than 15 years old.

"Dolly raised me. She taught me all about sex in exchange for me teaching her how to read," he smiled as he said this, "not that I learned very much from her."

"Where did they live?" Alfred asked, "From what I have read they lived in a ghetto, a location if I remember the name correctly."

"Emily and Sally both slept in the servant's quarters in the back yard of our house, a building that had two rooms. They had an outside lavatory and shower that were both pretty primitive, I must admit. Dolly went home every night to the Old Location where she lived with her family because she was a Coloured girl. On those nights when Emily or Sally were not there because they had gone to their families, Dolly babysat us when my parents went out. I would have to write her a pass, so that she could go home and not be arrested by the police, if she stayed later than the 9 p.m. curfew."

"So you as a young boy, you had authority over the movement of a young woman who was older than you and who worked for you?" Albert asked, not quite believing what he had heard.

"Yes, to us as children, this was the way of life. When I think of it now of course, I am horrified. I remember how on Christmas Day, the little African boys from the age of four to twelve would walk through town in their rags, looking for a handout. Christmas was the only day the police would allow them to do this, probably because they were all off duty, at home celebrating with their families. I, with my brother and sister, would stand in the street giving them sweets and whatever pennies my Dad had given us to give to them."

"And to you, this was acceptable?" Albert asked in amazement.

"Well, let us face it," Josh answered starting to get angry, "You Brits started it when you conquered the world and introduced colonialism. You declared all Blacks second-class citizens. Even Cecil John Rhodes, one of your great Englishmen, had a man deprived of his farm because he was a Coloured. Why? Because diamonds had been discovered on the farm. Rhodes wanted the diamonds for a company he formed, so he simply had a law passed stating that Coloureds were not allowed to own property and he took the farm in the name of Queen Victoria and the British Empire."

Albert shook his head and said nothing. He continued walking with them, thinking about what Josh had said.

Eventually Livvy broke the silence by asking, "Will you be here next week?"

"Probably," John answered, "I am usually at home every weekend."

"Oh, that is good," Livvy said. "You see, it is my birthday, and I would like you to come to my party."

"Livvy," Albert said, "you do know that Mom and Dad have prepared a special party for you. You will have to get their permission before you invite anyone."

"Well, I will ask them," Livvy said, sulking. "It is my birthday, not theirs."

"I have to go back to London tonight," Albert said to Josh. "I would very much like to ask you a great deal more about South Africa. I understand that it is a very beautiful country."

"Very beautiful," Josh said, "I love the country, and everyone I know who has visited it for the first time has fallen in love with it."

"Well, one day we should get together so that you can tell me more about it. Goodbye for now," and he held out his hand for Josh and John to shake. Then turning to Livvy he said, "We have to go home now, Livvy," and he walked off, Livvy trailing him, waving goodbye to them.

The invitation from Livvy never came, not that they had expected to receive one, and not that either John or Josh wanted to attend a birthday party for a thirteen-year-old girl, but they were both curious as to who Livvy was, especially now that they had met Albert. There was also no Livvy when they now walked through the fields whenever they visited Slough. This made them even more curious as to who she was.

"Well, you nasty pervert," Josh teased John, "Albert took one look at you and decided that your intentions were not honourable, especially with his thirteen-year-old sister."

John laughed and replied, "No sir, you have it wrong, Albert took one look at this wild African standing next to me, and that scared the hell out of him."

Josh continued to write a letter at least once a month to Marla, but she wrote to him less and less. She wrote and told him that she was at Wits University studying for a B.A. degree with the intention of majoring in sociology. Soon after, he met Sandra Greenstone, and was almost adopted into the Greenstone family. Sandra was "Audrey Hepburnish", the same slim look, hairstyle, smile and eyes that lit up a room with their pixie-like quality. Audrey Hepburn had recently conquered the world, and any and every girl who had a similar figure tried their best to copy her looks and fashion.

With Sandra as Josh's Audrey Hepburn, Marla slipped into a corner of his memory, almost forgotten.

Over the next six months, as winter approached, they visited Slough less and less. At Christmas, Josh was invited to their home for the Christmas Eve party. This would be the first time that he had ever attended one, especially at a home that would have a Christmas tree. His family always celebrated Hanukkah in December, a date that always changed because the Jewish calendar was a Lunar calendar. He bought a small gift for each family member, placing them under the tree when he arrived at the house, something he knew was customary.

That night, when dinner was served and they all sat around the table, Josh was shocked when Anne walked in from the kitchen carrying a plate with the head of a pig, an apple stuffed into its mouth. She placed it in front of Reg to carve.

"Because you are Jewish," Anne said to Josh as she walked back to the kitchen, "and I understand that Jews don't eat pork, I made a chicken for you," and she walked out of the kitchen with a small plate with a chicken on it. Josh never had the heart to ask whether or not it had been prepared in lard.

That night, after eating and drinking far more than he should have, for the first time in a long time, he dreamt of Marla. Sandra, who had gone to University in Dublin, Ireland, slowly slipped from his memory.

Chapter 8

On May 31, 1961, as a result of the referendum for White voters only that was held in January of 1960, South Africa declared itself a republic and was prevented from continuing as a member of the British Commonwealth. This was because of hostility from many members, particularly those in Africa, Asia and Canada, to South Africa's policy of apartheid. The prime minister, Hendrik Verwoerd, had Parliament vote to withdraw its application to remain in the Commonwealth as a republic, knowing that any such application would be rejected. This was what he had planned and the National Party was pleased that all ties with Britain would now be severed.

The next morning, Marla drove her car to the university as usual and struggled to find a space in the parking lot. This surprised her. She walked to her first lecture and looking around, thought that the corridors were very empty of students. With a parking lot full of cars, she thought this was strange.

"Where is everybody?" she asked the first person she saw.

"They are all protesting on Jan Smuts Avenue."

"What are they protesting about this time?" Marla asked. She had been studying far more than usual, and had lost contact with the student protest group.

"South Africa leaving the Commonwealth. Hendrik Verwoerd is apparently flying back to South Africa today from London, and the students want to make themselves heard. Didn't you know about it?"

"Well, we all suspected that it would happen eventually," Marla answered. "Once South Africa became a republic, it was simply a matter of time before they left the Commonwealth."

She walked toward Jan Smuts avenue where the protestors were lining the streets holding their placards. She stood at the entrance to the University watching them. Motor cars driving down Jan Smuts Avenue sounded their horns as they agreed with their protest.

She saw Costas with two other boys, leading the students into the street. They started walking towards the center of Johannesburg waving placards. Before Marla knew what was happening, she was caught up in the march. She squeezed her way out of the crowd of protesting students and managed to get to the pavement just as the police started to arrest those who led the protest. She stood there watching, amazed at what was happening.

The next morning Emma woke her. "Marla, I see that you were in the protest march at the university yesterday."

"No, Ma," she answered sleepily, "I just went to watch them."

"Well, my dear," Emma said sarcastically, "I have just had a phone call from Charlie Stuart. Apparently your photo is all over the papers showing you as a protestor."

"My what?" Marla said, sitting up in bed, wide awake, "Let me see, do you have a paper?"

"Here it is," Emma said. "I went out and bought one," and she handed Marla the newspaper. "There is your picture," and she pointed at a photo showing Marla standing slightly behind a student who was holding up a sign that read, "Down with Verwoerd."

Marla was horrified. "But Ma, that happened when I tried to get out of the crowd. I went to watch, and a group of students came up behind me and pushed me into the protestors. I moved away from them as quickly as I could and then stood on the pavement watching. Then I saw the police arresting Costas and other students, and forcing them into the back of the police vans." She looked down at the newspaper she was holding and read that over 100 students had been arrested. Just then the phone rang. Emma answered it.

"Hello, Irma," she said. "About the photo? No, she wasn't one of those arrested. She is OK. She tells me that she didn't even take part in the protest, but was an onlooker. Thanks for phoning, I will tell her. Talk with you later."

Emma walked back to Marla, who was sitting up in bed reading the newspaper, her face a picture of astonishment. "I think that you should stay home today," Emma said. "You know, I have begged you over and over again not to become involved in any political protest, no matter what your feelings are. I cannot have you draw attention to yourself."

"I am sorry, Ma," Marla answered, "but I was simply curious, that is all. I just wanted to see what was happening."

Emma walked out of her room downstairs into the kitchen. "Would you like some breakfast?" she shouted.

"Yes, please, Ma," Marla answered. She climbed out of her bed, put on her gown and walked downstairs into the kitchen. She looked at Emma, and saw a very beautiful but very angry woman. She often wondered why her mother had never married again, even though she had gone out on the occasional date, usually with someone arranged by Irma Rosen.

About two weeks later, they drove to Potchefstroom to spend the weekend with Charlie and Christa. Marie, Johan and their children were there, and both Emma and Marla were looking forward to see-ing them. As was the custom with Charlie, he prepared a braai, in the back yard. They all sat under the grapevine sipping wine while Charlie looked after the steaks and boerewors sizzling on the fire. Christa, as usual, was in the kitchen with her two maids preparing the vegetables, salads and dessert.

Charlie whistled as he barbecued his customary boerewors, with large steaks for himself and Johan. By now he knew the dietary habits of his family and didn't have to ask what they wanted to eat.

"So," he said to Marla as she stood watching him at the barbecue, "I see that you are becoming a typical Somerset Maugham follower."

Marla frowned and looked at him, puzzled. "What do you mean, Gran'pa Charlie?" she asked.

"Well," he answered as he turned over the boerwors, the fat crackling and spitting so that the flames licked the meat he was barbecuing. "Somerset Maugham was a very famous English writer. In one of his books, and I forget which one, he wrote that 'if you are a student and you are not against your parents; are not against society in general and are not against the government, then you belong in a mental asylum. When you are no longer a student, if you are against your parents, and you are against society in general and you are against the government, then you belong in a mental asylum,' or words to that effect."

Marla laughed. "You are talking about my photo at the protest march. Well, as I told Ma, I wasn't involved in it. I was just one of the many spectators. I did become angry when the police started to arrest the students who were in the march. Costas was one of those arrested. I understand that they kept him in jail for three days. Apparently he was one of the organizers of the protest."

"Were you one of those arrested?" Charlie asked looking at her closely to see if there was any reaction to his question. "You can tell me the truth."

Marla looked down at her hands. Then, after a few minutes she looked up at him. He was watching her closely.

"Yes Gran'pa," she said slowly, her face white with her consternation. "I was arrested, but after about two hours, I was released and allowed to go home." She frowned, thought for a few minutes then continued. "The others that were arrested with me, they were kept in jail overnight. I don't understand why I was released and no-one else was."

Looking at him, her face a picture of sadness, she implored him, her voice breaking as she spoke. "Please don't tell Mom, she doesn't know. If she found out what really happened, she would be very angry with me."

"Your mother tells me that you are starting to ask her a lot of questions about the politics in the country, and that you have formed some very definite opinions on what is happening here. Is this you, or is it your university friends that have given you your opinions? What have you concluded?"

"Well, Gran'pa," Marla began hesitantly, "for a long time I have been thinking about things in South Africa. That's one of the reasons why I decided to study sociology and go overseas when I am qualified. Do you remember Josh Stern?"

"Of course I do," Charlie answered.

"Well, before he went to London, a few of us went to a small party at his house to say goodbye to him and wish him well. Of course the conversation soon turned to politics, because of the policies that the National Party were putting into force. Costas, who was home for the weekend from Wits, was there, and he and Josh soon started arguing. Why, I don't know, because they both agreed that what the government was doing was wrong. Josh, to strengthen his argument, told us this story.

"Apparently, his father employs a Coloured woman called Dolly in the Pharmacy. Dolly started off as a housemaid, and has been with them for years. Josh told us that one night, after he had come back from serving in the Navy, he sat at the Pharmacy chatting to Dolly, and this is what she told him. But before I tell you what she said, I must add that Dolly is a Coloured girl and that means, according to the way Dolly told Josh, she is a person of a mixed race, half African and half European."

Charlie sat quietly, managing the braai; listening to what she said with interest.

"Of course, Josh knew that she was a Coloured but, according to Dolly, there are different types of Coloureds. There are those who look like Whites; those who look like Blacks, and those who look neither black nor white with their skin and facial features more like a light coffee colour than either black or white." She looked at Charles carefully before she continued, to see if he was listening to what she said.

"We all know that, and we also know that it can be confusing. But Dolly told Josh that she believes that there are Coloureds who are brilliant and extremely clever, and that there are Coloureds who are stupid and dumb. Nothing new, we see this even amongst us Whites. Josh told her exactly that. He also told her that there are Whites who are absolutely brilliant, like Albert Einstein, and that there are Whites who are stupid and dumb -- here he cited Hendrik Verwoerd as an example," and she laughed.

"Josh told me, Gran'pa, that Dolly argued that sometimes, the clever ones would look like an African, pitch black with kroes hair and a flat nose, and sometimes they would look like a White with straight hair and a pointed nose, and sometimes instead of being White, their skin would be coffee coloured. That you can never ever tell which colour is stupid and which is not. Josh told us that he then said to her, 'You are not telling me something new. Why is this so important? ' Dolly apparently answered that she believed that a true African Black is a stupid person and that they can only learn so much. But then you find one who looks like an African, and they are extremely clever, then you know that they are not a true African but a Coloured.

"'So you in actual fact are calling an African stupid,' Josh told us he said to her.

"'No,' she answered him, 'not stupid, stupid, but just not that clever. It is as if something is missing, something I believe that only the Whites have. When they have sex, the Whites with a Black, they sometimes pass that clever thing on, and sometimes they just don't. The African African and by this I mean the true black African, does not have that clever thing. You watch.'

Josh told us that Dolly believes that the Africans are taking over the countries that the British ruled, and they are going to make a mess of everything."

Marla looked around her. Charlie and Johan sat silently listening to what she said.

"Is Dolly that lady working in the back of the pharmacy?" Charlie eventually asked.

"Yes," Marla answered, "when the kids grew up, she left the house and went to work in the pharmacy. Josh told us that she was in charge of the stock, and that she was so good his father paid her a very good salary, in actual fact more than he paid some of his White salesladies. He said that even though she had four children, she was always at work and never missed a day."

Emma had quietly walked up behind Marla, and had listened carefully to what she had said. Charles looked at her, but she shook her head, so he said very carefully, "Do you believe all that nonsense?"

"I have often thought about it," Marla answered, "but then I think to myself that there are clever people all over no matter what their colour is, and there are people who are simply stupid. I remember my Ma always telling me that it is how you are educated that decides you. If you have a good teacher, or if you work hard at learning, then you will be clever, and be successful in life. If you don't work hard at school, or are taught badly, then you can only fail as you grow older and go into the world."

She thought for a minute, then continued, "the other thing Dolly told Josh, which surprised him, is that her brother lives in Johannesburg. He has been classified by the Government as a White and he works as a bank teller at Volkskas Bank. Ever since Josh told us this story, I have often wondered how a brother can be classified a White and his sister classified a Coloured. To me this shows that the whole race classification system really is a mess and should be abolished."

Charlie offered her a fork with a piece of boerewors. She shook her head.

"No thank you," she said. "You know I am a vegetarian."

"For a moment I forgot," Charlie answered, offering the boerewors to Johan.

"You know Gran'pa Charles, I often listen to the other students at the University, and sometimes I think that what they say is truly ridiculous. I just simply cannot fathom what they are driving at, or what they want and that is the point. There are a lot of them that criticize the government policies. Most of what they say is justified, but they don't come up with a solution to the problem. I agree that the country must get rid of apartheid, but, is a country that has one vote one person the answer? I don't believe that it is."

She frowned. "You know, next week, Helen Suzman is coming to talk to us. I very much want to go and listen to her. She is a very clever woman. Perhaps she can answer some of my questions."

Johan, who had carefully listened to everything she said, stood up and walking to the table, refilled his glass of wine. "You know," he said turning to Marla, "everything you say is something that many of us at camp used to talk about, but then being helpless to do anything about it, we just learned to live with the way things are. This apartheid regime will die, as all bad things die. The problem that faces us is what type of government will come afterwards."

Marla turned around to face him and as she did so, she saw Emma standing behind her, and smiled.

"Helen Suzman is a very clever lady," Johan said, walking to the barbecue. "She will give Verwoerd a lot of headaches. I have heard that one of Verwoerd's ministers asked her why she keeps asking questions in Parliament that embarrass South Africa. Apparently she answered, 'It is not my questions that embarrass South Africa, it is your answers.'"

They all laughed.

"Well said," Charlie grinned, removing the meat from the barbecue and putting it on plates. "The more headaches she gives them, the better. They are a bunch of verkramptes, and a clever Jewish woman is what they need to pull them straight."

"I have been fortunate in that I have met her," Emma said as they sat around the table preparing to eat. "Irma Rosen invited her to lunch one day, and she invited me as well. She is a charming woman, a true lady. I had a wonderful afternoon and really enjoyed talking to her."

"Ma, you never told me," Marla said, clearly upset. "Oh, Ma, I would have loved to have been there with you."

"She told us," Emma continued, "that her phone is tapped by the police. What she does is blow a whistle into the phone before she talks, and that soon fixes that."

"Clever idea," Johan laughed, "that must give plenty of eavesdroppers a nasty headache."

"When you think about it," Charlie said, "she is the only woman, English speaking and Jewish at that, in a parliament dominated by a bunch of Calvinist, Afrikaans-speaking men. That is one heck of a challenge. I take my hat off to her."

"She also told us, and I never thought about it before, "Emma continued, "that whenever the Nats decide to have their yearly general party meeting in Johannesburg, they arrange to hold it on the Jewish New Year. She jokes that this is to keep her from gate crashing the meeting, and asking them questions which they cannot answer."

Christa came out of the kitchen, with Marie and the two maids carrying the vegetables and salad. "Come on all of you, enough politics for now, let us talk about something nice," and turning to Marla she asked, "and how is University treating you, liefie? That was a good photo of you I saw in *Die Transvaaler*."

Later that night, as Emma lay in bed reading, Marla came to wish her goodnight. Emma put down her book and said to her, "Marla?"

"Yes, Mom," Marla answered, stifling a yawn.

"What that girl, Dolly, said is not true."

Marla sat on the edge of the bed, suddenly awake,

"Were you listening to what I said?" she asked, surprised.

"Yes, I was," Emma answered. "Dolly's story was wrong because people are all born with equal opportunities, with the exception of those that are born with brain damage. Yes, you will get some people more clever than others, that is genetic, but the average person, and let us not confuse them with the savant, or the Einstein, all have the same brain ability."

"But Mom," Marla answered her, "why are the Blacks in South Africa so... so... I don't want to use the word, but so backward?"

"I believe that the difference between them and us is in the education that they receive. Often that education is tribal, with tribal customs and traditions, and that is difficult to forget. For example, many tribes believe in polygamy, and I can understand why. History shows us that the men were raised to be hunters and fighters. If they were killed, their widow needed a hunter to supply food for her and her children and a man to care for them. She will then join a family where the hunter is strong and become a second, third, even fourth wife. Take their custom of a woman having to give birth to a male child before the man will marry her. That is very much a 'no-no' in our westernized society, but very much a 'yes-yes' in their society, even today.

"To my way of thinking, it does not matter what the colour of one's skin is, it is simply a matter of education. Never, ever forget that. I am sure that you learned at Wits, that evolution might change the physical appearance of one's body, and intersexual relationships between the various races can add to that, but the ability to learn among the different races throughout the world remains the same and depends on the quality of education received. We Whites have received a westernized education, in a democratic society where the state puts the welfare of its citizens ahead of the welfare of the governing individual, which I believe is the best form of government there is. But that is my personal opinion, and I am open to correction. I feel that Josh's Dolly is very wrong with her assumptions, and I must add that I am quite shocked at them. With all that I have said, there is one thing that worries me, though."

"What is that? Marla asked, looking at her mother as though seeing her for the first time.

"In a democratic society, the people elect the government. In South Africa, the Africans outnumber all the other racial groups. On the whole, they are uneducated. When they come to power, and they will come to power, there is no doubt about that, they will elect an uneducated man to run this country." She shook her head slowly.

"It will take three generations, if not more, before the Africans are westernized. Until that happens, the country could go to the dogs."

"Ma," Marla looked at her, astonished, "I never knew that you were so up in your feelings."

"There is a lot about me that you do not know," Emma smiled. "Now, goodnight my dear, and you sleep well," and she leaned forward and kissed Marla on her forehead.

Chapter 9

In November 1962, the United Nations adopted a resolution condemning apartheid. Marla and her friends held a party to celebrate the decision, feeling that their protests were achieving something.

"Ma," she said, after Emma once again lectured her over her student activism, "don't worry about me. I am working hard, and I will pass all my exams."

And pass she did, proud when the head of the department asked her whether she would not consider continuing her studies for a Masters degree and ultimately a Doctorate. She told him that she would think about it, but that she first needed a break from studying. She wanted to travel overseas and see a bit of the world before coming to a decision on how to plan her life.

Marla graduated from the University of the Witwatersrand with a degree in sociology. She had enjoyed being a student at Wits. Although Emma had asked her not to become politically involved in any organization, something any student would find hard not to do, she had initially been very active, but later had worked behind the scenes at every protest meeting against the policies of the Nationalist Government, simply because her friends were active. She did not want to be left out of the party scene.

.

The reality of where her future lay started to take precedence over political demonstrations. Yes, she had been in jail with her friends, and yes she became even more politically involved, but a lot more careful. Emma was continually begging her not to draw attention to herself and Marla always promised her that she would give up all political activity, but she didn't. The enjoyment of standing on the stage in front of a hall filled with rowdy students, shouting her political beliefs into a microphone, was something she enjoyed. She was constantly reminded of what Charlie Stuart had told her about the Somerset Maugham quotation, ' ...*but when you are no longer a student...*'

That December, she relaxed at the swimming pool at her home with friends or, more than often, without friends, catching up on her reading. She sat with Emma in the evenings as the sun set, with a glass of wine. She found her mother an interesting person to talk to, and delighted in being with her. Often, Irma Rosen and her family would come over for a meal, or they would drive to her home for the evening. It was all very pleasant and relaxing.

"So, what are your plans for the future?" Emma asked her one evening.

"Ma," she replied hesitantly, not sure how to tell Emma, "Before I go looking for a job, and settle down, I would like to travel and see a bit of the world. Professor Wilson at Wits has asked me to study further and get my Masters degree, but I don't think I want to do that just yet."

Emma's heart stopped. The fear of being found out even after all these years was still with her. She looked at Marla and saw, no longer a girl, but a young woman and knew that she simply could not say no. Marla would be 22 years old in a few months, a woman in her own right.

"When and where do you want to go?" she asked, not looking at Marla.

"A couple of girls I know from Wits, well, we decided that we would like to start by going to London. Josh is still there doing his apprenticeship, and he wrote and told me that he will find us accommodation and show us around. We would like to tour England and if we have the time, perhaps the Continent."

"For how long?" Emma burst out, amazed that Marla already had a plan in place.

"Don't know yet, Mom. I wrote to Josh about it and he wrote back saying that travelling and seeing England on its own could take anywhere from three to six months; that London alone with all its shows will keep us busy for at least two of those months, if not longer. I think I can say well, six months maximum, or until we get homesick or until the money runs out, whichever comes first."

"I think you should have a set plan or itinerary. If I can, I may even join you. I have always wanted to see London," Emma lied. She was far more protective toward Marla than she should have been.

"Thanks, Ma. I will work out an itinerary with Amy and Victoria, and let you have it. It would be wonderful if you did join us." Marla gave Emma a hug and felt the stiffness melt from Emma's body as she did so.

"Amy and Victoria? Do I know them?" Emma asked hesitantly, trying not to sound too controlling.

"Yes, Ma, both girls have been to the house."

"So many of your friends have come to swim," Emma said, "I just cannot remember them at all."

Marla smiled. "Amy is the girl you thought was so lovely. She is small and petite, on the plump side, with black hair, black eyes and a lovely smile. The two of you got on so well together. She helped you prepare lunch in the kitchen.

"Victoria is the girl you thought was a bit too muscular for a girl. She is the tall blonde, with light blue eyes that you felt were almost white. She enjoys working out in the gym, which is why she is so athletic. Do you remember?"

"Yes, now I do. Isn't Victoria the girl I thought was a lesbian?"

"Yes, that is right," Marla answered, smiling, "But I can assure you, she is far from homosexual, more likely the opposite. She is the one who takes the initiative and chases the boys."

Two months later, Marla, Amy and Victoria were on the RMS *Capetown Castle* en route to London. Emma had been stressed until

Marla's passport arrived, only then relaxing and bubbling with enthusiasm. Marla found this a bit strange, especially when Emma bought her far more clothes than she really needed and gave her a comfortable bank account.

She had written to Josh, telling him of their plans. He wrote back that he would meet them at Victoria Station. He would arrange digs for them and, with John Williams, would become their London tour guide.

The two-week trip to England was very relaxing, with most of their days spent lying in the sun at the swimming pool. The three girls shared a cabin with a porthole, which they kept open, enjoying the cool, fresh air as the ship sailed through the heat of the equator. There was always some form of entertainment in the evenings. When the ship crossed the equator, at a large ceremony, 'King Neptune' christened those passengers who were crossing for the first time by dunking them in the swimming pool.

Sailing through the Canary Islands, the ship docked for a day at Santa Cruz, allowing them to disembark and tour the island. They were thrilled, for the first time enjoying a culture that was not African. They found a restaurant near a lighthouse overlooking a beach of white sand. The menu boasted different types of fish and prawns prepared in a nest of parmesan cheese. Neither of the girls had ever eaten prawns, and they thoroughly enjoyed them, especially with a glass of cold Spanish white wine.

When the ship blew its horn, calling them all to embark, they were sad to leave, yet excited to be on their way once again to England. Marla bought a brightly coloured shawl from a vendor, who had halved his original price, as they walked up the gangplank into the ship.

As they sailed through the Bay of Biscay, known for the choppiness of the ocean, Victoria, much to her embarrassment, became seasick. She was very happy when two days later the ship entered the calm waters of the English Channel, docking at Southampton.

Marla loved London almost as soon as they arrived. Josh had bought them tickets for the show *My Fair Lady*, which was performing at the Drury Lane Theatre. Before the show they had dinner at Josh's favorite Indian restaurant, the New Assam in Chelsea, around the corner from where he had found them accommodation on Bayswater road. For them, the show with Julie Andrews, Rex Harrison and Stanley Holloway was a perfect introduction to England.

Josh had warned them that just living and sightseeing in London was a tour in itself. They walked the streets, marveling at the sights the city had to offer. They sat at Piccadilly Circus under the statue of Eros, trying to decide which street they should walk up first. Should it be Regent Street, Shaftesbury Avenue, Piccadilly or Coventry Street? Should they visit the National Gallery first and then Covent Gardens, or should they walk through Admiralty Arch into St. James's Park to Buckingham Palace? There was so much to see and enjoy.

That first Sunday, Josh took them to meet the Wises in Whitechapel. After a breakfast of fried eggs and chips prepared by Kaye, they spent the afternoon walking through the stalls in the East End, looking for bargains to take home as souvenirs. They spent a day catching a boat up the Thames to Kew Gardens, where they saw plants collected from all over the world in the large greenhouses. Windsor Castle, the official residence of Her Majesty the Queen was another must. Unfortunately the flag was not flying, telling them that the Queen was not in residence. They walked through the state apartments of the castle admiring the treasures from the Royal Collection, then sat and rested, eating the sandwiches they had brought with them in the gardens surrounding the castle, watching the changing of the guard.

John Williams invited them to spend a weekend in Slough with his family, and they walked through the fields behind the house, where Josh and John showed them the tower, and told them the story about Livvy.

On the advice of John and his stepfather Reg, they planned a tour of England. It was April, with spring blossoming throughout the country. They wanted to see as much of England, Scotland and Wales as they could and John and Reg helped them plan an itinerary. They would travel by train or bus and work their way slowly through the country, sleeping in youth hostels or bed and breakfasts.

"You have to visit Oxford and Stratford-upon-Avon," Reg said, "and work your way slowly up to Windermere in the Lake District. From there you can visit Edinburgh if you want to. You must see Scotland."

"What about Wales?" Marla asked, "I love the Welsh accent."

"Well, if you really like coal mines, I suppose you could go there," John laughed. "The countryside, I must say, is very beautiful. To get there you would travel through Hereford, and Josh knows all about Hereford," and he looked at Josh and laughed.

"What happened at Hereford?" Amy asked Josh.

"Well, two summers ago, over the holidays, I decided to earn some extra cash and took a job on a farm in Hereford for two weeks. It was a large farm, and there were three of us students. We slept in one of the stables in sleeping bags.

"The first problem I had was that I simply could not understand what the farmer was saying, his accent was so bad. When I thought I knew what he said, I was usually wrong. The first day we were there, he gave the three of us each a spade, and told us to move the horse manure out of the stables into the yard. We had to pile it on a cart. He would use it as fertilizer in the fields. Well, those stables had horse manure waist high because the horses had been stabled there all winter. It took us the whole day to clear it. By the end of the day we stank. When we asked the farmer where we could shower, he pointed to a tap in the yard with a basin. That was it."

They all laughed.

"Fortunately for us," Josh continued, "his wife came along while we were standing in our underwear, freezing, washing ourselves with water that was very cold. She took all our clothes to wash. She was a large woman, always with a smile. I must say that her breakfasts were to die for."

"Tell them about what happened to you when you went into the field," John said.

"OK, but I do feel embarrassed about what happened," Josh answered softly, almost to himself. "About the third or fourth day, we were taken to the field and shown how to use a hoe to work on the weeds. It was hot, and the farmer had an apple orchard, so he brought a barrel of apple juice for us to drink and quench our thirst. We were all thirsty and drank a lot. That was our first experience with apple juice and we all drank far more than we should have. That afternoon, they had to load the three of us into the wagon, to take us back to the farm. We were all so drunk we couldn't hoe straight, let alone walk straight. The farmer was very angry with us."

Josh frowned, not sure whether he should continue. After a moment's thought, he said, "The one bad day that I had was when we were baling hay. I was on top of the haystack, packing the hay into the baling machine as the two other students threw the hay up to me. One of the students was a Nigerian and when he learned that I was a South African, he kept ribbing me. He was bigger and stronger than I was and kept throwing the hay up to me far quicker than I could pack it, and then shouting at me because I was too slow. Unfortunately I lost my rag, and from the top of the haystack I threw my pitchfork at the ground in front of him. It landed on his foot. Fortunately for him and for me, the middle blade was only half a blade, so nothing penetrated his foot, but I will never forget his face. He never bothered me again, but after that I wasn't at all popular with the farmer."

He shook his head and looked at the map. "Don't go through Hereford," he pointed to the area on the map, "it is only farmland. Rather go north into the Lake District; that is so much more beautiful."

"From Stratford-upon-Avon you should go straight to Edinburgh, and see a bit of Scotland." John continued, taking over from Josh. "You can have a look at the bridge over the Firth of Forth, and if you want to, go into the highlands. The little villages are really beautiful, but I must admit that once you have seen one, you have seen them all. And then of course you must visit the pubs, where you meet the locals and England in its many dialects."

"But I only drink wine, not beer," said Victoria.

"That is OK," John answered, smiling at her. "You can ask them for a 'cuppa cha 'n a boen.'"

"A what?" Amy asked.

John laughed, "Cockney for a cup of tea and a bun. Sometimes when I am in a pub, especially up near Manchester or Birmingham, I wonder whether the locals indeed talk English."

"You know," Josh said, "I wrote my final exams in Edinburgh, and spent a few days touring there. I walked through the town and saw a shop advertising tartans for all the tourists. I walked in, and a very polite man with a heavy Scottish accent came up to serve me. Putting on the best Scottish accent I had, rolling my 'r's, I asked him if they had the McSterrrrnrr tarrrtan because I was looking forrr a kilt. He actually went to a register, and started looking through it, then he came back to where I was looking at the kilts, and said, 'sorrrry sirrrr, I canno' find one. Perrrrhaps you should considerrrr the Stuarrrrt tarrrrrtan."

"A good salesman," Marla laughed, enjoying the story.

That night they packed their kitbags and went to bed early because they wanted to catch an early train to Oxford. Josh came with a cab to collect them and their luggage, which he said he would look after until they came back. He then had the cab take them to the station.

Oxford would be their first stop. They planned to spend at least two days there wandering through the town. They found the city quaint with its individual colleges that made up the university. The buildings were very beautiful and historic. They took a walking tour of one of the colleges, each of which is protected by a high wall that opened up with courtyards and grass quadrangles. They walked alongside the River Cherwell that flows into the Thames, where they watched the university boat crews training.

Marla decided that she preferred London to Oxford and, after two days, was happy to leave. They worked their way to Stratford-upon-Avon, where William Shakespeare was born, and were lucky enough to get tickets for the play *Macbeth*.

"Let us go to Edinburgh and then work our way through the Lake District, as Josh said we should," Victoria said to them. "He really had fun in Edinburgh."

The very next day they caught the train directly to Edinburgh. They felt that looking at the grand architecture in the different towns was like looking at the same buildings, with the same shops and tourist attractions.

Edinburgh was different from London, a smaller city with cobbled alleys and shops geared to tourists, dominated by Edinburg Castle built on sheer granite cliffs overlooking the city. They paid for a guided tour of the castle, marveling at the panoramic views from the upper stories. When they walked through the Old Town, a medieval city crowded with multistoried tenements dating from the 15th century, they felt as though they had stepped back in time.

They caught a tour bus to the Firth of Forth to look at the bridge that spanned it.

"The tour guide says," Victoria said, reading the pamphlet she held in her hand, "that this bridge is made entirely of steel, and was built in 1890."

"Why is that so important?" Amy asked.

"The pamphlet writes that up until then, everything was built out of wrought iron. The Eiffel Tower in Paris is wrought iron. This bridge was the first major construction using steel."

"How interesting," Amy yawned.

After a few days they had walked and seen enough of Edinburgh. As planned, they caught the bus to Windermere in the Lake District.

Their hike started on the shores of Lake Windermere through a forest of oak trees, heading towards the village of Troutbeck, where they explored the beautiful 17th Century farmhouses spread along a narrow lane bordered by dry-stone walls. They then followed the narrow trail to Grasmere on the side of a mountain, with Grasmere Lake shimmering far below them. Marla wanted to find Dove Cottage, where William Wordsworth wrote his famous poem, "I wondered lonely as a cloud…," a poem that was a set piece for her matric year.

It was on their way there, walking on the side of one of the steep hills, that they realized they had taken the wrong trail to get to the youth hostel where they had planned to spend the night. From where they stood, they could see the hostel some distance below them. Because it was getting dark, rather than retrace their steps and walk back to the fork in the path, they decided to risk walking down the steep mountainside to the hostel below. As they neared the bottom, Marla slipped on the grass falling on her back. She grabbed at whatever she could to break her fall but nothing held. With a cry of pain she fell down the incline onto the lower trail, landing heavily on her left foot in front of three male hikers.

"I say, Bertie," one of the hikers said, "look at what dropped in."

Bertie looked at Marla as she lay on the trail in front of him, holding her ankle, the tears streaming from her eyes. "Eddie," he said, "it looks like this beautiful angel has hurt herself," and he knelt next to Marla. "Angel," he said to Marla, "let me help you," and taking Marla's foot he untied the shoelaces of her boot and very carefully slipped it off her foot. "Where does it hurt?" he asked.

"I think I may have broken my ankle," she sobbed. "It hurts terribly."

"George," Bertie called to one of the boys with him, "you are a fourth-year medical student. Have a look at this angelic ankle."

George knelt down, removed Marla's boot and examined her ankle, moving it slowly from side to side, listening carefully. "No, I don't think she has broken it," he said, "but only an X-ray can confirm that. I think that she might just have sprained it badly."

Just then Amy and Victoria appeared.

"Good heavens," Eddie said, "look at that, we have another two angels."

Amy and Victoria knelt next to Marla, concern all over their faces.

"Are you badly hurt?" Victoria asked.

Marla looked at her, her eyes full of tears. "I think I may have sprained my ankle," she said.

"Where are you headed?" Bertie asked, carefully removing her sock.

"The youth hostel," Victoria answered.

"Well then, Eddie, you take her back pack and boot and I will take her." Without any effort, he lifted Marla into his arms and walked down the trail toward the hostel. Amy, Victoria, Eddie and George followed them, soon chatting as though they had known each other all their lives.

Bertie looked at this girl he was carrying in his arms. She had her arms around his neck, and had rested her head on his shoulder. Her face was streaked with her tears, her bottom lip quivering with the pain from her ankle.

"She is as light as a feather," he thought, "and not only that, she is also a very beautiful girl."

"My friends all call me Bertie," he said to her, "and if you want to be my friend, then that is what you will have to call me."

Marla tried to smile, "I will remember that," she said through her tears.

"And what is your name, other than Angel?" he asked her, trying to coax a smile. "Consider, here I am carrying the most beautiful of all angels and we have not even been formally introduced."

"My name is Marla," she answered, "Marla O'Neil."

"That surname is Irish," Bertie said, "but that accent is…?"

"South African," Marla answered, grimacing with pain.

"Ah, yes," Bertie remembered, "I should have known that, but then I hardly know any South Africans, or even Australians for that matter, although I did meet a South African a couple of years ago with an accent similar to yours. Well, here we are," and he walked through the front door of the youth hostel, greeting the receptionist at the desk.

"Madam," he said, "I have in my arms a very beautiful angel, a Marla O'Neil who has hurt herself on the trail. She and her two friends are booked in here for the evening, but she does need a doctor. Unfortunately it is getting quite dark outside, so I do believe that we will only get to Grasmere and a doctor tomorrow morning." He pointed to Amy and Victoria, who had only just walked in with George and Eddie. "These two young ladies are with her, although," and he frowned as he looked at the two boys who both had happy smiles on their faces, "I really do not know for how long."

Looking at the register the receptionist replied, "Yes, sir, I have them here. If you three ladies could sign the register, I will show you where your room is."

"Uhh, Bertie," Marla said, "you can put me down now. I think I can stand on one foot without too much pain."

"Oh yes, of course," Bertie said, "just when I was starting to enjoy holding you so close." He put Marla down carefully, making sure that she could stand on one leg. Her ankle was starting to look swollen, so he said, "George, leave those two girls alone. I think you had better strap up that ankle. It is beginning to look a bit nasty."

He turned to the receptionist, "Madam," he said, "I am sure you have a first aid kit here. My friend over there," and he pointed to George, who was talking to Victoria, "is a fourth-year medical student, who I believe knows, or we hope he knows, what he is doing most of the time," and he frowned at George. "I know that he would like to look through it and see if there is anything he could use."

"Yes, we do have one," the receptionist said, and she reached under the desk and gave George a box with a red cross on it. George opened it, poked around and took out a crepe bandage.

"This will do nicely," he said, starting to unwrap it.

Marla carefully hopped over to the sofa, supported by Bertie's eager arm, his hand around her waist, and sat down. George looked at her ankle and slowly started to strap it. "Just tell me if it is too tight," he told Marla.

While George was busy with Marla's ankle, Bertie said to the receptionist, "Madam, we are three young hikers who came across this damsel in distress. Because the sun has now set, we will not be able to get to Grasmere, where we have a reservation. Is it at all possible that you have a room available?" and he gave her his sweetest smile.

"You are lucky; I do have a room. I had a cancellation early this afternoon. It has only two beds in it, but we can place a mattress on the floor, if that is acceptable," she replied. "I am sure that you all want dinner, which will be available in an hour's time, and is an additional charge. Shall I say dinner for six?"

"But of course," Bertie answered, "Where would you like me to sign?"

The three girls found their room very pleasant. Marla noticed that Victoria and Amy spent more time on their dress and makeup than they usually did as they prepared themselves for dinner. '*They must fancy the two boys,*' she thought and smiled to herself. '*I must say, that Bertie himself is quite good-looking. It was pleasant being carried by him.*'

When they went down for dinner, Marla leaning on Victoria's arm hopped slowly down the stairs. They found the three boys already sitting at a table, drinking beer.

"You are sitting here, next to me," Bertie said, walking to Marla and Victoria. Taking Marla's arm, he led her to a chair. Victoria and Amy looked at each other and smiled. Very soon, they were all chatting away, with the boys wanting to know more about South Africa. The meal served was nothing special, but was enjoyable. The fresh mountain air had made them all very hungry.

After dinner, they sat in the lounge drinking coffee, Victoria and Amy still talking about South Africa. Marla felt tired, the tension of the day's events starting to take its toll.

"You look tired," Bertie said, noticing how she felt. "Shall I help you up to your room?"

"I would like that," Marla answered.

Before she could say anything he lifted her in his arms and started to carry her upstairs. Marla blushed.

"Marla is tired," Bertie said. "I am taking her upstairs where I will put her to bed and tuck her in," he joked.

"Yeah, best of luck, old boy," Eddie laughed. "Just see that that is all you do." Victoria and Amy looked slyly at each other.

The next morning after breakfast, Marla, Victoria and Amy prepared to leave the hostel and make their way to Grasmere. Marla could hardly stand on her ankle, which did feel so much better after a night's treatment with ice packs. Bertie offered to carry her backpack and help her as much as he could.

They slowly made their way to Grasmere, with George and Victoria running ahead to see if he could find the doctor for Marla, who hobbled slowly, leaning on Bertie's arm.

The village doctor, a portly man with a very caring bedside manner, believed that her ankle was not broken, but that she had suffered a bad sprain which would be painful for a few days. He gave her some painkilling tablets and advised her to buy a cane at one of the shops down the road.

"Put as little weight on it as you can," he advised. "If you can fund a crutch, I would suggest you use it rather than the cane. I am sorry, but I do not have one to give you."

He then told her that if it still troubled her, she should have it examined at a hospital. George smiled with pleasure as his diagnosis was confirmed.

The girls then decided that Victoria and Amy would continue their hike into Windermere. George and Eddie offered to walk with them, while Bertie insisted on staying with Marla.

"There is no way that I shall leave you alone," Bertie said to her. "You need someone to walk with you, and I am he."

Marla laughed, surprised but pleased with his decision.

Wordsworth had described Grasmere as "the loveliest spot that man hath ever found," and Marla thought that he was right. She loved the village with its stone buildings dating from the 19th to early 20th Century. With Bertie alongside her, she hobbled slowly to the St. Oswald's Church, built sometime in the 13th Century. Marla went inside and sat in a pew, meditating and thinking about the events of the past few weeks. Bertie sat quietly next to her, not saying a word, but wondering what she was thinking. Every now and then he would sneak a peek at her profile as she sat with her eyes closed, as though praying.

"*I simply cannot believe what is happening to me every time I look at her,*" he thought, shaking his head. "*It is as though I am in a different world.*"

Eventually Marla stood up and they walked out of the Church, crossing the road to look at the inn called the Church Stile, where William Wordsworth had stayed with his brother, John, during their Lake District tour in 1797.

They made their way to the churchyard where Wordsworth was buried and stood looking at his grave, his wife, Mary, buried next to him. Both graves were marked by simple tombstones surrounded by lawns that were a yellow sea of daffodils.

"I can see how he could not have helped himself but write his most famous poem," Marla said to Bertie.

"So you know his work, then?" Bertie asked her.

"Yes," Marla answered, "we studied his poetry at school."

They sat in the churchyard for over an hour talking.

"Tell me all about yourself," Bertie asked her. "Leave nothing out."

Marla started talking about her life in Potchefstroom as a child, the different Afrikaans schools she had gone to and the friends she had made. She told him about her adopted grandparents, Charlie and Christa, and how much she loved them. About Irma Rosen and her family, how and why they had come to South Africa. She told him that her father had been killed in the war; how her mother, as a single Mom, had worked hard all her life; how Emma had moved to Johannesburg when she, Marla, went to university there. She didn't know why she was telling him all this, it just seemed so natural.

She told him about the politics of the country, how she detested the apartheid laws; how her dog Gamboo had been poisoned and how, to avenge Gamboo's death, she had taken an active part in the anti-government protests when she was at university. She even told him that she had been arrested.

He listened to her talk, not saying a word, all the time looking at her as she spoke. '*My God,*' he thought to himself, '*what is happening to me?*'

After a while, almost as though she was awakening from a trance, she stopped talking, sitting quietly looking at the daffodils around her.

"I think it is time we continued exploring," she eventually said, looking at Bertie.

He stood up and helped her to her feet.

Marla enjoyed his company, and his pleasantness. She thought that he was very good looking, with light, almost blond hair and a fair skin. His eyes were dark blue, and either side of his mouth boasted two dimples etched by his continual smile.

They soon found Dove Cottage, now a tourist spot on the outskirts of the village. The house was made from local stone with white limewashed walls boasting red rambling roses growing as high as the black slate roof. They walked slowly through the rooms, Marla feeling a comfort she had never felt before. *"Is it being in this room or is it Bertie?"* she thought.

At three o'clock, after a light lunch that Bertie insisted on paying for, they caught the bus to Windermere.

"Will I be seeing you tomorrow?" Bertie asked Marla as he took her to the hostel where they had arranged to meet Victoria and Amy. They were to spend the night there before catching the bus back to London.

"We are leaving for London early tomorrow morning," she said.

"At least allow me to buy all of you dinner," he asked.

"But you have spent so much on us already," she replied, frowning.

"Then we will make it a light snack," he said. "By the way, do you have a London phone number or address? I would like to keep in touch with you, to find out how your ankle is," he said quickly, almost as an afterthought.

"We are staying with a friend. Josh is looking after our luggage until we get back and find a place to stay. This is his phone number."

"Did you say his name is Josh?" he asked as he scribbled the number she gave him on a piece of paper. "And I suppose his surname is Stern."

"How did you know?" She asked, puzzled. "Do you know Josh?"

He smiled, and exclaimed, "In a way, yes, I do. I thought it must be fate, you dropping in like that. Now, I know for sure that it definitely was something written in the stars, something that was meant to be."

"What do you mean by that?" she asked, still puzzled.

"One day I will tell you," he answered with a smile. "I have never, ever believed in fate, but I see that I was wrong." He nodded his head thoughtfully, "I now have a great deal to do when I get back to London, and before I see you."

"See me in London?" she asked, hope showing in her voice.

"But of course," he answered. "One never argues with fate."

That night as she lay in her bed, she found that she simply couldn't sleep. She could not stop thinking about Bertie, what a pleasant person he was and how much she had enjoyed being with him. Lying in bed, she puzzled over what he had said about fate, and wondered at his obsession.

Eventually she got out of bed trying not to wake Victoria and Amy, who were fast asleep. She sat at the window thinking, looking out into the village, all lit up with a full moon, until the sun slowly showed itself, lightening up the sky. Then, stretching herself as though clearing her thoughts, she hobbled to the bathroom to wash the sleep out of her face.

Chapter 10

T he X-ray of her ankle taken at the London hospital where Josh was doing his pharmacy apprenticeship showed that she had cracked a bone. They put her ankle in a plaster cast.

"Girls, with my foot in this cast, I feel that I will be a handicap to both of you on your tour through Europe," she told Amy and Victoria when she saw them. "As much as I would like to go with you, I had better stay here until it is healed."

For some reason she had not yet been able to fathom, her heart was no longer in it. She was tired, and homesick. George had asked Amy and Victoria if he could join them in her place, and they were happy to have him with them. They left for Holland by ferry, their plan being to see as much of Holland as they could, then work their way slowly through Belgium and then into Paris, France before returning to London.

Marla waited for a phone call from Bertie. She had warned Josh that if someone phoned looking for her, he must please give him her phone number. With every day that passed, she started to assume that Bertie had forgotten her, and that she was just another passing fancy. Without realizing it, she became very depressed. She started spending most of her evenings at the Overseas Visitors Club in Earls Court, talking to anyone and everyone that wanted to chat with her. She hoped that by doing this she would stop thinking about him. Her plan worked well until she had to go to sleep, when she found that Bertie kept taking over her dreams.

It was just over a week later that he phoned her.

"May I speak with Miss Marla O'Neil?" he asked when she answered the phone.

She recognized his voice immediately, and her depression lifted. She felt wonderful. "This is she speaking," she answered, trying to hide the happiness in her voice.

"Marla, hello there, this is Bertie who you met on your hike in the Lake District. Sorry I took so long to get to you, but I was in Europe on business. I have only now returned to London. I phoned Josh for your number as you said I should, but it took a while to get hold of him. How are you keeping and how is your ankle?"

"My ankle? I cracked a bone and the doctor put my foot in a plaster cast, and..."

They seemed to speak forever on the phone. Eventually he asked her whether she would care to meet him for a coffee that evening. It was rather late but she agreed. They arranged to meet at a coffee bar on Kings Road close to where she lived.

"I am coming from Berkeley Square," he said, "so it should take me about a half hour to get there."

He wasn't there when she arrived, so she sat at a table waiting for him. When he did come, he was wearing a dress suit. He looked so dignified, so handsome that her heart skipped a beat.

"I must say that I am flattered that you should wear a tux to come and meet me," she said, stretching her foot with the plaster cast onto the chair next to her. "You do look very smart."

"Actually I was at a friend's wedding," he said. "I phoned from the desk at the hotel's reception, and sneaked away once you agreed to meet me."

She sipped at her coffee, trying not to look at him, scared that if she did, she would advertise her feelings for him. She was only now beginning to realize how much he meant to her.

"What took you so long to phone me?" she asked hesitantly, not sure if she should have asked him.

"I have only just returned from France. I told you before I left you that I had some urgent business to attend to. Tomorrow, I have to be in Germany for two days. It is all business. I have a lot of things to arrange now that I have met you. Well, I am almost there. Another week should see my schedule completed."

'*Is this his way of saying goodbye to me?*' she thought, '*Did he just call me to be polite, to inquire about my ankle?*' She felt a lump form in her throat. '*I must not cry. I must not show him how I feel about him.*' She gulped at her coffee, almost choking.

It was then, at the spur of the moment that she made a decision.

"Josh is returning to South Africa in a few days time and I have decided, because of my ankle, to go home."

He listened to her, his face a picture of sadness. Then, very earnestly and looking at her carefully he said, "I am truly sorry to hear that. Everything I am arranging now is because of meeting you. I will be very sorry to see you leave."

She thought for a minute and decided that she would make it easier for both of them if she showed that she did not care for him. "I would very much like to stay," she said coldly, looking at her coffee cup, not hearing what he was saying, "but I simply cannot, especially with this cast on my ankle. Better that I go home. She stood up, held out her hand and said, "Thank you, Bertie, thank you for being there when I needed you and thank you for…" and without meaning to, she burst into tears and hobbled out of the coffee shop down Kings Road as fast as she could.

He stood for a few seconds looking at her as she ran from him. Then, shaking his head, he ran after her.

"Marla," he said, "Marla…"

She turned to him. "Goodbye, Bertie," she said calmly. "I simply cannot stay in London anymore. I was leaving in a month's time at any rate, so now, because of my ankle, I am leaving a bit earlier than I originally planned." She held out her hand then withdrew it before he could take it in his. "Goodbye, Bertie, it was very nice to know you," and she hobbled away. He stood there watching her leave, his face a picture of utter dejection.

For the first night in a long time, Marla slept well, without dreaming of Bertie. He was now something in her past, forgotten and out of the way.

The next morning she went to the Union Castle Line offices, and managed to exchange her ticket for one on the same boat on which Josh was returning. She took the underground to the London hospital where the doctor removed the cast and bandaged her ankle. "As long as you take care and don't place it under too much stress for about a week, it should be fine," he advised her.

When she told Josh that she intended to sail back to South Africa with him, he was delighted. *'She must have got over her crush for that chap she met on her hike,'* he thought. *'Two weeks on a ship, having her all to myself, will be wonderful.'*

Three days later, Bertie jumped out of the taxi. Grabbing his suitcase, he ran up the stairs into his father's office.

"Mrs. Cartwright," he said to the secretary, "I have to see my father immediately." He put down his suitcase next to her desk. Without waiting for her to announce him, he opened the door to his father's office and walked in.

The office was paneled in wood dating back to the 16th and 17th centuries. On one wall above the fireplace hung a large painting by Thomas Gainsborough, framed by bookshelves holding a collection of first edition books. On the opposite wall was a painting by John Constable, an oil on canvas of Hadleigh Castle. Next to it hung a Gauguin with a van Gogh below.

Bertie stood quietly watching his father at his desk, arranged so that a view of the Thames and Houses of Parliament were framed behind him in the two heavily curtained windows. He was talking on the phone when Bertie walked in, and he beckoned to him to come in and sit down in one of the armchairs in front of a small bar, its counter boasting an assortment of liquor bottles and a vacuum holder of fresh ice cubes.

After a few minutes, he put the phone down, stood up and walked to where Bertie sat.

"Would you like something to drink?" he asked Bertie, walking behind the bar counter and taking a whisky glass.

"No, thank you, Father," Bertie said as Lord Winslow put three cubes of ice in the glass, then poured enough whisky to cover the ice. He twirled the glass, took a sip and then said, "Well, my boy, what can I do for you?"

"Father," Bertie said, turning to him, "I have rushed through the assignment the marketing department gave me for France and Germany. Meetings have been arranged for two weeks' time, and they will tell you with whom and where. I have also requested a two- to three-week leave of absence."

Lord Winslow raised his eyebrows and sat in the armchair facing Bertie. "But you have been on a week's leave. Why do you want another two weeks?"

"I have to visit South Africa," Bertie said.

"You have to visit South Africa?"

The surprise in his question caused him to spill a little of the whisky from his glass. He reached for a napkin and wiped his trousers dry. "Why the 'have to'?" he asked, "I have no intention or desire to open a branch there. The country is decadent, a disaster waiting to happen with its apartheid laws."

"If I told you why, you would never believe me," Bertie answered.

Lord Winslow narrowed his eyes, and looked at his son carefully. "Albert," he said. "I think I know you well enough to realize that it must be something serious. I sincerely hope that it has nothing to do with the politics of the country."

"No, Father," Bertie replied shaking his head, "it has absolutely nothing to do with the politics nor is it about opening a branch there."

"Then what? What is so important to you that you want to go to that godforsaken country?'

"It is to do with a girl, sir, a South African girl."

Lord Winslow choked on the whisky he was sipping.

"My God, Albert, are you serious? You want to go to South Africa because of a girl that you have probably only just met?"

"Yes, sir," Bertie replied.

"But who is she? What do you know about her?"

"Almost everything and almost nothing, sir," he said. "She is beautiful, has a lovely personality and ever since I met her, I cannot think of anyone or anything else but her. I am besotted. I simply can no longer think coherently. You know me, sir. I have dated plenty of girls. You and mother have even tried to match me with a few, but I always felt that those girls wanted me for my money, not for me alone. But with Marla," and his eyes took on a dreamy look, "with Marla it is somehow very different. I could feel it almost from the start, when I first saw her and held in my arms as I carried her."

"As you what? You carried her in your arms when you first met her?"

"Yes, sir," Bertie answered. "She virtually fell into them when she slipped and slid down the side of the mountain, breaking her ankle, so I carried her to the youth hostel."

"What do you know about her parents?" Lord Winslow asked, looking at his son keenly as though seeing him for the first time.

"Her father was killed in action in the war," Bertie answered. "She has been raised by her mother, Emma, who she told me is an agent that sells lingerie and dresses to various stores."

"Do they have any money?"

"That I don't know," Albert said. "I just know that she has mentioned that they have a beautiful home in Johannesburg, and that they have always lived comfortably."

"What is her surname?"

"Her name is Marla O'Neil."

"Would you like me to have a security check done? To learn more about whom they are? Does she know who you are?" his father asked hesitantly.

"No, sir, I don't believe that a security check is necessary. I would also prefer it if she didn't know who I am, not yet at any rate. I would like her to fall in love with me as Bertie, and not be influenced by anything else."

"Mmm…" Lord Winslow reached for a cigar. He held out the box to Bertie, but Bertie refused.

"So, what can I do for you?" he said, lighting his cigar and blowing the smoke in the air above him as he absorbed all that his son had told him.

"I need to catch the *Windsor Castle* leaving for South Africa this afternoon. I have tried to buy a ticket at the Union Castle Line offices, but they tell me that the boat is fully booked. I was hoping that you could pull some strings to get me on the ship."

"You want to go to sea to be with her? Good heavens Bertie, have you forgotten that after you graduated from Eton, following family tradition, I enrolled you in the Royal Navy? How you became so seasick every time you went to sea? That, my boy, was the end of your naval career. And now you want to go to sea to woo a girl? You must be crazy."

He looked at his son carefully. Bertie's eyes were begging him to help him.

"OK," he said. "You have convinced me. Let me see what I can do."

He stood up and walked to his desk. Picking up the phone, he said to his secretary, "Miss Cartwright, would you please find out who the manager of the Union Castle Line in England is, and put me through to him."

He put down the phone and said to Bertie, "Well, alright, I suppose you are old enough to make up your own mind. Have you spoken to your mother?"

"No, sir, I think it better to tell her only if something definite happens between us."

"You mean you are going to ask her to marry you?" his father asked, surprised.

"Yes, sir," Bertie answered. "She must accept my proposal knowing me only as Bertie, and nothing else. When, or rather if, she does accept my proposal, only then will I tell Mother. I feel that being in a captive surrounding like a ship for the time it takes to sail to South Africa, I will soon find out whether my feelings for her are infatuation or whether I truly care for her, and of course, she for me. If at the end of the two weeks, I still feel the same, only then will I ask her to accept my proposal of marriage."

The phone rang. Lord Winslow walked to his desk and picked it up. "Thank you, Miss Cartwright," he said, and then, "Mr. Summers, good morning. I sincerely hope that you can help me. My son, Albert, needs to sail with the Windsor Castle leaving for South Africa this afternoon. Can you assist me with accommodation on the ship for him?" he looked at Bertie while he waited for an answer. "Yes, I will hold," he said. After a few minutes he smiled, "You can? That is wonderful, I will tell him. His name is Alfred Winslow... yes,.. he does have a passport with him. I will tell him to leave immediately. Thank you very much. I will not forget your assistance."

He put down the phone and said to Bertie, "How do you intend getting to Southampton?"

"I was going to take a cab."

His father picked up the phone. "Miss Cartwright," he said, "please ask Farnsworth to take Albert to Southampton."

"Thank you, Father, I really appreciate it," Bertie said and he rushed out of the office. Picking up the suitcase that he had left at Miss Cartwright's desk, he ran into the street looking for the black Rolls Royce. Farnsworth was waiting for him. He took the suitcase from Bertie and put it in the trunk. Bertie climbed in, relaxing for the first time that day in the back seat of the car. Farnsworth drove as fast as he could to Southampton.

Bertie sat thinking about how, since meeting Marla, his life had changed. After leaving the Navy, much to his father's regret, he had gone on to Oxford University to study business administration and enjoy the fun of being a first-year student. As the years passed, he found that he enjoyed the course he had taken and started spending more and more time on study and less and less time having fun.

Once he achieved his degree, as expected, he joined his father in his business empire, Winslow (Pty) Ltd., that boasted a chain of stores in every major city in England. His father had started him in the marketing department, with the task of looking to establish branches on the Continent. It was on one of his yearly holidays with two friends that Marla had, so to speak, 'dropped in on him,' and changed his life.

Marla's cabin was a bit of a disappointment in that it was a lot smaller than the one she remembered having slept in, on the way to England. She looked at the two bunks and placed her smaller suitcase on the lower bunk, claiming it as hers should she be sharing. She felt claustrophobic. There was no porthole because the cabin was in the middle of the ship. Just the two bunks, one on top of the other, with a small washbasin and mirror. She couldn't wait to get out to the freedom of the upper deck and feel the cool breeze of the ocean.

When she reached the upper deck, she looked around to see if Josh was near, but he wasn't. She stood at the side of the ship, holding the guardrail and watched as the tugboat slowly guided the ship from its mooring into the harbour. Crowds that had gathered on the wharf, waving goodbye to friends or relatives slowly started moving away, as did those that stood around her on the ship. She stood there feeling sad that no-one that had come to see her off; not that she expected anyone to come all the way from London to Southampton, but she had hoped. She had said goodbye to the Wises, promising to write, enjoying one last plate of fried eggs and chips with them.

She felt sad to be going back to South Africa, sad because, "*let's face it,"* she concluded reluctantly, *"because of Bertie."* Since she had met him, she felt that her life had somehow changed; that she had changed. She had enjoyed his company – talking to him – listening to him when he spoke about everything in the world except himself. She shook her head and thought, *"God, I just wish that I could forget him. Time, though, will have to be the healer."*

She felt tears collect in the corners of both her eyes and brushed them away with the back of her hand. *"What is wrong with me?"* she thought. *"I have never cried so much in all my life. When I just think of Bertie I start crying. Ah well, I really liked him, more than anyone else I have ever met."* She closed her eyes with her memory. *"Well, that is life. Hopefully Bertie is now just a pleasant memory of my visit to England."*

She hugged herself as a cold breeze hit her. The ship was now underway on its own steam. She walked towards the lounge and looked around to see if Josh was there. He wasn't. She sat in an armchair near the door and reached for the diary in her handbag. She started writing down the events of the past two days.

She wrote how she had cried when she had hugged Amy and Victoria goodbye. They both promised to write to her from each city they visited. How on her last evening in London, she had slowly hobbled down Kings Road to Sloane Square, her ankle in the cast, not bothering her as much as it used to. That she had stopped at a shop displaying the latest craze in fashion, and on an impulse, bought a dress far shorter than what was presently worn in South Africa, wondering whether Irma Rosen was aware of the latest fashion. She smiled to herself as she wrote that when she walked out of the shop with her cane in her one hand, holding the package in the other, she saw a man looking at her, frowning, a man she thought she recognized. Just then a black cab had pulled up, and he got into it. When he looked at her again from the back of the cab only then did she recognize him as Peter Ustinov, the film star. She smiled to herself, pleased that at least someone famous had given her the eye.

She had then hobbled to the New Assam restaurant on Bayswater Road, a restaurant that served the curry and rice that she enjoyed so much. She wrote how she had dipped her thumb in the chutney, and left its imprint in a corner of the menu, as a sign of farewell.

Chapter 11

When they arrived at Southhampton, Bertie watched with despair as the *Windsor Castle* was being guided out of the harbour by a tugboat. Looking around desperately, he spotted another tugboat pulling to the side of the wharf preparing to moor. He jumped onto the tugboat, and ran to the bridge.

"Excuse me, Captain," he shouted above the noise, "I have missed catching that ship leaving the harbour. I will give you one hundred pounds if you could catch it and help me board her."

The Captain looked at him, then turned to look at the *Windsor Castle* as it was being guided to the harbour exit. "OK," he shouted to Bertie, "let us go for it."

Bertie ran back to the deck and grabbed his suitcase from Farnsworth's hands where he was standing on the wharf. "Thanks," he shouted. "Hope to see you soon." Waving his hand in a goodbye, he ran back to the bridge and asked, "Could you radio the ship's captain and tell him to wait for us? My name is Albert Winslow, and they are expecting me. Unfortunately, we were caught in a traffic jam; otherwise we would have been here on time.

He listened intently to the tugboat captain talking on the radio as he raced his tugboat towards the *Windsor Castle*, breathing a sigh of relief when he saw the ship slow down. Paying the one hundred pounds he had offered, and feeling terribly seasick, he boarded the ship, climbing up a rope ladder lowered over the side. His suitcase, tied to a rope, followed him. The lieutenant that welcomed him on board almost carried him to his cabin. He lay on the bed feeling terrible.

"Enjoying the trip so far?"

She looked up from her writing. Josh was standing in front of her, smiling.

"Like it so far? Comfortable in your cabin?" he asked.

"It is tiny," she answered.

"Cannot be smaller than mine," he said, "and to top it all, the man I am sharing it with is huge – overweight."

"Well I haven't met who I am sharing with," she answered, "at least not yet, but I have claimed the lower bunk."

"No such luck for me," Josh smiled, "I had to move to the upper bunk. Then again, when I think about it, would I want to sleep on the lower bunk, under a man that is obese?"

She laughed.

The dinner bell chimed.

"Hungry?" Josh asked.

"Very," she answered, collecting her diary and putting it in her handbag. "The sea air has an effect on me."

"Well, fortunately, for the first night we don't have to dress up," Josh said, "so let us go in and gorge ourselves." They stood and started walking towards the dining room. They noticed that a number of passengers had collected at the side of the ship, looking at something in the water.

"What is going on?" Josh asked one of the passengers on the deck.

"Oh… from what I have heard, someone, a VIP, appears to have missed the boat at Southampton and a tugboat has brought him to the ship."

"And they stop the ship for that? Amazing," Marla said, clutching herself as a cold breeze hit her. "He must truly be a very important person." She looked over the side and watched someone leave the tugboat, and climb up the rope ladder into the ship. The person looked vaguely familiar. '*Impossible!*' she thought, '*every person I see looks just like Bertie.*' She put the thought out of her mind and watched as the ship's officer pulled the rope ladder with a suitcase attached into the ship. The tugboat gave two hoots with its horn, and pulled away.

After dinner, she excused herself from Josh. She was tired, and couldn't wait to climb into her bunk. She found that an elderly woman had crawled into the bottom bunk, and was fast asleep. "*Well, that is the way it is,* "she thought as she undressed as quietly as she could, and climbed into the upper bunk. She tried to fall asleep, but found that she just couldn't. After about an hour of tossing and turning, she carefully climbed out of the bunk and dressed, trying to make as little noise as possible. She went back to the lounge to find a comfortable chair to relax in.

Sitting in the warmth of the lounge, she found that she was nodding off, and not wanting to sleep there she eventually stood up and made her way back to her cabin to find the lady she was sharing with throwing up in the basin.

"Can I help you in any way?" she asked the lady.

"No, no thank you," the lady answered. "Just go away and leave me to die in peace."

Marla smiled to herself. Fortunately she had never been seasick, but she knew what the lady was going through. Walking back to the lounge, she settled herself comfortably in an armchair, and fell asleep.

The ship was sailing through the Bay of Biscay, which could be very rough at times, causing many passengers on board to become seasick. She was lucky that it didn't affect her, but Josh was terribly nauseous and stayed in his cabin. It took him just over three days to get over it. Looking green around the gills, he eventually joined her where she lay at the swimming pool under a shade umbrella so that she would not burn too dark in the hot sun.

"You have changed," he said, sitting next to her. "You are not the Marla I have always known. Something in London has changed you."

"Changed?" she answered, smiling. "You have also changed. You seem to have a greenish hue around you."

He laughed. "Oh, I was so seasick," he mumbled, "you simply cannot imagine how terrible being seasick is."

"But I can," she answered. "I have a cabin mate that tells me every day that she is dying. I must add, though, that I am surprised that you were sick. Did you not tell me that you were in the South African Navy?"

"I was, and I was just as seasick for the first few days at sea," he answered. "After one month of basic training, I was posted to a frigate, the SS *Transvaaler*. The moment the ship left the harbour, while I was standing at attention on the foc'sle with five other sailors, saluting the Harbour Master, I started to throw up. I slowly worked my way to the quarterdeck, and squeezing under one of the vegetable bins, tied myself to it. Then with my head over the side of the ship I wretched, until exhausted, I eventually fell asleep. I woke up when it was dark, at the sound of lifeboats being lowered over the side and crawled out from under the bin, helping them lower the boats. The Petty Officer working next to me took one look at me and then shouted.

"Are you Able Seaman Stern?"

"Yes, sir," I answered.

"My god, man, those boats are out there looking for you!"

Marla laughed. She sat looking at the ocean, not saying anything. Then she asked him,

"You said earlier that I have changed. In what way have I changed?"

"You are quieter, as though thinking and remembering something, all the time. You are not the vivacious, excitable girl I know. What has happened?"

"Oh..." she said, turning her face from him. "It is a long story. It will bore you. I don't want to talk about it."

"OK," he said, turning away from her and reaching for the beer glass he had brought with him, "but if you do want a sympathetic ear, I am always at your beck and call. Taking a guess, though, because I know you so well, I would say that you have fallen in love with someone or something."

Surprised at what he said, she closed her eyes and turned her face away from him. Smiling to herself she thought about Bertie and for the first time realized that she had indeed fallen in love. She missed him; just being with him, his company, his idle chatter, his graciousness toward her. She missed his smile, his frown when he tried to explain something to her in his Oxford English accent.

'Ah, well,' she thought, 'Bertie is the past, I must now prepare for the future,' and closing her eyes, she closed the conversation with Josh, putting her memories behind her.

Two days after he had boarded ship, Bertie found that the movement of the ship was heaven compared to that of the tugboat, even though it only travelled a short distance before they had caught up with the ship. However, he was still scared that he would once again be overcome with sea sickness. Still feeling a bit nauseous, he stayed in his cabin until the green stranger he saw staring back at him from the mirror looked more like the face he had grown accustomed to. He plucked up his courage and walked up the stairs to the upper deck. The previous days of being seasick, lying on his bunk, wishing that he would die was something he struggled to put behind him. He would think of Marla and, gritting his teeth, wish himself to get well. Weak from hunger, but at least no longer sea sick, he could at last think coherently. At breakfast that morning, he had eaten sparingly, happy when everything stayed down.

The next day he decided once again to try the upper deck, feeling quite confident that he had overcome his seasickness. The ship had left the turbulent waters of the Bay of Biscay, sailing into the more peaceful waters of the Atlantic around Madeira. He walked into the lounge, then through all the decks and looked at each sunbather lying at the swimming pool, but could not find Marla.

Then the thought struck him: he was travelling first class. Marla would probably be second class. He walked to the second class pool on the quarterdeck and saw her lying under a shade umbrella, her foot still strapped in a bandage. She was talking to a man that was sitting next to her. His heart skipped a beat. Rooted to the spot, he stood watching her. He noticed that her black swimsuit made her skin look darker than he remembered. Her eyes were closed and with her hair blowing gently in the breeze he thought her more beautiful than he had remembered. He walked up to her slowly, enjoying just looking at her where she lay. Then, softly with a great deal of emotion in his voice, he said, "Aha, so there you are. I knew if I looked all over the ship I would be able to find you. I have been so seasick these last three days; otherwise I would have looked for you sooner."

Marla lay still, not believing what she heard. She had been lying in the sun thinking of Bertie, and suddenly someone was talking to her in his voice. She squinted at the figure standing in front of her, silhouetted by the sun so that she could not see who it was. She sat up, holding her towel in front of her, put on her sunglasses and then opened her eyes.

"Bertie?" she stuttered, recognizing the figure. "Bertie? My God, what are you doing here?" and then jumping up she threw herself into his arms. "Oh Bertie, Bertie," she screamed in happiness.

He kissed her, long and hard. "I just could not let you go," he said, and he kissed her again. "Marla, I love you, I absolutely adore you. When you told me you were leaving, I knew then I could not be without you."

"Oh, Bertie, I have missed you terribly. Oh, Bertie..." she whispered.

"This is Bertie?" Josh asked, "This is the chap you instructed me to give your phone number to? No questions asked? Good heavens, what a small world. Marla, this is Albert, Livvy's brother. Remember the story I told you about that young girl that John and I met in the tower?"

Chapter 12

"Bertie, my God," Marla asked after catching her breath and moving out of his arms. "What are you doing here?"

Bertie hesitated, looking at Josh. He did not recognize Josh. "I decided I had to see South Africa, and knowing that you were on this ship, I made up my mind at the spur of the moment to travel with you."

"Oh, Bertie, that was wonderful of you. I am so pleased you are here." Marla saw that he was staring at Josh, his look questioning as to who and what Josh was to her.

"Josh," she said, "this is Bertie. Bertie ... Josh."

"You look familiar," Bertie said to Josh, holding out his hand.

"We have met," Josh answered taking his hand and shaking it. "I know you as Albert. You were with your sister, Livvy, when we met. It was in a field in Slough."

"Oh, now I remember. You are that South African chap Olivia walked the fields with. I have never forgotten that. In fact, I believe it was fated that I should have met you and then met Marla. I am sorry, I just did not recognize you."

"Livvy is Olivia?" Josh asked.

"Yes," Bertie answered. "She likes to call herself Livvy. A nickname from childhood."

"Who are you talking about?" Marla asked.

"Albert...uh, Bertie's sister, Livvy. You remember, I told you the story of the little girl John and I met in the tower."

She turned to Bertie, "Why didn't you tell me when we were having coffee the other night that you were coming?"

"It was a last-minute decision," Bertie said, sitting down next to her. I finished the work I had to do and after what you had told me about South Africa, I simply had to see the country. Knowing that you would be on the ship, I felt why not join you."

"But then, why haven't we seen you earlier?" Marla asked, puzzled.

"Uhh ... Uhh, well," Bertie answered looking embarrassed. "The only ticket I could get was first class and uhh... well, uhh, I was indisposed."

"You mean you were seasick," Josh laughed. "So were we all when the ship sailed through the Bay of Biscay. I must say, though, that you still look a bit green around the gills."

"Not as green as I was a few days ago," Bertie mumbled to himself. "I thought that I was dying."

Josh burst out laughing.

"It is not something to laugh about, Josh," Marla said angrily. "When we first sailed out of Cape Town to London, for a short while I was just as seasick. Thank God your father had given me some Dramamine. When Ma and I drove to Potch, to say goodbye to the Stuarts, I went to the pharmacy to buy some cosmetics. I may still have some Dramimine left if you need it," she said to Bertie.

"Over lunch one day," she continued, "the Purser told me that sailing through the Bay of Biscay can be really nasty, especially in winter and spring, occasionally in summer. That the ship can often be greeted with high seas and strong winds and that very few passengers, even some of the crew, survive it without becoming seasick. He also told me that this ship should ride the waves relatively well because of its design, which is long, sleek and low. It is when the ship turns south and runs the waves broadside on, taking them on the beam, this is what causes the ship to roll from side to side, making one seasick. Those passengers who do not have their sea legs and travel from England to South Africa usually spend their first 36 hours on board, flat on their backs in their cabins wishing they were dead. Those travelling from South Africa to England, on the other hand, usually arrive in

Southampton looking rather green around their gills. He also told me that sailing through the Bay is the definition of true sea sickness."

"Thank you, Marla, for explaining so well why I became so sea sick, looking to death as a luxury," Bertie replied. "I will remember that for the future. I must say, though, that I do feel a lot better than I was, but I still feel that should the sea become slightly rough, my sea-sickness could start up again. At the moment, the sailing is really calm and pleasant, especially with the sun warming us up."

Josh laughed, "Well it should be. The ship is hardly sailing. It is approaching the island of Madeira, where the weather is a great deal warmer than that of England. If you were less focused on Marla, you would notice that she is sunbathing, and in a swimsuit, something difficult not to notice. She could only do this in warm weather. Furthermore if you look around you will see that all the sailors have changed their uniforms from the blue wool to white shorts with short sleeved shirts, white shoes and socks, their uniform in warmer weather."

"Ach, Josh, do behave yourself," Marla said angrily, "and don't be so sarcastic."

"Well I can't help it," Josh said, "he should look around instead of just hugging and kissing you."

Marla ignored him. "Josh and I were planning to tour the island tomorrow. Apparently we have the morning to shop, before she sails to South Africa in the afternoon or early evening."

"Tell me something, old man," Josh said, still showing his unfriendliness towards Bertie, "how is Livvy?"

"She is fine. From what my father tells me, she is back at school and enjoying it."

"From what your father tells you? You mean you never see her?" Josh asked.

"Quite honestly, I don't," Bertie answered. "She is so much younger than I am. The only time I see her is over the school holidays, and then only when I visit the estate in Slough. You see, she is in boarding school, and me? I have an apartment in London, and am rarely at my father's house.

"Tell me, would anyone like a drink?" And he snapped his fingers to get the attention of the steward.

"The last time we saw her," Josh continued, "she told us that it was her birthday in a few days and that she would send John and me an invitation, which of course never arrived. Now that I think of it, I do remember reading in the newspaper about the birthday of..."

"Would you like another beer?" Bertie interrupted, turning his back to Josh. "And what would you like to drink?" he asked Marla.

Josh frowned, trying to remember exactly what he had read, but with Bertie soon talking about the latest win of the All Blacks over England at Twickenham, he soon lost his train of thought.

They sat talking for the rest of the afternoon, relaxing at the swimming pool. Marla noticed that the tension between Bertie and Josh slowly thawed, and they were soon talking like friends. The rest of the afternoon passed really quickly, with Bertie insisting on paying for the drinks they ordered.

"I'm a working man, subject closed," he said laughingly. "You are both still students, or were students not yet earning a living. Either way, would you both join me for dinner this evening? I'm travelling first class, the only ticket that was available at the last minute. I promise to behave, and not throw up at dinner."

Marla looked at Josh. "We would love to," she said "but does that mean dressing up? I don't have anything fancy."

"Well, yes," Bertie replied, "but nothing too serious, more casual, and comfortable."

"That's very nice of you," Josh said, "but there is one condition."

"And what is that?" Bertie asked.

"That you show us around first-class. Never been there and would love to see it." Turning to Marla, "I'm sure you would also like to look around."

"I would love to," Marla replied.

"Okay, then," Bertie answered, "Let me see if I can pull some strings. Either way, I will pick you both up at six o'clock in your lounge and show you around before dinner. If you would like, I will try to arrange a visit to the bridge for another day."

Josh looked puzzled. "How will you be able to arrange all that?" he asked.

"Leave it to me," Bertie answered. "I am very persuasive."

"That I have noticed," Josh said, eyeing Marla.

"Well, I think we had better get going," Bertie said. "It is now half past five, which doesn't leave much time to arrange everything." He stood up, reaching out his hand toward Marla to help her stand.

"Okay, see you both in the lounge at around about six o'clock," and with a smile he squeezed Marla's hand and left.

"Mmmm," John whispered to Marla. "Now I can see why you have changed."

"Changed?" Marla said, blushing.

"But of course," Josh answered. "It is obvious to everyone around the pool that he is absolutely crazy about you, and you, crazy about him."

"Don't be silly," Marla said, her face turning crimson. "He is just a very nice, charming guy."

"Tell that to the marines," Josh answered laughingly, and they walked off to their respective cabins to prepare for dinner.

Bertie felt proud walking into the dining room with Marla on his arm; Josh, wearing a suit that needed ironing, a step behind them. Marla was dressed in one of Irma Rosen's formal evening dresses, a dress that had made her laugh when Emma had packed it for her.

"Ma," she had said at the time, "when do you think I am ever going to wear that?"

"You never know," she remembered Emma answering. "I have always believed that one must prepare for the inevitable."

Bertie, dressed in a dark blue suit, guided her to the captain's table. "The captain very kindly asked us to join him at his table, when I asked permission for you and Josh to have dinner in the first class," he whispered to Marla.

The captain stood up to greet her.

"Let me introduce you," Bertie said to Marla. "Marla, this is Captain Granger. Marla O'Neil from South Africa.

"Miss O'Neil," he said, holding out his hand, "it is a pleasure to meet you. Please, do sit down," and he pointed to a seat next to him. Bertie's seat was next to Marla, while Josh was seated at the far end of the table.

"It was very kind of you to invite us to join you," Marla said as Bertie helped her take her seat.

"The pleasure is ours," the captain replied. "I do hope you will enjoy your evening."

Dinner was very pleasant, with the menu far richer in variety than the menu in tourist class. She noticed that there were also fewer diners, but all were well dressed. Many were looking at her and whispering to each other. She dropped her eyes and read the menu. She knew that they were talking about her, and felt embarrassed.

"When the Union Castle Line offices phoned me to prepare..."

"Uh... Captain," Bertie interrupted before the captain could go any further, "what are the chances of us visiting the bridge?" He gave the captain a long, hard look reminding him not to say anything about him or his father.

"I will try and arrange it on a calm day, once we are out in the open ocean," the captain answered, smiling at Bertie. He then turned to answer a question from the guest seated across the table, and at their request introduced Marla and Bertie to everyone at the table. The captain looked at Bertie, smiled, and introduced them without mentioning their surnames. The dinner was very pleasant. Marla found it a bit too formal, though, and was pleased when it was over. They had to remain seated at the table with small talk, until the captain rose to return to the bridge.

The next morning they met on deck early, intending to go ashore to Funchal, but they found that the ship was besieged by local traders who came alongside in small boats, using a line with a basket to raise their goods up to the passengers on the open decks. A great deal was on display. They decided that rather than travel to the island, with the risk of Bertie becoming seasick as the small boat ploughed through the waves, they would stay on the ship and look at what was being offered. They were also intrigued by the local boys who would dive for coins the passengers threw overboard from the deck. The water was so clear that the coin was easily seen in the sand on the sea bottom. Josh had gone ashore. With so few passengers on board, Bertie took Marla to the first class swimming pool, where they lay on deck chairs, talking.

After about four hours, the ship blew its horn, calling everyone that was on shore back to it, and started preparing to sail on to Cape Town, a voyage that would take almost ten days at sea, out of sight of land, with just open, empty ocean.

They lost track of time and were never quite sure what day of the week it was. Mealtimes were announced by a gong over the public address system. They only knew that it was Sunday when the ship's officers dressed in their number tens. Occasionally the blank horizon would be broken by a passing ship, or a school of porpoises or flying fish. Whenever a whale was sighted, the bridge announced the sighting over the intercom, and all the passengers would collect on the side of the ship to try and spot the whales.

Entering the doldrums, a completely flat sea that was glassy without a ripple on the surface, a condition that usually occurred near the equator, they met with the *RMS Capetown Castle*, a sister ship passing about 1,000 yards from them. The ship was silhouetted against a red sky as it sailed towards London. It blew its horn to greet them, and their ship responded.

Every evening boasted films, dances, tombola sessions, quizzes with the odd special evenings that included cocktail parties, dinner dances, fancy-dress parties or live shows with officers dressed as minstrels performing a selection of songs usually followed by a sing-a-long.

Marla spent every waking moment of the day with Bertie. They soon became accepted as a couple by everyone on the ship. Josh, seeing that he had lost Marla, made friends with a girl from Wales.

The crossing of the equator ceremony was very traditional, with a King Neptune and his queen. A few victims, chosen from the passengers who had never before crossed the equator, were accused of some deep sea misdemeanor and sentenced to a form of punishment that ended with a ducking in the swimming pool. Bertie, crossing the equator for the first time, was one of the first to be initiated. He acted his part well to the amusement of all.

"Here is to King Neptune," he cried out as he was tipped backward into the water. "May he live..." and he gurgled through the rest of the sentence.

Marla toweled him dry when he came out of the pool, and he kissed her as a thank-you, picking her up as though he were going to hand her to King Neptune.

"I have already been initiated," she squealed, wriggling in his arms, "on the trip to England." Pretending that he had missed his step, he fell into the pool with her and kissed her again under the water.

"That kiss was for the benefit of King Neptune," he shouted as they both surfaced, Marla spluttering, pushing her wet hair out of her eyes.

"Bertie, just look at me," she said angrily as she stood next to him in the pool, looking at her wet dress. "I could kill you."

"Marry me instead," he blurted out.

It took a few minutes for her to realize what he had said.

"Marla, I love you very much," he said in a soft voice, filled with emotion. "I am sure that you know that by now. Will you marry me?"

"Is this a serious proposal," Marla asked, teasing him, "and not a part of King Neptune and crossing the equator fun and games?"

"Marla, you know that I am not joking. I am very serious. Will you please marry me?"

Marla looked at him, standing beside her waist deep in the swimming pool. Her face lost its smile as she saw the earnestness in his eyes. She thought about what he had asked her, and how she felt about him. How her whole being had changed ever since she had met him. How miserable she had felt when she thought he had ditched her.

"Yes," she answered.

"Please, do think about it. Please do... what did you say?" he looked her, not believing what he had heard.

"Of course I will marry you," she answered, her voice shaking with emotion. "Oh yes. Oh yes, indeed."

The passengers around the pool started clapping and cheering.

"Thank you, my dear," Bertie said softly, the emotion of the moment showing in his voice. "You have just made me the happiest of men, however there is one more thing I must beg of you."

Marla looked at him questioningly.

"I would like you to marry me now, on board ship and by King Neptune and the captain."

Marla was surprised. "Why now?" she asked. "Why the hurry?"

"Because firstly I am scared that you will change your mind once we get to Cape Town. And secondly, it is a romantic thing to do. I love you, Marla, you just don't know how much, and I want you for my wife, now, today if possible. We can have a second wedding in South Africa, with all the trimmings, if you want to, but this way I know that you will marry me as I am, just plain Bertie with no trimmings at all," and he stretched out his arms displaying his naked torso.

Marla thought for a minute. She stood back and looked at him. She saw in his face that he was deadly serious.

"Can it be done on board?" she asked.

"Yes," Bertie answered, "I spoke with the purser yesterday and he told me that the captain is charged with performing marriage ceremonies in deep ocean. At the moment, and for the next few days, the ship is far from the African coastline and is in deep ocean, so please, please marry me now."

"I know nothing about you," she said, "and the fact that you want me to marry you now, on board ship without me knowing anything about you, worries me."

"I promise you that you have nothing to fear from me. I have a good job, I earn a good living, and I own a flat in Chelsea. I am a respectable man and can support you comfortably for the rest of our lives. If I can get the captain to marry us tomorrow, will you agree?"

"Do you young lady take this man who I have only just christened to be your unlawfully wedded fishy husband?" King Neptune interrupted them as he shouted out above the applause.

Taking Marla's hand, Bertie moved her closer to where King Neptune sat.

"We do," they both shouted at him, laughing.

Queen Neptune then stood up and placed a ring of seaweed around both their necks.

"Then by all the fish in the ocean, and by the power vested in me by the whales, I pronounce you fish-man and fish-wife," King Neptune shouted as he stood up.

Bertie took a piece of seaweed from around his neck, and wrapped it around the third finger on Marla's left hand.

"What a beautiful ring," she said, "I will always treasure it."

Then holding hands, they climbed out of the pool to the applause and delight of the passengers.

Marla walked to the side of the boat, squeezing the water out of her dress. She stood looking out over the ocean at the moon. Whether it was the wine she had enjoyed earlier that evening, or Bertie standing next to her, or simply the romance of it all, she turned to him and said, "Yes, my darling, I will marry you on board this ship. No other ship, mind you. I still don't know why you are in such a hurry, though. You know absolutely nothing about me, or my family."

Bertie took her in his arms. "Marla, my fish-wife, I love you because of who you are, because you are the girl standing next to me. I don't love you for your family or for something that you could very well be. I am marrying Marla O'Neil, a girl who I love, a girl I want to spend the rest of my life with."

"One thing though, Bertie," she said, holding him at arm's length as he tried to kiss her, "I am agreeing to marry you tomorrow because when we met at the restaurant, I had not expected to ever hear from you again. When I left you standing there and I ran away from you, my heart nearly broke. I don't think I could live if for any reason I lost you for a third time. One thing you must promise me, though,"

"Anything," he answered.

"Please do not tell anyone that we are married until we have a church wedding. I would not want to hurt my mother."

"What about Josh? He will know."

"I will ask Josh to keep it quiet. He won't say a word."

He took her in his arms and kissed her, and she kissed him back.

"We do need Josh as a witness to the marriage," Bertie said. "Are you sure that he will be able to keep it secret?"

"Yes, I am sure he will," Marla said, "I have known Josh for many years and he will always do whatever I ask him to."

At no time did she think of asking Bertie about himself. It was only during the ceremony that she found out that Bertie's names were Albert, Charles, Angus and that her married name would be Winslow.

On a Thursday morning, at six a.m. the port of Cape Town, dominated by Table Mountain, emerged out of the morning mist as the ship sailed into Table Bay.

Chapter 13

Table Mountain, flanked by Devil's Peak to the east and Lion's Head to the west, forms a dramatic backdrop to Cape Town and Table Bay Harbour. As the *Windsor Castle* sailed into the Harbour, Table Mountain greeted them, covered with its tablecloth of cloud.

Almost all the passengers of the ship collected on the deck to admire the beauty of the scene. The 'Fairest Cape in all the World', as it has been known for centuries, lived up to its name, with its fynbos, one of the world's six floral kingdoms, painting the side of the mountains in vivid colours.

"My God, but what a beautiful sight," Bertie remarked, shivering in the cool morning air of the south-easterly wind, as he stood with Marla and Josh at the port side railing admiring the view.

"You are lucky," Marla said. "You are seeing Table Mountain with its tablecloth. There is the story that Van Hunks, a pirate of the 18th century, retired from piracy to the slopes of Devil's Peak. That is the mountain over there, on the right. He spent his days sitting on the mountain, smoking his pipe. Legend has it that one day a stranger approached him, and a smoking contest ensued which lasted for days. The smoke clouds built up and a strong wind blew them down towards the town. When Van Hunks finally won the contest, the stranger revealed himself to be the Devil, which is why that mountain over there, with a peak, is known as Devil's Peak. The cloud of smoke they left became Table Mountain's tablecloth -- the famous white cloud that you are now looking at."

"A nice story," Bertie said.

The ship carefully docked in the harbour, mooring itself with the help of two tugboats, while the harbour workers on the pier tied the ship to the wharf.

Josh, standing next to Marla, scanned the crowd of people that lined the quayside, trying to find his parents. They had written to him that they would drive up from Potchefstroom a few days earlier and enjoy the beach at Muizenburg before meeting him when the ship docked. They would then spend a week in Muizenburg with him before driving back to Potchefstroom.

He looked carefully through the crowd, shielding his eyes as the sun broke through the clouds. He saw Emma and turned to Marla, who stood next to him with Bertie. He pointed Emma out to her, but Marla had already seen her and was waving frantically, hoping to catch her attention. He turned to look back at the crowd, but found that he couldn't take his eyes off Emma. She had not yet seen Marla, and was still looking up at the ship trying to find her.

"My parents must be late," he thought as he carefully scanned the crowd below him on the pier, but couldn't find them.

He looked back at Emma, and frowned as he saw a harbour worker approach her and start talking to her. He watched curiously as Emma turned her back on him, ignoring him as she walked away. The harbour worker grabbed her arm. Josh thought that he said something to her that made her shrug him off angrily, but he persisted in talking to her. He saw Emma stop, and expected her to call for help and have the harbour worker arrested for harassment. Instead, she turned and said something to him, pointing up at the ship.

The harbour worker stood still for a few minutes, as though in surprise, and then he looked to where she pointed. Josh watched him shake his head slowly as though not believing what Emma had told him. He then turned and walked away, his shoulders bowed with what, to Josh, looked like disappointment.

"Did you see that Coloured chap harassing your mother?" he said to Marla, but she never heard him. She was talking excitedly to Bertie.

Then Josh saw his parents, and he forgot the incident.

The gangplank was lowered. Josh watched as the passengers started to disembark, walking into the main warehouse to have their passports stamped, and clear customs with their luggage. Eventually it was his turn and he waited for Marla and Bertie to go before him. They walked slowly in front of him, Marla excited yet nervous and displaying it, at the prospect of introducing Bertie to Emma.

As they approached the gangplank, the first lieutenant who stood at the exit held out his hand to Bertie and Marla.

"Thank you Mr. and Mrs. Winslow, for joining us. We hope you enjoyed the trip and look forward to seeing you again soon."

Bertie took his hand and shook it. Marla blushed and thanked him for his greeting, not yet used to being called Mrs. Winslow. Then remembering, she quickly removed the plain gold ring from her wedding finger, a ring that Bertie had given her when the Captain married them.

"*Marla*," Josh thought shaking his head as he looked at her and Bertie as they walked down the gangplank in front of him, "*I love you even more now. I just hope that you did the right thing in marrying Bertie the way you did.*"

He looked at her excited face as she turned and said something to Bertie.

"*Then of course, by marrying him, you have done very well for yourself. I cannot compete,*" he thought with a smile. "*But well, that is life,*" and he shrugged. "*I must admit though, that you have married a very nice fellow.*"

In the days they had got to know each other on board ship, Josh and Bertie had become very good friends. The three of them were inseparable until he met Gwenneth Jones, a Welsh girl on her way to a nursing job in a hospital in Johannesburg. She would be working there for a two-year stint with two other nurses. She gave him an excuse to leave Marla and Bertie alone. In the days that followed, he had a steamy relationship with Gwen, promising to contact her whenever he visited Johannesburg.

He looked around for her while Marla and Bertie walked ashore, but could not see her. He then walked down the gangplank and watched as Marla and Bertie cleared passport control and walked to where Emma was standing. He was curious as to how Marla would introduce Bertie to Emma, and stood watching them. A nudge behind him by a passenger, to hand his passport to the officer sitting at a desk in front of him, brought him back to reality.

"*I wonder what Marla is saying to Emma,*" he thought as he handed the officer his passport, "*and how she is introducing Bertie.*"

Then he saw his parents and forgot what he was thinking as the excitement of seeing them again after five years overcame him. He took his passport from the officer after it had been stamped, and rushed over to where they were standing. He hugged his mother, who beamed with joy at seeing him, and shook his father's hand vigorously.

"Oh, Mom and Dad, it is so good to see you after all these years. I have missed you both terribly."

His father asked him where his luggage was, and his mother started talking to him, but his curiosity got the better of him. Interrupting her he looked around to where Marla was talking excitedly to her mother.

"Excuse me for a second, Mom and Dad, Emma O'Neil is standing over there and I would like to say hello to her."

"Oh, how nice," his mother said. "Come on, Alf, let us go and say hello to Emma. We haven't seen her for ever so long," and they followed Josh to where Emma, Marla and Bertie were standing.

"Hi, Mrs. O'Neil," Josh said, holding out his hand to Emma. Marla looked at him, shook her head and frowned.

"Hello, Josh," Emma answered. "Hello, Mr. and Mrs. Stern. I understand that Josh was on the ship with Marla and Bertie."

"Hello, Mrs. O'Neil," his mother said. "We were not aware of that. Josh never wrote and told us that they were travelling together. He did tell us that he had seen your daughter in London, and had shown her around."

"Marla did write and tell me that Josh had found her a place to stay in London, and that he had been very kind to her. Josh, did you know Bertie in London?" Emma turned to look at Bertie, her eyes looking for an answer in his face, as she wanted to know more about him.

"Well, not in London, Mrs. O'Neil," Josh answered hesitantly, wondering how much Marla had told her, "but Bertie and I became very good friends on board the ship." He was trying to assure her that Bertie was a very nice person, and that she should not have any concerns about him.

Bertie smiled at Josh, and winked a thank you.

"Josh and I have become very close friends," Bertie said in his Oxford English accent putting his arm around Josh's shoulders. "I must say that he was an excellent chaperone to Marla," and he gave Josh's shoulders a squeeze.

"Bertie, let me introduce you to my parents," Josh said. "Mom and Dad, this is Bertie, who I met when I was in England. He is on a visit to South Africa, on a very personal issue."

"How do you do?" Bertie said, holding out his hand. "I must say that I enjoyed your son's company on board the ship."

Alf took his hand, shaking it. "Nice to know, my boy. Hope you like South Africa."

"It is a pleasure to meet you, Bertie," his mother said taking Bertie's outstretched hand and shaking it. Then turning to Emma she continued, "I must say, Emma, you look very pleased at seeing Marla," and without pausing for a breath and looking curiously at Bertie, she remarked, "Marla my dear, it is so good to see you after all this time. My, but you have grown into a beautiful young lady. Did you and Bertie meet on board the ship?"

"Oh, no, Bertie and I met in London. He decided to join us on our trip back to South Africa." Marla answered, looking up at Bertie.

"Are you and your parents returning immediately to Potchefstroom?" Emma asked Josh.

Josh turned to look at his parents for an answer.

"No, Emma," his father said, "We are spending a few days in Muizenburg, leaving only on Sunday morning by car. And you?"

"Well, you have a long drive ahead of you," Emma said, "I came down by train, and will be travelling back with Marla, and now Bertie, on the Blue Train in two days time. I prefer the train, even though it does take longer than by car."

"Well, enjoy the trip," Alf said, "I hear the Blue Train is the only way to travel nowadays, quite luxurious. Would you please excuse us? We are meeting family for lunch, and we have to arrange for Josh's trunk to be sent home by train. Hope to see you both the next time you are in Potchefstroom," and he started to walk away.

Josh and his mother stood for a while chatting with Emma. Then promising to see each other once they were back in Potchefstroom, they walked to where his father stood looking for Josh's luggage, as the porters piled the suitcases and trunks that came off the ship into the warehouse.

Josh looked back at Marla and Bertie and watched curiously as the harbour worker that he had seen from the ship walked up behind Emma and whispered something in her ear. He watched Emma's face turn pale.

Emma appeared to say something to Marla and Bertie and then walked away from them, standing behind one of the concrete pillars holding up the roof of the warehouse. The harbour worker followed her.

Josh's curiosity got the better of him. He sidled a little closer and heard the worker say to Emma in Afrikaans, "Emily, why don't you know me? Why are you ignoring me? You look like a White dressed the way you are, all posh and fancy. What are you doing here? Who is that girl and the boy that is with you?"

Emma suddenly started crying and took out a handkerchief, then pulling herself together she wiped away her tears. She stood for a minute, as though thinking, then turned, smiled and held out her hand to the harbour worker. Taking him by his arm, she walked with him back to where Marla and Bertie stood. She then said loudly in English,

"Marla and Bertie, this is Jonas," and then she lied. "Jonas used to work for us in Potchefstroom. It is a real surprise seeing him here. Excuse me a second, I have to talk to him about something."

Emma walked to one side, Jonas following her, not happy at what she had said. Marla frowned. She called after Emma as she walked away. Emma turned, walked to Marla, spoke to her and then carried on walking with Jonas.

Curiosity overcame Josh, and he watched them closely. He saw Emma talking to Jonas earnestly, gesturing to where Marla stood with Bertie. Jonas looked at them in amazement, smiled, then turned back to Emma saying something to her for a few minutes, his face very serious. Emma started crying again. Josh watched as Jonas reached forward as though to comfort her, but then stopped himself, and stood watching her cry, a frown on his face. The man appeared to say something else to her and then walked away. Emma stood still for a few minutes as she brushed away the tears from her eyes. Then, as though collecting herself, she walked back to where Marla and Bertie were standing.

"Shame, poor Jonas," Josh heard her say, her voice cracking as she spoke. "He told me that his mother is very ill, and could I help him with some money. I told him to come to our hotel tomorrow morning."

Alf called out to Josh. "Josh, is this your luggage?"

Josh walked over to Marla and whispered in her ear, "Have you told her yet?"

Marla shook her head.

"Best of luck, then; see you soon, Bertie," and he walked to where his father stood calling him.

"That young man with Marla," his mother asked, as he joined them, "he looks very nice."

"Oh," Josh said, "Bertie is very nice."

"Bertie who?" his mother asked.

"Bertie Winslow," Josh replied, "He and Marla met while she was hiking in the Lake District."

"And he joined you on the boat back to South Africa?"

"Well, yes," Josh answered.

"Winslow... Winslow, the name rings a bell," his mother murmured, then turning to Alf she said, "Alf, is that not the name we heard the other night on Springbok radio? They said that Lord Winslow's son, Albert was his name, was on his way to South Africa."

"Lord who?" Josh choked.

"Well," his mother continued, "last week Springbok radio announced that Lord Winslow's son, Albert, was coming to South Africa, looking to possibly open a branch of their business here. That he was supposedly travelling incognito, but as you all know, today nothing is incognito anymore."

"Business?" Josh said, amazement all over his face, "What business?"

"Well" his mother answered, "if I remember correctly, the name of the business was the same as his name, Winslow, and they announced that his father owns a chain of stores throughout England."

"But..." Josh said, "Winslow's is the biggest chain of department stores in England."

"Oh, I didn't know that," his mother said, turning away as though the subject now bored her.

"That makes Bertie the son of a multi-millionaire," Josh continued, "and that makes Marla... no I don't believe it... but then, when I think about it, he did travel first class, and the captain of the ship... Oh my God, I should have put two and two together, and she doesn't know."

"Know what?" his father asked.

"Mom, Dad, can you keep a secret?"

"Try us," his father said, not that interested as he signaled to a porter that he had identified Josh's luggage.

"Well," Josh continued excitedly, "but no one must know for at least three to four weeks."

"Know what?" his father asked as though bored with the conversation.

His mother turned to him, curious as to his excitement.

"Well," Josh said, "Mom, what you just told me explains a lot. Bertie travelled first class, and he showed Marla and me around the whole ship. He even got the captain to allow us to eat occasionally with the first class passengers, and it was as though the captain knew him. Then four days ago, he married them."

"He married who?" his mother asked.

"Marla and Bertie. The captain married them in a wonderful ceremony on board the ship. It was incredible, and to think she doesn't know that she is married to a millionaire's son."

"What?" his father said, no longer interested in the luggage.

"I don't believe you," his mother exclaimed, turning to him.

"It is true," Josh answered. "Bertie was insistent that they marry on board ship, and even agreed to a second wedding if she would marry him immediately. He said that it was so romantic if they did, something they would remember all their lives. Marla told me that he didn't have to spend too much time talking her into it. Bertie told me that he had to make sure she would marry him as quickly as possible, so he persuaded the captain to marry them and he did."

"But... but..." his mother said, "if I remember correctly, Springbok radio also said that Lord Winslow's wife, I can't remember her name, is a cousin to the Queen. If, as you say, Marla is married to Bertie, then she will be a guest at all of the Queen's functions. Good heavens," and she looked at Marla, "she could now be a part of royalty. I wonder whether she knows that?"

"I know she doesn't," Josh said excitedly. "It is all coming back to me. I remember reading an article in The Telegraph about an Olivia Winslow's thirteenth birthday party. The article mentioned that members of the Royal family had attended and that her mother is Princess something or other — I cannot remember her name. I just never put two and two together. I never dreamt that Livvy was short for Olivia."

"So, who is Olivia Winslow? Lilly asked.

"She is Albert — Bertie's sister," He turned to both his parents excitedly, "and that explains why he wanted to get married on the ship in a hurry. I think that he doesn't want Marla to find out that he is a member of the royal family, not until after they were married. What a bugger, but please, please don't say anything about them being married until they announce it, otherwise I am dead meat."

Chapter 14

Emma had arrived in Cape Town the day before by train, booking into a hotel near Clifton beach. She had wanted to visit her mother, but decided to do so only after she had met Marla at the harbour and settled her into the hotel. She reserved a table for two at a very smart restaurant for the next evening for dinner, as a celebration of Marla's homecoming, looking forward to seeing her and hearing about her adventures in England. She had missed her terribly.

Meeting Bertie with Marla at the harbour had been an unexpected surprise. Bertie looked a nice enough young man, and she was pleased that Marla had enjoyed herself on the voyage over. However, when her brother Jonas approached her while she was waiting for them to disembark, she had been shocked. She never knew that he worked at the harbour. Then, when he told her that their mother was dying, that the doctor had said there was nothing he could do for her and that they should allow her to go quietly, the joy of meeting Marla was lost.

"I am here to meet my daughter, Marla, who has come home from a holiday in England," she told him when he asked her who she was meeting.

"But you never told us that you had a daughter or even that you may have married," he had said in astonishment. He had looked at her, at the way she was dressed. "My God," he had said, "looking at you, I believe that you are living as a White!"

She had said nothing, the thought of how quickly she could visit her mother foremost in her mind.

After Marla and Bertie cleared their luggage, she took them to the hotel. Fortunately there was a room for Bertie, en suite with the one she and Marla would be sharing. Then, seeing that they were settled, she excused herself by saying that she needed to go shopping.

Without dressing down, as she usually did whenever she visited her parent's home, she caught a taxi and made her way to her mother's house, in District Six. Over the years, she had helped her parents financially in renovating the house that she had grown up in, but with all the rumours circulating that the government would most likely move all the Coloured and African families living in District Six to a separate township, they did not want to spend more money on the house.

Her arrival by taxi made the neighbours look out of their doors and windows, wondering who she was. The grape vine that she remembered at the walkway to the front door had grown since her last visit, boasting the large juicy black grapes that she remembered so well. She walked into the house without knocking, surprising a young woman whom she did not know, who was in the kitchen, preparing lunch.

"Where is my mother?" she asked in Afrikaans, her Cape Coloured dialect automatically coming to the fore.

The young woman looked at her, not quite sure who she was.

"Your mother?" she asked.

"Yes," Emma replied, "the lady who lives in this house. My mother."

"In the bedroom," she replied, looking at Emma curiously.

Emma walked up the passage, opened the door to the bedroom and walked in. She was shocked when she saw her mother. She looked so very frail, so very old, lying in her bed, her eyes closed.

"Ma... it is me, Emily," she cried in Afrikaans, reaching for her mother's shriveled hand, the blue veins showing through her paper-thin translucent skin.

"Emily... Emily... is it really you?" her mother said, her voice tremulous with the emotion of seeing her daughter as she opened her eyes.

"Yes, Ma, it is me. I am here, with you."

"Oh, Emily, I am so sick."

"Yes, Ma, Jonas told me."

Emma comforted her. She watched her mother's eyes light up as she told her the truth about her life in Johannesburg. She poured it all out, not quite sure whether her mother understood or even heard what she was saying.

"I always knew that you were a child that was different from the others," her mother said softly, her voice quivering as she spoke. "I knew it, because you were born in a hospital, not at home like your brothers and sisters. I could see it in you as you grew up. Oh, you make me so happy." She closed her eyes, a smile on her face.

Emma spent the next hour holding her hand, watching her sleep, worried about her health. She was happy that her mother had recognized her and spoken to her. Then, leaning over, she kissed her on her forehead, then walked out of the room to go back to the hotel before the rest of the family arrived home from work. As she walked to the front door, she told the young woman who was still in the kitchen, unsure of whether she was family or not, that she would return the next day.

"You are Emily?" the girl asked, obviously having eavesdropped when Emma spoke to her mother.

"Yes," Emma replied.

"Oh Missus Emily…oh Missus Emily," the girl said, her voice filled with adoration, "you are so, so beautiful."

Emma smiled. Walking to the door, she turned and said, "Don't forget now, tomorrow. I will be back tomorrow," and she climbed into the taxi that waited for her. It had attracted a large number of young children around it.

The next morning, after Marla and Bertie had gone to sunbathe on Clifton beach, she went back to the house. There was now no longer any reason to dress down, so she dressed smartly, taking great care with her makeup and her hair.

When the taxi pulled up at the house, she saw that the house was full of family, most of whom she did not recognize. Jonas was waiting to meet her, and he helped her out of the taxi. As they walked through the crowd he introduced her to those members of the family she did not know. She hugged her sisters, shook hands with her brothers, and smiled at those cousins she knew, as she made her way to her mother's bedroom. They were all curious to meet this member of the family who, they had learned from Jonas, had broken the colour barrier.

They waited while she sat with her mother, eager to hear all about her, and her family. She showed them pictures of Marla that she had brought with her and told them about what she did for a living but she never told them that she had once lived in Potchefstroom, a predominantly Afrikaner town, only that she lived and owned a house in Johannesburg.

"Please, bring your daughter to visit us," they all begged her, and without much persuasion from them, she agreed to bring Marla to the house the next day.

That night, at the hotel, after enjoying her usual Johnny Walker Red Label with Marla and Bertie, she said, "Marla, I have something that is very personal to tell you."

"And Bertie and I, we have something to ask you," Marla replied, looking at Bertie. Before Emma could say anything, Bertie continued.

"Mrs. O'Neil -- Emma, Marla and I would like to marry. We want you to give us your blessing."

Emma was shaken. She had thought of Bertie as simply a boy who Marla had met on board ship, just like one of the many boyfriends she had had over the years. That it was a short friendly relationship. She had not thought that it would become this serious. It took her a few minutes to catch her breath and put her thoughts in order. Then, talking slowly as though looking for words to say the right thing, she replied.

"Bertie and Marla, this is wonderful. Yes, you do have my permission. I am so very happy for both of you."

"Oh, thank you, Ma," Marla rushed up to her mother and gave her a hug. "Thank you Ma." I knew that you would like Bertie. He will make you a wonderful son-in-law."

"Thank you, Emma," Bertie said, not quite sure whether he should hug and kiss her or not.

Then remembering what she wanted talk to Marla about, she wondered whether or not it would affect their planned relationship.

"Bertie," Emma asked in a quiet voice that Marla had learned meant that something serious was coming, "please excuse Marla and me for a few minutes. I do have to talk with Marla about something first. It is nothing to do with you and Marla, you both have my blessing, and I am so terribly happy for both of you, but I have to talk to Marla seriously about another matter."

"With pleasure," Bertie said, and then plucking up his courage, he kissed Emma on the cheek and left the room.

"What is so urgent that it cannot wait?" Marla asked.

"Sit down," Emma said. Marla, hearing the seriousness in her voice, sat down apprehensively.

"Do you remember that man who spoke to me at the harbour?" Emma began. "The man called Jonas who I told you worked for us?"

"Yes," Marla answered, puzzled, "but I found that strange, because I cannot place him at all."

"Well," Emma continued, walking to the window and looking out over the bay, "I lied to you. Jonas never did work for us. Jonas is actually my brother."

Marla looked at Emma, her face showing her disbelief. "But…but he is a Coloured man," she stuttered.

"Yes, that is correct," Emma replied, agitatedly turning to look at her. "He is a Coloured and for that matter, so am I." Marla looked shocked, her hand in front of her mouth, her eyes wide as she took in what Emma had just said.

"You see," Emma continued, her voice shaking with emotion as she spoke, "when I was a teenager, I found that being restricted; being classified a second-class citizen by the government, was more than I could bear, so I decided to jump the racial barrier and become a White, a European. I refused to allow myself to be categorized simply because of the colour of my family's skin. My skin was white and my hair was straight, not crinkled like theirs, but straight and above all brown. In those days as a young girl, I dyed it blonde so that I could sunbathe on Clifton beach as a White, with no questions asked."

Emma walked up and down the room nervously as she spoke. Marla sat in the chair, not quite believing what she heard.

"As a young girl," Emma continued, "I kept asking myself, 'what have I done to these people who rule South Africa and who persecute me and those like me, not because of my intellect, which was far superior to many of theirs, but simply because I was born into a family they classified as second class?'

"They went to church on a Sunday and so did I. They prayed to the same God that I prayed to, but they came out of their church believing that they had the right to separate the people of this country into various racial groups because of the colour of their skin. They could place legal restrictions on what we may or may not do or possess. That God had given them this divine right. What utter nonsense.

"When the Second World War ended, the world learned how Adolph Hitler and the Germans had classified the Jews, the Gypsies, the Russians and any race that they believed was inferior to them, including lesbians, homosexuals and any mentally handicapped person. And then they slaughtered them, like so much vermin, in their gas chambers or shot them in mass executions to be buried in open mass graves. Since then I have always wondered why Jan Christian Smuts, who was prime minister at that time; who fought the Germans, and saw what they did in Europe, did not repeal any of the hateful classification laws. Laws that the British had put in place. Then when Smuts lost the election to D.F. Malan and Malan appointed Hendrik

Verwoerd, a man I believed was influenced by the Nazis when he was a student in Germany, as Minister of Native affairs, those laws were intensified to the point of persecution. I have always wondered whether the National Party Government is going to follow Adolph Hitler's final solution, by first categorizing the South Africans, and then slaughtering those who are not the same colour as they are, in gas chambers like the Germans did."

She shook her head and continued, the bitterness showing in her voice. "They won't, of course, not because they don't want to but because they need cheap slave labour, so that they can continue with their comfortable lifestyle."

Emma had become very emotional as she spoke, her eyes blazing vehemently. Marla sat quietly listening to her mother, a mother that she had never before seen like this.

"I am sorry, my girl, perhaps I am overreacting, but I become very emotional on this subject." After a few minutes, with Marla sitting quietly watching a side of her mother that she had never known, Emma continued.

"Were you to ask me why I ran away from my family, a family I loved, then I must answer that it was to give myself a better life and to try and give them a better life. I never attended my father's funeral, because I never knew that he had died until after he was buried. They never, ever knew where to contact me. I even stole for them. That vase on the mantelpiece at home, the one I would never let you touch when you were growing up, that vase was full of uncut diamonds. Stop!" she held up her hand. "Don't ask me where they came from. I stole them, even though I did not know it at the time. Over the years I would sell them and send the money home to my father and mother so that they could educate my brothers and sisters, and give them a better life than they would have had if they had no money... the type of life I grew up with as a child. I have also used the money in many donations to help give both Blacks and

Coloureds a better education than they were receiving. That vase, with all the many coloured marbles; that vase is like South Africa, with its many different coloured peoples. The diamonds represent opportunity.

"When I was a teenager, I learned about apartheid when I was not allowed to go to the bioscope in Cape Town, or even sit on Clifton Beach, because it displayed a 'FOR WHITES ONLY' sign. I then thumbed my nose at apartheid and those hateful laws, and you, my beautiful daughter, you are the result of everything that I hoped and prayed you would be.

"One day, this stupid ridiculous regime will end. One day, everyone in this beautiful country of ours will be free, to live as equals. My only concern is that the government in charge will be a Black one, full of hate and revenge, and not educated enough to run this country efficiently. A black African is a black African is a black African, not a stupid African, but an African taught by tribal tradition to look after himself and his family first, and everyone else second. I know them well. I grew up knowing how they think.

"So my dear, I gave you what I had to fight for all my life. And in doing so, I had to forsake my family. But it was worth it. You are all I could have wished for. I did come to Cape Town at least once a year to see my parents and the family. And it was hard, hard to leave them when I had to. Please, don't judge me badly; please don't convict me for leaving my family – it was a decision I made at that time, and to be quite honest, I would make exactly the same decision today. I was a young girl who rebelled, a girl who would not accept apartheid and laws that I feel the world will, in years to come, condemn."

She sat down in the chair opposite Marla, who sat quietly listening to her, and took both her hands in hers.

"Years ago, I remember when on one of my sales trips, I had to go to Mbabane in Swaziland. I went to watch the traditional reed dance, where the King of Swaziland chooses a new wife from among the many young girls who dance before him. There was a black American, a Negro standing in front of me. He turned at the end of the ceremony and said with pride, 'These are my people.' I told him that the only thing he had in common with them was the colour of his skin, absolutely nothing else."

Emma paused, looking at Marla carefully.

"My darling," she said softly, her composure restored. "I tell you all of this because my mother is dying, and I would like her to meet you before she passes away."

"And here I thought you were telling me all this because you didn't want me to marry Bertie," Marla said.

"Good heavens, no, not at all," Emma answered, frowning. "He is a lovely man, and I welcome him with open arms as a son-in-law."

"Well," Marla continued, "he is already your son-in-law. Bertie and I had the captain of the ship marry us."

"You what?" it was Emma's turn to be shocked. "You and Bertie are already – married?" Her body started shaking with the shock. "But – but," she stammered, "what will he say when he finds out about what I have just told you? That your mother is a Coloured!"

"Let us find out what he will say," Marla said. "Let me call him."

She ran downstairs to fetch him and told him everything that Emma had told her. When he walked into the room, he walked up to Emma and said, "Emma, I love Marla. I love her as she is, for who she is and what she is. Were she an alien from Mars, it would not matter. I love your daughter, and I have loved her from the minute I first saw her."

"Ma," Marla said, putting her arm around Bertie, "if you want to, we can have a second white wedding here, in Cape Town, with your family, or in Johannesburg with the other family, whatever you want."

Still shaking with shock, Emma was surprised at how well both Marla and Bertie were taking it all. She answered, "Let me think about it," and then she laughed. "I suppose you will want to share a room with Bertie now, and not with me." And with the tension breaking, they all laughed.

"Well," Emma said after a few moments, scratching her forehead, "I suppose there should be another wedding, but let us have it in Potchefstroom, and nowhere else."

"Do you really want to, Mom? With the expense and all that…and why Potchefstroom, of all places?"

"But of course, darling, you must have a beautiful wedding! And your grandfather, Charlie, must give you away. I have a lot of friends in Potchefstroom, more than I have in Johannesburg, most of them Afrikaners. Some are even Nationalists, mind you, but they are Afrikaans-speaking friends that over the years I have learned to love. That is one of the reasons I always insisted that you must attend an Afrikaans school. A number of us are even preparing for the end of apartheid. It may take a number of years, but it will definitely come."

"You sound so sure of that," Marla said.

"Oh, there is no doubt about it," Emma answered. "To give you an example, one of us who is in the government is promoting a law to declare that the children of White fathers will be classified as White. I know that this sounds silly, but it is far better to work slowly, and achieve slowly than to oppose absolutely, and achieve nothing."

"You talk about 'us'," Marla said. "Who is 'us'?"

"I am sorry, but that I cannot tell you. It is a well-kept secret. I will tell you, though, that very soon, hopefully in the next few years, we will have a few of our sympathizers starting the difficult task of rewriting the South African constitution, leaving out any and all racial segregation. Now that is all I will tell you, so do not ask me for more."

"Do Gran'pa Charlie and Gran'ma Christa know about you, and everything you have just told me?"

"Yes," Emma said, "he is the one who helped me originally and he still helps me, which is why we are so very close."

Marla stood up, and gave Emma a hug.

"I love you, Mom," she said. "You will never, ever know just how much."

"I love you too, baby," Emma answered, hugging her.

The next day, she took Marla and Bertie with her to the house in District Six. She smiled to herself when she saw the curious faces of the family as she walked into the house, how they all looked at the three of them, some smiling, others not. She laughed happily as her brother, dressed in his Sunday clothes, leaned over and kissed her, and tried to peck at Marla's cheek.

Emma greeted everyone, in fluent Afrikaans with the Coloured accent, something Marla hadn't believed she was capable of doing. She guided Marla and Bertie into her mother's bedroom and after giving her mother a passionate kiss on the forehead, said to her, "Ma, this is your granddaughter, my daughter, Marla, and this young man is her husband, Bertie." Turning to Marla, she said with tears in her eyes, "Marla, say hello to my mother, your real grandmother."

Chapter 15

Emma's mother passed away the day after she had met Marla and Bertie. Emma delayed their departure by Blue Train back to Johannesburg by a week. The funeral that took place three days later was a small one, with only members of the family present. At the house, where the family met after the funeral, she found that she had become a curiosity, with many of the family asking her how she had jumped the racial barrier. She told them the truth, that she had simply moved to Johannesburg, where everyone assumed she was a White because she dressed, behaved and acted like a White. She did not tell them about the help she had received from Charlie Stuart and evaded further questions on the subject as much as she could.

The family looked at Bertie and Marla with curiosity. Bertie, in turn, was fascinated by them. They spoke Afrikaans, which he did not understand. The one or two who did talk with him in English did so with their beautiful Malay accent, which he told Emma afterwards he found most enjoyable and fascinating.

"Why do so many of the young women have their two front teeth missing?" he asked Emma when they were back at the hotel. She smiled and told him that it was the fashion amongst the young Coloured girls. "It is called a passion gap," she said, looking at him, not sure whether he understood.

Marla giggled, and burst out with, "Ma-a-a-a!"

Bertie thought for a minute. "Of course you are joking," he exclaimed.

"Not at all," Emma laughed, "I am quite serious."

He shook his head and said, "Well, if that is the custom, then it is a strange one."

Bertie enjoyed meeting her family, developing a strong friendship with one of the sons of Emma's brother Jonas, who had a wonderful sense of humour. He was shocked to see how the laws of South Africa discriminated against these people, forcing them to live in, what he felt, were slums on the outskirts of Cape Town.

"Apartheid is horrific," he told Marla later that evening. "To classify a person because of the colour of their skin as a second-class citizen is absolutely sick. My father fought in the war, and taught me never to forget what Nazi Germany did with their horrific discriminatory laws. And here in South Africa, they practice exactly the same thing?"

He looked at her, and held her by her shoulders so that she could see the seriousness in his eyes. "I want you never to forget that I love you. I love you because of who you are, and who you will one day be. I will always love you and nothing in this world will ever change that." She moved into his arms, and he held her close to him.

Bertie admired his mother-in-law even more and, as he got to know her, he respected her for having beaten and bested the system. He could see where Marla had got her determination and personality. He enjoyed talking with Emma and learning more about the political tragedy of South Africa from her.

"I will be very happy to take Marla away from this sick country," he told her, "and I sincerely hope that you will come with us."

She smiled gratefully, but said nothing.

In the train, on their way back to Johannesburg, they planned the wedding. It would be within a month, if they could get the church. Emma belonged to the Methodist church, and on occasion when she lived in Potchefstroom, had helped out as secretary, so she felt that they would oblige her. Bertie, however, was an Anglican, a member of the Church of England. He asked Marla if she would agree to marry in the Anglican church. This meant that Emma would have to ask Charlie

Stuart, who was also an Anglican, to reserve St. Mary's Church for her. The church was a small one, built entirely of stone. It was the first Anglican church in the Transvaal, and boasted beautiful stained glass windows.

"Will you be sending invitations to the family in Cape Town?" Marla and Bertie asked.

"No," Emma answered. "In Potchefstroom that will not work. Better to have a separate celebration with the family in Cape Town."

'*Not quite true,*' she thought, '*but better not to take any chances.*'

"When the two of you return to Cape Town to catch the boat back to England," she told them, "then we can throw a party, or simply have a small family gathering. That is, if you still want to."

"I would very much like to," Bertie replied, then looking at Marla, he asked, "Don't you agree, Marla? They are our family, and should share in our celebration."

Emma was pleased with his answer. She truly liked her son-in-law.

Once they arrived in Johannesburg, Bertie phoned his parents and told them of the intended wedding. He never told them that he and Marla had been married on the *Windsor Castle*. They were pleasantly surprised and said that they would fly out and celebrate with them. The flight would take almost 24 hours from London to Johannesburg, with stops in Paris, Rome, Cairo, Nairobi, Brazzaville and Salisbury.

He had still not told Emma and Marla who his parents were, and Emma had not pressed him as to his background. He had told her, though, when she did ask, as any mother would, that he could keep her daughter in the style she was accustomed to.

"I have a flat in Chelsea," he told her. "As soon as Marla has settled and familiarizes herself with London, we shall look for and buy a house. I have a very good paying job. Money is no object."

Emma, on the other hand, felt that there were enough diamonds left in the vase to help them get started in life if they ever needed a hand.

They spent the next few days showing Bertie Johannesburg, also introducing him to the Rosens. A week before the day of the wedding, they drove to Potchefstroom to conclude all the arrangements for the wedding and reception. Charlie and Christa Stuart insisted that they stay with them, and with Marie and her family coming from Pretoria, the house was very full. At eighty four years old, Charlie was no longer that active, spending most of his days fishing at his favourite spot at the Potchefstroom dam. One would find him fast asleep in his canvas chair, reeking of citronella oil and garlic to keep the mosquitoes away, his line cast in the water, looking for a bite that seldom came. Although he now found it more difficult to braai, his arthritis troubling him, he still enjoyed entertaining. He especially enjoyed sitting under the grapevine chatting, drinking sherry, wine or beer after eating a thick well-done steak, with boerewors and pap or whatever else Christa and her two maids prepared in the kitchen. Bertie was fascinated by him, and enjoyed talking to him as he sat there with a glass of beer in his hand nibbling at pieces of biltong.

"What is this that you are eating?" Bertie asked, taking a strip of biltong and carefully tasting it.

"That is biltong," Charlie said. "Biltong is raw meat that has been salted and dried, another delicacy that the Boers introduced us to."

"Hmm, it is quite tasty," Bertie said, nibbling at the piece. "I can now understand why all your rugby players are big and healthy men. With all this wonderful meat and beer, one can only be big and tough."

Charlie and Johan, who had joined them, both laughed and Charlie, stretching his Scottish accent to the full said, "My frrrriend, you forrrrget that I am frrrrom that bonnie Scotland. I only learrrrrned this custom of brrrrraaing from the Boerrrrs."

The day before the wedding, Irma and Solly Rosen met Peter and Isabel, Bertie's parents, at the Jan Smuts airport in Johannesburg. They arrived in the late afternoon after travelling all night by plane, and were tired from the journey. Irma drove them to her house in

Houghton, where they were to spend the night and freshen up before driving to Potchefstroom early the next morning for the wedding.

Over dinner that evening Irma offhandedly asked Isabel, "What does Bertie do for a living?"

Peter, remembering Bertie's request not to say too much about themselves, cleared his throat to remind his wife.

"Well," Isabel answered, her husband jabbing her in the side with his elbow. "Ouch!," she exclaimed. "Uhh, well, Bertie was always a bit of a wild one as a young boy. He rebelled, taking life as it is, and enjoyed it to the full, giving Peter and me plenty to worry about. He was almost expelled from Eton in his final year, but my husband fortunately managed to pull some strings."

Peter gruffly cleared his throat and Isabel took two steps away from him.

"He enjoyed hiking through Europe, almost as though he was running away from home. He even preferred remaining at boarding school with his friends, and he had many of them, rather than be at home with us, perhaps because of our social.....uuhhh," and she grunted as an elbow caught her in her side again.

Irma looked at both of them, not understanding what had happened.

After a few seconds, and standing a little further away from Peter, Isabel continued. "He went to Oxford University to study law, but rather than join a legal practice when he was qualified, he joined Peter's company. I must say that in the past two years, what he has achieved is something quite remarkable. He has become a great deal more responsible and respected amongst all his friends. Wouldn't you agree, Peter?"

"Forgive me for asking," Irma asked, "but does he earn a good salary? Marla is a wonderful person and is as much my own daughter as she is Emma's. We love her dearly, we all do. We only want to make sure that she will be well looked after when she is married."

Isabel Winslow looked at her husband and smiled. "She will be well looked after," Peter answered, nodding his head. "Of that, I can assure you."

"I must say that when Bertie told me he was marrying a South African girl, I was at first, very apprehensive," Peter said to Solly later that evening. They had walked outside after dinner and were sipping sherry while sitting in the garden under the huge Jacaranda tree. "But from what my son has told me about Marla, she sounds like a very fine person."

"She is, she really is," Solly answered, "she will make you a wonderful daughter-in-law. We will all miss her terribly. But tell me, why would her being a South African girl have troubled you?"

"Hmmmppp," Peter grunted, clearing his throat, "just never sure whether they will adapt to our social life." Then changing the subject, he continued, "If her mother is going to miss her, then she will simply have to join us and spend more time in London. We have a large house in Berkley Square, and she can have her own suite of rooms with a separate entrance."

"*My girl,*" thought Solly, "*your daughter's future parents-in-law own a house with a separate suite of rooms in Berkley Square. Not bad, not bad at all. If I could ever have been told a Cinderella story, then I have just heard one. Emma, my dear, from living in the shanty towns of Cape Town, to living in the poshest of houses in London. How absolutely magnificent.*"

The next morning, Solly and Irma drove the Winslows to Potchefstroom for the wedding. They found the countryside, with its khaki coloured grass and rolling hills, fascinating.

"I always thought South Africa would be wild, teeming with game," Isabel said, "yet we haven't seen any animals other than a few cows."

Solly smiled. "The game has been mostly confined to game reserves, but in the Northern Transvaal, on the Limpopo River, they still wander around freely. A friend of ours has a farm there, and we often go hunting on his farm in the winter. The last time I was there, last

July in fact," Solly continued, "as I was stalking a koedoe bull, a lioness with cubs crossed about twenty feet in front of me. I stood absolutely still. After she had passed, I waited about a quarter of an hour before I continued walking."

"Weren't you scared?" Peter asked.

"I nearly wet myself," Solly replied, "but the two boys that were with me, well, they were so scared that it took them about five seconds to climb up a thorn tree, and twenty minutes to climb down."

They all laughed.

As they approached Potchefstroom, the scenery changed to the green of willow trees on the banks of the Mooi River. Isabel couldn't help but remark as they drove over the bridge into the town, "After driving through all that brown, khaki, what do you call it, 'felt'? What a beautiful town this is. The gardens are full of flowers, and everything is so green."

"That is because there is a large dam at the top of the town, so they are never short of water for the gardens, even in the driest of seasons," Irma told her.

Solly drove them to the Kings Hotel, where they booked into the rooms Emma had reserved for them. Bertie was pleased to see them. He was stranded at the hotel by that marriage rule, 'thou shalt not see thy bride on thy wedding day until the ceremony.'

Once they had dressed for the wedding, Solly drove Isabel and Peter to the Stuarts' home to meet Marla and Emma. Charlie, in a Scottish kilt that he only wore on special occasions, met them at the door.

"Mr. and Mrs. Winslow," he said jovially, "welcome, welcome to Potchefstroom and my humble abode. Marie, Emma, Christa," he shouted down the passage of the house, "come and meet your daughter's future parents-in-law."

Turning to Peter, he asked, "and what would you prefer, a Black Label, or a glass of bubbly?" He took Peter by the elbow and led him, followed by Isabel, Irma and Solly, into the lounge. He walked to his liquor cabinet, where he popped a cork on a bottle of champagne and poured glasses, which he handed around the room without waiting to hear what their preference was.

Emma, Christa and Marie, with Johan following them, walked into the lounge.

"Let me introduce you," Charlie said to Peter and Isabel. "This is your future daughter-in-law's mother, Emma. And here is my wife, Christa, and daughter, Marie, with her husband, Johan. Everybody, this is Peter and Isabel Winslow. Introduce yourselves."

Marla, looking absolutely beautiful in a white wedding dress, walked into the room followed by her two bridesmaids. She was anxious to meet Bertie's parents.

"And here," Charlie boasted, walking up to Marla where she stood with Laura and Ingrid, "are my three beautiful granddaughters." Laura, holding Marla's hand, looked very much like her mother, Marie, with dark brown hair captured by a crown of flowers. Ingrid, a year and a half younger, stood behind her. She was tall, like her father. Her blonde hair, also crowned with flowers, made her look even taller. Both girls were bridesmaids, wearing blue satin dresses trimmed with gauze that Christa had hastily sewn.

"It is a pleasure to meet you at last," Isabel said, walking up to Marla. "Albert has told us so much about you, but you are far lovelier than he could have ever described you."

They stood around talking with Isabel, making a point of talking to Marla and Emma.

"Our house in London is always open to you," she said to Emma. "Bertie's flat is rather small, but until they have bought a house, should you come to London you will have to stay with us."

"Thank you," Emma replied. "I really appreciate your offer."

"Well," Charlie interrupted, "more of all this later. We have to be at the church in a half hour, so let us enjoy our drinks first. Marla, Johan will be driving you with your two bridesmaids, so just see that you are all ready. You will be the last to leave. Johan, you are driving the bridal car. You must drive slowly. Take a long route around to get there. A bride must always be late for her wedding…but not too late, mind you," and he ushered the three girls back into the bedroom.

The church was hidden behind the buildings of King Edward Street, close to a poplar tree forest. Floral bouquets surrounded its entrance. With the flowering dahlias in the small garden, the scene was a welcoming delight to the guests, all of whom had to walk down a small lane between the Ackermans' clothing and Bortz' furniture stores to get to the church.

It was clever of Emma to have the wedding in Potchefstroom. Over one hundred people, including the mayor and his wife, all of them friends, were present when Charlie Stuart gave Marla away. After the ceremony, Marla and Bertie with Emma, Isabel and Peter stood at the entrance shaking hands with their guests as they walked out of the church.

Alf and Lilly, with Josh, were among the last to leave.

"Are you perhaps not Lord Peter Winslow?" Lilly Stern asked as she shook Peter's hand. Bertie, who was standing next to his father, almost choked.

"Err, uhh…yes," Peter answered gruffly, looking at Bertie.

"Then you are Lady Isabel Winslow," Lilly said, taking Isabel's hand. Turning to Alf, she continued, "You see, Alf, I was right."

Everyone that heard her looked at each other, astonished.

"I don't understand the importance of what Lilly just said," Emma said to Charlie.

"Good heavens," Charlie interrupted her. Turning to Peter he asked, "Are you the Lord Winslow of…?"

Peter looked embarrassed. "Uhh…Yes," he interrupted Charlie.

"My God," Charlie said in astonishment. "That means that…"

"Yes," Peter said again, not allowing him to finish.

"What is going on?" Emma whispered in Charlie's ear. "Charlie, what is this?"

"Well," Charlie swallowed and whispered, loud enough so that Marla who was standing next to her could hear. "You had better relax and be prepared. You see, my dear Emma, your daughter has just married the son of the richest man in England, possibly the fifth richest in the world, and above all, a member of England's royal family."

Emma would never forget the look that Marla gave Bertie.

"Is this true?" Marla asked, astonishment written all over her face. "Is your father really the Lord Winslow?"

Bertie looked embarrassed. "Well, uhh, yes," he answered.

"But…why didn't you tell me who you were?" she asked angrily.

"I didn't want you to marry me for my money," Bertie answered, "I wanted you to marry and love me for me, and me alone, and now you have; twice, as a matter of fact."

"But how could you keep it from me? What if I felt that being part of your family, and a member of the royal family, was not what I wanted? What if…?"

"Marla," Bertie said, taking her into his arms, "do you love me?"

She looked at him, her anger melting. "Yes," she said softly.

"That is all that matters," he answered. "Nothing else does. Oh, by the way, you don't have an engagement ring. I never ever gave you one. Mother brought me this one to give to you. It was my late grandmother's ring." He took a ring, mounted with large blue-white diamond in a setting surrounded by smaller pink diamonds, out of his pocket. "Please do wear it." He took her hand and placed it on her ring finger. "A little bit large," he said. "Your fingers are very slim."

She looked at it, astonishment on her face. "It is really beautiful," she said. "It must be worth an absolute fortune."

The reception in the town hall continued until midnight. Everyone was tired and happy. Saying goodnight to each other, they promised to meet for a late breakfast at Charlie and Christa's home the following morning.

The next morning, after enjoying a hearty brunch at the Stuarts' house, Peter and Isabel left with Bertie and Marla on their honeymoon. Bertie had insisted that they join them on a tour of the Kruger National Park before returning to London. He wanted them to get to know Marla and for Marla to find out exactly who the family was that she had married into, and the society she would be joining when they returned to London.

Two weeks later, Marla and Bertie left South Africa for England. Marla had packed all her personal mementoes into crates that Emma promised to send to her. Bertie told Marla to bring as little of her clothes with her as she needed. The family would take her shopping once she was in London for the latest in fashion.

"Are you telling me that my taste in fashion is wanting?" she asked him, teasingly.

"No…not at all," he answered, not sure whether he had hurt her or not. "It is just that somehow, here in South Africa, my mother said that the fashion appears to be about a year behind that of England. I just thought you would like the latest, not that it means that much to me."

She smiled and hugged him. "Thank you. I will enjoy the shopping experience, hopefully with your mother, if she will take me."

"I am sure she will," Bertie said, wiping the sweat from his forehead, pleased that he had not slighted her as he feared he may have.

The day before they caught the *Edinburgh Castle* back to Southampton, they gave a small party to the Cape Town family, who were pleased to see them. As they boarded the ship, Emma promised Marla that she would visit her in London once she was settled. Emma tried not to cry, but she simply could not hold back the tears that streamed down her face as she hugged her daughter goodbye.

Emma spent a week with her family before catching the train back to Johannesburg. The house in Parkhurst was empty with Marla gone, but she was pleased to be home. She stood in front of the mantelpiece and looked at the vase holding the marbles and the last of the diamonds. She rearranged the display of roses in the vase, and added a dahlia she had cut in the garden.

"*You have served me well over the years,*" she thought, "*I have simply to look at Marla's face to see that. She has turned out to be quite a remarkable child.*" She smiled to herself. "*To think that after all these years, no-one knew that you were there, and now, with Marla's marriage to a very nice young man, you have also brought a great deal of happiness.*"

There were only a few stones left in the vase, but her financial dependence was no longer tied to the diamonds. Over the years, she had invested wisely and had built up a very sizable portfolio with stockbrokers in Johannesburg.

She walked outside and sat on the verandah, looking at the swimming pool. It was only then that she started to feel really lonely. Yes, she had her friends in Johannesburg, but living alone at home would never be quite the same. The shock of finding out that Bertie's father was one of the wealthiest men in England, and that Bertie himself was a very wealthy man in his own right, with Marla moving into the top echelon of English society, had almost worn off.

"*Well, I must say it has been a hectic three weeks full of surprises,*" she mused as she sat on the verandah, a glass of Johnnie Walker in her hand. "*So much has happened. It is nice to have a son-in-law that I like — actually when I think of it I do like him very much. But I am sad as well, because he has taken my daughter away from me, and to England.*"

She sighed, a tear trickling down her cheeks. "*But, I suppose, that is life. I will have gained a son, but I will have also lost a daughter.*" She thought of the vase. "*Well, you will now have to help me plan future trips to London, and I never wanted to leave South Africa. Life definitely has its twists.*"

She took another sip at the glass of whisky she held in her hand,

and watched a stork fly from the chimney of the house next door, across the swimming pool to perch on the tree close to where she sat. *"Is this a sign?"* she asked herself.

Feeling lonely, even though she had spent a few nights at dinner with Irma and Solly, she decided to visit Potchefstroom and the Stuarts that weekend. As usual, they sat in the back garden under the grape vine while Charlie braaied his steak and boerewors and Christa worked in the kitchen.

"So, what are your plans?" Charlie asked her after they had all eaten.

"I want to go to London and visit Marla," Emma said. "That means that I have to apply for a passport, and I am scared that it will identify me as a Coloured."

"So what?" Charlie said, "Go to London, and live there permanently. If necessary, become a British citizen. You have achieved a great deal for us here, and in London, you could help us even more."

"How?" Emma asked. "How can I help you in London?"

"The same way you helped us here. By talking to people and by appealing to influential people; by presenting your story to anyone and everyone that will listen to you, that is how. Legislation where children of White fathers will be classified as White is a foregone conclusion, thanks to your hard work. Also, thanks to you, Black school children realize that they can only succeed in running this country effectively after they receive a proper and decent education. The limited education the Government insists they must have is a joke. I think you have done a great deal in your own small way.

"By the way, I asked an old friend of yours to come over for a visit. I must admit that I believe he frightened you at the time, but he was just doing his job. He is now retired, so he doesn't have to pretend any longer."

"Who is he?" Emma asked.

"Wait until he comes," and as Charlie said this, Brigadier Grobelaar walked into the garden. He was a lot older, and being out of uniform, it took Emma a while before she recognized him.

"Good evening Mrs. O'Neil," he said in his deep, gruff voice, a voice that Emma had never forgotten. He held out his hand, smiling at her, his steely blue eyes that had been so cold when she first met him now laughing and friendly.

"Good evening, Brigadier. My God," Emma said shocked, "Charlie, who else is a member of your organization?"

"That, my dear," Charlie said, "you will never know. Not even I know, especially now that I am no longer active."

"Brigadier Grobelaar," Emma said, turning to him, "how can you ever face me after you murdered my dog?"

"That, my dear lady, was not I. I was very upset when I heard about it, and the officer who did it was transferred into the bundu."

"Then why did you not tell me? Why did you allow me and my daughter to hate you all these years?"

"You had to," he replied. "If you did not, I would no longer have been in the position I was. A large number of people hated me, and I had many a sleepless night about that, but I do think that in the years I served, I prevented a lot of people from being killed. "

"Prevented being killed?"

"Yes, a lot more people would have been killed had I not been there."

"Do you sleep at night?" Emma asked looking at him with disdain.

He never gave her an answer. Then he reached into his right pocket and pulled out an envelope.

"This is for you," he said, holding it out to Emma.

"What is it?" Emma asked, not taking it from him.

"It is your passport."

"My what?" she looked at him in astonishment.

"Your passport."

Emma looked at him, then at Charlie, confusion in her eyes.

"I learned many years ago that family comes before friends," Charlie said, amused at her obvious confusion. "I knew that it was just a matter of time before you would want to join Marla in London. Also, as I told you, we need someone like you in England. The quicker you leave, the better for all. We now need you there."

Marla looked at him, tears in her eyes. "I love you, Charlie," she said gratefully. "You are truly a wonderful man."

Charlie smiled.

"I have news for you," Brigadier Grobelaar interrupted. "We found that there is only one place where he does not have security guards around him. That is in parliament."

"That is interesting," Charlie said. "I would never have thought of that."

Emma thought for a few minutes about what he said. "If you are talking about what I think you are talking about, I think I can help here," Emma looked carefully at Charlie and the Brigadier as she spoke. "I will have to make a few phone calls, but leave it with me. I will let you know what can be arranged in a week's time."

Epilogue

It took Emma a little less than a year to sell her house in Parkhurst, tie up her affairs and say goodbye to all her friends in South Africa. She hired a firm of movers to transport all her furniture to her brother in Cape Town, to be distributed amongst the family, rather than sell it. But she kept a certain vase with its marbles and stones.

In that same year, sad to say, Charlie Stuart passed away. When he did not return home from one of his fishing trips, Christa and her two maids went looking for him. They found him in his chair at his usual fishing spot, a smile on his face, a fish pulling on his rod. One can only say that he died a happy man. Emma attended his funeral, with Marla and Bertie flying in from London. It was a large one, the church filled with people from all over the country, few that Emma knew.

Solly and Irma Rosen threw a small farewell party for her. She was sad to say her goodbyes, but she told them that she would visit South Africa as often and whenever she could. They, in turn, were planning to emigrate to Canada, and promised to stop over and visit her in London. She was going to live with Isabel and Peter until she found an apartment. She had been advised to sell the few uncut diamonds she still had in the vase in Amsterdam, if ever she needed the money, which she didn't because she was financially comfortable.

Once she had settled in London, Peter Winslow offered her a job, as buyer for women's clothes for his organization. This meant that she was often present at fashion shows, both in London and Paris. She was always a guest at his house with any function that he and Isabel gave, and it was at one of these functions that she met John Milne, a widower. John was a Member of Parliament and a cabinet minister in the present government. After a short courtship, they married. As his wife, Emma had a strong influence over British parliamentary feelings towards South African apartheid, expressing her viewpoint liberally at functions whenever she was asked.

In that same year Marla gave birth to the first of her three children. She and Bertie bought a house in Hampstead, a house that Marla was very happy with. When, at the age of seventy, Bertie's father, Peter, retired, Bertie took over the chairmanship of the board of Winslow's.

Emma, with the help of her husband, John, became more involved in finding ways to bring an end to apartheid. She joined the anti-apartheid movement in the United Kingdom, and was instrumental in debating the imposition of economic sanctions in order to weaken the Botha government. In spite of her anti-apartheid feelings and becoming more and more into contact with black African Nationalist Party leaders, she became more convinced than ever that the country would be on the road to ruin under Black leadership. She started considering that perhaps the way to prevent this was for South Africa to form a government of proportional representation of the three racial groups, Black, White and Indian, with the Coloureds being part of the White group.

"It has always worried me," she confided in her husband, "that under the apartheid regime, the Indian and Coloured community prospered, becoming doctors, scientists, educators and professionals, even though they were suppressed. But the Blacks, who were equally suppressed, remained but for the odd few, hewers of wood."

In 1998, when she was 78 years old, Emma returned to South Africa for the last time. Over the years she had had numerous visits from members of her family, and had visited them in turn, helping her brothers and sisters financially when they moved into Cape Town proper, once apartheid was abolished with the election of Nelson Mandela as president. She was heartbroken when she toured the centre of Johannesburg to find that the City Centre, Hillbrow, Yeoville and suburbs in which she had spent a great deal of time, had become slums of squalor, with buildings boarded up and squatters occupying any accommodation they could find. Successful businesses were all operating from shopping malls, to her a sign that White-, Indian- and Coloured-owned business areas were better managed and more secure than the businesses in the Black-run municipal areas.

When she visited Potchefstroom, on a memory trip, she was hurt to see that Kerk Street, now named Walter Sisulu Street, was as much a slum as that of the Johannesburg centre, with all the major businesses moving to newly built shopping malls surrounding the town. She wrote a letter to the mayor expressing her sorrow at the inability of the Town Council to manage the town effectively. She received a very polite letter of response from the mayor, promising nothing.

That she had been correct in her feelings, namely that the Blacks in South Africa, when they came to power, would be unable to govern effectively, disappointed her. Her continual belief that it would take three to four generations of education for them to bring their standards up to that of the Whites was justified in what she saw. South Africa, she felt, was on the road to ruin, a second Zimbabwe. Tribal instinct of looking after oneself and one's family first, and everyone else second, was ingrained with all the African tribes.

Cape Town, she felt, was a different kettle of fish, because it was a city where the city council was heavily weighted towards the White, Coloured and Indian communities, and not overwhelmingly Black. She wondered how long that would last and felt that the end, when it came, would be sudden.

Emma returned to London a heartbroken woman, disappointed that although her years of work, as small a part as it had been in removing apartheid from the country, was successful, the country was decaying fast, with the Black leadership placing their personal bank accounts ahead of the welfare of the citizens. The increase in criminal activity in the country also worried her, which she took as a sign that the government was unable to look after its citizens effectively. Four years later, at the age of 82, she passed away peacefully in her sleep.

Marla and Bertie, following the instructions in her will, had her body cremated. They flew to Cape Town, where, when hiking on Table Mountain early one morning, they allowed the wind to settle her ashes.

Today, should you visit the home of Albert and Marla Winslow, you will see in the entrance hall a vase of flowers on a specially designed pedestal. The stems of the flowers are held in place by a large number of coloured marbles, amongst which is one small uncut diamond carefully mounted on the inside of the vase above the waterline. Whenever anyone asks Marla about the vase, she always tells them the following.

"That vase always stood on the mantelpiece above the fireplace in my mother's home for as long as I can remember. It was always filled with marbles of many colours, amongst which were a large number of colourless stones, which I later learned were uncut diamonds. The vase boasted a flower display that my mother personally arranged every day.

"The vase is like South Africa, a country filled with people of many colours, a few who are truly uncut gems. The flowers represent hope for a prosperous future, also displaying the incredible beauty of the country. The gems represent those few who worked so hard over many years to repeal the apartheid laws, putting the welfare of the people of the country ahead of any personal greedy needs, something the present African leaders have still to learn. My mother was one of those gems, and that little stone that you see there, in the vase with the flowers, is all about my mother's life."

The Politics

In 1962 The United Nations called for an arms embargo on South Africa. This was the start of an arms industry in the country that eventually led to the successful development of an atom bomb.

In November of 1963, President Kennedy of the United States was assassinated. Many in the non-white community were devastated, because they believed that a possible saviour was no more.

In 1964, the leader of the banned African National Congress, Nelson Mandela, was sentenced to life imprisonment. Black protests against apartheid grew stronger and more violent. In the same year, South Africa was banned from competing in the Olympic Games.

In 1965, South Africa officially declared that children of White fathers were to be considered White. This law made many who worked against apartheid feel that they were slowly winning the battle.

On February 11, 1966, District Six was declared a Whites-only area under the Group Areas Act with removals starting in 1968. The Government gave four primary reasons for the decision. The main reason was their belief that interracial interaction bred conflict. Most of the residents believed that the government sought the land because of its proximity to Cape Town's city centre, Table Mountain and the harbour. The more than 60,000 residents were relocated to the sandy, bleak Cape Flats township complex approximately 25 kilometers away from Cape Town. The old houses of District Six were bulldozed to the ground. Places of worship were allowed to remain.

On September 6, 1966, Dr Verwoerd entered the House of Assembly at 2:15 p.m. As he made his way to the front bench, he exchanged greetings with those around him. Just as he was taking his seat, a uniformed parliamentary messenger, Dimitri Tsafendas, a Coloured, walked briskly across the floor from the lobby entrance. Without warning, Tsafendas drew a sheath knife from under his clothing. He bent over Dr Verwoerd and raised his right hand high into the air. With his left hand, he plucked off the sheath and then stabbed Dr Verwoerd four times in the chest, killing him.

After Verwoerd's assassination, Balthazar Johannes Vorster was elected by the National Party to replace him. Vorster had in his youth attracted notoriety by opposing South Africa's intervention on the side of the Allies in World War II and speaking favourably of Adolph Hitler's Nazi regime. In 1942 he was detained for involvement with the Ossebrandwag, a pro-Nazi organization. He continued with Verwoerd's implementation of apartheid legislation and in 1968, the last four parliamentary seats that had been reserved for White representatives of Coloured voters were abolished. He was, however, more pragmatic than Verwoerd in that he pursued diplomatic relations with African countries, allowing African diplomats to live in White areas. His rationale was that if they could accept and acknowledge the apartheid regime, the rest of the world would follow.

It was also during this period, 1966, that the Angolan Bush War started in South West Africa, between South Africa and the National Union for the Total Independence of Angola (UNITA) on the one side and the Angolan Government, South-West Africa People's Organisation (SWAPO) and their allies, the Soviet Union and Cuba, on the other side. This war was to last until 1989, a war that ate heavily into South Africa's finances and ended with South West Africa's independence from South Africa and the formation of Namibia.

South Africa experienced its own scandal similar to the Watergate Scandal in the United States, known as the Muldergate Scandal. It was named for a cabinet minister, Dr. Connie Mulder. He was behind the 1976 effort to establish an English-language newspaper called *The Citizen* that would favour the National Party. The businessman set up to operate the paper was Louis Luyt, an entrepreneur who made his fortune in the fertilizer business in Potchefstroom, but was best known for running the nation's rugby union organization. When it came to light, the Muldergate Scandal forced the resignation of B.J. Vorster after his having served for 12 years as prime minister. Vorster was elected honorary state president, but by mid-1979, he also had to resign from that office in disgrace after it was revealed that he had known everything about the scheme. He died a mere four years later, at age 67.

Eschel Rhoodie, the Secretary of Information, was instrumental in organizing this project, which was called Project Annemarie, after his teenage daughter. When the scandal was aired, Rhoodie fled South Africa to France, but was extradited back to South Africa and sentenced to 12 years in prison for fraud, serving only 3 years after an Appeal. He then emigrated to the United States of America, where he died in 1993.

In 1976 an uprising in the black township of Soweto spread to other black townships, and left 600 dead.

Stephen Bantu Biko famous for his slogan, "Black is beautiful," was an anti-apartheid activist in South Africa in the 1960s and 1970s. As a student leader, he founded the Black Consciousness Movement, which would empower and mobilize much of the urban black population. In 1977, he died in detention. He became a martyr of the anti-apartheid movement. The ANC used his image as an imitation of "Che" Guevara, the major figure of the Cuban Revolution.

In 1978, Pieter Willem ("P.W") Botha, with a nickname Die Groot Krokodil (Afrikaans for 'The Big Crocodile"), became Prime Minister.

In September 1979, a double flash over the Indian Ocean detected by a U.S. satellite was suspected of being a South African nuclear test in collaboration with Israel. No official confirmation was made. The explosion was clean and was not supposed to be detected. To many, it was ironic that a National Party regime that started life leaning towards Nazism should look to a Jewish state for assistance in armament development.

In 1983, President Botha proposed a new constitution accepted by the White South Africa voters. Though the proposed new constitution did not implement a federal system, it created two new houses of parliament, one for the Coloureds (House of Representatives) and one for the Indians (House of Delegates).

The new Tricameral Parliament theoretically had equal legislative powers, but the laws each house passed were effective solely for its own community. The plan included no chamber or system of representation for the Black majority. This was because Blacks were relegated to their bantustans, a homeland for each black ethnic group that was to move gradually to a greater state of independence within South Africa. The system was based, and similar to, the First Nation Reserves created in Canada for the various Indian (Native American) tribes. The belief was that if the world could accept it in Canada, then they could do so in South Africa.

Interracial marriage was legalized and the Group Areas Act, which banned non-Whites from living in certain areas, was relaxed. Botha also authorized contacts with the ANC leader, Nelson Mandela. However, he would not cede power to the Blacks.

It was during this period that a number of lecturers at the Potchefstroom University secretly began rewriting the South African constitution, leaving out all forms of discrimination and apartheid.

During the 1980's Dr. Desmond Tutu, a Christian cleric, rose to fame as a South African activist and opponent to apartheid. As the first black South African Anglican Archbishop of Cape Town, he used his pulpit as a platform in the defense of human rights. In 1984, he received the Nobel Peace Prize.

The same year, President Botha became the first Executive State President.

During the late 1980's, foreign investment in South Africa declined, and disinvestment began to have a serious effect on the nation's economy. The war against SWAPO on the South West Africa/Angolan border was costly, and with money no longer coming into the country, a solution to end the war had to be found.

On Feb 2, 1989, President Botha suffered a mild stroke and resigned as leader of the National Party. F. W. de Klerk was selected by parliamentary caucus as leader. In March 1989 he was elected as State President but because President Botha refused to resign, even though incapacitated, on 15 August, 1989, he was sworn in as acting State President, and only the following month was nominated by the electoral college to succeed Botha in a five-year term as State President.

F. W. de Klerk was far more liberal than anyone in South Africa had anticipated, arranging the release of Nelson Mandela and the dismantling of the apartheid system. In 1993, Frederik Willem de Klerk and Nelson Mandela were both awarded the Nobel Peace Prize for their work in the peaceful termination of the apartheid regime and for laying the foundations for a new democratic South Africa.

On 27 April, 1994, South Africa's first racially inclusive democratic elections were held.

Acknowledgments

The two books that make up the VASE WITH THE MANY COLOURED MARBLES, EMMMA, and MARLA, could not have been written free of factual errors without the assistance of Dr. Jonathan Singer, who checked and rechecked historical errors I made. The editing of the book, by Lynn Thompson, with suggestions and improvements made by her in my writing, especially with the scenic beauty of South Africa, was a learning curve. My gratitude will always be with her.

Finally to a friend of many years who lives in Potchefstroom. A friend that did the final editing, pointing out numerous errors I had made and, knowing many of the characters in the book, helped with numerous suggestions.

In writing the two stories, I consulted books, newspapers and websites, as well as delving into my memory of past events during my life in Potchefstroom. Re-living many of the events was not easy, and I had many nightmares and regrets as to whether the outcome may have differed had I taken a different route. I decide to stick to the original facts of my life, and those family and friends that make up the story.

Yes, the people mentioned in the book are people who lived in Potchefstroom, and did truly work against the Apartheid policies of the National Government, hating Hendrik Verwoerd for his National Socialist ideology, always scared that he would tilt towards extreme Nazism. Yet, when he was shot by David Pratt, his wife, Betsy, ran to a Jewish friend for comfort in Johannesburg. I shall not mention her name, but only say that she was a part of my family.

Did the characters in the book truly exist? Yes, they did. However

I used a writer's license to create their conversations and interactions with each other. I have also changed names, with the exception of various businesses.

The story about the girl in the elevator being promoted to senior buyer because of the way she dressed, truly happened. It was one of the rules my sister agreed to follow when I offered to help her after her divorce.

"You will always dress as though you are on the front cover of Vogue Magazine," was the first rule.

The second rule, "You will go out with anybody and everybody who ever asks you out, no matter who they are or what they look like," led her to meet her present husband. They have been happily married now for 29 years.

The story about John Orr and the material truly happened. My father-in-law, who escaped from Germany with his family exactly as written, saw an opportunity to make a great deal of money and took it. The money allowed him to open a chain of gents' outfitters.

The story of the uncut diamonds also really happened, only it wasn't Emma who found them, but the one partner who stole them from his friend. I still remember his words, words that swept through Potchefstroom as the story was told and retold. "What diamonds?" he asked when his partner accused him of stealing them.

The story of the teenage boy who gave Robie Leibrandt a hiding because of anti-Semitic remarks, is also true. As a young boy, every summer I lived at the muncipal swimming pool, and actually saw the fight.

The death of Gamboo, poisoned by the Security Police as a warning, happened to me and my family, one of the reasons why I encouraged my children to emigrate, with my wife and me following once they had settled themselves. I had refused to give the Security Police the names of certain children who organized the throwing of stones at their school during a protest. Here I must mention that a senior Member of Parliament and cabinet minister of the Nationalist Government, was a good friend. When I told him that I had been threatened by the Security Police, he made sure that it never happened again.

The South African constitution was rewritten by lecturers and senior students at Potchefstroom University, leaving out all mention of racial segregation. Whether the rector and professors of the university were aware of this is not known. However, a close friend who was seriously involved had to resign his position and take up a post at Stellenbosch University for some or other reason.

The story of Livvy is also true. My friend and I met her in the fields in a white tower behind his house in Slough. She was royalty, a princess, niece to Queen Elizabeth, which I later learned by seeing her photograph in an English newspaper, celebrating her 13th birthday. Yes, John and I were not invited to her party.

Finally, the tragedy of South Africa was the normal way of life we Whites accepted and lived with. Yes, we, the majority of English-speaking and many Afrikaans-speaking South Africans, were not in favour of the apartheid the conservative Afrikaner insisted on, but we still favoured separate development, with our black servants using separate lavatories and bathrooms; sleeping in outhouses in the back yards, and living in locations without electricity and other facilities, that we the Whites enjoyed and accepted as the norm. They worked in our stores as hard as the Whites, but for a pittance, happy with what little they earned. They cleaned our houses, made our beds and prepared our meals. They even raised our children, and all for the leftovers of our meals, which they were allowed to take home to their family in the Location, plus a very small salary.

The tragedy of South Africa is still seen today in many countries throughout the world, where people are discriminated against because of their religion, or their sex. They refuse to accept the lessons the collapse of apartheid in South Africa gave them, but time is against them, and they will learn the hard way. Not every country has a Nelson Mandela.

Finally, my debt is to my wife, as she is my love. She put up with all my moods as I wrote this book, but understood me, and allowed me my eccentricities.

South Africanisms

The words below are South Africanisms, commonly used in day to day talk.

AAfrikaans	The language spoken by White minority in South Africa.
Afrikaners	white South Africans, descended from the Boers, who speak Afrikaans.
ag	um; the Afrikaans spelling, pronounced as 'ach',
ANC	African National Congress, a left-wing political party that fought the South African apartheid Government in a war on the Angolan border. They were supported militarily by East Germany. Today the ANC is a left-wing political party in post-apartheid South Africa.
Baas	the name used by Africans to address their employer; the Afrikaans word for "boss", pronounced 'barse'.
Ballottee	Someone called up for military training. The government held a lottery every year to decide who would do military training. If a student decided to attend University, then they applied for University leave and did their training once they left the university.
Bantu	the name given by the government to Africans.
Bantustan	the name given by the Government to an artificially created homeland for Africans.

Biltong	raw salted sun-dried meat, similar to pemmican but a great deal tastier.
Bioscope	movie theatre, cinema.
Black	an African.
Boer	the Dutch settlers of the Cape Province who trekked North to escape British rule. They founded the Boer Republic, pronounced like tour . 'bour',
Boere	Afrikaans plural for Boer
Boerewors	a sausage with spices, very popular and tasty when barbecued, pronounced 'bourrevorse' ,
Broederbond	a secret society in South Africa devoted to advancing Afrikaner interests in South Africa, from 1918.
Bundu	the boondocks; an uninhabited wild region far from any town.
Chinese	one of the ethnic groups in South Africa, originally brought by the British to South Africa from China to work in the fields.
Coloured	an ethnic group of mixed-race people who possess some sub-Saharan African ancestry. Many came from Malaya and were called Cape Malays. The South African government classified them as a separate race group.
Coolies	unskilled labourers brought to South Africa from India by the British, to work in the sugar plantations of Natal.
Corset	girdle
Costume	when applied to swimming, a swimsuit.
Doek	head covering often worn by blacks, similar to a bandana or scarf tied around the head to cover the hair, pronounced 'dook'
Dominee	Afrikaans for minister of a church, pronounced 'Doomoney'

English	by South African race laws, one of the types of South African Whites.
Fancy Dress Party	costume party
Foc'sle	forecastle, the ships deck near the bow.
Fynbos	fine bush. An Afrikaans word referring to the natural shrubs and vegetation in the Cape area of South Africa, pronounced 'fainboss'
Genoeg	enough, pronounced 'cgenooch'
Gramophone	phonograph; record player.
Gown	bath robe.
Habonim Camp	A camp for Jewish children
Hindu	One of India's religious groups.
Hostel	Dormitory. House of residence or lodging for students.
IDB	Illegal Diamond Buying
Indians	South African residents with bloodlines going back to India. The British brought coolies from India to work in the sugar plantations of the province of Natal. Many became businessmen and shop keepers. They were refused entry into the Orange Free State.
Jacaranda tree	type of tree in South Africa that blossoms with purple flowers.
Japanese	people from Japan who settled in South Africa. Due to business with Japan after World War II, the South African government classified them as part of the White community.
Kaffir	refers to Xhosa speaking peoples – black persons. This has for many years been a highly objectionable word – Arab traders in the 18th century are reported to have referred to southern African peoples as 'cafars'. In the 19th century it became the

normal term for a member of the Xhosa speaking peoples and gradually extended to designate all Africans. Today the word has become a swear word.

Kerk	Afrikaans for Church
Koedoe	a species of deer.
Kroes	African curly- kinky hair identifying one with African ancestry.
Lekker kuier	,pleasant visit. Often used as a greeting, pronounced 'lecker keyer'
Liefie	darling; dear one; beloved, pronounced 'leafy'
Malays	South African of Malaysian descent. They were racially classified with the Coloureds.
Matric Dance	graduation dance, the prom.
Matric Year.	senior year. the last year of high school.
Matriculated	graduated. Exams are set by the government, so they are universal. Results are published in the newspapers.
Matric Results	graduation results, commonly published in the newspapers.
Melktert	a pie made with milk; a traditional South African recipe similar to custard pie, pronounced 'melktehrt'
Muslim	followers of Islam, the Muslim religion.
Nats	short for members of the Nationalist Party of South Africa.
Number tens	uniforms that a ship's crew wore on Sundays.
Ossewabrandwag	secret society; a pro-Nazi anti-British group formed in South Africa during World War II, prounounced 'orse-se-va- brunt-vag' ,
Outfitting	haberdashery, men's clothing and furnishings.
PAC	Pan Africanist Congress, afar more radical organi-

	zation than the ANC that originated as a movement for South African liberation.
Pap	Oat Porridge, pronounced ' pahp'
Passion gap	a fashion followed by female Coloureds who removed their two front teeth.
Pavement	sidewalk
Picannins	small young African boys.
Platteland	, Afrikaans for the rural areas of South Africa, pronounced ' plahttelahnd'
Prize Giving	awards ceremony
Range of lingerie	a line of lingerie
Republiek	republic.
Rivier	river, pronounced 'rifeeeeer',
Skelm	rascal, rogue, pronounced 'skehlem'
Spruit	small stream, pronounced 'spruyt',
Standard 8	Grade 10.
Standard 9	Grade 11.
Stoep	verandah, porch, deck, pronounced 'stoop'.
SWAPO	South West Africa People's Organisation, a political party formed in 1960 to represent the Africans of South West Africa, now Nambia.
Tickey	two and a half pence.
Tombola	A raffle game. Pay , then draw a ticket. The number on the ticket gives a prize with the same number.
Transvaaler, Die	An Afrikaans newspaper that supported Afrikaner Nationalism.
Treason Trial	A court case where 156 people were arrested and accused of high treason, trying to overthrow the government and replace it with a communist state.
UNITA	Portuguese acronym for the Union for the Total Independence of Angola, the 2nd largest political party in Angola.

Uitlanders	foreigners, pronounced 'uytlahnders,'
Vaal	Khaki colour. Faded, dim, drab, dreary, pronounced 'faal'
Veldt	Fields. Pronounced 'felt'
Verkramptes	Conservative Afrikaaners, pronounced 'fercrumptes'
Voortrekkers	South Africans of Dutch descent. They ran away from British rule in the Cape to form their own Republics in the North of the country. Founders of the Boer Republics of the Orange Free State and the Transvaal. Pronounced 'foortrehkers'
White	a person of European descent classified by the South African Government as a primary citizen with full voting rights.
Wors	sausage, pronounced 'vors'
Written Matric	graduated from high school.
Yislike	'good grief!' exclamation of surprise, pronounced 'yuslike'

About the Author

JACOB ASHER SINGER WAS BORN in 1935 in the small town of Potchefstroom, 72 miles west of Johannesburg, in South Africa. After attending school at the Potchefstroom High School for Boys, he studied Pharmacy at the Chelsea Polytechnic in London, England, qualifying in 1958 and returned to South Africa.

In 1960, he married Evelyn Jackson, and practiced successfully as a pharmacist for the next 25 years, retiring in 1985 and emigrating to Canada in December 1992.

His first book, BRAKENSTROOM, is a book of short stories about Potchefstroom. This book, The Vase with the Many Coloured Marbles is his second book, based on true life experiences and people he knew in Potchefstroom. "There are so many stories to tell about South Africa" he says. "South Africa is a beautiful country, with a fascinating although controversial history. Unfortunately with the increase in criminal activity and tardiness in controlling violence it is rapidly falling into the 'Africa trap.'

Jacob was never politically active, but he personally met and knew many of the active players on both sides of the political fence. When threatened by the security police for not giving them certain confidential information, he encouraged his children to emigrate, and joined them in Canada once they had established themselves.

After a lifetime of living in a country torn apart by politics and intrigue, he admits that he does find Canada rather boring.

Fresh pulecils . cer
w + any/v 1
m beers

CPSIA information can be obtained at www.ICGtesting.com
Printed in the USA
BVOW031033110112

280248BV00004B/38/P